COVERT AFFAIRS 2

Also by

ELIZABETH CAGE

Covert Affairs

COVERT AFFAIRS 2

SPY GIRLS ARE FOREVER • DIAL "V" FOR VENGEANCE • IF LOOKS COULD KILL

ELIZABETH CAGE

SIMON PULSE

NEW YORK   LONDON   TORONTO   SYDNEY   NEW DELHI

alloy**entertainment**

Produced by Alloy Entertainment

151 West 26th Street, New York, NY 10001

SIMON PULSE

An imprint of Simon & Schuster Children's Publishing Division

1230 Avenue of the Americas, New York, NY 10020

This Simon Pulse paperback edition August 2014

CONTENTS

SPY GIRLS ARE FOREVER

To Sean, George, Roger, Timothy, and Pierce —

a few good men who know a Spy Girl when they see one.

ONE

"Beam me out of here," Jo Carreras muttered as she and Theresa Hearth entered the now familiar white plastic conference room of The Tower for another debriefing. "This place needs a major makeover. The latter-day mother ship motif is *way* out."

"Tell it to Uncle Sam," Theresa replied. She gently set her laptop on the pristine white conference table that stretched the length of the entire room. It had to be at least twenty feet long. "Maybe he'll turn you loose with The Tower platinum card."

"Yeah, right. Only if we save the world just one more time." Jo flipped her long black hair out of her face. Then she snatched a blueberry muffin from a small tray of juice, bagels, muffins, and other breakfast treats in the center of the conference table. The tray was the only thing in the room that hinted at warmth. Let alone humanity.

Actually, there was a time when the sight of this conference room/bad *Trek* set creeped Jo and Theresa out. Now it wasn't eerie so much as tacky. But back then, they were just raw recruits thrown together to save the Free World from Evil and other capitalized words. They'd been so green when the organization known only as The Tower had trained them as secret agents.

Naturally, their enemies underestimated three teenage girls. But the adventures had been intense. Dangerous. Thrilling. Terrifying. And exhausting. They had defused bombs, fallen out of airplanes, hacked into top secret computers, run from the law, and trotted the globe using false identities. They had used gadgets that would make James Bond drool. They wore fabulous couture that would make him drool even more. Soon they stopped being just girls.

They became the Spy Girls.

Jo glanced around and blinked her large ebony eyes. "Where's Caylin?"

Theresa shrugged.

Then they heard a high-pitched *"Kiii-yai!"*

The door at the opposite end of the room flew open, and Caylin Pike burst in, blond ponytail flipping, fists wrapped in athletic tape. She danced back and forth, boxing the air and twirling while she executed a series of wicked roundhouse kicks.

"It's about time," Jo murmured.

Caylin whooshed past Theresa and headed toward Jo's seat. She punched with each step—"Ya! Ya! Ya!"—all the way up to Jo. Then Caylin launched a final sidekick that came within an inch of Jo's nose.

"Now *that's* what I'm talking about." Caylin grinned, holding the foot in front of Jo's face. Jo didn't even flinch—except to wrinkle her nose.

"Ever hear of foot-odor spray?" she asked.

Caylin swung her foot back to the ground and stood in place. Her shoulders slumped. "I do *not* stink!"

"Your feet do," Jo replied with a wry smile.

Caylin ignored her, choosing instead to plop her foot on the conference table, bend forward, and stretch her hamstring. "This tae-bo stuff is unreal. It's total body kamikaze. You guys have to try it. You'll die."

"Just what I want out of a workout," Theresa said.

"No thanks, Van Damage," Jo added. "You work out enough for all of us."

"You don't even know what working out is," Caylin scolded, massaging her calf. She paused to snag a bottle of water from the tray.

"Working out?" Theresa asked, looking confused. She turned to Jo, shrugging. "Never heard of it."

"You know, weights, treadmills, ambulances," Jo quipped. "You've seen the infomercials."

Theresa widened her gray eyes in mock surprise. "*That's* working out? Ew!"

"God forbid you break a sweat," Caylin grumbled.

"You break the sweats, I'll break the codes," Theresa replied, patting her laptop.

"So what does Jo break?" Caylin asked.

Theresa grinned. "Wind."

"Hey!" Jo erupted, throwing a muffin. It exploded against Theresa's arm, sending chunky crumbs across the spotless white table. "You're supposed to be the quiet one!"

"*You* should try quiet sometime," Theresa said with a laugh, brushing crumbs away.

"Very funny," Jo said with an exaggerated toss of her dark hair. "The only thing I break is hearts, Spy Geek. Don't you forget it."

"Yeah, I heard that enemies of state all over the world are paying big bucks for the latest satellite pics of you sunbathing on The Tower roof," Caylin pointed out.

Jo blinked. "They are?"

Caylin and Theresa exploded in giggles and groans. "Yeah, *right!*"

Jo sighed melodramatically and shook her head. "It's so hard being beautiful, brilliant, and top secret."

"Ahem," came a deep voice from all around them, as if from within the walls.

The Spy Girls froze.

"Uh-oh," Caylin said, glancing about. "The Sam-man cometh. Cease all fun."

The lights dimmed. A large video screen emerged from

the far wall, blinking and humming. Gradually the pix-elated image of Uncle Sam, their boss, came to life before them. As usual, they couldn't make out any of his features.

"Greetings, Spy Girls," Uncle Sam said. "How are the debutantes of détente today?"

"My word, Uncle Sam," Jo gasped. "What have you done with your face?"

"I always look like this, Jo," Uncle Sam replied.

Jo rolled her eyes. "That was a joke. You know—what have you done with your face . . . like, 'where is it?'"

"I know what you meant, Jo," Uncle Sam replied dryly. "Do you think you're the first operative to come up with that one?"

"Yeah, yeah, yeah," Jo grumbled. "Dish it, Sammy. What's this week's crisis?"

"Well, it's a crisis, all right," Uncle Sam replied. "But it's a little different this time out."

"Different?" Theresa asked.

"Let me guess," Jo interjected. "Forty nuclear warheads have been stolen from Russia, and we have to infiltrate the Moscow mob. Dressed as nuns."

"No, that's not it," Caylin said. "We have to go to Nepal to rescue the Dalai Lama from a band of rebel Sherpas."

"Dressed as nuns," Jo repeated.

"If you two are finished?" Uncle Sam replied coldly.

"We have to go up in the space shuttle!" Caylin went on.

"Go undercover as Dallas Cowboy cheerleaders!" Jo countered.

"Now *that* would be cool," Caylin agreed.

"That's *quite* enough!" Uncle Sam exclaimed.

The girls paused, staring at the screen. Finally Jo muttered, "He is *so* decaf this morning."

"As I was saying when I was so *rudely* interrupted," Uncle Sam continued, "your next mission is a bit different. I assume you are all familiar with the Mediterranean principality Zagaria, along with its royal family."

"Princess Kristal," Theresa replied.

"Correct. The eighteen-year-old princess. Her mother, Queen Cascadia. And Prince Arthur, who just turned fifteen."

"Lucky kid," Caylin commented. "That's big bucks."

"Who'd want to be a royal?" Theresa scoffed. "Talk about lack of free will."

"Funny you should say that, Theresa," Uncle Sam said. "Because it's exactly free will that has the palace in an uproar. It seems Kristal has been exercising her free will a little too freely these days."

"How so?" Caylin asked.

"Let me guess," Jo piped up. "It has something to do with her boyfriend, Rook."

"Exactly," Uncle Sam replied. "How did you know?"

Jo smiled. "I read the newspapers."

"Ha!" Theresa replied. "Like the *International Trasher*?"

Jo scowled. "That's *Tracker*, giga-girl! If you spoke any language other than Java, you'd *know* that it keeps its finger on the pulse of pop culture like no other newspaper."

"At a second-grade reading level," Theresa argued. "There's not enough soap in the cheesiest of operas to wash the dirt out of *that* rag."

"Ladies!" Uncle Sam said. "If I may?"

Jo and Theresa fell silent.

"Here's the situation: Kristal has run off to Schnell to do a little skiing in the Swiss Alps. The royal family is fairly certain that Rook is with her. Queen Cascadia fears that this could lead to more complicated—and permanent—romantic matters."

"Like marriage?" Caylin offered.

"Like marriage," Uncle Sam confirmed. "It's no secret the queen doesn't like Rook. If Kristal and Rook marry, the implications for the monarchy would be huge. Her Majesty has requested that The Tower locate the princess and return her to Zagaria."

"Schnell," Jo said in awe. "That's the most exclusive ski resort in Europe."

"With the best snowboarding in the world," Caylin added.

Theresa shook her head at her comrades' enthusiasm. "Doesn't the royal fam have bodyguards to handle this kind of stuff? I mean, why do *we* have to go?"

"Are you nuts, Theresa?" Jo demanded. "This is a cakewalk right into the jaws of luxury. It's *Schnell*!"

"The point, Theresa," Uncle Sam replied, "is that Kristal doesn't want to be found. Surely you know her reputation. She'd rather be the rock star that she is than a princess. She and Rook have been on the front cover of every tabloid in the world. This is her way of rebelling against her upbringing. Schnell isn't that big a town, but there are many intimate places for a girl like Kristal to hide. She goes there often, so she must have dependable people willing to keep her whereabouts discreet for a bribe. She would see royal bodyguards coming a mile away. On the other hand, three American girls who are fans just might be able to get close to her."

"Skiing and jet-setting," Caylin mused. "Sounds like a choice little mission."

"My advice would be to follow the paparazzi," Uncle Sam suggested. "They know the clubs where Kristal has been giving surprise concerts."

"Cool," Jo said.

"Lame," Theresa countered.

"What's your malfunction?" Jo asked. "Nothing's going to blow up, no one's going to die, and the world is still safe for democracy."

"That's the point," Theresa replied. "Shouldn't we be doing something a little more challenging? We've proven ourselves. Isn't there a *real* crisis out there somewhere?"

"Yeah, in your head," Jo muttered.

"I'm serious."

"T., we couldn't ask for a better mission." Caylin paused. "Actually, after our little fiasco in Seattle, we very well *should* ask for a better mission."

"Ask and ye shall receive," Uncle Sam said. "Theresa, relax and enjoy this one. If you pull it off, there's a whole week of rest and relaxation in Schnell for the three of you, courtesy of the royal family and The Tower."

"Are you kidding?" Jo squealed. "That is totally Gandhi of you, Uncle Sam! I take back all the things I said about your face!"

"Thank you, Jo," Uncle Sam replied. "But there is one thing. . . ."

"Uh-oh," Caylin moaned.

"Oh no," Theresa breathed.

"What, pray tell?" Jo asked.

The pixels in Uncle Sam's image multiplied into a mischievous smile. "You have to find the princess in seventy-two hours."

Theresa snorted. "Three days? Yeah. Okay. Sure. Nothing

like chasing a spoiled brat through a maze of clubs full of Euro-snobs smoking cigarettes that cost more than my haircut."

"We'll do it," Jo declared.

"No problem," Caylin agreed. "Sorry, T. You might actually have to go outdoors on this one."

"Ha ha," Theresa replied. She glumly raised her glass of orange juice. "Here's to world peace."

"Nah, here's to cool slopes and hot tubs," Jo shot back.

"Good luck, Spy Girls," Uncle Sam declared. "I'll contact you when you reach your home base in Schnell. I think you'll find your accommodations quite . . . accommodating."

Caylin stood and raised her drink as well. "Let's rock and roll, ladies!"

Two juice glasses and one water bottle clicked together. And then the Spy Girls were off.

TWO

I don't think I've ever seen snow so white," Jo marveled as she and her compatriots arrived at the front door of their base of operations. It was a stunning A-frame at the base of the mountain, only a few hundred yards from the Schnell Ski Lodge. They literally could ski right to their front door.

The Alps surrounded them, as tall as the sky and covered with a fresh blanket of snow from the night before. Schnell was nestled in a remote valley in Switzerland, a quaint collection of old-country buildings combined with state-of-the-art resort fare. You could get Swiss chocolate on one corner, a mud bath on another, and a confidential bank account on yet another. Everything in the town was designed to cater to the rich and foreign. Charm might have been Schnell's first name, but money was its middle.

And here the Spy Girls were, in front of one of the choicest chalets in the valley.

"Okay, guys, it's four o'clock," Theresa announced after the Schnell clock tower chimed four times. "Uncle Sam told us that'd be our official mission kick-off time. Time's running out!"

"Oh, stop, Nervous Nellie," Caylin said with a laugh. "Wow, you can actually smell how clean the air is up here." She took a deep breath. "Man, I can't wait to hit the slopes."

"Why don't we hit the house first," Theresa suggested grumpily, shifting her bags on her shoulders. "I'd like to put this gear down sometime before my arms fall off."

Caylin rolled her baby blues and fished an electronic key card out of her pocket. She slid it into a slot by the doorknob, and the door opened. "Maybe you shouldn't bring so many computers, T."

"Really," Jo agreed. "Does Bill Gates know you stole his mainframe?"

"Someone has to do the homework," Theresa replied.

"I did all the homework we need on the plane," Jo

declared, brandishing a copy of the latest *International Tracker*. "Now it's time to *west* and *welax*."

She nudged the door open with her foot, and the trio entered what was going to be their home for the next three days—and hopefully the week after that.

Jaws dropped all around.

"Holy Richie Rich, Batman," Jo whispered. "Can you say, 'Cinderella'?"

"Do you realize that you just subreferenced three cartoon characters in one sentence?" Theresa mumbled, her voice full of awe at the sight before her.

"Who cares," Jo replied dreamily.

The roof of the A-frame rose to a point three stories above their heads, all of it immaculate, dark-stained wood. Several ceiling fans spun, lazily moving the toasty-warm air. A spiral staircase led to the second and third floors. To the right was a kitchen fit for a chef. To the left, a roaring fire was set in a magnificent stone fireplace that was big enough to stand in. And straight ahead? A wall of glass facing the mountain, one of the most spectacular views the girls had ever seen.

Caylin dumped her bag and broke for the almost invisible glass doors, which opened out onto the backyard. Theresa was mesmerized by the wall of gadgetry in the entertainment center. Jo simply drifted to the center of the room and spun, staring at the ceiling.

"I can't believe this," Theresa gushed, indexing the array of electronic hardware that surrounded the giant screen TV. "CD, DVD, Blu-ray, HDTV, and the new network system that allows access to every single television station in the world." She hefted a remote control that had more buttons than the cockpit of a 747. "Jo, do you realize that we can watch *Friends* reruns in Finnish, Russian, and Swahili *simultaneously?*"

It was as if Theresa hadn't even spoken. Jo just whispered, "It's not fair. How are we supposed to complete the mission in three days when we can't even bear to leave the house? I mean, think of the party we could have tonight!"

Behind her, the sliding glass door flew open. Caylin stomped in, huffing clouds of breath. She appeared to be in a daze, as if she'd just been hit on the head. "There is a hot tub out here. You can do *laps* in it. I mean, this is a serious hot tub. I've never seen a hot tub like this. We're talking a hot tub big enough for Rook's entire entourage."

Theresa had torn one of her laptops from its nylon case and was feverishly plugging in adapters to the rear of one of the electronic components. "I could break into the Pentagon with this stuff."

"I checked out the backyard, too," Caylin said. "There's a garage back there. Ask me what's in it."

Jo's eyes locked on Caylin's like lasers. "What's in it?"

"Snowmobiles."

Jo let out a high-pitched squeak. "Did you see the make?"

"Does 'Snownuke 667' sound right?"

Jo screamed and launched herself at the doors. She disappeared in a fluff of snow.

"This is ridiculous," Caylin grumbled, some of the excitement wearing off. "This is the coolest pad The Tower's given us yet. How are we supposed to concentrate on our mission with all these distractions?"

Theresa stopped fussing with wires and gazed at her friend. "Maybe that's the point. Maybe this is a test."

"Give us a cream puff mission with a time limit, and see how professional we are?"

Theresa shrugged. "Makes sense."

Caylin sighed and slumped into one of the stunning leather sofas. "I think we'd better get out of here tonight and search for Kristal before we do anything else. I mean, don't even unpack."

"Good idea," Theresa replied. "That sounds like a plan."

"Promise we won't let each other slack?" Caylin offered.

Theresa marched over to Caylin and held out her hand. They shook. "Promise. Spy Girls get the job done."

"Yes, ma'am."

Just then they heard a roar outside. Jo ripped by on a sleek black Snownuke, her fist raised in the air. White chunks spun up from the snowmobile's track, and they heard a distinct *"yeeeeeee-haaaaaaa!"* before Jo disappeared around the corner.

Theresa sighed. "This is definitely going to be harder than we thought."

The Schnell Ski Lodge was far more than just a ski lodge. It was a full-fledged resort with conference areas, two nightclubs, six restaurants, and a five-star hotel. People of all nationalities roamed the hallways, some dressed for skiing, some dressed for dinner, some dressed strictly for business.

"This is wrong," Caylin said as the trio wandered through the complex. "Kristal is a worldwide celebrity. She wouldn't be caught dead just walking around here."

"I agree," Theresa replied. "There're too many people around. Someone would spot her, and the jig would be up."

"Not to mention the crowd that would form," Caylin added. "She'd be mobbed."

"Do you have any suggestions?" Jo said.

"We need information," Theresa commented. "We need to know where she's been, what clubs she's hit, and then—"

Theresa's mouth dropped open.

"T.?" Caylin asked. "What's wrong?"

"No way," Theresa said incredulously. "No way. Nuh-uh. Can't be."

"*What?*" Jo demanded.

"Dr. Eve is here!"

Jo and Caylin shared a clueless look. "Who?"

"Dr. Eve!" Theresa replied. "She's giving a lecture at eight. What time is it?"

"Quarter to," Jo replied.

"Oh, man, we have to go. We just *have* to. It'll be so cool, guys, seriously. You *have* to go with me!"

"Whoa," Caylin said, holding up her hands. "Who is Dr. Eve, and tell me again what you think we should be doing?"

"Is she like Dr. Ruth?" Jo asked.

Theresa moaned and rolled her eyes. "She's only one of the foremost female scientists in the world! She won the Nobel Prize for her work in space."

"She's an astronaut?" asked Caylin.

"Cosmonaut," Theresa corrected. "She's Russian. Her full name is Dr. Eve Dankanov, but she just calls herself Dr. Eve. She lived on a space station for over a year. She's one of my idols. We *have* to go see her."

"Uh, hello?" Caylin scolded. "Weren't *you* the one saying

that we should concentrate on the mission? We have three days to find Kristal. And that's it."

"This won't take *that* long," Theresa pleaded. "An hour, tops. If you're bored, you can leave. In fact, forget it. I'll go alone."

"We shouldn't split up yet," Caylin warned. "We don't know this place well enough. What do you think, Jo?"

"I think those two guys are staring at us," Jo replied, gazing across the lobby.

They weren't just guys—they were identical twins. Tall, dark, unbelievably foxy identical twins. And they were definitely staring at the Spy Girls.

"I think I'm in love," Jo said huskily. "Wow. Double your pleasure, double your fun. Two great tastes that go great together. Two all-beef patties, special sauce, lettuce, cheese—"

"What are you, a walking jingle machine?" Theresa asked impatiently. "Come on! *What's the plan, people?*"

Jo tensed. "They're coming this way!" She quickly ran her hands through her hair. "How do I look?"

"Terrible!" Caylin said in mock disgust. "How do you face the mirror every morning?"

As the twins approached, their features became clearer—and they became even more handsome. They had thick dark hair that was tousled and spiky. They had deep-set brown eyes that seemed to pierce whatever they looked at and chiseled features right out of a couture ad. They dressed all in black: black turtlenecks, black sport coats, and black slacks. The only hints of color were the bloodred silk handkerchiefs in each of their breast pockets.

"*Buona sera,* signorinas," one twin said, extending his hand. "I am Santino. You are American?"

Jo stepped forward and shook his hand, which was strong and warm. A chill went through her. "Yes, American." She flashed a sexy little grin. "And you're Italian."

"Sì," said the talking twin. "This is my brother, Carlo. We're twins."

Jo's eyes lit up. "Really? You're kidding. That's so cool."

"Oh, can it, Scarlett," Caylin growled, stepping forward. "I'm Cay—uh, Caroline. This is . . ."

"Tish," Theresa chimed in.

"Yeah, Tish. And this," Caylin said, referring grandly to Jo, "is *Joan.*"

Jo shot Caylin a venomous look over her shoulder. *"Joan?"* she mouthed in disgust.

"Hello to you all, ladies," Santino said. "You are here for Dr. Eve's speech, I hope?"

"Yes," Theresa said immediately. "We wouldn't miss it for the world."

"You follow her work, then?"

"I do," Theresa replied "These two just kind of—"

"Of course we follow her work," Jo interrupted. "I've always found it fascinating how someone can live for such a long time in a weightless environment."

"You mean like in your head?" Theresa muttered.

Jo ignored her. "It looks crowded. I hope we can get a seat."

"Have no fear," Santino replied. "Carlo and I work for Dr. Eve. We're her assistants. We can see to it that you have seats in the front row. That is, if you don't mind sitting next to us?"

"I don't mind a bit," Jo said. "You don't mind, do you, ladies?"

"Guess not," Caylin said, resigned. She caught the silent

Carlo staring at her. She smiled, and he looked away.

"Carlo is a little shy," Santino said, giving his brother a playful tap on the head. "He doesn't talk."

"Much," Carlo added with a slight smile.

"What do you say, signorinas?" Santino asked. "Shall we take our seats?"

"Cool," Theresa said. "Let's go."

As they entered the auditorium Caylin snagged Theresa's arm and pulled her close. "Shoot. I *totally* blanked on the alias thing," she whispered. "I just . . . improvised. Think we're okay?"

"I guess so," Theresa replied. "I'm sure the Wonder Twins here wouldn't know the difference if you'd said you were Caylin, Caroline, or Captain Kirk. I'm sure Uncle Sam will understand."

"If you say so. I know better than to ask Jo when there's flirting to be done, but what about the stupid mission?"

"We're here—let's just go with it," Theresa said. "We can scour the clubs for Kristal afterward. But I've been dying to see Dr. Eve forever. She's my idol. Besides, I think Carlo likes you."

Caylin smiled. "He is kind of cute. Well, they *both* are, but I tend to gravitate toward the strong, silent types."

"Hmmm. Looks like Jo thinks otherwise," Theresa said. "Check it out."

Jo already had her arm linked with Santino's as they strode down the auditorium aisle. She was animated and chatty—as always—and Santino was so smooth. Two master flirts doing what they did best.

Theresa felt a rush of adrenaline as the twins led them to the front row. She couldn't believe she was about to be *this close* to *the* Dr. Eve Dankanov!

They settled into their seats, and the twins excused themselves to make sure everything was in place.

"Isn't Santino a doll?" Jo gushed when they left. "I mean, did you see those eyes?"

"Yeah," Caylin replied. "Carlo has the same ones."

Theresa burst out laughing. The other two gaped at her.

"What's so funny?" Jo asked.

"You two," Theresa replied, trying unsuccessfully to hold in her giggles. "It's amazing what you guys will tolerate for a couple of chiseled chins. I mean, you guys *hate* the sciences—biological, physical, metaphysical—"

"Who's going to listen to the lecture?" Caylin retorted. "I couldn't care less about Dr. Eve."

"The only science I'm interested in is chemistry," Jo added. "And maybe the elements of attraction. Paramones."

"Pheromones." Theresa laughed again. "I hate to break the news to you, but these guys are probably borderline PhDs in astrophysics and mathematics. It might be a good idea to listen to the lecture so you don't sound like a couple of idiots when they try to talk to you about it later."

Jo sighed and stared longingly at the curtain, behind which the twins had just disappeared. "T., I hate it when you're right."

"I don't mind it one bit," Theresa replied, smiling.

The lights dimmed and a hush came over the audience. Then Santino marched confidently onstage to the podium. He politely tapped the mike to make sure it was on. *"Buona sera. Buenas noches. Guten Abend,"* he began, rattling off "good evening" in eight different languages, ending with English. "It gives me great pleasure to bring to the stage a true pioneer in astrophysics and zero gravity research. The Nobel Prize winner and former cosmonaut commander, Dr. Eve Dankanov."

The auditorium erupted in applause. Theresa clapped violently and tried to stand, but Jo and Caylin yanked her back down into her seat.

Santino met up with Carlo at stage right, and the twins returned to their seats next to Jo and Caylin. Santino flashed a bright smile at Jo, who winked at him.

Theresa rolled her eyes.

Meanwhile, Dr. Eve marched proudly to the podium. She was a tall, powerfully built woman who obviously was used to being in charge. Her face was deathly pale and equally serious. Her jet-black hair was pulled back in a bun so tight, it arched her eyebrows. Her ice-blue eyes barely registered the crowd, focusing only on the podium and notes before her.

"Someone needs a makeover," Jo commented.

"Shhh!" Theresa scolded.

"In space, no one can hear you accessorize," Caylin

prodded, referring to Dr. Eve's plain gray suit. There was no jewelry in sight. Not even earrings.

"She doesn't have time for *surface* stuff," Theresa stated. "She's far too busy with her work."

Jo sniffed.

Finally the applause died down and Dr. Eve greeted the crowd. Her voice was deep and commanding, and she spoke perfect English with just a touch of a Russian accent.

"Greetings, ladies and gentlemen, science symposium guests, and members of the press. I am Dr. Eve Dankanov. Tonight I wish to discuss Zimmerman's theories regarding the behavior of gas in a vacuum, such as space, versus its behavior in an atmosphere, such as the earth's. As some of you have guessed, I intend to expose Mr. Zimmerman's theories as antiquated and incorrect. He is, quite simply, wrong in all areas."

"Who's Zimmerman?" Jo asked.

"Someone who obviously ticked off Dr. Eve," Caylin whispered.

"He's a hack," Theresa responded. "Dr. Eve's research pretty much destroyed his theories. She's the real deal. She did her research in outer space. Zimmerman never set foot in an airplane. He hated to fly."

"I'm so glad you're here to tell us these things," Jo muttered, sinking into her seat.

"She's right," Santino said bitterly. "Zimmerman was an imbecile."

Dr. Eve continued her presentation, proving with a slide demonstration how Zimmerman's theories were worthless. Theresa was hypnotized, hanging on every word and nodding when she agreed with something Dr. Eve said. Which was pretty much everything.

Then a strange slide appeared on the screen behind Dr. Eve. The previous slides had displayed pie graphs and flowcharts, as well as photos of Dr. Eve working on the space station. But this one was different. It displayed a long, complex formula.

"What's that?" Theresa wondered.

"Uh-oh," Santino said.

Theresa noticed the twins sharing a panicked look.

Dr. Eve didn't spot it at first. She continued her lecture. Then she noticed the shift in the crowd. They, like

Theresa, were all trying to decipher the meaning of the word *meggidion,* which was printed below the formula.

Dr. Eve whirled at the screen, then leveled a stare of pure rage at the twins. She barked a long, harsh phrase in Russian and dramatically pushed the handheld button that changed slides. The next one was another flowchart about her lecture.

Santino and Carlo sank into their seats, as if trying to melt away.

"I apologize, ladies and gentlemen," Dr. Eve said with an unhappy sigh. "If you'll allow me to continue . . ."

"What's wrong?" Jo whispered.

Santino smiled weakly. "Wrong slide."

"What's meggidion?" Theresa asked.

"It's a component of one of Dr. Eve's unsuccessful experiments," Santino replied. "It's rather embarrassing for her, you see."

Carlo punched Santino on the leg. "We are forbidden to talk about it, Santino."

Santino smiled again. "As my brother said." He gestured to the podium. "Please, the lecture continues."

The Spy Girls turned back to Dr. Eve. No other strange slides appeared, and the twins said nothing during the rest of the lecture.

When it was over, they all stood and stretched. "That was so cool," Theresa gushed. "Thanks for getting us in, guys."

Santino bowed. "Our pleasure."

"Well, we should get going," Caylin suggested.

"Wait," Santino said, holding up his hand. He turned to his brother and uttered something in Italian. Carlo smirked and nodded. "Would you like to meet Dr. Eve?"

Theresa's eyes bugged. "Are you kidding? I'd give my right arm."

"I dunno," Caylin replied. "We have something we have to do. Something *important*, girls. Remember?"

"Come on," Theresa pleaded.

"It can't be tonight, anyway," Santino said. "Dr. Eve wants to get back to her chateau early. But tomorrow night she is hosting a reception for special guests of the symposium. Would you like to come as our guests?"

Jo smirked. "Guests?" she asked, implying she preferred the term "dates."

The twins grinned sheepishly at each other. Carlo muttered something in Italian. Santino laughed. "The . . . *appropriate* word would be 'guests.'"

Jo winked. "I get it." She turned to her partners. "What do you say, ladies?"

"We're there," Theresa declared. Caylin nodded.

"Fine," Santino said, his dark eyes glittering seductively. "Dr. Eve's chateau is the last house on Hauptstrasse, up on the mountain. Eight o'clock. And it is a formal affair. You will want to dress."

"Don't worry." Jo flashed a sexy little grin. "We will."

Someone barked a scathing order from the stage. They all turned and spotted Dr. Eve standing offstage, glaring at the twins.

"We have to go," Santino declared. "We will see you tomorrow night."

"Count on it," Theresa replied.

Santino yanked Carlo by the sleeve and they hightailed it up to the stage. Then they all disappeared behind a curtain.

The Spy Girls headed for the exit.

"I can't believe we're going to actually be at Dr. Eve's house!" Theresa said excitedly. "It's too cool."

"And the twins are too hot," Jo added. "Have you ever seen such sexy eyes?"

"Okay, guys," Caylin said. "How about a reality break? I think Carlo's hot as a pepper, too, okay? But we have a princess to find, and the clock's ticking."

"We have all day tomorrow to find her," Jo reassured her. "And hey, you never know. Dr. Eve is sort of A-list. Maybe Kristal will be at her bash."

"If you believe that, I have this white house in Washington to sell you cheap," Caylin replied.

They came out of the auditorium into the lobby. Dozens of people milled about, chatting up the lecture. Outside the massive front windows, the lights of Schnell Mountain made the snowy slopes glow.

"Man, it's not fair. We should just hit the slopes now," Jo said. She gestured at the crowd. "I mean, all these people can just slap on the skis whenever they—" Suddenly Jo paused, frozen in midpout.

"What?" Theresa asked.

Jo's eyes widened, and she frantically grabbed at the arms of the other two Spy Girls. "There, there, right over there," she whispered harshly, pointing.

"What?"

"It's Rook!"

THREE

"Let's get him!" Caylin ordered.

The trio plowed through the crowded lobby. But they weren't the only ones who spotted Rook. His dark looks and brilliant green eyes were legendary throughout the world. It was as if every person in Schnell descended on him at once.

Several burly bodyguards surrounded him and roughly plowed him forward, away from the surging crowd.

"They're heading for that nightclub!" Caylin warned. "We have to hurry!"

Theresa grunted, trying to push through the throng. "No way. It's not happening." She watched helplessly as the bouncers ushered Rook and his party around the velvet ropes and inside.

All at once the crowd dispersed. Jo sighed in disgust

and straightened her hair. "If this is what it's going to be like whenever Rook comes into a room, we're going to have a very hard time with this mission."

"I say we go into the club," Caylin suggested.

"I am *not* dressed for that," Jo countered, brushing imaginary dust from her sweater sleeve. "I look like I just did a shift at a fast-food joint."

"None of us are dressed for it, Jo, let alone up for it," Theresa argued. "But Rook is in there right now. We've got him cornered. If we can get in there, it'll be dark. You might even manage to get past his bodyguards if you tease your hair a little."

"Thanks so much," Jo muttered. "Why don't we go back to the A-frame and do some serious preening? We'll get right in."

"There's no time," Caylin replied. "Rook could leave. And I don't think anyone has a better suggestion at this point. We have to try."

"Fine," Jo grumbled. "What a waste of a perfectly good nightlife."

"You'll live," Theresa said. "But you'd better turn on the

charm because those guys look like they've heard it all."

Indeed, the four bouncers were megamen, each over six feet three and solid as brick walls in their heavy black turtleneck sweaters. As the Spy Girls approached, the lead bouncer's gaze focused on them from under deep eyebrows. His mouth curled into a smirk, and he folded his arms.

"Young Americans," he proclaimed in a thick German accent. "Looking for a good time, no?"

Jo turned up the wattage on her smile and stepped forward. "As a matter of fact, we are, Herr . . . ?"

"Dieter," he replied, his smirk growing.

"Dieter," Jo repeated, her eyelids fluttering seductively. "How sweet."

"Do her eyes just *do* that, or does she have to work at it?" Theresa whispered to Caylin.

"Shhh," Caylin said, nudging her.

"We couldn't very well visit Schnell and not grace Rik's with our presence," Jo continued, referring to the name of the club. "It is the fabulous place to be, is it not?"

"*Ja*, it is," Dieter replied with a chuckle. "But I must say *nein* to the young American girls."

Jo almost flinched. *"Nein?* Are you serious?"

"Perhaps the young American girls would like to come back when they are young American women," Dieter suggested. "Perhaps that would be better, *ja?"*

"Ja?" the trio repeated simultaneously.

Dieter leaned into them menacingly. *"Ja!"*

"Dieter, you're single-handedly setting international relations back about five years," Jo complained.

"Sehr gut. In five years you might be able to get into the club," he replied. "Until then you must go, fräulein babe chicks."

"Fräulein *what?"* Caylin growled, taking a step forward. "Could you repeat that, you Cro-Magnon excuse for a sexist pig?"

Dieter chuckled. "How threatening."

Theresa tugged on Caylin's sleeve. "Maybe it's time to go, girls."

"No, I want to know exactly what a *babe chick* is," Caylin retorted, fists balled tight.

"It's definitely time to go," Theresa demanded, stepping

between Jo, Caylin, and Dieter. "We live to charm another day, okay? Say good night, Dieter."

"Good night, babe chicks," Dieter said, waving.

Once out in the cold night Caylin cut loose. "Can you believe him? *Babe chick! Babe chick!*"

"At least he was polite enough to call you fräulein," Theresa offered.

Caylin scowled. "Oh, save it."

"This is ridiculous," Jo commented. "I mean, look around." She gestured at the magnificent mountains all around them. The slopes glowing under their lights. The happy couples walking arm in arm to romantic dinners. The boisterous groups heading out for a night on the town. "We've got to get serious. Uncle Sam made this mission sound like a cakewalk, but it's going to take some serious spying. I don't know about you guys, but I want that extra week here."

"Me too," Caylin said glumly.

"We need some gear," Theresa stated. "Uncle Sam set us up with toys. We'll need the skis, but the snowmobiles and hot tub and big TV are useless. Even my computers can't help us much."

"What are you thinking?" Caylin asked.

Theresa smiled. "Let's get back and call the man. You'll see."

"So," Uncle Sam finally said, "that's all?"

Theresa chuckled. "How about a Cobra attack helicopter so Caylin doesn't have to use the ski lift?"

"Cool," Caylin chimed in. "I'll take it."

"Sorry," Uncle Sam chided good-naturedly. "I'm afraid not."

"Well, then I think this list will cover it," Theresa said.

"It's either this or you make us A-list movie stars overnight so we can crash any party in town," Jo added.

Uncle Sam's distorted image nodded and shifted from side to side in the large mirror above the fireplace. "That, Jo, I cannot do. You'll have the gear by morning. Plus you might even have a few surprises. However, I suggest you use the rest of your time wisely."

"If you would've supplied us with this stuff from the beginning," Jo said gruffly, "we might not have had to waste an entire night already. We'd be in that club talking to Rook as we speak."

"Easy, Jo," Caylin warned.

"She's just mad that her charms didn't work on Dieter," Theresa replied, smiling. "Her one-hundred-percent rate is down the drain."

Jo shot her an acidic look but said nothing.

"All right, Spy Girls, that's enough," Uncle Sam said. "You'll have your hardware soon. I'll expect a princess on my doorstep in two days. Good luck."

Uncle Sam disappeared, and the mirror reflected the room once again.

Jo sighed. "What a great mission."

"It'll get better when we have that gear," Theresa said. "We should have requested it before we did anything."

"Well, I don't know about you guys," Caylin said wearily, "but I'm taking a nice, long soak in the hot tub. Then I'm crashing. We've got slopes to hit tomorrow."

"You really think Kristal will be skiing tomorrow?" Theresa asked.

Jo nodded. "Every other picture of her in the *Tracker* is on skis. She'll be out there."

The Spy Girls nodded in agreement, but none of them felt very confident.

Jo opened the front door of the A-frame before seven the next morning. A large trunk stared back at her.

"Gear's here," she proclaimed.

Caylin looked over Jo's shoulder, her hot chocolate steaming in the cold air. "How do they do that? I didn't hear a thing last night."

"That's because you snore like an elephant," Jo replied.

"Elephants don't snore," Caylin replied icily. "And neither do I."

"Like an elephant," Jo repeated. "Ask T."

Caylin made a growling noise and grabbed a handle on the trunk. "Take an end."

Jo smiled and grabbed a handle. "My, my, aren't we touchy."

They hauled the trunk into the middle of the main room and popped the lid. Theresa joined them as they sifted through their equipment.

"Here's a standard cosmetic kit for all of us," she said, passing them out. "Includes lipstick camera, compact communications, and mascara."

"What's the mascara do?" Jo asked, opening hers.

"Just mascara," Theresa replied.

"And not even a very good brand." Jo sniffed.

"That's the government for you," Caylin replied.

"Here's an assortment of bugs and miniature video cameras," Theresa declared, "which would have been perfect last night for Rik's. If we can get one of these on Rook or his bodyguards, we'll always know where he is. And that means Kristal, too."

"What are these boots for?" Caylin asked, holding up a beautiful pair of winter hiking boots. "They're gorgeous."

"We didn't ask for them," Theresa replied.

"There's a note from Uncle Sam," Jo said, scanning a piece of paper. "Dear Spy Girls—Enjoy the boots. They're a bonus if you happen to have a princess sighting and no means of transportation. Simply click your heels and you're off. And let's hope you never have to use the belts. They are standard equipment for mountainous terrain. Just click open the buckle and pull. Regards, Uncle Sam."

Caylin clicked open a belt buckle and gave it a yank. A line of black mountain-climbing rope came out. "Whoa, cool! There must be a hundred feet in this little belt. How do they make this stuff?"

She pressed a button in the buckle, and the rope snaked back into the belt automatically.

"Let's check these out," Jo urged. She held a boot in each hand and firmly clicked their heels together. With a loud snap, two-foot lengths of ski erupted from each boot.

"Ski boots!" Jo cried. "These are so stylin'!"

"Great," Theresa muttered.

"What's your problem?" Jo asked. "We finally have some cool stuff we can actually use."

"Maybe *you* can."

Jo and Caylin glanced at each other. "What are you talking about, T.?" Caylin demanded.

Theresa looked away, setting her boots back in the trunk. "Nothing."

Jo leaned forward in anticipation. "Oh no. I don't think it's nothing. Not a chance."

"Lay off, Jo," Theresa warned.

"I agree with Flirty Spy," Caylin chimed in. "It's definitely not nothing. So talk, T. Or we'll request truth serum from Uncle Sam. And you *know* he'll have it here by lunch."

Theresa glowered at her cohorts. Her jaw worked back and forth, grinding.

But they still stared.

"Okay, okay." Theresa relented. "You were bound to find out anyway. I mean, we're in the Alps."

"What?"

"Spill it!"

Theresa's nostrils flared, her eyebrows quivered, her lips curled back in a snarl . . . and she said it:

"I can't ski."

FOUR

Caylin blinked. Jo's eyes bugged. Then they both giggled.

"T., don't take this the wrong way," Caylin said, holding her belly, "but you really, *really* need to get a life."

"Hey—" Theresa began.

"Really, T." Jo added, "I mean, other than tailgating, skiing is the single best sport for meeting guys! How can you have lived this long and missed out?" Jo's eyes turned dreamy. "The fluffy snow, the swoosh back and forth as you fly down the slope. Maybe the guy's in front of you, maybe he's behind you, but either way it's always better than flirting face-to-face. I mean, you get some hot ski pants, throw your hair back in the wind, add in the big boots, poles, and planks, and, girl, you suddenly realize that you've never looked hotter. Trust me,

Theresa, the lift line is better than any school dance I've ever been to."

Caylin snickered. "Oh, no no no, my dearest Josefina. You have it all wrong." Caylin jumped up on the coffee table and struck a surfer's pose. "A snowboard is the only true way to experience everything a slope has to offer. Take the balance and coordination you need to ski and multiply it by about six hundred thousand. Then you *might* be on the same planet as boarding. I mean, on a board you can literally *fly*."

Caylin leaped off the table, kicked out at an imaginary foe, and landed on the carpet without a sound. She turned to Theresa and smiled. "Meeting guys is just the gravy, T. The trip is the real trip, you know?"

"Whatever you say, ninjette," Jo scoffed.

Theresa sank back into the sofa. "I think we should just find Kristal. That's what I think."

Caylin flopped onto the sofa next to her. "And how do you propose to do that? Jo and I can hit the slopes. What can you do? Hack into the lift ticket computer to see if Kristal bought one today?"

Theresa's eyes narrowed in anger. "For your information, I have very specific plans today. I doubt you two have ever made a specific plan in your lives."

"What were you going to do?" Jo asked. "Not that your partners should know or anything."

"I signed up for a ski lesson," Theresa replied defiantly. "The school here says I can be up on the regular slopes by lunch."

Caylin laughed. "Up's the easy part. How did they say you'd be getting down?"

This sent Jo and Caylin into mad gales.

Theresa scowled. "Oh, come on! I mean, really! How hard can it be to ski?"

Theresa felt the world spin out from under her. Her heart shot into her throat, her belly lifted into the air, and her lungs deflated.

Then she hit the ground.

"*Oof!*"

"Still think skiing's easy, T.?" she heard Jo call out.

Theresa sat up. Her equipment was all around her.

A ski. A glove. A pair of goggles. A pole, slightly bent.

How could she fall? She wasn't even going that fast. In fact, she was only a few yards from the A-frame.

"Are you in pain?" Caylin called from up the hill. "Pain's good. You should learn to like pain."

"You're sick, Cay," Jo replied, shoving off with her poles toward Theresa's crash site.

"Hey, I'm just trying to help," Caylin offered, slapping her snowboard against the slope and moving forward. "She needs it."

"I'm fine!" Theresa growled.

Jo cut her skis into the trail just in front of Theresa as she stopped, spraying her with several pounds of snow.

"Sorry, I couldn't resist," Jo remarked, giggling.

"You two are the cruelest people I've ever met!" Theresa sputtered, brushing snow off her.

"Hey, what did I do?" Caylin said, sliding in next to Jo. "At least you learned the first rule of skiing."

"What's that?" Theresa asked.

"When in doubt," Jo replied, "fall."

"Thanks a lot."

"Can you make it to the lodge okay?" Caylin asked. "Seriously."

Theresa nodded gruffly, collecting her gear. "I'll make it. Even if I have to walk."

"Well, we have the communications and surveillance gear now," Jo commented. "Let's keep in touch. And find us a princess. What do you say?"

Jo put out a hand for Theresa. She grabbed it and stood up on her skis. Shakily.

Finally Theresa managed a smile. "I say okay."

"Good," Jo replied.

"Remember," Theresa said. "No matter what happens, we're still going to Dr. Eve's party tonight, yes?"

Jo grinned seductively. "I'd hate to disappoint the twins."

"Well, that's that, then," Theresa said, popping off her skis. "I'm going for my lesson. I'll talk to you guys later."

"Hey, T.," Caylin called.

"What?"

Caylin grinned. "Break a leg!"

"I must look ridiculous," Theresa muttered as she trudged through the snow, approaching the lodge. She carried her skis and poles in a sloppy bear hug, stumbling every once in a while in her Frankenstein-like ski boots. She noticed several people pause to stare at her. "What's the matter? Haven't any of you ever seen an American before?"

Finally she made it to the ski school. Or at least to the sign that said Ski School Meets Here in several languages.

No one else was there.

Theresa sighed and dropped all of her gear in a heap. The skis and poles clattered, but she didn't care. Her arms were exhausted.

"That's no way to treat a brand-new pair of K2 skis," came a deep voice with a pronounced British accent.

Theresa turned, and when she saw him, she couldn't help it: She actually gulped.

The guy stood about six feet two. His hair was golden blond. His eyes dark brown. His cheeks were rosy from the cold, but his boyish smile said that the weather didn't bother him one bit.

"Here," he said, bending down and fetching her skis. "Like so."

He stuck them into the snow so they stood up to make an X. He stuck the poles next to them. "If you throw them around like that, you'll rough up your edges. Don't want that."

"Oh," Theresa replied, staring dumbly at him.

"Are you Tish, by any chance?" His eyes stared right into hers.

"Um . . . yeah," she stammered, looking away. "I mean, yes. I am." Why couldn't she talk?

"Perfect," he said, taking off his glove and extending his hand. "I'm Patrick. Your instructor."

"Oh," she said again. She blinked, felt horribly stupid, and then clumsily removed her own glove to shake his hand. His handshake was so warm and firm. The warmth seemed to course into her veins. "Nice to meet you."

"You've never skied before?" he presumed.

"No," she replied sheepishly. "Well . . . unless you count on the way over here. But I fell."

He chuckled. "That's all right. You should prepare

yourself. You're going to fall quite a bit today."

Theresa returned the chuckle. "I can't wait."

She *still* couldn't talk! What in the world was she saying? Was she going to talk in one-syllable words all day?

"You're British, aren't you?" she managed.

"Yes, from London," Patrick replied. "I'm on leave from Oxford."

Theresa tried to keep her eyes from popping out of her head. A real, live Oxford man was teaching her to ski! Jo loved her diamonds. Caylin loved her workouts. But Theresa's magic words went strictly along the lines of Harvard, Stanford, MIT, Princeton, and of course, Oxford.

She actually had goose bumps.

"Is there much skiing in England?" she asked.

Patrick shook his head. "No. My family used to come to the Alps quite a bit when I was younger. I learned on these mountains. Now I teach here while on holiday." He grinned. "Are you ready, then?"

Theresa smiled nervously. "No, not really."

"Oh, relax," Patrick replied. "I haven't killed anyone. At

least, not yet." He pulled her skis out of the snow and laid them side by side on the ground. "There you are. Step on in, and off you go."

Theresa stutter-stepped to her skis. She gingerly popped her skis onto her boots—the only part of the process that she really knew how to do.

"Wasn't that easy?" Patrick asked gently. "Didn't hurt a bit, did it?"

For the first time Theresa held his gaze. "I'm not six, you know."

He held up his hands. "Sorry."

"That's better." She couldn't help cracking a smile. "So what do you study at Oxford?"

"Archaeology, political science, and computers," he replied. "Not necessarily in that order, of course."

"Of course," she echoed.

"How about you?"

"I dabble a bit in computers myself," she said playfully, not mentioning the more colorful places she'd hacked into.

"Splendid," Patrick replied. "We'll have much to talk

about." He gestured toward the beginner slope. "Shall we?"

Theresa's gaze followed the gentle slope all the way down to the distant chairlift at the bottom. It might as well have been Mount Everest. "Just like that? Don't I have to pass a written exam or something first?"

Patrick laughed. "Of course not. It's not so bad. You have to start with the basics. It's called the snowplow. You simply point your toes in, forming a triangle with your skis. Then you push out with your edges to slow yourself down. Like so."

He demonstrated, effortlessly moving ten yards down the hill as slow as a snail. But Theresa had a tough time keeping her eyes off his muscular legs. The butterflies in her belly intensified.

"You want me to do *that*?" she asked, her fingers nervously flexing on her poles.

"I promise you won't get hurt," Patrick said, gesturing her forward. "All you have to do is remember one thing."

"What's that?"

"When in doubt, fall."

"I've heard that somewhere before," Theresa muttered.

Patrick waved her on. "No worries. Just point your tips

toward me and push with your poles. Off you go, then."

Theresa drew in a deep breath . . . and pushed. She felt herself moving, picking up speed, faster, faster. Panic crept into her body, and she wanted to flail her arms. Patrick got closer and closer.

A low sound came out of her throat—something totally embarrassing that would be a full-fledged scream in two seconds.

Then Patrick was right there. She braced for a bone-crushing impact, but he simply hooked his arm around her waist and brought them both to a gentle halt.

"There, you see?" he said calmly. "You just skied."

Theresa smiled nervously. "Yeah, but if you weren't here, I'd be dead meat down in those pine trees."

Patrick gave her a playful wink. "Don't worry. If you got hurt, I wouldn't be able to live with myself."

She smiled, noticing how natural his arm felt around her waist. And how her heart sank when he took it away.

"Ready for your next challenge, Tish?"

She gripped her poles, smiled, and nodded. Maybe skiing wasn't so bad after all.

That night the Spy Girls took a taxi to Hauptstrasse and hoofed it up the driveway to Dr. Eve's chateau. Jo and Caylin complained the whole way that they hadn't seen hide nor beautiful blond hair of Kristal that day. She and Rook simply weren't making themselves public. The Spy Girls would have to take more drastic measures if they were going to—

Silence took over when the chateau came into view.

The trio just stood there and stared. And stared. And stared.

"Will you look at this place?" Jo marveled, breaking the silence.

Every window was lit from inside, casting a warm golden glow over the snow. The chateau seemed to be built into the mountain itself. It was designed in a definite alpine motif, with dark wood frames rising up to points all over the place. In many ways it was like a castle, but not made of stone. The front of the building was all windows, curving out over the hill to provide a breathtaking view of the valley below.

"Big bucks," Caylin whispered.

"See?" Theresa said. "Even science geeks can live like movie stars."

"You wish," Caylin replied.

"Well, even we'll manage to dress this joint up," Jo boasted. "As usual, girls, we all look fabu. One good thing you can say about The Tower: They know how to dress an agent."

The Spy Girls were decked out to the nines and tens—full-blown evening wear, cashmere overcoats, the works, even though the high heels were a little treacherous on the icy patches.

"The twins won't know what hit them," Jo said playfully.

"We're about to meet one of the most amazing women in the world," Theresa muttered, "and it still comes back to the boy toys."

"It always does, Theresa," Jo teased. "Speaking of which, do tell us more about your studly ski instructor."

Theresa felt her cheeks flush. "You've heard enough."

"Yeah, right," Caylin said. "You practically drooled all over your dress while we were getting ready. I think someone's got a crush."

"Cut it out," Theresa replied wearily. "He's an Oxford man. Your everyday, ordinary brainiac."

"Oooh, then T.'s *definitely* crushing big time," Jo chimed in. "But how did you find an Oxford man who knows how to ski? Shouldn't he be locked up in a computer lab somewhere, cleaning his screen?"

"Har-dee-har-har," Theresa retorted, even though she knew all too well that Patrick had never left her thoughts since she left him that afternoon. On their last run she'd actually made it all the way down the beginner slope without falling. Patrick had been so sweet, so patient, and so complimentary.

But the lift rides were the best part. That's when they talked about other things. Like Oxford. School in general. Computers. Dreams.

Patrick and Theresa were so alike. Caylin and Jo were right—she *did* have a crush on him. But unfortunately she had a mission to attend to. She couldn't spend every hour of the day getting ski lessons . . . could she?

"Do you really think there's a chance that Kristal will be at this party?" Caylin wondered.

"You never know," Theresa replied.

"There *are* a lot of limos in the driveway," Jo observed.

"Let's go find out," Caylin declared.

The trio reached the beautiful mahogany double front doors and rang. As they waited for an answer, Caylin stiffened.

"Do you see that?"

"What?"

"Up there, by that tree." Caylin nodded without being obvious. "Two men."

Indeed, two men clad in black leaned against a tree trunk several yards from the front door. The girls couldn't make out any other details.

"Relax, guys," Theresa said. "Dr. Eve has bodyguards. She's worked on a lot of big-time projects. Plus I'm sure her guest list is loaded with big names. Security is a must."

The front door was opened by a distinguished-looking man in a tuxedo. He said some curt words in German. *Guten Abend* was not among them.

"Go ahead, Miss Science," Jo prodded. "This is your show."

Theresa stepped forward and smiled. "Hello. We were personally invited by Santino and Carlo. The twins. I'm sure everything's in order."

The man at the door said nothing. He didn't budge.

"Um, is there a problem?" Caylin asked. "Do you speak English?"

"I speak perfect English," the man replied. "Yet I react to what I do not see. And I do not see invitations."

"Yeah, but Santino and Carlo invited us last night," Jo replied. "You didn't see that, either, but it happened."

"Josef," came a voice. "Let them in." Santino—or Carlo—appeared over Josef's shoulder, smiling in his tux. "They are my guests."

Josef nodded stiffly and stepped aside. The twin immediately snatched up Jo's hand and kissed it. "You look positively radiant. Which is *molto pericoloso*. Very dangerous. You could melt the snow and cause an avalanche."

Definitely Santino.

Jo giggled. "That's the nicest thing anyone's ever said to me . . . *today*."

Santino grinned. "Ah, touché."

The Spy Girls checked their coats and were escorted by Santino into the main living room—the front room with the floor-to-ceiling windows overlooking all of Schnell. Guests milled about, sipping champagne and sampling hors d'oeuvres. Everything was cocktail dresses and bow ties. Everyone was reserved and professional—as if they did cocktail parties for a living.

"I apologize for Carlo," Santino said. "He's indisposed at the moment. But he will be here shortly. Make yourselves comfortable, and feel free to mingle. Dr. Eve is looking forward to meeting you."

"She is?" Theresa asked, taken aback.

"Yes. I mentioned that Carlo and I had met three remarkable American women who follow her work closely. She was intrigued."

"Wow," Theresa replied. "Intrigued."

"Easy, girl," Jo joked.

"If you will excuse me, I must help with some of the preparations," Santino said. "I'll rejoin you in a few minutes."

"Take your time," Caylin replied casually.

"But not *too* much time," Jo added, smiling slyly.

Santino smiled back. "I promise."

As he disappeared, Caylin turned toward the food table. "Cool. Let's nosh."

Jo grabbed her arm. "Show some class, fräulein. This crowd eats their treats one at a time . . . *with a fork.*"

"Give it a rest," Caylin scoffed. "They eat like everyone else. For free."

They pored over the food table, sampling everything. Jo scarfed caviar. Caylin stuck with shrimp. Theresa, however, just hovered, tapping her feet. Her gaze moved steadily across the room, in search of Dr. Eve. She couldn't believe she was going to actually meet her. This woman who had accomplished so much. Who knew so much and meant so much. This was truly a once-in-a-lifetime—

Theresa froze.

Her eyes locked on a figure across the room. But it wasn't Dr. Eve. It was Patrick!

He spotted her, too. He smiled and gave a small wave. The tux certainly suited him, no pun intended. To Theresa, he was a showstopper.

And like the first time she saw him, she gulped.

"You see a ghost, T.?" Caylin asked through a mouthful of shrimp.

Theresa didn't answer. She just kept staring at Patrick.

"No, Caylin," Jo replied. "She saw *that*."

All three Spy Girls locked eyes on Patrick, mouths agape. Caylin and Jo didn't realize it, but that meant their chewed food was showing.

"Who's that?" Jo demanded.

"Patrick," Theresa whispered.

"*That's* Patrick?" Jo said. "The geekly ski instructor from Oxford who likes laptops and fossils?"

"That's him," Theresa confirmed.

"I take back everything I said about you, T.," Jo gushed.

Theresa snatched a glass of champagne from a passing tray and stepped out. "See you guys later."

"I wonder," Caylin replied as Theresa approached Patrick. "Can you believe her, Jo?"

"Some girls have all the luck," Jo replied. "But remember, we have two hunky dates of our own. In fact, I think I'm going to go find Santino. He's neglecting his guest."

"Hey, what about me?"

"Carlo is lurking somewhere," Jo suggested, already on the move. "Plus there are a couple dozen shrimp left. Have a day."

"Thanks a lot."

"Be careful," Patrick warned. "That stuff goes right to your head."

Theresa shrugged. "I don't even know why I picked it up," she said nervously. "I don't drink."

She put the glass back on the same waiter's tray she had just plucked it from. The waiter rolled his eyes and moved on.

"If I may," Patrick said, "you look absolutely stunning."

Theresa blushed hard. "Thank you. So do you."

"I'm used to seeing you covered with snow."

"But I improved. You're a good teacher."

"You're a better student. You'll be on the big slopes in no time." He smiled. "If you decide to keep skiing, that is."

Theresa smiled back. "I'd like to. If you'd teach me."

Patrick cocked an eyebrow. "I'm not sure. I'm terribly in demand, you know."

"I'm sure," Theresa replied. "So what brings you to this party?"

"Naturally, I'm a fan of Dr. Eve's work in space. It's fascinating. When I saw that she was lecturing at the science symposium, I thanked my good fortune. As for the invitation, I sort of gleaned one from a rather wealthy dignitary who needed help with his slalom skills."

"I see," Theresa replied, spotting an opening. "So you must deal with a lot of wealthy people who want to learn to ski?"

"Some," he replied.

"Anyone famous?"

Patrick smirked. "Perhaps. Who did you have in mind?"

Theresa playfully made a circle on the carpet with her toe. "Well, I heard that Kristal is in town. And I'm a huge fan of her music."

Patrick chuckled. "No such luck, old girl. I'm afraid Kristal is the phantom of Schnell. Of course, the tabloids think she's here. But no one knows for sure where she'll pop up next."

Theresa sighed. "I guess I'm a little starstruck. I mean, meeting Dr. Eve is more than I dreamed of. I couldn't imagine meeting two of my idols in one week."

"You like the princess that much?" he asked.

Theresa nodded. "How can you not admire her? She has the perfect life. Anyone would die for that life." Sure, she was lying, but it was for a good cause. She *was* on a mission, after all.

Patrick nodded back. "I never thought of it that way."

Theresa hated deceiving Patrick. She wished she could tell him what she *really* thought—that Kristal was just a spoiled royal. But she had to find clues wherever she could. Patrick seemed to have the town wired. She figured maybe he knew someone or something. No such luck. And now he thought she actually adored the princess! She was making herself into a class-A dork in no time at all.

"If you'll excuse me, Tish," Patrick said. "Not to be indelicate, but I really must . . ."

Theresa smiled. "I think I get the picture."

"Right. Be back before you know it."

She watched him stride toward one of the back hallways. She let out an enormous sigh. Between finding Patrick, falling all over the slopes, meeting Dr. Eve, and trying to track down Kristal, Theresa couldn't believe she was still sane.

As the same waiter passed again she reached out and snagged back her glass of champagne. This time the waiter stopped.

"Would you rather have the bottle?" he asked snidely, in a thick Russian accent.

Theresa chuckled lamely and returned the glass to the tray. "Guess not."

Jo slipped down a long hallway where there were no guests in sight. She'd glimpsed Santino going this way, but now he was nowhere to be seen.

She turned left, moved farther down the hall, and made another right.

"Don't get lost," she warned herself. "He's just a hunky Italian guy, after all."

She smiled to herself. "All the more reason to forge ahead."

She came to a spiral staircase. What to do? Up or down? She gazed up, but saw only darkness. There was light below and carpeting.

She went down.

She found herself in a den. The room was deserted. The furnishings were warm and luxurious. A fire roared in a fireplace even larger than the one they had in the A-frame. A huge stuffed elk's head hung over the mantel, its antlers reaching out like long, spindly fingers.

"Poor Rudolph," she whispered.

She spotted a doorway off to the right and went through it. A short hallway led to a closed door. Light filtered through the cracks from beyond.

Should she open it?

"Well . . . you can always just say you're looking for the bathroom," she convinced herself.

She turned the knob, then paused.

Was Santino really worth getting caught over and totally embarrassing herself? Not to mention getting the Spy Girls kicked out of the only thing resembling an A-list party they could get invited to?

On the other hand . . . she *was* just looking for the bathroom. Right?

She pushed open the door.

She was at the top of another spiral staircase, overlooking a room that was considerably less charming than the den. There was a long conference table, a speaker-phone centerpiece, and a dozen chairs. The far wall was all blackboard. Totally clean. Portraits of other famous scientists lined the other walls. Einstein. Well, Einstein was the only one Jo recognized. She assumed they were scientists, but famous was a relative term.

She caught movement on the other side of the room.

Santino!

At least, she *thought* it was Santino. It could've been Carlo. Either way, that twin was hot in his tux!

He marched toward the blackboard wall, his back to Jo. She thought to call out to him, but waited.

Maybe she should sneak up on him and do a "guess who?"

The thought gave her shivers. Maybe he'd turn around and kiss her then and there!

She took a step down the spiral staircase.

Santino didn't hear her. He stopped at the blackboard and made a strange movement with his hand.

Jo's eyes bugged when an entire section of the blackboard turned inward.

Her inner compass told her that the blackboard wall faced into the mountain. Was there more to this chateau than met the eye?

Santino disappeared, and the blackboard slid back into place.

"How cool," Jo whispered.

She quickly descended the staircase and approached the blackboard. She ran her hands along the edges of the slate and its frame. There were no seams or switches or any other visible signs of a door.

It was totally hidden.

"This is *so* wild—"

Suddenly a series of loud pops came from the stairs. Jo's heart leaped into her throat. She gasped. She knew exactly what they were.

She'd heard those sounds before.

Gunshots!

"I'm outta here," Jo whispered.

FIVE

Jo sprinted up the spiral stairs into the den. The place was still deserted, but the screams and chaos from the main room told her that she didn't want to be discovered here. There would be too much to explain. Even if it really *had* been a bathroom trip.

Adrenaline coursed through her as she marched down the hallway toward the party. She didn't have to worry about getting lost. All she had to do was follow the noise.

Suddenly a burly man dressed in black appeared before her. He held a semiautomatic pistol in front of him with both hands, battle ready.

She gasped, freezing in her tracks.

"Who are you?" he demanded, threatening to raise the gun.

"Don't shoot!" she squeaked, putting her hands up. "I'm just . . ."

Oh, what the heck, she thought.

". . . looking for the bathroom! Were those, like, gunshots?"

The man shoved past her. "Get back to main room. The party is over!"

He disappeared.

Jo sighed. What on earth had happened?

She found Theresa and Caylin in the main room. The guests were silently congregated in a tight group near the center of the room. Jo spotted Dr. Eve in the far corner. Several armed guards stood by her, their guns held loosely in their hands.

"What's going on?" Jo asked urgently.

Theresa shrugged. "We don't know. We were just standing here and some guns went off outside. The guards came rushing in and told us all to stay here."

"Who did the shooting?" Jo wondered.

"The guards," Caylin replied, her fists clenching anxiously. "I saw one of them pop in a new clip before."

"I didn't think the party would be this exciting," Jo said dryly. "You sure can pick 'em, T."

"Hey, I aim to please," she replied.

"Excuse me, everyone," came a voice.

The crowd turned. It was Dr. Eve.

"I wish to apologize for this outburst," she announced. "It seems to be a false alarm. But my security people feel it is best that we conclude this affair a little early. I am sorry for those of you who traveled so far to be here, but I assure you this is for the best. It seems my work has as many detractors as it does supporters. I am grateful to all of you, but unfortunately I must say good night."

The crowd dispersed. Drinks and food plates were set down. Low mutterings replaced the spirited conversations from mere moments before. Dr. Eve personally bid each guest farewell.

"Now's your chance to meet her, T.," Jo said.

"Great timing," Theresa replied. "Where are the twins to introduce us?"

"I don't know about Carlo," Jo commented, "but I found Santino downstairs. Before I could say anything to him, he disappeared through a secret door in a blackboard."

"Really?" Caylin said. "That's weird."

"Why is it weird?" Theresa argued. "Considering what just happened, you don't think Dr. Eve has to keep her work a secret? Of course she's going to have secret rooms."

"Whatever you say, T.," Caylin replied.

Then it was their turn to bid farewell to Dr. Eve. Jo and Caylin hung back, allowing Theresa to speak for them.

She cleared her throat, trying not to be nervous. But her words came out in one long blurted sentence: "Hello Dr. Eve my name's Tish I'm a big fan of your work and your accomplishments I think you're brilliant and your lecture last night was right on the mark. Basically."

Theresa paused, blinking, hoping she hadn't just made a fool of herself.

No one said anything for a moment. Dr. Eve stared at Theresa, taking it all in. Then, slowly, she saw Dr. Eve smile for the first time.

"Thank you," Dr. Eve replied. "I think."

"I—I'm sorry," Theresa stammered. "I'm a little nervous. You're, uh, one of my idols."

Dr. Eve looked at her thoughtfully. "Thank you . . . Tish, was it? I am a little nervous myself. I'm not used to gunplay outside my window."

"Um, me neither," Theresa replied.

Dr. Eve sighed. "The world is such a violent place. Too many people. Too much suffering. The pressure just builds and builds, and it needs to be released one way or the other." Dr. Eve smiled at Theresa again. "I'm glad you could come tonight, Tish."

"I'm sorry they—whoever—crashed your party," Theresa replied. "I was kind of hoping I'd get to talk to you tonight sometime. But I guess that idea's shot. Er, *gone*." She smiled sheepishly. "Sorry."

Dr. Eve chuckled. "You say you follow my work?"

"For a long time."

"Well, perhaps we can talk."

Theresa's eyes went wide. "We can?"

"I don't see why not. I have to make up for being such a careless hostess. I'm having some young students at my home the day after tomorrow. Perhaps I can give you a bit of a tour. In return, you can tell me your opinions on my work. I would be grateful."

Theresa's jaw dropped. "*You* would? Are you *kidding*?"

"I'll take that as an acceptance?"

"Absolutely. I'd be honored."

Dr. Eve nodded. "Very well. The day after tomorrow. Over lunch?"

"I'll be there," Theresa said, grinning from ear to ear. She shook Dr. Eve's hand vigorously.

"Good night, Tish and friends," Dr. Eve said, pulling away and waving. "I'm sorry it wasn't more of a pleasure."

Theresa waved as Jo and Caylin pushed her toward the door. They picked up their coats and followed the crowd outside.

"Wasn't that cool?" Theresa gushed. "I mean, as cool as there ever was cool?"

"What it is, is cold, T.," Jo complained, shivering in the frigid air. "We'll never get a taxi at this end of Hauptstrasse."

"We'll have to hoof it into town until we flag one," Caylin said.

"Great," Jo continued as they made their way down the icy hill, slowly, in their heels. "What a great party. No dates, no fun, and nothing to show for nothing. Remind me why we listen to you again, Theresa?"

"You can't do it tonight, Jo," Theresa announced. "I'm a happy girl right now, and there's nothing you can do about it."

"I'm so glad you're happy," Jo muttered. "Your happiness, as always, is my happiness. Maybe when we get home and amputate our frostbitten toes, we can all be happy together!"

"You talk too much," Theresa retorted.

"And you—"

Jo was cut off by a cry from up the hill. Then a dark figure darted from the trees in front of them. It dashed across the road into the woods on the far side. Several guards pursued, flashlights bobbing.

"Halt!" one screamed.

The guard squeezed off a shot. The noise hit the Spy Girls all at once, like three invisible fists.

The guards flashed their lights into the trees, but it was too late. The figure was gone. The guards reluctantly retreated back onto Dr. Eve's property.

"There must have been an intruder," Caylin whispered.

"That shot scared the life out of me," Jo replied, quivering. "I hate guns. They're so *loud*."

"Let's get out of here," Caylin urged.

"I'm with you," Jo said. "Theresa?"

Theresa didn't budge. She stared at the section of trees where the figure had disappeared.

"Hel-lo?" Jo prodded, waving her palm in front of Theresa's eyes. "Tower to Theresa. Do you copy?"

"What's wrong, T.?" Caylin asked. "You look like you've seen the proverbial ghost."

"I know him," Theresa replied, her voice distant.

"Who?"

"The intruder."

"You do?"

"Who is it?" Caylin demanded.

"It was him," Theresa said. "It was Patrick."

• • •

Back at the A-frame, Theresa and Jo lounged in their sweats, sipping hot chocolate. Caylin stoked the fireplace with fresh logs. Gradually the chill left them.

"What would Patrick want with Dr. Eve?" Theresa wondered aloud. "He's just a student."

"Who cares?" Jo remarked.

"I care," Theresa replied gruffly. "If he's trying to sabotage her work somehow, I owe it to her to find out as much as I can about him."

"I thought you were in love with him," Caylin said with a humorless chuckle.

Theresa smiled lamely. "That's the thing. I can't get him out of my mind."

Jo stood up angrily. "I've had it with this. Theresa, we have a mission, okay? And it has nothing to do with Dr. Eve, or Patrick, or the fate of humanity itself. It's a simple mission, one that I'm sure you remember. We have to find Kristal, and that's it."

"I seem to remember a certain Spy Girl falling all over herself to find a handsome young twin at the party tonight," Theresa replied bitterly. "And wasn't it you who suggested that Kristal might actually be at the party? I've heard some rationalizations before, but that's a whopper."

"We wouldn't have even *been* at the party if it wasn't for you, T.," Jo argued. "You just *had* to go to the lecture. You just *had* to meet Dr. Eve, your idol."

"We wouldn't even have gotten into the lecture in the first place if you weren't so obsessed with the twins!" Theresa fluttered her eyelids mockingly. "Oh, we have to meet them, oh, they're coming over, oh, how's my nail polish?"

"Yo!" Caylin interrupted.

Jo and Theresa fell silent.

"You're both out of line!" Caylin said, angrily tossing one last log on the fire. "We wasted an entire night on this party. And you're both to blame. Okay, we *all* are. No one twisted our arms, no one put a gun to our heads. Now we have less than thirty-six hours to locate Kristal and find some way to get her out of here. And I don't have to remind you that we don't have clue one where she is. I mean, we defuse bombs and steal secrets and prevent world wars. All of a sudden we're stumped?"

"I agree," came a familiar voice.

"Oh no," Jo muttered.

"Uncle Sam!" Theresa cried.

Their superior came into focus in the mirror above the fireplace. At least, as in focus as the computer distortions would allow.

"Caylin is right," Uncle Sam said grimly. "You've all behaved shamefully and unprofessionally."

"That's not fair," Jo argued. "This mission isn't exactly a world saver."

"That doesn't matter," Uncle Sam replied. "You are professionals, and you have been charged by The Tower to complete your mission according to the parameters set forth. It doesn't matter if you are recovering nuclear warheads or rescuing a cat from a tree."

Uncle Sam paused. When the Spy Girls didn't reply, he continued.

"Now listen carefully, ladies. Theresa, you will stop worrying about Dr. Eve's business. She has her own problems and her own people to take care of them. And if you need a ski lesson, ask Caylin."

Theresa didn't say anything. She just hugged a pillow and scowled.

"As for Jo and Caylin," Uncle Sam went on, "you will forget about meeting every handsome male on the slopes. You will focus on your mission, start looking for the princess, and stop acting like a bunch of giggling schoolchildren. That is the deal, and that is as good as it gets. Do you understand?"

Theresa stood up, tossed the pillow aside, and marched out of the room.

"I certainly hope Theresa is on board by morning, girls," Uncle Sam warned.

"She will be," Caylin said confidently, even though she felt anything but.

"Good. Because if you can't pull together as a team and finish this mission, you'll be of no use to The Tower. Do you know what that means?"

Jo and Caylin exchanged alarmed glances. "I can guess," Jo said.

"You'll be out of the spy business for good," Uncle Sam said.

The screen winked off, and the mirror became a mirror once again.

"I've heard *that* one before," Jo muttered.

Caylin flopped down onto the leather sofa. "Yeah, but I think he really means it this time."

Jo sighed. "Two strikes—"

"—and we're out. Game over. End of story."

Jo awoke with a start.

Someone had spoken to her. Or was it a dream? Her pillow was still there, the blankets were pulled up to her ears, and she still felt like sleeping for six more hours.

Everything was normal.

"Hey! Wake up!"

Except for Caylin shaking her.

"Go away," she replied grumpily.

"Wake up, Jo!" Caylin was already dressed in her ski pants and turtleneck. Showered, fed, and ready to kick butt. Jo hated her for it.

"Go run a triathlon or something," Jo growled. "I'm sleeping."

"Theresa's gone."

Now Jo's eyes were open.

"I'm dreaming, right?"

Caylin shook her head. "I just checked the whole place. Her jacket and skis are missing."

"I'm going to kill her!" Jo cried, sitting up. "What time is it?"

"Oh-seven-thirty," Caylin replied.

Jo bristled. "Do we need the oh? We're not marines. Just say seven-thirty, okay?"

"Don't take this out on me," Caylin warned. "Theresa's the jerk here."

Jo sighed. "What are we going to do? Should we look for her?"

"After what Uncle Sam said last night, I don't think we can afford to. She could be anywhere. We should forget about her and look for Kristal."

Jo nodded. "You're right. Give me a few minutes to join the living, and we'll jam." On her way to the doorway Jo stubbed her toe. "*Owww!*" she screamed, dancing on one foot. "Oooh, I'm gonna *kill* that girl!"

Caylin snorted. "Not if I get to her first."

• • •

Jo and Caylin surveyed the ski lodge from a table at the centrally-located cafe, sipping their hot chocolate.

"This is useless," Jo concluded. "We tried it before, and it doesn't work. Even if Rook or Kristal walked through here, we'd never get near them. We have to try something else."

"I'm open," Caylin replied. "But to what?"

Jo's eyes narrowed as a man strode by with a big camera around his neck.

"I think we should start thinking like the paparazzi," Jo said.

"How so?"

"Think about it, Cay. We've been issued some of the most advanced surveillance equipment known to humanity. Cameras, microphones, infrared, the works. Let's use 'em."

Caylin nodded. "Sounds juicy. But what good does all this stuff do us if we don't even know where to start?"

"I bet you a Swiss franc that we do."

Caylin laughed. "You're nuts."

"So you take the bet?"

"Sure, why not?"

"Pony up, ninja girl," Jo said, holding out her hand. "I'll show you."

Caylin fished a few coins out of her pocket and handed the cash to Jo, who stood. "I'll be right back!"

"Not if you're in a *Scream* sequel."

"Har, har."

A minute later Jo returned with a stack of newspapers. She dumped them on the table with a flourish. "Ta-da! Welcome to the real world of journalism."

"You've got to be joking," Caylin scoffed. She picked up a copy of *Celebriteez* between thumb and index finger, as if it were contagious. "You want me to *read* this?"

"We're going to read them all," Jo said, flipping through the issues of *International Tracker, Infamous,* and *Cheese!* she bought at the newsstand. "Whenever you see something on Kristal, tear it out. We'll make a pile. Any lead that mentions Schnell, we'll follow up. Easy, right?"

"Whatever you say," Caylin replied, opening *Celebriteez* and making a sick face. "Ugh! I can't *believe* the stuff they print in these rags!"

Jo flipped through the pages of *Cheese!* and laughed. "Hold your tongue, sister. Here's a story I *know* you're going to like." She tore out a photo of Kristal and Rook, accompanied by a short piece on a recent spat in a Schnell club.

"What club?" Caylin asked.

"Guess."

"Rik's?"

Jo nodded, flipping pages like a madwoman. She and Caylin continued through the whole stack, grimacing and groaning at some of the more ridiculous headlines:

OVERWEIGHT MAN STALKS BROADWAY
STAR—AND HE CAN'T EVEN WALK!

ALIENS BUY DELAWARE!

SHOCKER ROCKER SPOTTED BACKSTAGE AT
DISCO DIVA'S DEBUT—NAKED!

When they were done, they had a half dozen stories relating to Kristal and Schnell. Caylin slumped back in her chair. "I feel dirty," she muttered. "You actually like that stuff?"

"It's fun," Jo replied, picking up the first article. "And if it leads us to the princess, I expect you to subscribe."

"Over my dead body," Caylin retorted. "What's that one say?"

"Just that Kristal gave a quick concert at Rik's two weeks ago. She played a new song."

"Big whoop," Caylin replied. "What else do we have?"

"Kristal at Rik's, Kristal at Rik's, Kristal on the slopes, and Kristal—"

Jo paused, scanning the article hard.

"Well?" Caylin prodded.

A smile curled Jo's lips. She handed the piece to Caylin. "Read it and leap."

"'A source close to the royal family states that Princess Kristal and her longtime beau, Rook, have taken refuge in the honeymoon suite at the ultraexclusive, ultraswank Zürich Haus resort in beautiful Schnell. A spokesperson for the royal family in Zagaria flatly denies that Kristal and Rook have secretly wed and refuses to comment on the issue any further. Meanwhile, the happy couple has been spotted all over the trendy eateries and clubs of Schnell.'" Caylin looked at Jo. "You don't think they're married already?"

Jo shrugged. "Who knows? But that paper came out today. It gives us a place to start. It says that the honeymoon suite at Zürich Haus is actually a luxury chalet out in the woods. If we could find it, maybe we'll find Kristal."

Caylin folded the paper. "It's a long shot."

Jo huffed. "We're running a girl short, we're in the doghouse with Uncle Sam, and we're getting our leads from tabloids. Everything we do from now on is a long shot. Let's go."

They bought a map of the town from the newsstand and located the resort, which was mostly a series of private, exclusive chalets in the woods. The honeymoon suite was the most remote one. Caylin scanned the ski lift map and pointed to one near the resort.

"I say we take this lift to the top, then ski down into the trees here. If we cut across the mountain, we should run right into the cabin from the back. Sound good?"

"It's our only choice," Jo replied. "We'll never get in the front gate."

They zipped up their coats, flipped out their ski passes, and marched to the lift they wanted. When it was their turn, they scooted into position and waited for their chair.

"Mademoiselles!" a French-sounding lift attendant cried. "You have no skis!"

Jo and Caylin glanced at each other and smiled. They simultaneously clicked their heels. Their ski boots snapped to life before the man's eyes.

"*Sacre bleu,*" he whispered.

"Bye, now!" Jo waved.

The chair whisked them away.

It took Jo and Caylin two hours of trudging through two feet of snow, but they found it.

The chalet was tucked into a cul-de-sac at the end of a narrow road. It was a one-story little cabin with a carport, a hot tub, and an outdoor shack that appeared to be a sauna.

There were no signs of life.

They slipped in closer and saw the back end of a black sports car in the carport.

"It's a Lotus," Jo whispered. "Supposedly that's what Rook drives. Confidentially, I prefer the Lamborghini myself."

"You think they're home?"

Jo shrugged. "There's only one way to find out."

They edged closer to the chalet, slipping between trees. The snow masked their sound, but they knew they were hardly invisible. Hopefully no one would look out a window.

Finally they had their backs against the back wall of the cabin. There was a small open window a few feet above their heads.

"Use the camera," Jo suggested.

Caylin unlooped what looked like a five-foot section of vacuum cleaner cord out of an inside pocket. Yet it held its shape like a pipe cleaner. She plugged one end into a handheld mini-monitor and snaked the other end up the side of the building. It stood on its own, and in seconds the camera embedded in the other end was peeking in the open window. The picture on the LCD screen was perfect.

"The bathroom," Caylin whispered.

"I can see that," Jo remarked. "Zoom in on the shower door."

Caylin did.

"It's wet," Jo said. "And the mirror has some steam on it. Someone just showered. They probably have the window open to air out the steam."

"Bet you a Swiss franc that they're still home," Caylin replied.

"You lost that franc fair and square," Jo chided. "Okay. What do you want to do?"

Caylin thought it over. "Let's go in."

"We can't get in that window. It's too small."

"Let's go around. We'll find one. Or maybe a door's open."

"Ha! Nothing's that easy."

They circled the cabin, checking windows as they went. Every one was locked, every shade drawn. The only window without a curtain was the sliding glass door leading into the living room. They could see a dying fire in the fireplace, along with some room service trays with scraps of food and champagne glasses.

"Look out!" Caylin whispered, shoving Jo out of sight. "Someone's there."

"Who?"

Caylin shrugged. "All I saw was shaggy black hair and a bathrobe."

"Rook. That shaggy do is world famous."

"Don't you mean Scooby?"

"You're a riot, Cay. But I have an idea."

"Let's hear it."

Jo paused, glancing back the way they came. "I think I can fit in that bathroom window. Kind of drop in for a visit. What do you think?"

Caylin shook her head. "I think we're both totally postal. This will never work."

"Do you have any better suggestions?" Jo snapped.

"If we screw it up, Kristal and Rook will bolt. They'll dig a hole for themselves on some South Pacific beach, and we'll never find them."

"All the more reason to go in there now," Jo reasoned. "Because we *won't* screw it up."

"Okay, okay, let's go."

They retraced their steps. The window was about three feet above their heads and looked smaller than ever.

"A toothpick couldn't get in that window," Caylin

grumbled. "And I'm sorry, but you're no toothpick."

"I beg your pardon!" Jo growled. "You just boost me up, blondie. I'll get in that window."

"I don't know if I can lift you," Caylin said.

"Oh, shut up."

Caylin snickered and made her hands into a stirrup. Jo put her boot in it and pushed up. Caylin let out an exaggerated groan.

"Shhh!" Jo scolded.

She reached up and grabbed the windowsill, pulling herself up to chin level. The screen lifted easily.

"I'm in," Jo whispered down to Caylin. "Give a push!"

Caylin shoved the bottoms of Jo's boots. Jo slid her arms inside, planted her hands against the wall, and pushed. The fabric of her ski jacket hissed against the window frame, but she slid in several inches.

"Harder!" she pleaded, trying not to make too much noise. "I'm almost in!"

Caylin heaved against Jo's legs and feet. She slid in farther, almost to her waist.

And stopped dead.

"What are you doing?" Jo cried. "Push!"

"I am!" came Caylin's strained reply.

Jo's eyes bugged. She tried to move any way she could—in, out, anything. Nothing happened.

Panic gripped her. She wiggled like a trapped worm.

"I'm stuck! I can't believe it! I'm actually stuck!"

She felt Caylin leap up and hang on her legs, trying to pull her out. It did no good. Caylin dropped off into the snow, and Jo hung there, arms and legs flailing.

"I'm gonna kill you, Caylin! Get me out of here! Do you hear me, you ESPN2-watching freak? I said—"

Jo stopped in midpanic.

A beautiful blond woman in a bathrobe stared at her from the bathroom doorway, jaw sagging. She was immediately joined by the man with the shaggy black hair.

The woman was not Kristal.

The man was not Rook.

All three stared at one another for a few seconds.

Then Jo smiled, waved, and said, "Hi!"

SEVEN

The sun set behind the Alps, throwing massive orange shadows across the snow. Theresa came skidding to a halt at the bottom of the slope. One of the big slopes.

Patrick slid in next to her.

"I can't believe I just skied down that mountain!" she gushed, her cheeks bright red from the cold. She slammed her poles into the snow happily.

"I told you so," Patrick replied. "Would I lie to you?"

Theresa laughed, but she truly wondered if Patrick really would lie to her. She took an awful risk blowing off Jo and Caylin. But she didn't care about the princess—not from day one. And Dr. Eve's work was important to her. To humankind. If Patrick was somehow trying to sabotage her, Theresa wanted to know. Now *that* was an important mission! Better than hounding a spoiled royal like a bunch of hyperactive groupies.

Unfortunately, her day with Patrick had been long on skiing and laughter but way short on answers. Every time she directed the conversation toward last night's party, Patrick steered it back to something else.

The truth was, Theresa didn't really mind. Even if Patrick was up to something sinister, spending the day with him had been wonderful. If there ever was a guy who spoke her language, Patrick was the man. And the fact that he was gorgeous didn't matter a bit—yeah, *right*!

Still, Theresa knew she had to try one more time to get some scoop. It was her duty, after all. Sort of. In a lunatic-fringe-loner-acting-alone kind of way.

"I still can't believe you didn't hear any of the gunshots," she probed.

Patrick shrugged. "I guess that bathroom was on the far side of the chateau."

"How did you get out? I didn't see you."

"One of the security guards escorted me out. I walked down the hill and flagged a taxi. Though I have to admit, it was rather alarming stepping out of the loo to see a man pointing a gun at me."

Theresa laughed. "I bet."

Patrick cocked an eyebrow. "Why are you so curious?"

A slight wave of alarm passed through her. She had to be careful. Was she being too nosy? She smiled, shrugging shyly. "I don't know, Patrick. I was . . . well, worried about you."

Patrick grinned. "Were you?"

Theresa blushed. She couldn't believe she just said that! She nodded, feeling like a total dork.

"It was rather frightening," Patrick said, sliding closer on his skis. "I wish you would have been there to protect me."

Theresa giggled. "You are too smooth."

"And you are too beautiful."

She froze. She didn't know what to say. Her throat felt like one big knot. Patrick stared deep into her eyes, rooting her to the spot.

"Is something the matter?" he asked.

"N-no one's ever said that to me."

Patrick smiled, brushing a gloved finger along her cheek. "It's true."

Theresa's stomach did flip-flops. There weren't just a

few butterflies in there. There was a swarm. She wanted to kiss Patrick so bad. But she couldn't . . . not if he was still a suspect.

There was so much about him she didn't know.

But he was so perfect. . . .

Then she had an idea. It might not have been a brilliant idea, but it was the only thing she could think of. She had to know the truth about Patrick once and for all. And there was only one way to do that.

"I think you've got the wrong girl," she whispered.

He shook his head. "I've never met anyone like you, Tish. I know we've only been acquainted with each other for a short time, but you're definitely the right girl."

"Maybe, Patrick," she replied, pulling away. "Maybe I'm the right girl. But this is definitely the wrong time."

Patrick blinked, caught off guard. "Tish, I can't think of a better time. We've had a wonderful day. There's a beautiful sunset. We could have dinner, or—"

"No, Patrick. We did have a wonderful day. But let's not spoil it by pushing our luck." She reached out and touched his hand. "I have to go."

"Why?" he asked softly.

"I just do."

Theresa smiled, but she felt as though a fistful of daggers had slowly worked their way into her chest. She turned away—as gracefully as she could on skis—and pushed off. She didn't stop until she'd passed around the corner of the lodge.

Then she took a deep breath.

"I can't believe I just did that," she whispered, eyes shut tight. "I'd better be right."

She opened her eyes, turned around, and carefully peeked around the corner of the lodge from where she came.

Patrick stood where she left him, motionless. He stared toward the sunset. He looked so sad.

Theresa swallowed the lump in her throat, remembering her mission. "You had to do it," she told herself. "You *had* to."

After another minute Patrick lifted his poles and pushed off, heading away from her.

Now was her chance to meet the real Patrick. This plan

was her only option, and she had to make it work. She just hoped she could keep up with him on skis.

Theresa gripped her poles and followed him.

"I can't believe you got stuck!" Caylin said with a giggle. "I would've given *anything* to see the expression on your face. But seeing your feet flailing like crazy was pretty good, too."

"I bet," Jo muttered, tossing a frozen-pizza crust onto her plate. "We're just lucky I popped out of that window when I did. The guy had the phone in his hand. I wouldn't want to have to explain that one to Uncle Sam."

"Think that guy called the cops?" Caylin wondered.

"Who cares. I've never skied so fast in my life."

"Fast? That was nothing. One time at Vail, I—"

Jo held up her hand. "I don't care, okay, Cay? I really don't. All I care about is the fact that we're a bunch of total morons, complete and unabridged. Theresa's AWOL, and we can't even infiltrate a honeymoon chateau without humiliating ourselves. I mean, what kind of spies are we?"

"We just had a bad day," Caylin reasoned. "Everyone has bad days."

"No, this trip has been a disaster since we got here. Uncle Sam is going to kill us. Or at least ship us to remedial spy school or something equally terrifying."

"You know, Miss Doomsday Device, we still have time."

"What's your plan? Break into the espresso bar and read bad poetry? We couldn't even do that without getting thrown in jail."

"Actually, I was thinking of taking on Dieter the bouncer again," Caylin suggested. "But this time we make it a little more fair for us fräulein babe chicks."

Jo's eyes narrowed. "What do you mean?"

Caylin grinned mischievously. "Come on. I'll show you."

"Now this is what I call using all resources at our disposal," Jo said naughtily.

She and Caylin entered the lodge and marched directly to the entrance of Rik's. A line of about twenty people waited behind the velvet ropes, looking hopeful.

"I think Dieter's about to have a heart attack," Caylin predicted.

"Oh yeah," Jo agreed. "Tonight we *own* this place."

The Spy Girl duo had changed tactics. They left the down jackets, ski pants, and clunky boots back at the A-frame. This time they raided the well-stocked closets for tight, slinky dresses, spiked heels, and full-length mirrors. Jo wore all red. Her black hair flowed around her face with a life of its own. Her face glowed with a paint job fit for a supermodel. Caylin chose a black spaghetti-string number, with her blond hair moussed, spritzed, and teased to the point of perfection. Lush, glitzy fake-fur wraps completed their ensembles.

When they neared the entrance, all eyes turned on them—the guys' opening wide, the girls' narrowing to slits.

They strode right to Dieter at the head of the line.

He grinned and held the velvet rope open for them. He gestured grandly with his hand.

"*Wilkommen zum* Rik's, fräuleins. *Haben Sie Spass!*"

Jo sniffed and brushed him aside. "What*ever!*"

"Babe chicks coming through," Caylin announced.

Once inside, they basked in the moment, giggling madly.

"Oh, that was so choice," Jo gushed. "I'd give my top secret clearance to have that on video."

"It's pretty sad, if you ask me," Caylin said. "What was wrong with all those other people waiting in line?"

"They don't have government-issue Gucci," Jo replied. "Come on, let's take over."

They entered Rik's.

"Whoa," Caylin whispered. "Not bad."

House music thundered all around them from invisible woofers. Cocktail waitresses darted back and forth with full trays. The center of the place was the dance floor, packed with all the Euro-cool cats money could buy. They moved methodically, staring intensely into each other's eyes, but never smiling. Nine out of ten wore black.

The rest of the place was a maze of small tables and deep, dark booths.

"Do you see anyone?" Jo asked, squinting into the darkness.

"Someone definitely sees us," Caylin replied, gazing over at the main bar to their right. "Check it out."

"Why, hel-lo there," Jo said smartly.

The twins, Santino and Carlo, waved at them from two bar stools.

"Hello, ladies," Santino greeted, standing when the girls arrived. He kissed Jo's hand. "So nice to see you again. It's a shame our evening was cut short last night."

"It was a shame," Jo replied coolly. "I hope they caught whoever was responsible."

Carlo shot Santino a look. Santino smiled and said, "Yes, it was all taken care of. Perhaps you would like to dance?"

Jo's eyes lit up. "Indeed, we would."

"We would?" Caylin asked, shooting Jo a look of her own. "Don't we want to soak up the atmosphere a little first? You know, check out the *crowd*?"

Jo scowled and dragged Caylin toward the dance floor. "We can check out the atmosphere from the dance floor, can't we?"

So they danced, hopping and gyrating and flirting. Jo and Caylin indeed felt many eyes on them, but they didn't care. The music and the moment overtook them. By the time they made it back to their seats, an hour had passed.

"Whew, that was killer," Jo said, wiping her brow.

"You broke a sweat from that?" Caylin asked, barely winded. "You have to work out more."

"As if what you say will change the world," Jo muttered. She turned to Santino. "Do you guys hit the clubs often?"

"Yes, fairly often," he replied. "Our hours are long, so when we do get time off, we enjoy it."

"Do you see a lot of famous people in here?" Jo asked. "I mean, this is, like, the hottest club in the hottest ski resort in Europe. You must see a lot of glitterati."

"Some," Santino replied, his eyes darting from Jo's.

"Like who?"

Santino shrugged. "I don't know their names. I don't follow things like that."

"How about Tristan and Edith? Antonio and Lola? Colin and Vivica? Joel and Jane?" Jo asked, rapidly listing all the celebrity couples she could think of.

Santino stared stupidly. He obviously had no clue.

"How about Kristal and Rook?" Caylin asked.

That registered. Santino blinked and glanced at Carlo.

"No, no one like that," Santino said.

"Bummer," Jo replied. "We're big fans. We heard that

she did some surprise concerts here. We hoped maybe we'd get lucky."

"No, I'm afraid not," Santino said curtly.

"Santino," came a voice. "It's time."

It was Carlo.

"You talk!" Jo said kiddingly.

Carlo gave her a dark stare. "Sometimes."

Santino caught his look. "I'm sorry, ladies. We must be going. We have an early morning tomorrow."

"So soon?" Jo moaned. "We were cooking out there."

"Again, I'm sorry. Perhaps another time?"

"Okay," Jo replied.

The twins dropped some money on the bar and disappeared into the crowd. Jo scowled.

"He didn't even kiss my hand good-bye," she said.

"Do we smell or something?" Caylin asked.

"Well, *you* do. I've been telling you that for weeks."

"Stand-up comedy is not your forte," Caylin said. "Maybe we should get out of here. Kristal's not going to show. She's—"

Jo poked Caylin in the ribs.

"Ow! What was *that* move?"

"Shhh!"

"You're shushing me in a hundred-decibel nightclub? Did you have a thrombo or something?"

"Don't make a big deal out of it," Jo said, "but check out the guy in that dark booth over there in the corner and tell me we didn't just catch a big-budget break?"

Caylin peered into the smoky gloom. The man's face was illuminated by a tiny, dim lamp in the center of his table. Caylin saw shaggy dark hair, razor stubble, and shadowy, brilliant green eyes.

"It's Rook!" Caylin exclaimed.

"Shhh, if you freak out, he'll run," Jo warned.

"Where's his entourage?" Caylin wondered. "No security, no leeches, no nothing. He's all alone."

"He's all ours, you mean," Jo corrected, slipping off her stool and straightening her hair. "Turn on the charm, Spy Girl. We're going in."

They crossed the floor quickly, dodging dancers and waitresses. With each step they expected to be stopped by burly bodyguards. But Rook grew closer.

No one stopped them.

When they reached his booth, Jo slipped in on one side, Caylin on the other. Rook couldn't have escaped if he'd wanted to—and they both figured he'd definitely want to.

His tired eyes came to life when they edged in next to him.

"You're very cute when you're depressed," Jo commented.

"Oh, please, just go away," Rook grumbled, dismissing them with a wave. "Take your autograph-seeking, gold-digging selves as far away as those little spike heels will carry you."

"We don't want your autograph," Caylin replied, smiling at Jo.

"You want my blood, then?" Rook muttered. He rolled up his black sleeve and exposed his veins. "Take it. You're all a bunch of vampires."

"We don't want your blood, Mr., uh, Rook," Caylin said awkwardly. "We just want to talk."

"What my tongue-tied friend here is trying to say," Jo said, her flirtatious expertise taking over, "is that you looked very lonely all by yourself. You look like you could use some friendly company."

Rook snorted, knocking back the remaining liquor in his glass. "I have too many friends already. I don't need any more."

A waiter lurking in the shadows immediately set another drink in front of him, then disappeared.

"Good service here," Caylin mused.

"It pays to have roots," Rook replied caustically. "They know what I drink, how much I drink"—he paused to glare at them—"and when I want to be left alone."

He gulped at his new glass.

"It seems to me that you don't have much to be unhappy about, Rook," Jo suggested. "You're rich, you're famous, and you've got one of the most beautiful women in the world to go home to."

Rook laughed bitterly. "You know it all, don't you? The *International Trasher* and all the others tell you everything there is to know about me, right? How much money I have. Where I'm spending it. Who I'm spending it on. Whether or not this weekend was the big weekend when I secretly got married. All of it. Am I right?"

Jo squirmed. "Not, like, totally."

"So, did you?" Caylin asked.

"Did I what?" Rook replied.

"Get married."

Rook laughed again and shook his head. He took another deep sip of his booze. "You certainly have the look down, I'll give you that. But you're too impatient."

"What are you talking about?" Jo asked.

"The two of you," Rook said. "You're beautiful. You've got someone buying very expensive clothes for you so you can get past a monster like Dieter. So you can get to me."

Jo caught Caylin's look: *Are we busted?*

"How much are they paying you?" Rook demanded, looking around. "Where's the hidden camera?"

"What are you talking about?" Jo asked again.

"You must think I'm stupid," Rook said. "You're reporters. Or you're stalkerazzi trying to get photos of me alone with two beautiful women." He raised his glass to the imaginary cameras. "Well, get a good shot. And for the benefit of your tape recorders, my official statement is, no, Kristal and I are not on our honeymoon. No, Kristal and I have not even been married. No, Kristal and I haven't spoken for days."

He downed the rest of his drink. The waiter in the shadows emerged with another. Rook snatched it from his hands and tossed him the empty.

He stood and raised the new drink. "Take heart, beautiful single women everywhere," he announced. "For alas, my beautiful princess has fled. I am alone. Kristal has left me!"

EIGHT

Jo grabbed Rook by the arm and forced him to sit down. If he made a scene, she and Caylin would be the ones kicked out, not Rook.

He slumped back into his seat, chuckling.

"We're not reporters," Jo stated.

"And we're not stalkers," Caylin added.

Rook's eyes narrowed. "Then who are you? You're too obvious to just be groupies."

"*That's* good to know," Caylin said, rolling her eyes.

"We're . . . um, operatives," Jo said lamely.

"Operatives?" Rook mumbled.

"Covert operatives," Caylin said. "Our assignment is to find Kristal and return her home."

"Return her home," Rook echoed. "So you're secret agents?"

"Basically," Jo replied.

"And whose idea was this 'mission' of yours?"

Caylin paused before answering. "Queen Cascadia."

"Aarrgh!" Rook roared, pounding the table. "*I knew it!* Her mother! She thinks she has such the iron fist. That monarchy is such a joke. But she must have gotten to Kristal. She must have!" Rook slouched in his seat and covered his face with his hands. "Unbelievable."

"Kristal just up and left you?" Jo asked, not quite believing it.

Rook leaned forward. His eyes were bloodshot. He looked totally defeated. "I guarantee it. You see, Kristal is very used to being loved. By everyone. She can't stand someone having a bad opinion of her, even if it's deserved. This is her way of calling it off. Just leaving me without a word." Rook snorted derisively. "All that cold royal blood, and she didn't even have the courage to dump me face-to-face."

"That's not an easy thing to do sometimes," Jo offered.

"Save the sentiment," Rook replied. "I need to be alone."

He motioned to the shadowy waiter. The man emerged and pulled the table away from the booth so Rook could escape. He was very drunk and nearly fell. Caylin grabbed his arm to steady him.

"Are you all right?" she asked gently.

His gaze met hers. His hard, bloodshot eyes softened slightly. "I'm destroyed."

Caylin helped him stand, then whispered in his ear, "We're not the enemy, Rook. We're here to help. Can we contact you if we find out anything?"

Rook let out a deep sigh. He eyed Caylin suspiciously for a moment. Then he nodded. He told her the address of his chateau and what to say to the guards at the gate.

"Don't come near me before noon," Rook warned. "I will be hung over."

"Gotcha." Caylin stepped back. Several security guards/hangers-on had emerged from the shadows like the waiter. He really was never alone. They surrounded him, moved him forward, and disappeared into the crowd.

Caylin pulled Jo aside. "I have his address."

"Will you remember it?"

Caylin smiled and held up her handbag. "I activated one of my bugs. The whole conversation was recorded."

"Just like he thought," Jo stated.

"Oh, well."

"This doesn't make sense, Cay. He thinks the queen got to Kristal."

"If she did, we would have heard about it," Caylin replied. "Our mission would have been called off."

"You're right. I think this is worth a phone call."

"You're right, Spy Girls," Uncle Sam agreed from the A-frame's big mirror. "Queen Cascadia has had no contact with Kristal. I checked with her this evening. What does that tell you?"

"Maybe Rook knows more than he's saying," Jo offered.

"I don't know," Caylin said. "I'd say his broken heart performance tonight was pretty real. His whiskey breath sure was."

"Either way," Uncle Sam replied, "there's a big piece of this puzzle still missing. I want you to contact Rook again tomorrow—when he's sober. Check him out, check his place out, get a vibe. And Spy Girls?"

"Yes, Sammy?"

"Forget the three-day time limit. Just get the job done."

Jo couldn't contain her grin. "You got it! Not a problem!"

"As I said, *get the job done.*"

"We promise," Caylin replied.

"Good," Uncle Sam replied. "Now, Spy Girls, I have only one more question before I say good night."

"Let's have it, double-oh-Sammy," Jo chirped.

"Yeah, lay it on us," Caylin said.

The distorted image of Uncle Sam shifted, some of the pixels in his face turning an angry red. He crossed his arms, and they could feel his glare upon them.

"Where's Theresa?" he asked.

Theresa sat crouched inside a thick copse of evergreen trees, staring through her tube of Tower-issued breath spray that also happened to be a very powerful infrared telescope.

She was watching Patrick. She'd tailed him to one of the most remote ski lifts on the mountain and followed him up. The sun had just been setting, and while the view was like nothing she had ever seen, she noticed that the slopes below her got steeper and steeper. She didn't know where Patrick was going, but the trip down the mountain would be rough. And judging by the failing sunlight, dark.

However, once at the top, Patrick took off to the left, into the trees. Wherever he was going, he wasn't taking the normal slope.

Theresa did her best to follow, ducking under tree limbs and using her poles to keep from falling into the deep powder.

She failed several times, eating her share of flakes.

Luckily Patrick took his time. She ended up falling one last time into her current hiding place, brushing herself off, and spotting the dark shape of Patrick a few dozen yards away.

"Okay, dreamboat," she whispered. "What's your deal?"

She popped the cap on her zoom lens and zeroed in on him.

He was studying several large steel vents that seemed to grow out of the mountainside. The snow had melted around the vents, exposing the ground.

"What's that all about?" Theresa wondered. She clicked

the record button on the telescope and captured the moment for posterity.

Theresa scanned the mountainside for more vents, but saw nothing.

Hmmm . . .

She capped her spy gear, grabbed her poles, and pushed off toward Patrick. If she could get closer, maybe she could see more. Her little telescope was only so powerful.

If she could just stay quiet enough to—

Theresa's left ski hit a patch of ice beneath the powder. She lost control of that entire side of her body, pitching wildly. Her poles flailed, and it was all she could do not to scream her head off.

She picked up speed, faster and faster. Trees whipped by her, branches stung her face, and she burst out of some evergreen branches to see Patrick. Faster than light and larger than life.

Bam!

They went down in a hail of equipment. Poles flew, goggles spun, and limbs tangled.

When they came to a stop, Theresa found herself on top of Patrick, staring right into his wide eyes.

"Uh, hi."

Patrick blinked. "Tish?"

"In the flesh." She shrugged. "And snow."

He shoved her off and rolled away. "Are you mad? What are you doing here? You could get us both killed!"

"My skiing's a lot better," she replied. "Killing us is a little extreme, don't you think?"

"That's not what I—" Patrick sighed and gathered up her equipment. "Look, just get your skis back on. I'll make sure you get to the bottom of the hill safely."

Theresa didn't budge. "What are you doing up here, Patrick?"

Patrick glared. "I could very well ask you the same thing."

"I followed you," Theresa replied defiantly.

"Why? I thought you made it painfully clear that you didn't want to see me again."

"I did?"

"You most certainly did!"

Theresa shrugged. "I guess you're just irresistible, Patrick."

"Not bloody likely." His eyes narrowed, and he took a step forward. "A girl who can't ski doesn't follow someone to the most remote part of the mountain without a good reason."

Theresa grabbed her orphan ski from him. "The other person must have a pretty good reason for going to the most remote part of the mountain in the first place."

Patrick popped his own skis back on and hefted his poles. "Don't you suppose that's none of your business?"

"Maybe." Theresa nodded as she clicked her ski on. "The same way these big vents are none of *your* business."

"You really shouldn't be here, Tish."

"Neither should you."

Patrick scowled. "You don't understand. If we get—"

"Hey!" came a gruff voice from up the hill.

"—caught?" Theresa finished for him.

"Yes," Patrick replied. "Caught was *definitely* the word I was searching for!"

NINE

Who is that up there?" Theresa whispered.

Two figures emerged from the trees above the vents. Both were on skis. But neither of them had poles.

They had submachine guns.

"Uh-oh," Theresa moaned.

Patrick slowly pulled his goggles down over his eyes. He clicked a button on the side, and Theresa swore they came to life. They hummed, and a dim green light glowed from inside them. She'd seen that before.

Night vision.

The armed skiers closed in.

"Tish?"

"Yes, Patrick?" she whispered nervously.

"You're about to get the skiing lesson of your life."

He shoved her down the hill. Theresa screamed and almost fell immediately, but regained her balance enough to see Patrick pass her. He was crouched in a downhiller's pose, poles back, head down. Full speed ahead.

"Stop!" came a voice from behind them.

A gunshot rang out.

"Oh man, no guns! No guns!" she cried.

She didn't look back. She didn't stop. She couldn't have if she wanted to.

All Theresa could do was point her skis downhill, follow Patrick, and pray.

The wind whipped her face. She hadn't had time to retrieve her own goggles, and now her eyes watered badly in the cold. In seconds she could barely see. She wiped at her face with her glove, but it didn't help.

Panic gripped her.

A tree shot by. Her right ski grazed it.

Another shot rang out somewhere behind her.

Up ahead, Patrick was gone.

"Oh no."

She was a goner for sure. But she couldn't stop. The gunmen would catch her and kill her. How did she get herself into these things?

Another tree raced by, too close. If she hit one of them at this speed . . .

Then she remembered: the first rule of skiing.

When in doubt, fall.

But she was going too fast!

What was worse, getting shot or slamming into a tree? Equally bad, she thought. Both options would leave her dead. And falling? How about a broken neck?

A third shot rang out.

Theresa yelped—the slug took a chunk out of a tree just in front of her. Bark sprayed her as she passed.

"Patrick!" she screamed.

He seemed to emerge from the trees themselves. It was actually him. He was skiing next to her, a reassuring hand on her arm. Where did he—?

"Steady!" he called. "Grab my waist!"

He pushed just ahead of her. His movements were smooth and calculated. In a split second he'd stepped in front of her. She grabbed his waist, trying not to lose her balance. If she did, they'd both buy it.

Patrick guided Theresa through trees, over moguls that nearly threw them both in the air, and down a mountain that Theresa couldn't have skied alone without serious injury. Patrick made her feel as if she could do anything.

Several more shots rang out.

Something whizzed over Theresa's head.

"That was too close!" she called.

"We need speed!" he yelled back.

He suddenly crouched in front of her and slowed down.

Slowed down?

"Patrick, what are you—*whoaaa!*"

When he slowed, Theresa bumped into him, almost flipping right over his head. Just then he stood up sharply on his skis. Theresa felt her body lift with his. Her skis left the snow.

She was riding him piggyback.

"Hang on, old girl!" he said.

"Don't caaaall me thaaat!"

Their speed rocketed. Theresa wanted to close her eyes, but she just couldn't. She had to see.

More shots exploded behind them. But Theresa swore they were more distant. No bark exploded in their faces.

"Hope you're bullet-proof!"

"Shut up and ski, you idiot!"

He did. Theresa chanced a glance behind them, but the trees were a blur. She spotted something far to her right, up the hill. Lights. Glass. A house. It looked familiar.

Dr. Eve's chateau!

They were that close?

Just then they hit a massive mogul. Theresa's stomach lurched. She felt weightless.

They were airborne.

The world went super slo-mo.

This was it. They would land. Fall. Break legs. Get caught. Be shot. Every fear pumped through her. All Theresa could do was grip Patrick tighter.

When they hit, she felt the air rush out of him. His legs buckled. Snow sprayed up into her face, blinding her. But the wind kept whipping her. Their speed didn't waver.

They didn't fall!

Theresa howled in triumph and hugged Patrick. They

soared into a thick stand of evergreens. The branches reached out at them, snapping and yanking their clothes. But nothing could stop them now.

They burst through the trees. Just below them twinkled the lights of the town.

Theresa looked over her shoulder. All she saw were trees and the trail of Patrick's skis.

"We made it!"

They finally stopped just outside of town, in the shadow of a hundred-foot fir tree. They were invisible from the road. Patrick collapsed in the snow. Theresa landed on top of him.

"My bloody legs are on fire," he muttered. "How much do you weigh?"

"Didn't anyone tell you that it's not polite to ask a girl her weight?"

"Why don't you get off me and I'll consider it."

Theresa rolled off Patrick and stood uncertainly. Her own legs felt like butter. There had to be more adrenaline in her veins than blood. She couldn't stop her hands from shaking.

Patrick rolled over and massaged his legs. "Are you all right?" he asked, huffing. "No bullet holes?"

"I'm okay. But who *were* those guys?"

Patrick chuckled. "Ski patrol. We were undoubtedly in a restricted area."

"Very funny. What were you doing up there, Patrick?"

"Seeking new downhill challenges," he replied smoothly. "The expert slopes are dead boring. Don't you think?"

"I think I'd like to turn next time I go down a slope."

"Well, I know one thing," Patrick offered, standing up.

"What?"

"I'm one fantastic ski instructor. You were great."

Theresa laughed. "Not great. Just alive."

Patrick nodded. "I think we'd better get moving. Who knows what will come down that mountain after us. Do you think you can make it on your own?"

A pang of alarm went through her. Not because she couldn't make it home alone, but because she didn't want Patrick to leave. She felt electrified after their ordeal. She just wanted to kiss him silly.

"Um, I guess I'll be all right," she said.

"Tish, I think . . . I think it's best that we don't think too much about what just happened. Okay?"

"Yeah, *right*," she replied. "I'm not shot at every day. Something serious is going on, Patrick, and I think you owe me an explanation."

"Tish," Patrick replied, a pained look on his face. "It's really best that you don't know."

"That's not fair!" she cried. She bent down and retrieved one of her ski poles. "We just—"

When she turned back, she froze.

Patrick was gone.

"Patrick?" she called.

No answer. Just a silent, snowy night. He had completely disappeared.

Theresa sighed. "No fair."

Theresa skied back to the A-frame, thinking back on her exciting night. It had been like no other. Usually girls her age were thrilled just to be able to go to the prom with their boyfriends. But tonight Theresa had followed the man of her dreams up a mountain and skied down with him while being shot at.

"Not bad, Spy Girl," she whispered to herself as she locked her skis in the ski rack. "Not bad."

Still, she knew there were too many unanswered questions. Questions she couldn't ignore.

She clomped into the A-frame with her ski boots still on. She didn't even get a chance to close the door.

"Nice to see you, Theresa," Caylin said, arms folded, foot tapping.

"Where have you been, young lady?" Jo demanded, not a hint of humor in her voice.

"Let me guess," Theresa replied wearily. "You were worried sick."

"You wish," Jo said. "But Uncle Sam was *very* interested in your whereabouts. I'm never lying for you again."

Theresa glared back at her. "I never asked you to lie in the first place."

"What's the story?" Caylin asked angrily. "You owe us an explanation, Theresa. You let us down today."

Theresa sighed and bent stiffly to unbuckle her boots. "You wouldn't believe me if I told you. I'm dying for a hot bath."

"Try us," Jo ordered.

"I decided to continue my investigation of Patrick. Something is definitely up with him and Dr. Eve. I owe it to her to find out what."

"You *owe* it to her?" Jo asked incredulously. "Are you serious? You don't even know her!"

"I know her work, Jo. It's more important than rescuing any princess. I mean, what are we, a bunch of Luke Skywalkers?"

"It doesn't matter what you think of the mission," Caylin reminded her. "You're not supposed to think about it. Just do it."

"Shoe commercial sentiments from the jock," Theresa muttered. "How quaint."

Caylin took a step forward, but Jo put up her hand. "So what is it, T.? Really. Are you in love with this guy, or what?"

Theresa shot Jo a withering look. "Dr. Eve's mission

in life is to help humanity, Jo. And she has the power and knowledge to actually do it. As a student of science—and a human being—how can I stand by and watch someone try to hurt her? How?"

"Uncle Sam said it himself: Dr. Eve has her own people to handle that," Caylin explained. "You were ordered to back off."

"Yeah, back off and chase Kristal, I know." Theresa angrily tossed her ski boots in the corner. "Real humanitarian aid. Well, I'm not doing it."

Jo blinked. "What did you say?"

"You heard me."

"No way," Caylin argued. "You're helping us with Rook tomorrow."

"You finally found him?" Theresa asked.

"No thanks to you," Jo replied. She quickly explained their encounter with Rook in the nightclub, along with Uncle Sam's orders to contact him the next day.

"I'm happy for you guys," Theresa said. "But I'm still not going. Dr. Eve invited me to her chateau, remember? I'm not passing that up."

"You're playing with all our lives, T.," Caylin warned. "If we fail, we're through. Do you understand that?"

"I'm sorry, Cay. But I think helping a Nobel Prize winner continue her work safely is more important than returning a spoiled royal to her mother, who was once a spoiled royal herself."

"You're forgetting something," Jo said.

"What?"

"You're a Spy Girl. Like it or not, you're part of a team. And this team has a mission."

Theresa shook her head. "That mission isn't for spies. It's for baby-sitters. I'm the one with the real mission. So you know what that makes me?"

"What?" Caylin asked.

"The *real* Spy Girl."

TEN

At noon the next day Theresa took a taxi to the end of Hauptstrasse and walked up the long driveway to Dr. Eve's chateau. The whole time all she could think about was the previous night.

She didn't know what would happen with the Spy Girls. She left before they were awake and ate a long breakfast at the lodge. No matter how many times she ran it back in her head, she still couldn't bring herself to work on the Kristal case while she could help Dr. Eve. It went against everything she stood for.

So many questions . . .

She was sure that the gunman the night of Dr. Eve's party had been Patrick. But what was he doing near those vents? And what were the vents for?

They'd skied right past Dr. Eve's chateau last night. That

couldn't have been a coincidence. And Patrick had been too well prepared. No one skied with night-vision goggles.

Nothing added up.

She approached the beautiful mahogany double doors of Dr. Eve's chateau and rang the bell. She saw no armed guards. Nothing unusual. The butler answered the door and showed her in immediately.

Theresa entered the main living area. It was even more spectacular during the day. Outside the windows were miles and miles of snow-capped mountains and evergreen forest. The natural light in the room was almost blinding.

Dr. Eve was there too. A cluster of students Theresa's age surrounded her. Special guests from the science symposium, no doubt.

Dr. Eve strode over as soon as she saw her.

"Tish, so wonderful of you to come!"

Theresa shook Dr. Eve's hand, and all of her worries instantly disappeared.

Jo and Caylin rode the Snownuke 667 over to Rook's place. Actually, Jo drove. Caylin held on for dear life.

"This isn't funny anymore!" she cried as Jo nearly side-swiped yet another car. "We're not supposed to ride this thing in the middle of town!"

"Relax," Jo muttered. "You act like I've never done this before."

Jo blew through town and across an open field to get to Rook's. While crossing the field, Caylin got a glimpse of the speedometer: 105! Wait—that was kilometers. But still . . .

She closed her eyes and prayed.

Finally Jo slowed down as they entered the posh neighborhood where Rook hung his hat. And these days, his head.

They found his house without a problem. It was gorgeous. A sprawling mansion behind a tall stone wall. There was an intercom at the front gate.

Jo buzzed it.

"What?" a gruff voice demanded.

Jo said the password that Rook had given them the night before and told the voice that they were there to see him.

There was a moment of silence on the other end.

Then the gates creaked open.

Jo drove the sled up the snow-covered driveway and parked it next to Rook's black Lotus.

"Wow," Jo marveled, running her hand over the Lotus's hood. "What a sweet ride."

"Come on, speed demoness," Caylin urged.

The front door was open a few inches. A thunderous techno riff roared out at them. They pushed the door open wide and went in.

Immediately they were hit with the smell.

"Oh, man, there is definitely a bachelor in the house," Jo grunted, wincing.

"It's like cigarettes, body odor, and really old socks mixed together," Caylin added.

Indeed, the house would have been beautiful under normal circumstances. But Rook was obviously living very alone, no matter how many hangers-on he had. Take-out food cartons, dirty clothes, and torn newspapers littered the living room. Beyond that was a den with a cathedral ceiling. A massive stereo pumped the music through speakers as tall as the Spy Girls. The tune echoed off the high ceiling, making them feel as if they were in a concert hall.

Rook padded out of the kitchen in a wrinkled muscle shirt and pajama bottoms. He held a cup of black coffee. His eyes were even redder than they'd been the previous night. Medusa would have been envious of his hair.

"I guess I wasn't dreaming last night," he muttered, sipping the coffee. "You were real."

"Yeah!" Jo hollered over the music. "Can you turn that down? We can't hear you!"

Rook nodded and pointed a remote at the stereo. The sound receded.

"Doesn't that hurt your head?" Caylin asked.

Rook chuckled. "Not that song."

"Why not?"

He sighed, stepped down into the den area, and slumped into an easy chair. He didn't offer them anything, and he didn't ask them to sit.

So they sat, anyway.

"It's the last song I ever heard Kristal sing before she left," he explained. "She sang it to me."

"When was the last time you saw her?" Jo asked.

"The night she left me, obviously," Rook replied bitterly.

"What happened?"

Rook rubbed his eyes. "We were at Rik's. Partying hard, like usual. Then some noisy fans demanded that Kris get up and sing. She felt like it, so she did. The last song she sang was this one." He gestured at the stereo. "It's called 'Eve of Destruction.' She's going to release it as the first single off her new album. Anyway, she sang the song. She stared at me the whole time. I mean, you know how that girl is famous for her blue eyes. We've been together for years . . . and those eyes still melt me, you know? She had me in the palm of her hand while she sang that song. And she knew it. When she finished, she smiled at me from the stage. Then she walked backstage. And I haven't seen her since. She walked right out on me." He chuckled angrily. "Sometimes I still can't believe it."

The song ended. There was a pause, then it began again.

"Is that a demo?" Caylin asked.

Rook nodded. "It's the only copy I have. I don't know if I'll have the heart to buy the CD when it's released next month."

Caylin stood and approached the stereo. Jo ignored her, concentrating on Rook.

"Why would she leave you, Rook? Everything I've read says you two were happy. Total Cinderella factor."

Rook scoffed. "Everything you read, huh? Well, we *were* happy. I guess that makes me Cinderfella. The only time we ever fought was when the press got too close. Or when her family stuck its royal nose where it didn't belong. They must have finally gotten to her."

I don't think so, Jo thought. And that was right from the queen's mouth.

"I need more coffee," Rook said. He got up and shuffled to the kitchen, swinging the door behind him.

"What do you think?" Jo asked Caylin.

"Shhh," Caylin replied. "Listen to this."

She upped the volume on the stereo. Jo really tuned in to the song for the first time.

Her eyes widened.

Caylin saw the reaction and nodded urgently. "Do you hear what I hear?"

"Affirmative, Sporty Spy," Jo said breathlessly. "Could it be true?"

"There's one way to find out."

Rook came back in with fresh coffee. He didn't look any better.

"Rook, what's the story behind this song?" Caylin asked.

Rook stared blankly. "The story?"

"What does it mean?" Jo clarified. "What was Kristal talking about when she wrote it?"

He shrugged. "She's gone gonzo for this environmental stuff. She said something about donating all the proceeds from this song to enviro-warriors or something. I can't always keep track of what's in her head most times. I just love the song."

"Do you have a lyric sheet?" Jo asked.

"Nope. Don't need one. I know this tune by heart. Want me to sing it?"

"No thanks," Caylin declined. "But could you write it out for us?"

"You think it'll help?"

Jo and Caylin glanced at each other.

"Totally," they said in unison.

Rook found some paper and scribbled out the lyrics. He handed it over to the girls with a bewildered look on his face.

Caylin read the chorus aloud: "'She'll find what she's looking for/Find the key to a worldwide door/She'll open it up and spread the gloom/Unleash the poison that seals your doom. . . .'"

Caylin paused, but Jo gestured for her to continue.

"'Call it pain/Call it knowledge/Call it rain/Call it college/It's the world gone bad/It'll make you sad/It's a global reduction/Called the eve of destruction. . . .'"

"Kris kept talking about poison when she wrote that," Rook said. "You know, how the world is being choked off. Stuff like that."

"I think Kristal's talking about someone specific," Caylin said, her face pale.

"What?" Rook asked.

"Her name is Eve," Jo said grimly. "Eve of Destruction. But you can call her *Doctor* Eve."

"I'm glad you decided to stay behind after the main tour, Tish," Dr. Eve said. "You show a lot of enthusiasm and promise."

"I hope so," Theresa replied. "Your lab is amazing. You actually built it into the side of the mountain. I've never seen anything like it."

It truly *was* amazing. After lunch the other students departed. But Dr. Eve had invited Theresa to stay behind. She offered to show her the real laboratory. The one on the tour was just for demonstrations.

Theresa was so excited at the offer that she only nodded over and over. She didn't want to open her mouth and sound like a dweeb.

Dr. Eve led her downstairs and through several rooms, one of which looked like a hunter's trophy room. A massive elk's head hung over the fireplace. Soon they were in the large conference room that was part of the original tour. Dr. Eve approached the blackboard and touched the frame.

An entire section of the wall opened inward!

Theresa's eyes bugged. "Whoa!"

Dr. Eve showed her many things. Some of her current work on the long-term side effects of weightlessness. Space colonization theories. And her crowning achievement: water purification.

"I study space for population purposes," Dr. Eve explained. "We will have to live in space eventually, for there will be no room for us down here. And I study water for the subsequent pollution that accompanies population growth. If we do not have pure water, we will die."

Dr. Eve led her through several chambers, each relating in some way to her research. Several lab techs milled about, ignoring them.

Theresa walked by a ventilation grate and felt a cold breeze hit her face. That was strange. Where would cold air be coming from?

She recalled the large vents on the mountain. Was this what Patrick was looking for? An entrance to Dr. Eve's lab?

Dr. Eve's head whipped around. "What are you looking at, Tish?"

ELEVEN

Jo and Caylin raced back to the A-frame on the Snownuke. Jo pushed it even faster than before, forcing Caylin to hold on tight. She screamed into Jo's ear as they went.

"I hate it when Theresa's right!"

"Me too," Jo yelled. "But she's got it backward! She's trying to *help* Dr. Eve!"

"You think this Patrick guy is trying to expose Dr. Eve?"

"Who knows? We have to get back to the A-frame and find Theresa before she goes to see Dr. Eve!"

"She was long gone this morning," Caylin reminded her.

"You're right. But Dr. Eve's invite was for lunch. Theresa might be back already."

"Maybe if you wish real hard, that'll happen," Caylin muttered.

When they reached the A-frame, they leaped off the snowmobile and ran inside. They called out for Theresa, but there was no reply.

"She's not here," Jo said.

"That leaves only one option," Caylin replied.

Jo nodded. "Dr. Eve's chateau."

"Let's roll."

"Wait—leave the lyrics on the table. If we missed Theresa and she shows up here, I want her to see the song for herself."

Caylin nodded and tossed the lyrics to "Eve of Destruction" on the coffee table and zipped up her coat.

They headed out.

But once outside, they stopped dead.

Santino and Carlo waited for them, astride a pair of idling snowmobiles.

"Whoa," Jo blurted. "Hi, guys."

"You know, this *really* isn't a good time," Caylin said. "We're kind of busy."

"We thought perhaps you might like to go for a ride?" Santino suggested.

Jo chuckled. "Um, no thanks. Like she said. We're busy."

Carlo reached into his jacket and pulled something out.

Jo and Caylin gasped.

It was a gun.

"We insist," Carlo said menacingly.

"I—I'm sorry, Dr. Eve?"

"You seem very interested in something, Tish," the doctor said. "What is it?"

"This air. It's cold," Theresa said, putting her hand up to the vent.

Dr. Eve nodded. "There are vents leading up to the surface. Not much fresh air would get down here otherwise. Sometimes there are fumes."

"Fumes from what?"

"Many things. Natural gas. Chemicals. Anything you might find in a busy laboratory, Tish."

So the vents *did* lead down here, Theresa thought. Patrick must have figured that out.

"This must have been expensive to build," Theresa marveled. "Who paid for all of it?"

Dr. Eve cocked an eyebrow. "It was expensive. But I receive many grants from many governments. A lot of people would like to see me succeed in my work."

"I can imagine," Theresa replied. "If science paid half as well as pro sports, you'd be able to afford a castle."

Theresa heard a loud hiss. She followed the sound with her gaze. There was a large steel door in the far corner, behind some large equipment. A technician came through the door dressed head to toe in white. What struck Theresa as odd was the tech's full-head gas mask.

The tech shut the steel door, locked it down, and flipped a switch. It hissed again, then was silent.

"What's in there?" Theresa asked.

Dr. Eve paused. The tech passed them. The way the man breathed in his gas mask, Theresa felt as if Darth Vader had just walked by. He disappeared into another chamber.

Dr. Eve cleared her throat. "It is a decontamination area."

"For what?"

Dr. Eve smiled. "Beyond that door are many computers and other supersensitive machines. We need a completely dust-free environment. That is why I can't show it to you."

"Oh. Why was that man wearing a gas mask?"

Tension crept into Dr. Eve's voice. "Sometimes we work with extremely hazardous chemicals. The technicians need to be protected."

"What kind of chemicals?"

"Do you always ask so many questions, Tish?" Dr. Eve demanded.

Theresa nodded. "I'm just curious. I thought you wanted me to ask questions."

Dr. Eve's expression darkened. "Unfortunately, curiosity is the curse of the scientist. That is the one lesson you will learn, Tish."

"Really?"

"Oh yes. Sometimes we learn more than is safe. And we get much more than we bargained for."

Dr. Eve sneered and slowly slid her hand into the pocket of her lab coat. Her face contorted strangely.

A wave of alarm shot through Theresa. Why did Dr. Eve suddenly seem so angry?

TWELVE

Dr. Eve kept reaching inside her pocket. Her sneer intensified.

Her eyelids fluttered.

She pulled a handkerchief out of her lab coat and violently sneezed into it.

"Gesundheit," Theresa said.

Dr. Eve honked and replaced the hanky in her pocket. "Thank you. I hope I'm not coming down with something."

Theresa relaxed. Dr. Eve's sneer was just a presneeze buildup.

"Shall we head back to the surface?" Dr. Eve offered. "You've seen quite a bit."

As they retraced their steps Theresa continued to thank

Dr. Eve for the tour. "I know how private you are. Not everyone gets to see your lab the way I have."

"You're right, Tish. But your dedication and enthusiasm are obvious. In fact, you remind me a lot of myself when I was your age."

"Wow—thanks!"

They exchanged pleasantries all the way to the front door. Theresa felt as if she were floating.

"Now I really must say farewell, Tish," Dr. Eve said. "Be sure to keep in touch. I'd be happy to offer any recommendation letters you may need toward your education."

"Omigosh! That would be so great of you!"

"I would be more than happy to oblige."

Theresa shook the doctor's hand vigorously and thanked her once again. Before she knew it, she was outside, walking three feet above the snow-covered road toward town. She mumbled one supergeeky phrase over and over, not caring who heard her:

"Dr. Eve is the coolest person in the world!"

• • •

Santino and Carlo rode their snowmobiles at a steady clip, side by side, a Spy Girl perched behind each of them.

"This is ridiculous!" Jo barked. "What's with the guns? All you had to do was just ask us out."

"We're not laughing, Joan," Santino called over his shoulder. "If that's your real name."

"Hey, don't make fun of my name! I didn't pick it!" Jo grumbled, elbowing him.

"Oh, shut up for once," Santino replied.

"Kidnapping's a serious offense," Caylin added.

Santino shot Carlo a sly smile. "We're familiar with it."

"So you don't care about going to jail?" Jo asked.

"I should ask you the same question," Santino said. "We saw you on the doctor's surveillance video snooping that night of the party. You followed my brother to the door in the blackboard. Why would you do that, Joan?"

"I was looking for the bathroom!"

"Of course. We also saw the two of you talking to Rook last night at the club. Were you asking him where the bathroom was, too?"

"For your information," Caylin replied gruffly, "we were just getting his autograph."

"Were you getting his autograph at his home this morning as well?"

Jo and Caylin didn't answer.

"Finally: *silence!*" Carlo cheered.

"Yes, you are such big fans of Kristal, always asking if she's around, if we would know where she might be. Well, guess what, girls. We know *exactly* where she is!"

"Easy, Santino," Jo remarked. "Your ego is showing."

"Oh, be quiet." He grunted. "There is something going on that is bigger than all of you. And we're here to make sure that you never find out what it is."

Jo caught Caylin's eye. It was true about Dr. Eve! Caylin saw it, too. She reached down and tapped her boot. Then she jerked her thumb over her shoulder.

Jo knew exactly what she meant and nodded.

She grimaced, then forced herself to lean forward and softly kiss the back of Santino's neck.

"What are you doing?" he demanded.

"I'm just sorry things have to end this way between us, Santino," Jo said, pulling closer. She scowled, puckered up, and kissed him again.

The snowmobile slowed down ever so slightly.

That's when Jo leaned forward and said, "Consider that a good-bye kiss, chump!"

Then she and Caylin simultaneously flung themselves off the backs of the snowmobiles.

"Hey!" Santino yelled.

When they landed, they rolled on their backs, raised their boots in the air, and clicked heels.

The skis snapped out, and both Spy Girls launched themselves down the mountain.

"Faster, faster!" Jo hollered, looking behind her. "They're coming!"

"What I wouldn't give for a big fat snowboard!" Caylin screamed, crouching.

They shot down the slope full bore. The wind roared in their ears, but they could still hear the snowmobiles revving behind them.

"Head for those trees!" Caylin ordered. "They won't be able to keep up in there!"

Jo nodded and they turned hard for a stand of evergreens. She looked back. Santino and Carlo were right on their tails.

They plunged into the trees, cutting hard on their tiny skis. They lost a lot of speed, but then so did the twins.

"Are they still there?" Caylin called.

"Are you kidding?"

The snow deepened to over a foot. They sank in almost to their knees. They might as well have been skiing in a swamp.

"The skis are too small!" Caylin bellowed as the snowmobile engines revved louder. "We have to get out of this!"

They half-skied, half-stepped through the snow, eventually breaking out of the trees and ending up back on the open slope.

"Hurry!" Jo urged.

They picked up speed again. Behind them the twins burst out of the trees, catching some air. The snowmobiles came down with loud thumps and continued the pursuit.

"If we can make it to the lodge, we have a chance," Caylin urged.

"That must be a mile away!"

"You have a better idea?"

"Yeah! Go home!"

"Come on, it's that way!"

"No, it's *that* way!"

Both pointed in different directions.

Jo cut left. Caylin slashed right.

And they collided head-on.

Both girls went down in a storm of snow and limbs. They rolled hard, tangled up like two dolls. A ski snapped off Jo's boot, clattering away. Snow coated their faces, invaded their mouths, choked off their breath. They coughed and sputtered.

Finally they came to a halt.

"Ouch," Jo mumbled.

"Ditto," Caylin said.

They heard the twins pull up and dismount. They opened their eyes.

Carlo aimed his gun at them. Santino rummaged around in his pocket.

"All right, signorinas," Santino said. "Let's try this one more time."

He brought his hand out, held up two pairs of handcuffs, and smiled.

The twins had added to Jo and Caylin's misery by putting ski masks on them, but backward so they couldn't see. Caylin assumed they were taken to Dr. Eve's chateau. That had been the general direction in which they'd been heading before they jumped off the snowmobiles.

Caylin was taken off the snowmobile and roughly escorted inside. She could hear Jo complaining beside her. They all marched for a while, turned left and right several times, and then she heard a heavy door being opened in front of her.

"What's this?" Jo asked.

"Shut up," came Santino's voice.

The ski masks came off. Then they were shoved forward into a dark room.

The steel door clanged shut behind them.

It was pitch-black.

"Cay?"

"Right here." She reached out and touched Jo's shoulder.

"Where are we?"

"My guess is the chateau. Somewhere inside the mountain."

"Figures."

Something moved off to their left.

"Did you hear that?" Jo whispered.

"I heard that."

"What was it?"

"Why don't you ask it?"

"I don't want to seem too forward," Jo replied. "I'm starting to think that flirting is one of my fatal flaws."

"What a breakthrough," Caylin muttered. "Is someone there?"

She was answered by a light, quiet voice, singing. A soft melody, slower than how Caylin had heard it before, but one that was immediately familiar.

"'Eve of Destruction,'" Caylin whispered.

The singing stopped.

"How do you know that?" came a gruff female voice. "That song hasn't been released yet! Did you bootleg it?"

Caylin's eyes had adjusted to the gloom, and she made out a shape approaching her. Short. Shapely. With what looked like long blond hair.

Jo let out a big, exhausted sigh. "Princess Kristal, I presume?"

Theresa walked back to the A-frame in a happy daze. The town buzzed around her, but she didn't notice any of it. Meeting Dr. Eve had been a dream come true for her, but actually talking with her and befriending her? That was totally unbelievable!

She was so wrapped up in her thoughts that she didn't notice the person who suddenly appeared next to her. He matched her step for step.

Finally he grabbed her arm.

Theresa jumped, but the guy had too firm a grip on her for her to back away.

"Hey, who—?" Her eyes widened. "Patrick!"

He nodded, moving her along. "Just keep walking."

"What do you think you're doing?" she demanded, trying to shake off his hand.

"It's time we had a heart-to-heart, Tish."

He guided her in another direction, away from the A-frame.

"Where are we going?"

"My place," he replied.

Theresa gazed into his face. Patrick refused to look at her. His expression was grim. There was no flirtation, no twinkle in his eye. Nothing.

Theresa remembered that he was most likely the enemy. He had something against Dr. Eve.

She had a feeling she was about to find out what.

THIRTEEN

Patrick had a tiny flat above a jewelry store on the outskirts of town. Three rooms—a living room with a sofa bed, a kitchen with a small collection of Vietnam-era appliances, and an unappealing bathroom. There was no TV or stereo, but ski equipment and magazines were scattered everywhere.

A card table was set up in the main room with several items Theresa recognized immediately: the same brand laptop that she had, with a ski-bum screen saver; three different passports from three different countries; and a variety of small surveillance knickknacks.

She glared at Patrick. "Who are you?"

"The question is, who are you?" he countered. "Has Dr. Eve hired you to protect her?"

Theresa blinked dumbly. "What are you talking about? I'm just here on vacation."

"Oh no, you're not. You're far too involved with that woman to be just a simple tourist. You've seen her several times. You followed me all over the mountain last night after telling me that you never wanted to see me again. You lied to me."

"I didn't expect to be caught," Theresa replied indignantly. "And what about you? Were you using me to get closer to Dr. Eve? All those lessons. All that attention. Did you think that I would lead you right to her?"

Patrick paused. "That has nothing to do with it."

"It has *everything* to do with it. It makes you ten times the liar and a hundred times more scummy."

Patrick blinked at that one. "Scummy?"

Despite her anger, Theresa felt herself blushing. "You know what I mean."

"The point is, Tish, that I wasn't using you. In case you hadn't noticed, I'd managed an invitation to Dr. Eve's that night without you. And I got on fine by myself up on that mountain." His expression softened slightly. "What does that tell you?"

Theresa sighed. "This is all just double-talk. If you

weren't using me, then why did you spend all that extra time with me?"

He didn't answer at first. He looked away.

"Patrick?"

"You're infuriating."

"*Me? You're* the one running some kind of scam! *You're* the one dragging me off by force!"

"I needed to know the truth about you. You can't just be here on vacation. There are too many coincidences."

"So you thought kidnapping me might solve everything."

"You're in no danger here. I won't hurt you." He swallowed hard. "I couldn't."

"You couldn't? What does that mean?"

"Because I care about you too much already!"

Theresa froze. He didn't just say that. He couldn't have said it. Because it couldn't be true. No one she ever had feelings for had returned them. And Patrick? For all of his deceptions, she knew he was her dream guy.

"Y-you *care* about me?"

"Isn't it obvious? You had me frightened to death last night because I thought you'd get shot. My head's been spinning since I met you. I'm lucky if I can concentrate five minutes at a time without thinking about you."

Theresa gulped. The belly butterflies had returned full force. "Really?"

He moved closer. Too close to be polite. "Really."

She gazed up into his eyes, and that was it. Her pulse pounded in her ears and her mouth went dry . . . which was bad . . . very bad . . . because she couldn't lick her lips . . . which was even worse . . . because he was about to . . . about to . . . kiss her.

Time stood still. She wrapped her arms around his neck and pulled him close. Every care left her. All she could think about was how wonderful his lips felt against hers.

Someone cleared his throat.

Impossible. No one else was in the dingy little apartment.

The kiss continued.

Someone cleared his throat again.

Patrick broke the kiss. "I hear you," he muttered.

"Hear who?" Theresa asked.

"Him," Patrick replied, pointing an angry finger at his laptop screen.

Theresa gasped. It was Uncle Sam!

But no—it wasn't Uncle Sam. Not quite. He didn't quite look the same. His face was distorted as always, but the shape was rounder, plumper. This man was heavier than Uncle Sam.

"Hello, Richard," he said, a perfect and proper British accent coming through.

"Richard?" Theresa shrieked.

"Hello, Jack," Patrick replied glumly. "Your timing is impeccable as always."

"Quite so, it seems. Found a friend, did we?"

"Yes."

"What is this?" Theresa demanded. "Who are you working for? Are you a good guy or a bad guy or what?"

"I'm a good guy," Patrick said.

"Sometimes he is," the man called Jack interjected. "I don't know about now. Who is this tart, Richard, and why is she suddenly a part of this operation?"

Theresa's jaw dropped. "Excuse me? Tart? Did you just call me a tart?"

"Indeed I did."

"Listen up, you pixelated piece of—"

"Okay, okay!" Patrick blurted, trying to cover Theresa's mouth. Theresa shoved him away.

"Who is this person, Richard?" Jack demanded.

"I think I can answer that, Jack," came yet another voice.

"Uh-oh," Theresa moaned. "I think I'm in trouble."

"What?" Patrick asked, confused.

Theresa recognized this new voice. Knew it well—too well. She felt Uncle Sam's presence in the room even before his distorted face appeared next to Jack's, split screen.

"Sam, is that you?" Jack asked.

"Who else?"

"What's going on here?" Patrick said angrily. "Who *are* all you people?"

"My name is Uncle Sam, Richard. I'm Theresa's boss."

"Theresa? Who—what? *Her boss?*"

"Yes, Theresa's one of mine, Jack. Theresa, I'd like you to meet Union Jack, my counterpart in British intelligence."

"British intelligence?" she asked. She glared at Patrick. "You're a spy, too?"

"What do you mean, *too*?" Patrick asked, incredulous. "How many spies arc in this town?"

"What is one of your operatives doing in one of my safe houses, Sam?" Union Jack wanted to know. "She has no clearance here."

"Theresa's working on Princess Kristal's disappearance," Uncle Sam explained. "At least, she's *supposed* to be working on it. Seems she's taken a shine to your boy here."

Theresa squirmed, smiling weakly at Patrick.

He nodded at her, smiling. "That sheds some light on a few things, doesn't it?"

Theresa nodded as well. "So if you're the good guys, what could you possibly have against Dr. Eve?"

"We've been investigating Dr. Eve Dankanov for several years now," Union Jack commented. "For what, I can't say. It's classified even for you, Sam. I apologize. But it occurs to me that your girl Theresa has actually been inside Dr. Eve's lab. She has earned Dr. Eve's confidence. She could be useful to us."

"Hey—" Theresa began.

"She has a mission of her own, Jack," Uncle Sam replied.

"One that she's been *ignoring*. However, under the circumstances, she is the ideal candidate. You couldn't ask for a better covert operative when the operative has already infiltrated the enemy."

"I haven't infiltrated anything!" Theresa growled. "Dr. Eve trusts me because my interest in her work is real. Not because I have some twisted plot in mind. She showed me her work. She's totally dedicated to helping humanity. I'm sure of it."

"She was like that," Patrick said. "Once."

"Listen to Richard, Theresa," Jack urged. "Eve Dankanov has stepped off into another realm. One time, she was dedicated to helping solve the world's problems. But that is ancient history, I'm afraid. Trust us."

"You can't trust spies," Theresa retorted.

"Theresa, I am hereby ordering you to assist Richard in his investigation," Uncle Sam declared. "Do you understand?"

Theresa scowled. "This stinks."

"Duly noted," Uncle Sam continued. "But for once you will swallow your stubborn pride and follow orders. Work with Richard. You've been partners for two days, anyway. Simply continue. And round up the other Spy Girls as well. This mission is your new priority. Do you understand?"

"Yes, sir," Theresa said reluctantly. She wanted to tell him "I told you so," but thought better of it. She wasn't totally right, after all. A mission involving Dr. Eve was more important than finding Kristal. But she still refused to believe that her hero and mentor was an enemy of humankind.

It was impossible.

"All right, partners," Union Jack said. "Time to fly."

"Welcome to the team . . . Theresa," Patrick said, a wry smile playing across his face. He extended his hand. "It's a pleasure to be working with you. Officially, of course."

Theresa returned his smile. "Of course, uh, Richard."

He winked at her.

"All right, you two, that's quite enough of that," Union Jack scolded.

"You have a couple of Spy Girls to locate," Uncle Sam added. "Get cracking."

"Where does one find a pair of Spy Girls?" Patrick asked.

Theresa sighed. "That's a very good question."

"Well, before we get started, may I ask you a small favor?"

"What?"

He looked down at the floor. "May I continue to call you Tish?"

"If I can keep calling you Patrick," Theresa said with a smile. "We *are* spies, after all. Wouldn't want to blow our cover or anything."

"It's a deal, then."

"Mission accomplished, Jo," Caylin joked. "We found Kristal. Does this mean we can ski now?"

Jo snickered, bumping her head against the cinder block wall of the cell in frustration. "Cowabunga."

"Who are you people?" the princess demanded.

"Allow us to introduce ourselves," Jo replied. "I'm Jo. This is Caylin. And we're here to rescue you."

"Rescue me?" Kristal scoffed. "How can two little girls rescue me?"

"We're *not* little girls, *Princess,*" Jo griped. "We're the same age as you."

"And you can start by telling us how you ended up in here," Caylin shot back. "What do you have to do with Dr. Eve?"

"No, I think *you* should tell *me* how you ended up in here," Kristal corrected. "Who are you working for?"

Jo sighed. Then she explained that they worked for "your basic, garden-variety intelligence-type organization." She told the princess how her mother had requested that the Spy Girls find her and return her home.

Kristal laughed bitterly. "You never would have gotten me to go. Even if you could have found me."

"We *did* find you," Caylin corrected.

"By accident," Kristal scoffed. "You probably spent all your time chasing after Rook."

Jo shot Caylin a tedious glance. "Why don't you tell your story now. We told you ours."

Kristal shrugged. "All I did was sing a song."

"'Eve of Destruction,'" Jo said.

"Yes. I sang the song for the first time in public at Rik's. Do you know Rik's?"

"We're familiar with it," Caylin replied dryly.

"I sang it so well, too. I sang it to Rook. He was so happy that night. Then I took my bows and went backstage. That's when they grabbed me."

"Who?" Jo asked.

"Those rude twins. Santino and . . ."

"Carlo," Jo finished.

"You know them?"

"We're familiar with them," was the reply, this time from Jo.

"Anyway, they took me at gunpoint. All of my security was still out front at our table. They weren't prepared for me to sing that night. It was a bit of a surprise, even for me. The champagne, I guess. They brought me here. That's the story."

"But why?" Jo asked. "It doesn't make any sense for a world-class scientist to kidnap a princess. Does she want ransom?"

"No, it's nothing like that," Kristal replied. "I think Dr. Eve isn't sure what to do with me. It was kind of a misunderstanding, you see."

"What was?" Caylin asked. "The lyrics?"

"Yes. You heard the song?"

Jo nodded. "Rook played it for us. He wrote out the lyrics by heart."

Kristal grinned. "He can be so sweet sometimes."

"I think you need to get back to him soon," Caylin urged. "He's not bathing."

Kristal chuckled. "Yes, that's Rook. He's so lost without me."

"So what's with the lyrics?" Jo said anxiously.

"If you read them, you must have made the same connection that the twins did when they heard me perform at Rik's that night. Somehow, without knowing it, I made references to something Dr. Eve is working on. The twins thought I was some kind of spy, so they kidnapped me. Dr. Eve herself thought it was ridiculous, but she had me sing the song for her. I didn't sound very good, but it certainly shook her. I could see the anger in her eyes. Whatever she's working on, it must be top secret. And dangerous. Why else would she keep someone of my stature prisoner?"

Jo nodded, ignoring Kristal's ego trip. "That makes

sense. But you had no clue that Dr. Eve was doing something nasty?"

"Not at all," Kristal replied. "It was a coincidence. Who knew I was such an ecological savant?"

"We have to find a way out of here," Caylin declared. "And soon."

"Oh, don't worry," Kristal replied. "Someone will come for me. If you two managed to find me, my bodyguards will certainly come soon. And no one will stop them."

Jo glanced at Caylin. Of course. Kristal lived in a different world, where people served her every wish. It was natural for her to think that way. Natural, and wrongheaded.

"I think we have a bigger problem than just getting out of here," Jo warned.

"What's that?" Caylin asked.

"Maybe the princess can answer that for us," Jo suggested. "Kristal, what's Dr. Eve working on that's so dangerous?"

"I don't know," Kristal whispered. "I really don't know. But it's bad. We're talking Armageddon, end-of-the-world bad."

FOURTEEN

It was late afternoon when Theresa and Patrick returned to the A-frame. When they entered, Patrick whistled.

"This is your safe house?"

Theresa nodded. "Nice, huh?"

"It's ludicrous! You live here in pure luxury while I toil away in squalor, sleeping on a lumpy mattress and eating canned soup!"

Theresa shrugged. "We eat frozen pizza sometimes," she said lamely.

"So I see," Patrick muttered, picking up a discarded box. "*Gourmet* frozen pizza with real cheese. I think I need to have a word with Union Jack regarding accommodations."

Theresa called out for Jo and Caylin. No answer.

"They're not here," Theresa said. "They've been chasing Rook all over the mountain. They could be anywhere."

"Hold it," Patrick said. He held up a sheet of crumpled paper he found on the coffee table. "Take a look at this."

Theresa read it. It was a set of lyrics to a song called "Eve of Destruction." A note was scribbled in the upper-left-hand corner: "T., check this out. Still think she's a goody-goody?" She recognized Jo's handwriting.

Theresa read the lyrics.

Slowly her eyes widened. Her heart sank. She desperately wanted not to believe it. But the evidence was mounting against her hero.

"Do you understand that?" Patrick asked.

Theresa barely heard herself. "Yes."

"You should know that the lines 'key to a worldwide door' and 'seals your doom' are pretty specific references. I can't tell you to what. But you have to trust me."

"There's that word again," Theresa muttered. "*Trust.* Trust should be a four-letter word."

Patrick turned her to him. "This is serious, Tish. I know you don't want to believe it, but it's true. I swear. And we have to do something about it."

Theresa nodded, swallowing the lump in her throat. "If it is true, then I know where Jo and Caylin are. They went looking for me at the chateau."

"Then that's exactly where we have to go," Patrick replied.

They waited for the sun to set. Then they set out for Dr. Eve's chateau. But instead of skis, this time they took the snowmobile.

"A beautiful house, new skis, new snowmobiles," Patrick grumbled from behind her. "You girls have it made. I had to *buy* my skis."

"We're just lucky, I guess," Theresa replied, steering up the hill between trees. She was constantly aware of Patrick's body behind her. His strong arms around her. She sighed and tried to focus on the problem at hand.

But it wasn't easy.

They left the snowmobile a few hundred yards from the vents so the sound wouldn't attract any guards. They approached silently, using hand signals.

Finally the vents came into view. Patrick used his

night-vision goggles to make sure there were no guards nearby. There weren't, as far as he could tell. They stayed low and sneaked up to the first vent.

Warm air puffed out gently.

Patrick examined the cover to the vent. "It doesn't seem to be fastened," he whispered.

He carefully bear hugged it and lifted. The metal made a loud creaking sound as it came loose. To Theresa, it sounded loud enough to start an avalanche. She glanced around, but she saw no movement, no guards.

Patrick gently set the vent cover down in the snow and peered into the hole. It was definitely wide enough for a person to climb down. His hair fluttered in the warm breeze, and Theresa could see a golden glow on his face— there were lights below.

"This leads right into the lab?" he asked.

She nodded, immediately undoing her belt. Patrick paused, staring at her.

"Calm down, Mr. Bond," Theresa chided. "We're on a mission, remember?"

"Please don't call me that, old girl," Patrick retorted.

This time Theresa winked at him, and she began unwinding the climbing rope from her belt.

Patrick smiled and undid his own belt. His did the exact same thing. "Standard issue for mountainous terrain, right?"

"That's right," Theresa replied. "I just hope your government didn't cheap out on your rope the same way they did on your safe house."

"Very funny," Patrick remarked.

They tied the ropes end to end to be sure of the length, anchored them to a tree, and slowly lowered themselves into the vent.

The warm air felt good as it rushed up beneath her. It was like being in the barrel of a gentle blow-dryer.

Finally Theresa hit bottom, and Patrick was right there with her. A series of ducts led off in different directions. There was a vent right in front of them. They crouched down and peered through it.

"That's the main lab," Theresa whispered.

"Looks deserted," Patrick observed.

"It's night. Even Dr. Eve has to eat and sleep, right?"

Patrick slid his fingers through the steel grate and

slowly worked it loose. After several seconds it popped outward. Patrick climbed out, dropped to the floor, and set the grate aside. He motioned for Theresa to follow, then replaced the grate.

The lab was indeed deserted.

"Is this the entire lab?" Patrick asked, fingering some equipment. "There's not much here."

Theresa remembered the air lock. A "decontamination" area, Dr. Eve had said. She pointed across the room at the door in the corner.

"That's supposed to be some kind of sterile room," Theresa said. "I wasn't allowed in there, and Dr. Eve got a little antsy when I asked her about it."

"Okay, then."

Patrick examined the mechanism. "It's a standard air lock. Supposedly all one has to do is press this button—"

The door let out a gigantic hiss that made Theresa flinch. *Someone* had to hear that!

"—and presto." The light above the door changed from red to green. Patrick unclamped the lock and swung open the door.

They stepped into a small, closet-size chamber with another door immediately ahead of them. This one was more modern-looking, made totally of thick Plexiglas.

Patrick closed the first door and clamped it. There was another loud hiss as the air lock compressed. Theresa's ears popped.

Then the light above the glass door went from red to green. Patrick opened it, and they stepped into a much larger lab.

"Whoa," Theresa whispered. "I never knew what state of the art meant until now."

All the equipment was pristine. The odor of fresh plastic was in the air, as if the computers had just been pulled from their boxes. And what computers! Some of them Theresa had never seen before. She was dying to turn one on and play, but there was no time.

"Over there," Patrick said, pointing. "That's what we want."

"The refrigerator? Why?"

"You'll see."

The refrigeration unit was massive, floor to ceiling,

and sealed with a lock with a full-alphabet keypad. A tiny screen above asked for a password:

Patrick typed *Eve* and hit enter.

Access denied.

"Um, this could take a while," he muttered.

"Try *Mikhail 1515*," Theresa suggested.

"Really?"

"Just try it."

Patrick typed it in. The computer paused, then printed *access granted*. The lock clicked open.

"How did you know that?" Patrick demanded.

"That was the name of the lab Dr. Eve built in the space station." Theresa smiled. "What on earth would you do without me, Mr. Bond?"

Patrick waved a finger at her. "I'm warning you, old girl. . . ."

Theresa ignored him and pulled open the refrigerator, which was actually a liquid nitrogen deep-freeze containment unit. Steam from the nitrogen poured out of the shelving unit. Patrick waved aside the mist and put on one of his ski gloves. He reached in and plucked a small vial of a clear liquid from a collection of twelve.

He held it up to examine it. The heat of the room caused the glass to fog up. He wiped it away and showed Theresa.

"See that?"

"The liquid? What is it, poison?"

Patrick shook his head. "Look what's floating inside the liquid. In that tiny capsule."

"Uh-oh," Theresa whispered. "Looks like Dr. Eve discovered aspirin."

"This isn't funny. That one capsule could contaminate the drinking water in all five boroughs of New York City."

Theresa's belly filled with lead. Her jaw dropped open. After all the posturing from Dr. Eve, all the lectures on purifying polluted drinking water . . . she had the ability to contaminate it!

"What *is* this stuff?"

Patrick shrugged. "No one knows for sure. It came back from space with her. Maybe she concocted it up there, maybe she just collected it up there. This is the closest anyone has gotten."

"Are you going to take it?"

Patrick nodded. "All of it."

He pulled a foot-long, flat steel case from a Velcro pocket in his thigh. He popped it open. A tiny rack hissed out on its own microwave of nitrogen mist. The case could hold twelve vials. Patrick started loading them up.

The air lock let out a massive hiss.

Theresa froze.

Someone was coming!

They had seconds before the outside door opened and they could be seen. Patrick had loaded only seven vials, but he slammed the refrigerator door shut, balancing the steel case in his free hand.

"Over here," Theresa whispered. "Under this table."

They slid across the floor and dived beneath a table next to the wall. If whoever came through that door didn't turn on many more lights, they would be pretty invisible.

The outside door clanked open. Someone stepped into the air lock.

Patrick struggled to close the steel case. In his haste a vial had wedged itself in the hinge. Theresa tried to help him free it, but he slapped at her hands, causing the unthinkable. . . .

The vial squeaked out from their fingers and flipped through the air.

Too far away to catch.

Too fast to stop.

All they could do was watch with wide eyes as their death hit the floor.

But the vial didn't break.

Theresa blinked.

The air lock hissed and opened. A white-coated lab tech walked in, someone Theresa had never seen before. He was younger, with shaggy long hair and black geek glasses. He held a clipboard and a cup of coffee.

Theresa and Patrick watched in horror as the vial slowly rolled across the floor toward the tech.

They didn't move. Didn't breathe.

The tech didn't notice it. He crossed the room, searched a table momentarily, and came up with a fancy-looking pen. Smiling and satisfied, the tech turned back toward the air lock.

Theresa relaxed. He only lost his pen!

Meanwhile, Patrick pried her claws out of his arm. She retracted them and sheepishly mouthed "sorry" to him.

The tech moved closer to the air lock.

And the vial still rolled.

Theresa spotted it. Saw the timing of the tech's steps. And clawed Patrick's arm again.

The tech's shoe came down on the vial with a crunch.

He cocked an eyebrow and looked down.

He saw what he did.

And he screamed.

"Move!" Patrick yelled. He threw aside the table and dove for the far wall. Theresa didn't see what he had in mind at first. Then she saw: gas masks.

A pair hung from a hook near the air lock. Patrick snagged them and hurled one at her. It hit her in the stomach and dropped to the floor.

Theresa held her breath.

The tech saw them, and his eyes registered fear and confusion. Then they focused on the far wall. Theresa saw it too. A big red alarm button.

He went for it.

Theresa scooped up the gas mask and strapped it on. Patrick grabbed her by the arm and dragged her toward the air lock. She saw tiny, smokelike wisps coming up from the crushed vial. Whatever was in it was now in the air.

She felt sick. What had they done?

They reached the air lock just as the alarm siren sounded. Patrick slammed the door shut and hit the button. Again the hiss. Again the ear pops.

In the lab the ceiling seemed to explode with jets of white steam. She'd read about something like that. A system for labs that worked with bio-hazardous gases. When a contaminate was unleashed, the jets cleaned the room.

She couldn't stop trembling. What had they let loose? Were they contaminated?

Something slammed into the glass door. Theresa screamed.

The tech.

He pounded limply on the door. His face had turned an ashen gray, as if the blood left his flesh. His teeth stood out yellow against his lips. His glasses hung on one ear.

Slowly he slid to the floor. Mouth agape. Hands clawed. Convulsing.

After another eternal moment, he lay still.

"We killed him," Theresa whispered.

"It was an accident," Patrick replied breathlessly. "He walked into a sterile biohazardous lab without a gas mask or suit? What was he thinking?"

"He was just getting his pen!"

"Would you rather it was you?" Patrick asked pointedly.

Theresa shivered, shaking her head.

"Remember that."

Suddenly the alarm shut down. The steel door clanked on its hinges.

"Uh-oh," Patrick whispered.

"Busted," Theresa replied.

The door creaked open. Dr. Eve, the twins, and three more security guards stared in at them.

"Tish," Dr. Eve said, shaking her head slowly. "You have *no* idea how disappointed I am."

FIFTEEN

They had all been rounded up in the front lab: Theresa and Patrick, along with Jo, Caylin, and Kristal. Theresa had run to embrace her friends when they'd been brought in, but the twins had separated them roughly.

The twins and the guards hung back, giving their boss the floor. Dr. Eve walked through the group of prisoners, speaking as she sized them up.

"So this is the best the world has to offer," she said haughtily. "Either the powers that be don't take my work very seriously or the intelligence recruiters of your countries have gone short on intelligence."

She focused this last remark on Theresa. The Spy Girl simply stared back, refusing to back down.

"You no doubt have something to say, Tish," Dr. Eve surmised. "By all means, indulge me."

Theresa took a deep breath and uttered only one short syllable: "Why?"

Dr. Eve grinned and leaned into her. "Why not?"

"That's a pretty childish answer," Theresa replied.

"To a childish question. A girl your age can't possibly understand what the future holds for all of us."

"Why not enlighten us," Jo suggested. "You love to lecture, after all."

Dr. Eve chuckled, but didn't bite.

"You're going to poison the world's water supply, aren't you?" Theresa asked.

Dr. Eve nodded.

"Why?"

"Why not?"

They all stared at each other for a moment.

"Should we start over?" Patrick asked. "You're going to contaminate the world's water supply, aren't you?"

Dr. Eve nodded. "I'll sum it up in one clean sentence so your short attention spans can absorb it."

"Talk about clichés," Jo muttered. "MTV hasn't destroyed us yet."

"It won't have the chance, if I have anything to say about it," Dr. Eve growled.

"So what's the deal?" Caylin asked.

"Put simply: A planet can support only a finite number of inhabitants."

"I can't believe it," Theresa said. "This is your idea of population control?"

"It's only temporary," Dr. Eve assured them. "We'll spread our little present around selected areas of the globe—areas that have the most to gain from population control—and let nature run its course. Human beings need to drink, after all. Then myself and a few key scientists shall live in space for a few months, formulating a cure."

Patrick nodded. "A cure that you've already discovered."

"Precisely," Dr. Eve replied. "We come back, population is down as well as global morale, and we administer my cure to the world's water supply. The human race goes on. And I live like a queen for the rest of my days."

"You're no queen," Kristal growled. "You don't even know the meaning of the word."

"Neither will you, Your Highness," Dr. Eve replied.

"You'll be dead long before you can ascend the throne. Such that it is."

Kristal fumed but said nothing.

Dr. Eve walked over to Patrick. "I believe you have something that belongs to me."

She tore open the Velcro flap on his thigh pocket and withdrew the steel case holding the vials.

"Thank you very much." She turned to the twins and the guards. "Gentlemen, why don't you take our guests back to their cell? And be sure to leave them a gallon of fresh water. You know, some of the experimental water from the lab. I'm sure as the days go by, they will become quite thirsty. It will be interesting to see who'll break down and drink it first."

Dr. Eve retrieved the last remaining vials from the refrigerator, placed them carefully inside the case, and marched toward the exit. The guards took a step toward them.

"Excuse me," Theresa called after her. "Dr. Evil?"

Dr. Eve turned and glared at her. "Yes, Tish?"

Theresa reached into her pocket and pulled out a small

vial-shaped object. She made sure they all got a glimpse of it before she closed her fist around it and held it up.

"You forgot one," she said.

A wave of nervousness went through the room. Including the other spies.

Dr. Eve stood her ground. "I thought you were smarter than that, Tish. If you kill us all now, nothing good will come of it. But if you give me that vial, I can promise you a long life. You can grow up to be a scientist, too. Just like me."

"I'd rather die of thirst," Theresa spat.

She turned and whipped the object into the far corner as hard as she could.

The place went crazy. The armed guards screamed and ran for the exit. Dr. Eve hugged the steel case of vials to her chest and followed.

One of the twins punched a red alarm button, and the air was filled with sirens. The huge jets exploded from the ceiling, blinding them.

Everybody ran for the exit.

Theresa grabbed Patrick. He tried to force her gas mask

back on her. She shook her head and screamed over the noise, "It was my lip balm! It wasn't a vial! We're not going to die!"

"What?" Jo called.

"We're not going to die!" Theresa repeated.

Everyone heard her this time.

Including the twins. They stopped in their tracks, turned, and glared.

"Uh-oh," Kristal said.

"Dr. Eve's getting away," Theresa urged, pushing Patrick toward the door. "Come on!"

"Go," Caylin told her. "We have a little unfinished business with our boyfriends here."

Theresa and Patrick ran around the far side of the lab and reached the door. The twins remained, eyeing Jo and Caylin.

"Alone at last," Santino said, cracking his knuckles.

"You wouldn't hit a girl, would you?" Caylin asked innocently.

"Never," Santino replied. "But in your case, I'll make an exception."

He lunged at her. Caylin sidestepped him, caught his

fist, twisted it behind him, and bent him over. His face slammed against a hard lab tabletop.

Santino howled and fell to the floor, his nose gushing blood. He kept screaming, "Oh, my nose, oh, my nose," over and over.

"Your turn, Jo," Caylin said.

"What kind of girls are you?" Kristal asked from behind them.

"Spy Girls," Jo replied.

Carlo charged her. Jo let him. At the last second she grabbed his shirt and fell back, dragging him forward. Then she planted a foot in his gut, rolled backward on her back, and flipped him over her head. He landed hard, the air rushing out of him.

Jo stood, ready to face him again.

But as he stood, Kristal stepped forward and slammed a beaker over his head. Glass exploded everywhere.

Carlo dropped like a sack.

"That's for being rude," Kristal announced, dusting off her hands.

"Amen, Your Majesty," Jo replied with a grin.

• • •

Theresa and Patrick sprinted out the front door of the chateau. It was hard to see in the failing light, but they caught a glimpse of Dr. Eve turning the far corner near the garages.

"That way!" Theresa ordered.

Suddenly the air was shattered by the roar of an engine. As Theresa and Patrick rounded the corner, Dr. Eve sped off on a snowmobile.

"We have to catch her!" Theresa said.

"There's another one," Patrick said, pointing. "Get on! I'm driving this time."

"Chauvinist," Theresa growled.

Patrick turned the ignition and revved the engine. "Not at all. I've seen you drive, that's all."

"Hey—"

Patrick cut her off by peeling out. They flew up the hill, following Dr. Eve's trail.

The lights of the chateau quickly faded, and the farther out they headed, the darker it became. All they had to guide them was the headlight and the fresh path carved by Dr. Eve's snowmobile.

Patrick gunned the machine for all it was worth. The wind whipped Theresa's hair, stinging her cheeks and lips.

"I think my face is frozen!" she screamed.

"Just hang on! I see her!"

Theresa looked over Patrick's shoulder and saw a dim red taillight up ahead.

"Where is she going?" Theresa asked.

"I know exactly where," Patrick replied. "There's a reservoir not far from here."

"Oh no! It probably serves the whole valley!"

"Not just that," Patrick said. "They bottle the water, too. They sell it all throughout eastern Europe."

Theresa's stomach tightened. "She'll kill millions!"

"That was her point, yes," Patrick replied.

Gradually the terrain flattened out. They were topping the mountain. In front of them was a huge flat expanse of white.

The lake.

"Is it frozen?" Theresa asked.

"I hope so!" Patrick blurted as they launched off a short

rise. Theresa's stomach lurched, and they landed hard on the ice.

It didn't crack.

Patrick went full throttle and gained ground on Dr. Eve. In seconds they were pulling alongside her sled.

"Stop!" Theresa called.

Dr. Eve snarled and pulled something from her coat.

Theresa gasped. "Gun!"

Dr. Eve fired. The bullet sailed over their heads, but the sound made Patrick swerve. They slammed into Dr. Eve's snowmobile violently.

Plastic shattered. Engines revved.

And Theresa felt the whole world pitch sideways.

All of them hit the ice.

Theresa caught a glimpse of a snowmobile flipping in midair. Patrick was nowhere. Dr. Eve spun across the ice in front of her.

Finally they all came to rest.

Theresa just lay there, panting, wondering if she was really alive. She must have been because the ice was *freezing* under her.

She raised herself up on one elbow and looked around. Dr. Eve was a few yards to her left. To her right, a capsized snowmobile. That was all she could see.

She turned back to Dr. Eve. She was moving. Blood trickled from a cut on her forehead. But Theresa stared at her hands. She was fumbling with the opened steel case, collecting spilled vials off the ice and placing them safely inside.

Theresa crawled toward her. She tried to count the vials as Dr. Eve picked them up.

Seven . . . eight . . .

She got to eleven and slammed the steel case shut. She stuffed it inside her coat.

"That's only eleven," Theresa gasped, fumbling toward her on the ice. "Where's the other one?"

Dr. Eve grinned. She held up her hand and showed it to her.

"Don't!" Theresa begged. "Don't drop it!"

"I have to," Dr. Eve replied. "Don't you see that?"

The ice shifted beneath them. A long, loud creak came up like the howl of a wolf.

Dr. Eve locked eyes with Theresa for a split second, triumph spreading across her face.

Then the ice caved in.

Theresa dove forward with it, simultaneously slamming into Dr. Eve and reaching for the vial.

She felt it slip from her fingers, and she and the doctor both fell into the water.

It seemed as if a hundred knives stabbed Theresa. The water was beyond cold, beyond anything she could ever imagine.

She grabbed at everything, praying to find the vial, picking up sharp chunks of ice. Feeling her hope dwindle as she slowly sank into the frigid depths.

This was it.

She was going to die.

She and millions of others.

Because she failed.

Suddenly there were hands on her, pulling her up.

She was out of the water, breathing air. But she was paralyzed. Legs stiff, fists balled tight.

She was so cold . . . so cold.

"Tish, it's Patrick. You're all right. Do you hear me? You're all right."

"The vial," Theresa mumbled. "I lost it."

Patrick grinned and put his lips to her ear. They were so warm.

"The vial's in your hand, Tish," he said, holding her fist up to show her.

Sure enough, there it was, frozen to her glove.

"Ha . . . I caught it," was all she could say before she blacked out.

As the music faded, the applause got louder. Kristal raised a fist and saluted the crowd at Rik's one last time. Then she marched backstage and leaped into Rook's waiting arms.

It was a kiss for the ages.

"That is so sweet," Jo remarked.

"Being a VIP is so sweet," Caylin replied, sipping her carrot-apple-celery cocktail and fingering the backstage pass around her neck. "I could get used to this."

"We have a whole week," Jo countered. "We could do a lot of damage in a week."

"Look how much damage we did in three days!" Caylin cheered.

"I know!" Jo mimed wiping her brow. "But, boy, that was a close one. When we got back to the A-frame and called Uncle Sam, we'd just scraped the seventy-two hour mark."

Caylin raised an eyebrow. "I have a feeling we'd have gotten our week's vacation, anyway."

Jo nodded. "It's not like we don't deserve it or anything. I mean, in addition to saving the world's water supply and stuff, we not only found Kristal—"

"And reunited her with her boyfriend—"

"But we reunited her with her family, too," Jo finished, smiling as Queen Cascadia embraced her daughter, then Rook. "Looks like the royals might be loosening up a bit."

"Well, now they know Rook's a good guy," Caylin mused. "He's cleaned up his act, and he helped us find Kristal. Now they know he has her best interests at heart."

Jo sighed. "Isn't it romantic?"

"Oh, it's the *most*, my *deah*," Caylin drawled.

They clinked glasses and celebrated.

"Speaking of romantic, where's Theresa?" Jo asked.

"Where do you think?" Caylin replied, gesturing over at the corner.

"That was a great show," Theresa said with a shy smile. "And I mean that, really. No lie."

"It was," Patrick replied. He leaned his shoulder against the wall and brought his head down close to hers. "Thanks to you, the world is safe for rock and roll once again."

She smiled, shivering. She still felt so cold sometimes. But they said that it would go away eventually. She'd just have to wear a lot of sweaters in the meantime.

"Are you okay?" Patrick asked.

Theresa nodded. "It's not every day I go swimming with the frozen fish sticks."

"You'll be fine."

"Yeah, but it'll take years to live down Jo and Caylin's *Titanic* jokes. So there were icicles in our hair—so what? We don't look a thing like Kate and Leo!"

Patrick laughed at first, but then his expression turned serious once again.

It had been doing that all night.

"You're leaving, aren't you?" she asked.

He nodded.

"I thought so."

"Now that Dr. Eve is in the hands of the proper authorities, I have another assignment. I catch a plane in an hour."

Theresa wanted to reach out and hold him, but instead her hands stopped short and merely straightened his collar. "You take care, Mr. Bond. You hear?"

Patrick smiled and nodded. "Your wish is my command, old girl."

He swept her into his arms and kissed her. A proper spy kiss that put Kristal and Rook to shame. It was a kiss Theresa would never forget.

She ignored Jo and Caylin's catcalls.

"Good-bye, Theresa."

"Good-bye, Richard."

He strode away. But before he hit the exit, he turned back to her.

"Perhaps our paths will cross again," he suggested. "The club we belong to is a pretty exclusive one. Just don't burn out on me."

Theresa grinned. "Not a chance," she whispered as she watched him disappear behind the door.

She stood alone for a moment and sighed. Then she took a deep breath and joined her fellow Spy Girls near the refreshment table.

Jo wrapped Theresa in a conciliatory hug. "Them's the breaks, lover girl," she said. "You going to be okay?"

"I think so," Theresa murmured. But she wasn't quite sure.

"We're sorry we doubted you, T.," Caylin offered as she lightly punched Theresa on the shoulder. "Let's never fight again. Promise?"

"Promise," Theresa replied with a smile. "So, how's the grub back here, anyway?"

"Fit for a princess," Jo quipped. She held up a gold foil-wrapped box. "But I think *this* little item has your name all over it."

"Chocolate!" Theresa gasped. "Ohhh, just what I need

right now." She tore into the box. "Wait—there's no chocolate in here."

"What?" Jo and Caylin replied in stereo.

Theresa held up a package of Brazil nuts and a CD of samba music. "Can anyone say, 'Uncle Sam was here'?"

Caylin smiled. "I bet I know what this means."

"Whoo-hoo!" Jo cheered. "Rio de Janeiro, here we come!"

DIAL "V" FOR VENGEANCE

For Gage and Wendy — congratulations!

ONE

"Maybe Uncle Sam is finally going to reveal his true identity to us," Jo Carreras suggested to her fellow Spy Girls as the trio walked down the long hallway leading to their boss's office. "We've never been summoned directly to his personal headquarters."

Jo was endlessly awed by the rooms and corridors that constituted The Tower. Unlike most government agencies, The Tower was all about future shock—clean lines and smooth surfaces. There were massive, sectional leather sofas all over the place, and a seriously impressive collection of modern art lined the walls. Kind of like something she pictured when she read the book *1984,* but without all that nasty totalitarianism stuff. Jo couldn't wait to get inside Uncle Sam's office—no doubt, the place would be totally decked out.

"Yeah, right." Theresa Hearth snorted, responding to Jo. "You *know* why the great one has summoned us."

Okay, so there was no way in you-know-what that Uncle Sam was going to let them see his face. A girl could dream.

"Get ready, *chicas*," Caylin Pike announced, flipping her blond hair over one shoulder. "We're about to learn all about mission number five."

Caylin and Theresa were right, of course. The dynamic trio had been back at Tower headquarters in D.C. for almost two days. Their Swiss mission had been successfully completed, and now it was time for a new assignment.

Jo felt a flutter of excitement as the girls neared Uncle Sam's office. Nothing got the old adrenaline flowing like the prospect of yet another top secret mission. She picked up her pace, impatient to reach Uncle Sam's lair.

And there was no doubt that her fellow Spy Girls were equally anxious to find out the itinerary of the next adventure. Over the past few months Jo had more or less mastered the ability to read Caylin and Theresa's minds. It was hard to believe that less than a year ago, the three young women had been strangers.

Jo would never forget the morning she had arrived at The Tower for the first time. She had thought she was about to matriculate in an elite East Coast college. Uh, try not! Long story short, it turned out that Jo (the linguist)— along with Caylin (the athlete) and Theresa (the computer nerd)—had been carefully selected by the U.S. government to be trained as a top secret super-duper spy team. After some of the most intense training Jo could have imagined, the girls were officially inducted into The Tower. Voilà! The Spy Girls were born, and the ride of a lifetime had begun.

"Ready or not, here we come," Jo called out as she pushed on Uncle Sam's heavy metal door.

Yep. The office was ultraspiffy. Huge glass desk, a Rothko hanging next to a floor-to-ceiling window, and several long leather couches.

"Greetings, Spy Girls." Uncle Sam's gravelly voice— gravelly-sexy, not gravelly-gross—was loud and clear, but as per usual, The Man himself was nowhere to be seen. Instead a digitally programmed, ultrapixelated version of

Uncle Sam's silhouette appeared before the trio on a large screen. "You're all looking extremely well."

Jo plopped onto a black leather sofa. "So, where are we going next?" she asked. "Dallas, Texas? Zimbabwe, Africa? Sydney, Australia?"

"We'd like to go somewhere warm," Theresa said. "I've been hoping for a chance to try out one of those solar-powered laptops."

"And headquarters complete with an Olympic-sized pool wouldn't be too shabby," Caylin added.

Uncle Sam laughed. "You're going to Brazil."

"Brazil, as in home of the samba and incredibly good-looking Latin lovers Brazil?" Caylin asked.

"That's the one," Uncle Sam confirmed. "But go easy on the good-looking Latin lovers. You all will be there to work."

"So, what are we going to be doing in South America?" Jo asked. "Besides working on our tans, of course."

Uncle Sam cleared his throat—a sure sign that he was about to impart a piece of crucial, possibly terrifying, information. "The Tower has received an anonymous tip from an informant in Rio," he said solemnly. "We have every reason to believe that this informant has influence within Rio de Janeiro's thriving underworld."

"And what does said informant claim is going down?" Theresa asked. "Tell us exactly what we're dealing with."

As usual, Theresa was the Spy Girl most concerned with getting facts, details, and an outlined plan of action. In Jo's experience, attention to minutiae was a trait common to most computer geekettes.

"The informant promises to lead us to the head of one of Brazil's largest drug-smuggling rings," Uncle Sam stated. "If you girls complete this mission successfully, some of the most dangerous people in South America will be rendered powerless."

"Wow . . . big-time stuff," Caylin murmured.

"That's right," Uncle Sam agreed. "This drug lord has the blood of hundreds—if not thousands—of people on his hands."

Jo felt as if a small, homemade bomb had just exploded in her stomach. Drugs. Drug lords. Drug cartels. The words had a powerful effect on her. All visions of bikinis and cute guys faded from her mind. In their place was the face of her father. Four years ago Jo's beloved dad, a highly respected Miami judge, had been murdered—all because he had been presiding over a case involving a powerful drug lord. Since then, nothing had been the same. . . .

"This so-called tip sounds a little thin," Caylin said. "I mean, does this informant have a name?"

"Maybe someone is setting a trap," Theresa agreed. "This whole thing sounds too good to be true. Fly to Rio. Meet informant. Bring down major drug lord, all as easy as one-two-three."

"Good point, Theresa," Uncle Sam said. "It's always possible that informants have ulterior motives." He paused. "I'm counting on you three to discern whether or not the informant's motives are trustworthy."

"We won't let you down, Sam," Jo promised. To heck with the informant. She would track down the underworld baddie herself if necessary. "We'll bring these people down . . . no matter what the cost."

•　•　•

"So much for the concept of R and R," Caylin muttered an hour later. "I'm beginning to wonder why we ever bother to unpack."

The trio had gone straight from Uncle Sam's office to their Tower dorm room, the floor of which was now covered with clothes.

"I still have shinsplints from skiing in Switzerland," Theresa said, picking up a pair of mud-splattered jeans. "Jeez, where have these *been*?"

Caylin tossed aside a limp, tattered bikini. "Let's hope we each get a complete new wardrobe at the Rio headquarters. I have nothing decent to wear."

"How about you, Jo?" Theresa asked. "Are your duds in the same sorry shape as ours?"

"Yeah, no—I mean, sorry, what did you say?" Jo sounded dazed, as if she had heard nothing of Theresa and Caylin's fifteen-minute discourse on the nonlucky series of events that had led to their too quick departure from The Tower.

Caylin tossed a pair of fraying cotton panties into the trash can and glanced at Jo. She was sitting on her bed, staring at the still empty suitcase in front of her.

"Are you all right, Jo?" Caylin asked. "'Cause we're, like, under some major time pressure here."

"This is going to be our most dangerous mission yet," Jo predicted darkly. "Drug lords don't mess around."

"Why doesn't Sam have something more solid for us to go on?" Caylin asked, struggling unsuccessfully to keep the whine out of her tone. "I mean, we're just supposed to jet to Rio and meet some random informant in a nightclub called El Centro."

"That's not a lot of information to go on," Jo agreed. "But it will have to do."

Theresa slipped her laptop computer into its carry-on bag. "All we know is that we're supposed to look for a red flower and gray-streaked hair." She paused. "Is the old guy going to be holding a rose between his teeth or what?"

"Look on the bright side," Caylin said. "If the informant is going gray, we're pretty much guaranteed that we won't be distracted by any pesky romantic notions."

"Nobody said being a Spy Girl was going to be all fun and games," Jo said sharply. "Let's remember what we're going to South America to accomplish."

"Easy, Carreras," Theresa admonished. "Caylin and I take our missions just as seriously as you do."

Then something clicked in Caylin's head. Man, she was an idiot. And so was Theresa. How could they have been so insensitive? Going to Brazil to fight a drug lord wasn't going to be just another mission for Jo. In many ways, she would be evening a score.

Caylin shot Theresa a warning glance. They both needed to let Jo know but pronto that they would be behind her every step of the way as she confronted the demons of her past. Yes. It was definitely time for an official Spy Girl powwow. Unless they all addressed what Jo was going through, their fellow James Bondette might not make it through this mission with her sanity.

Jo stared into space, reliving in vivid Technicolor the day of her father's murder. She closed her eyes against the painful memory, but the images wouldn't go away. For probably the thousandth time since Judge Carreras died her freshman year in high school, Jo found her mind replaying each tragic detail.

· · ·

"Be good today, Josefina," Mr. Carreras commanded. "I don't want to hear from Ms. Pinsky that you got sent to the principal's office again."

They were sitting in the front seat of Mr. Carreras's aging car in front of Josefina's Miami high school. As he did every morning, Mr. Carreras was dropping off Jo on his way to the courthouse, where he would spend the day listening to prosecutors and defense lawyers pleading their cases before a court of law. Josefina had expected her dad to be in an awesome mood today—he had just finished a high-profile drug case that had consumed his every waking moment for six months.

And he was in a good mood. Unfortunately, on this particular morning Josefina's father also seemed determined to give her a lecture on the virtues of being an obedient member of the student body.

Josefina sighed. "Dad, I'm not going to apologize for getting into trouble last week. I don't believe in cruelty to animals, and I absolutely refuse to dissect a poor, defenseless frog."

Mr. Carreras raised one bushy eyebrow. "Even if that means you will fail biology, Josefina?"

She nodded vigorously. "I will not back down on this issue, Dad. It's too important."

Mr. Carreras laughed, then reached over and patted Josefina on the head. "My daughter, the crusader." For a moment he stared into her eyes. "I want you to do well in school . . . but I also believe in standing up for what you believe in." Again he paused. "Someday you're going to make a difference in this world, Josefina."

She grinned. She knew her father would come around eventually. He had devoted too much of his life to doing good to undermine his only daughter's efforts—however humble—to change the world.

"Thanks, Daddy." Josefina leaned forward to hug her father before she left the car. Then suddenly, the peace of her morning was shattered.

Pop. Pop.

She whirled around and screamed.

A man had placed a gun to her father's head and pulled the trigger. Two terrible shots that changed Josefina's life *forever. As she rushed to her dying father's side, his last words echoed through her mind. Someday she would make a difference. Someday.*

"Jo? Are you okay?" Theresa's soft voice broke through Jo's tortured memories, and her eyes fluttered open.

"Yeah, I was just . . . remembering." She was surprised to see that tears were falling onto the legs of her jeans. Jo hadn't even realized that she was crying.

"We know this is going to be tough for you," Caylin said.

Jo dried the tears from her cheeks as sadness was replaced with anger. "I still can't believe that the man who shot my father never went to jail."

Theresa shook her head in sympathy. "I don't understand how the defense claimed there was a lack of evidence. Somebody must have paid off an official."

Jo shrugged. "Who knows?" She tried not to dwell on the details of the investigation surrounding her father's murder. In fact, she had blocked out most of the time immediately following that horrible morning. She simply couldn't deal with the injustice that had allowed her father's killer to go free.

"But the police were positive that your father's murder was connected to the trial of a drug lord," Theresa said. "Which probably means this mission is going to be extra hard on you."

Jo nodded. She knew firsthand how ruthless the drug trade was. The people who got rich selling white powder didn't care how many lives they destroyed. As long as they had their fancy cars and mansions, they were happy.

"I just have a bad feeling about going to Rio," Jo admitted to her friends. "We've been in over our heads before . . . but this is different."

"Theresa and I won't leave your side for a moment," Caylin said reassuringly. "Besides, we may fly to Brazil and discover that the informant's information is no good."

Theresa nodded. "Yeah, we could be on a plane heading back to The Tower two days from now."

"I have to confess that there's a part of me that hopes this trip *doesn't* pan out," Jo said softly. "As much as I despise everything having anything to do with drugs, I also have a feeling that this whole mission is going to be an emotional roller coaster."

"That's not the Jo I know," Caylin answered. "You're usually the first one of us who's ready to risk anything to fight the bad guys."

Caylin was right. Jo remembered the steely resolve she had felt in Uncle Sam's office. This was an important mission. Jo couldn't allow her personal history to get in the way.

"We'll be with you every step of the way," Theresa reminded her. "The three of us will get through this mission together."

Jo smiled. Bonding with Theresa and Caylin had been the best part of her new life as a spy for The Tower. They filled a place in her life that had been emptied when her father was killed. They made her feel safe and secure—no matter how dire any given situation seemed on the surface.

"You guys are right on," Jo said. "If it turns out that the gray-haired guy is for real, then I'll fight with everything I've got to put this drug lord where he belongs—in memory of my dad."

"He would have been so proud of you, Jo." Theresa plopped down next to Jo and threw an arm around her shoulders. "I'm sure he'll be watching over us while we're in Brazil."

Jo took a deep, calming breath. From this moment forward, she was going to put her all into this mission. For her father. For justice.

"Enough gloom and doom," Jo announced suddenly, bouncing up from the bed. "Life is for the living!"

Caylin shoved her suitcase into the corner. "You said it, Spy Girl. Let's do something fun—preferably an activity that doesn't involve packing."

Jo hooked up her iPod to the stereo and scrolled through her playlists. "All right, *chiquitas*. It's time you learned how to samba!"

Theresa stood up, kicking aside a pile of clothes to make room. "Me, dancing?" She laughed. "Now *this* is going to be dangerous!"

TWO

"I think I'm going to like this mission more than I expected," Jo commented the next afternoon. "The guys in Rio simply define the word *hot*."

Theresa surveyed the crowded airport over the rims of her large black sunglasses—part of the glam-girl disguise she had been assigned back at The Tower. "I don't like to encourage obsession over testosterone, but you're right."

Caylin pulled a tube of lipstick out of her leopard-print handbag. "Anyone else care for a touch-up? You never know when Mr. Wonderful is going to appear."

"There will be plenty of time to give each other makeovers later," Theresa said. "Right now, let's concentrate on finding our headquarters."

"I know *Theresa* is uptight, but does 'Trixie' ever let

her hair down?" Jo asked, wiggling her eyebrows underneath the wide brim of an orange straw hat.

Theresa groaned. She wasn't thrilled with her latest alias. Who was going to take a girl named Trixie seriously? "Listen, *Jacinta,* I'm still Theresa underneath this thousand-dollar outfit."

"Personally, I *like* being Corinne, wealthy New York debutante," Caylin chirped. "It's a trip. And yet not too far from the truth."

"Ha ha." Theresa adjusted the rhinestone-studded collar of her jacket. During the past few months she had gotten used to doing the changing-skins thang. The Tower insisted the three Spy Girls use different disguises for each mission—still, she missed her old khakis and T-shirts. "Can't I be a poor, badly dressed deb?" Theresa lamented.

Caylin shook her head. "Poor debutantes aren't interested in pouring tens of thousands of dollars into drugs to take back to the United States."

"Oh. Right." Faking an interest in "getting into the

business" was going to be tough, but she had to do what she had to do. "So, are we going to figure out where we're going, or are we going to stand around here and talk fashion all day?"

Jo glanced at the electronic organizer that held the girls' immediate instructions. "Our wheels should be right outside this door." She pointed left.

The girls walked out of the airport and into the fading Brazilian sunlight. The air was warm and moist, tropical. Theresa had heard about Rio's famous Carnival season, and she could see that this was the perfect place for extended celebration. People streamed across the airport sidewalks dressed in bright clothes, laughing and greeting one another with hugs and kisses.

"Hello, babe mobile!" Jo shouted. "I think *that* pretty little thing is our ride for the next few days."

"Nice!" Caylin yelled, running toward the black Alfa Romeo that Jo had discovered. "I think I'm *really* going to like being a wealthy New York debutante."

"Give me a black Alfa Romeo and a fabulous new wardrobe, and I'll curtsy for as many stuffed shirts as you want me to," Jo agreed. She slid the key she had been handed at their final Tower briefing into the driver's-side door of the Alfa Romeo. "Score. It's ours."

Theresa placed her laptop in the tiny backseat of the Alfa Romeo and climbed inside. "It's a good thing Uncle Sam called our room and said we didn't need to worry about packing much. I don't think we could fit more than one small garment bag in this thing."

Caylin got into the car and slammed the door shut. "I've never really pictured myself as a Euro-flash kind of chick before, but I think I could get used to this."

"Do we have the address?" Theresa asked.

Jo pushed a red flashing button on the dashboard of the Alfa Romeo. Instantly an electronic map of Rio appeared on a miniature screen. "Check."

"Then let's hit it," Caylin said. "If this is our car, I can't wait to get a look at our pad."

Jo twisted her black hair up into a topknot and revved the engine. "Home, James!" She put the Alfa Romeo in gear and peeled out of the Rio airport with her usual dramatic flair.

For the next half hour Theresa relaxed against the Alfa Romeo's black leather seats as Jo navigated the car through the streets of Rio. Despite her semi-nervous breakdown the night before, Jo seemed to have rallied. Thank goodness for that. Since Jo was the only one of the three teens who could speak Portuguese, it was imperative that she be in top form. Not that Theresa had entertained doubts about Jo's ability to rise to the occasion. The girl had guts coming out of her nose.

"Okay, girls," Jo announced finally, slamming on the brakes of the Alfa Romeo. "Four-fourteen Hacienda Drive. Home sweet home."

Theresa opened her eyes and looked out the window. "I thought we were staying at a house! This place is a hotel."

Caylin laughed. "Wrong, my friend. *This* is the kind of place three footloose and oh-so-fancy-free debs rent for a stint in South America."

Theresa whistled softly. The house wasn't a house. It was a bona fide mansion. And it was pink. In front of the place was a huge circular drive and a large fountain. "I feel like Cinderella at the big ball. What happens at midnight?"

Jo switched off the engine. *Vámonos,* Spy Girls. Our mansion awaits."

"We can look at our new clothes and practice acting vapid," Caylin said as she opened the passenger-side door. "Like, hi, I'm, like, Corinne, and I, like, love to shop and go sailing on my million-dollar yacht."

"Hey, this is going to be a piece of cake," Jo said. "All we have to do is leave our brains in the walk-in closet."

Theresa climbed out of the Alfa Romeo and followed her friends toward the ten-foot-high front doors. Whether their personas were vapid or not, this was going to be one mission to put in the record book.

"Rio, here we come," she murmured. "Ready or not."

Remember the mission. Remember the mission. Jo repeated the mantra to herself again and again as she applied yet one more layer of black mascara to her long eyelashes. She was in a white marble bathroom, wearing a five-thousand-dollar beaded designer dress. A week ago those two facts would have added up to heaven on earth in her mind.

But Jo couldn't shake the foreboding that had descended upon her as she, Caylin, and Theresa had explored their decked-out deb den. Yes, their over-the-top house had been outfitted by The Tower in order to provide them with an airtight cover story. But Jo knew that there were many other mansions in Rio that were even more elaborately decorated. And each piece of avant-garde furniture had been paid for in cash—cash earned from selling drugs. The notion made her nauseous.

A tap on the door interrupted Jo's gloomy interior monologue. "Hey, *Jacinta,* can we invade your private space?" Caylin called.

Jo set down her mascara wand and pasted a fake smile on her face. "Yeah, *entre.*"

The door opened, and Theresa tottered into the bathroom, wearing a pair of five-inch stiletto heels. "I don't know how much help I'm going to be tracking down our mystery informant if I trip and break my ankle on these things," she moaned. "Don't debs ever wear, like, high-tops?"

Caylin perched on the edge of the sunken marble

bathtub and regarded her own rhinestone-covered high heels. "I've worn some tootsie tighteners in my day, but these are ridiculous. Is Uncle Sam trying to torture us or something?"

Jo turned from the mirror. "Hey, you guys are supposed to be wearing happy faces to prevent me from sinking into some kind of posttraumatic stress syndrome attack. Remember?"

"Oh yeah," Theresa said, readjusting the strap of her shoe. "I guess I'm just feeling a little bit nervous about pulling this whole thing off."

"If anyone guesses that we're not who we claim to be, we'll end up with our throats slashed faster than you can say 'Spy Girl to the rescue,'" Caylin agreed.

"Gee, thanks for the news flash." Jo headed out of the bathroom, Theresa and Caylin trailing behind.

"Seriously, Jo, how are you holding up?" Theresa asked as they entered the large master bedroom, where Jo had set up camp. "You look a little . . ."

"Pale," Caylin finished. "Do you feel all right?"

"Physically, I'm fine. Mentally . . . I've had better

moments." Jo pulled a tiny sequined handbag out of her enormous closet.

She was usually totally pumped at times like this. The adrenaline would flow through her veins as she prepared for a mission, always expecting the unexpected. But tonight she was aware only of a vague sense of dread and the fact that a clump of mascara had wedged itself in the corner of her left eyelid.

Theresa paced back and forth across the lush green wall-to-wall carpeting that covered Jo's bedroom. "It's imperative that we all put aside our doubts," she said, stopping mid-stride. "We have to face tonight like it's any other night."

"Right," Caylin agreed. "If we don't force ourselves to rev up, this night is going to be a disaster."

There was no arguing the wisdom of Theresa and Caylin's words. Jo knew that her job allowed little room for excess emotional baggage. "I'll come through, Spy Chicks," she promised.

"We know you will," Caylin said. "You never have to doubt our faith in you."

"On that note, I think we need to get in a bit more

dance practice before we descend upon El Centro," Theresa exclaimed. "Let's get ready to sambaaaa!"

Theresa turned on the stereo and tuned the radio in to a Brazilian salsa station. As the fast-paced music played, Jo demonstrated the groove for Theresa and Caylin. The heaviness she had felt earlier evaporated as Jo watched her friends struggling with the new dance steps.

"Your hips should move *naturally*," Jo explained. "You two look like you're being jerked around by a sadistic puppeteer." Losing herself in the music of her childhood, Jo continued to dance.

"I think I'm getting it!" Caylin yelled after a few minutes. "Samba, samba, samba." She moved across the carpet, swaying her hips as if she were in a music video.

"Great!" Jo laughed as she watched Caylin get into the Latin groove.

"How am I doing?" Theresa asked. She still looked as if she were dancing with a straitjacket on.

"Uh . . . more hips." Theresa was never going to be able to put the samba on her dance resume, but Jo admired her effort.

"Like this?" Theresa thrust out her left hip. Too much. Her feet flew out from beneath her, and she landed on the carpet face first.

"Um, no, not exactly." Jo tried to hold back her giggles as she helped Theresa stand up.

But there was no stopping the laughter. First Jo, then Caylin, then Theresa gave in to a fit of hysteria.

"You better tell people dancing is against your religion," Caylin advised. "Otherwise we're going to get kicked out of the club as a health risk."

"I'll just stand to the side and look sultry." Theresa pouted her lips and let her eyelids droop. "Is this sexy?"

"We'll find out soon enough," Jo told her. "The witching hour has arrived."

They headed out to the Alfa Romeo, still giggling. "Drugs, money, beautiful clothes. I feel like I've walked into a movie about shallow twenty-somethings trying to quote unquote find themselves," Caylin commented as she slid into the car.

"Well, at least we look our parts," Jo said, getting behind the wheel. "We have never been hotter babes than we are right now."

"As long as my role doesn't require the samba, we'll all be up for Academy Awards," Theresa predicted.

Jo stepped on the gas. If it turned out that this informant could lead them to a drug lord, she could *guarantee* an Oscar-winning performance. "Next stop, El Centro."

"Talk about living out our lives as if we were on the set of a movie! This place is truly outrageous." Caylin had to shout over the music in order to communicate with her fellow Spy Girls. They were standing pressed against the bar, waiting for a round of nonalcoholic piña coladas from the oh-so-very-cute bartender.

Theresa gazed around the crowded club. "One thing is definite. Any gray-haired dude roaming around this place is going to be easy to spot."

"No kidding," Jo agreed. "I think we've walked into a Beautiful People's Anonymous group."

El Centro was packed with young men and women, all dressed to the hilt in outfits that looked as if they had sprung fully accessorized from the pages of *Vogue*. Caylin couldn't see anyone over the age of twenty-five in the whole place.

"Maybe our informant got spooked," Theresa suggested. "This could turn out to be nothing more than a night out on the town."

Jo picked up one of the large, frosty drinks the bartender had placed before them and took a long sip. "I have to admit that I'm starting to enjoy myself."

Caylin felt as if she were on the spring break trip of the century. Pounding music, hot guys, tasty drinks . . . all sans parents. If it weren't for the fact that they were very possibly on an incredibly dangerous mission, this scenario would be too good to be true.

"I'd like to offer a suggestion," Jo announced, raising her drink.

"Be our guest," Caylin said. She wanted to hear what Jo had to say, but she also wanted to engage in flirtatious eye contact with a gorgeous blond guy who was dancing a few feet away from them. Oh, well. Who was to say she couldn't do both? "Proceed."

"I move that we split up, search for hotties, and enjoy ourselves," Jo suggested.

"What about the informant?" Theresa asked.

Jo shrugged. "If he's here, we'll find him."

Caylin glanced at the babe to her left. "Jo's right. I mean, as long as we keep our eyes open for a geezer holding a red flower, I don't see what else we can do."

Theresa took a sip of her piña colada and stared off into space for a long moment, thinking. "Okay. But if we do spot someone who seems like he could be our informant, then we drop Operation Scam immediately."

"Of course," Jo agreed. "We'll do the texting thing, then meet back here to consult before proceeding."

Caylin set her drink on the bar. "Happy hunting, girls." Without a backward glance, she glided toward the dance floor. The mission might be a bust, but if blondie was half as sweet as he looked, the night was going to be an unqualified winner.

THREE

"Baby, baby, baby . . . oh yeah, baby, baby, baby." Caylin sang slightly off-key to the pounding music.

She wasn't doing the samba, but her hips had definitely found a life of their own. Unfortunately, the blond had been a dud. But Caylin had discovered that dancing with herself was just as fun as the partner thing.

"You dance very well, pretty lady." A deep but oily voice interrupted her solo groove.

Caylin moved her head to take a gander at her new admirer. Yikes! He was older, and his hair the kind of salt-and-pepper look that was commonly referred to as "distinguished." Could it be?

"Hello?" Caylin responded. "Um, are you looking for someone?"

"I think I've found her." His English was perfect, and

the suit looked expensive. The man had definite informant possibilities.

"Tell me more." Caylin moved closer, her nerves jangling.

In a flash, the man's hands encircled Caylin's waist. He pulled her close, pressing his hips against hers and breathing hot, stale air into her ear. Yuck. This wasn't dancing; it was wrestling.

"Whoa, tiger," Caylin shouted over the music. "The forbidden dance really ain't my style."

"Ah, yes, I see the lovely girl is a bit shy." He winked and grabbed a long-stemmed silk rose from a small bud vase on a nearby table. "If you will allow me, I'll buy out an entire florist's shop and offer its contents to the lady who smells as sweet as a rose."

Ooh. Caylin had heard of going deep undercover. But this was beyond any superspy stuff she had ever seen. There was simply no way this Ricardo Montalbán look-alike was any kind of informant. He did, however, redefine the term *cheesy*. Exiting the situation seemed like a primo idea.

"Adios, amigo." Okay, so her limited Spanish wasn't

Portuguese. At least she was *attempting* to blend. Caylin saluted Rico Suave and melted into the crowded dance floor. Next!

El Centro was brimming with guys who looked as if they might have at one point posed for *GQ*, but Jo couldn't focus on finding a hot Brazilian guy to show her the sights of Rio. Everywhere she looked, Jo saw possible informants. So what if their hair wasn't gray and there were no signs of a telltale red flower?

And there, by the bar, was another likely prospect. Aha. There was some actual gray hair on his head. Finally she was getting warmer. Jo sauntered toward the bar, rehearsing her opening line. Excuse me, sir, have you informed on any drug lords lately? Hey, dude, how about telling me what Rio is *really* about? Hmmm. Maybe a bit more subtlety was in order.

"Hey, there," Jo greeted her prey. "Come here often?" Okay, she wasn't going to win a lot of points for originality, but Jo thought her voice was sounding fairly smokin'. She would certainly get the guy's attention.

The gray-haired daddy stared at her in confusion. "Eh?"

Interesting. The man didn't speak English. Good thing Jo was the one who had spotted him. Caylin and Theresa would have been at a loss for words—literally.

"Are you looking for someone?" Jo asked in flawless Portuguese.

He nodded. "I'm meeting a woman here. But we've never met before." His eyes scanned the crowd as he spoke.

"Are you two going to have a *secret* rendezvous?" Jo asked, fluttering her lashes.

He raised his rather bushy gray eyebrows. "Secret? No."

Jo bit her lip, wondering how to proceed. The old dude wasn't jumping at her bait. Then again, a lot of people had a hard time digesting the notion that spies could be as young as the Trio Grande. She would push further.

"Do you have a flower to give me?" Jo whispered. "If so, we could go somewhere private and . . . uh . . . talk about it."

Mr. X frowned, squinting his bright green eyes at Jo. "Young lady, you are an affront to your generation."

"Uh, what?" Jo was accustomed to being described as one of those rare sterling examples of America's youth.

"I'm old enough to be your grandfather. These flirtatious comments are simply outrageous." He was getting more and more worked up as he spoke. Uh-oh. If the man had a heart attack, Jo had no one but herself to blame.

"Sorry, I, uh, didn't mean . . ." Her voice trailed off as she felt her face turning crimson. Flirting with a geezer—talk about mortification!

"You Americans don't know where to draw the line!" the man finished. "Now go home and wash that revolting paint off your face." He pivoted away from Jo and strode toward the other side of the club.

Jo stared at the man's retreating back, wishing the floor would open up and swallow her. This night was going absolutely nowhere at the speed of light.

Theresa twirled a miniature parasol between her fingers and mentally recited the entire times table. She had been officially bored for over half an hour. Sure, the fellas here were oh-so-fine to *stare* at, but she hadn't had much success with actual conversation. The guys either didn't know how to speak English or were only interested in discussing various parts of her anatomy.

And there was *no* way Theresa was going to hit the dance floor. There weren't enough strobe lights in Brazil to make her dancing look anything but totally embarrassing. She had finally resorted to sitting at a tiny table, hoping against hope to catch sight of someone with gray-streaked hair and a red flower.

"I'll get another drink," Theresa said to her parasol. "Maybe a virgin strawberry daiquiri this time." The parasol didn't respond. Typical.

Theresa relinquished her chair, wondering how long spy protocol dictated that the trio hang out at El Centro. This pounding music was giving her a major headache. She glanced toward the source of the music, a large glass-enclosed DJ booth on the second level of El Centro. Huh. There was someone dancing in the window of the booth. Someone with gray-streaked hair and a red silk shirt.

Theresa squinted, staring at the booth. Wow. The hair was now obscured, but even from where she was standing, Theresa could make out that there was a flower pattern covering the shirt. Alert! Alert! This was not a test!

Theresa pulled her tiny ever present cell phone from her small purse. "Sorry to interrupt your scamming, Spy Girls, but Trixie may have hit the jackpot."

"Are you sure you saw the informant?" Jo asked Theresa five minutes later. "Because I've had a few bum steers."

Theresa shrugged. "I'm not *sure*. I mean, I didn't charge up there and say, 'Hi, are you the anonymous informant I'm looking for?'"

"It does seem weird that the guy would be hanging out in the DJ booth," Caylin commented, glancing toward the large window.

It was empty. "Still, we might as well check it out."

"Gee, thanks for your confidence in my ability," Theresa responded. "I'm telling you, I saw gray-streaked hair and I saw a red flowered shirt."

"So what's the plan?" Caylin asked.

"I'll do the talking," Jo offered. "We don't know how much English the guy is going to know."

"Sounds good to me," Theresa responded. "I'll be ready with the mascara cam in case photos seem like a good idea."

"And I'll keep my eyes open for suspicious underworld types hanging around," Caylin said. "We have to be extra vigilant about possible traps."

"Wonder-triplet powers activate!" Jo said. "Let's get this thing over with."

The girls walked single file up the wrought iron staircase that led to the DJ booth. Caylin's heart hammered in her chest. If Theresa's instincts were correct, then the girls were about to start their mission for real. The idea was equal parts thrilling and terrifying.

At the top of the narrow flight of stairs, Jo knocked on a heavy, metal door. "I doubt anyone can even hear us in there."

"Unless the person inside is *waiting* for our arrival," Theresa pointed out.

Jo shrugged, then pounded on the door for several seconds. "I guess there's no one—"

Suddenly the door flew open. Caylin peered over Jo's shoulder, her heart thumping wildly. But the guy at the door didn't have gray-streaked hair. He was tall, cute, and very blond. The guy was also wearing a pair of huge headphones. Aha. The DJ.

"False alarm," Caylin said to Theresa over her shoulder. "But hey, I think we just found the best-looking guy in the place."

Then the guy moved aside, revealing a young woman who was sitting in a plush armchair. Caylin's eyes lit on her hair, which was very coifed and very black—aside from a two-inch-wide skunk streak straight down the middle. And yes, she was wearing a red flower-patterned shirt.

"False alarm?" Theresa whispered. "Doesn't look like it to me."

"Wow . . . he's a she," Jo said. She seemed powerless to walk into the booth and begin questioning this latest candidate. "And she's no older than we are."

The young woman stood up and walked toward the trio as the dude with the headphones retreated to the high-tech sound board lining one end of the small room.

Skunk Chick didn't seem surprised that three American debutantes had arrived, unannounced, at the door of the DJ booth. In fact, she wore a welcoming smile.

"Congratulations," the stranger said in smooth, perfect English. "I see you've found me."

"Bingo," Caylin whispered.

FOUR

"This mission is getting weirder by the second," Theresa whispered to Caylin. "Where are we *going*?"

The supposed informant was leading Theresa, Caylin, and Jo through a maze of hallways and tiny, hidden staircases. Apparently El Centro was constructed like a giant labyrinth.

Caylin shook her head. "I have no idea where she's taking us—I just hope there aren't any men with guns waiting for us at our destination."

At last the young woman stopped in front of a door. She began to usher the Spy Girls into a large, circular office that overlooked El Centro's large dance floor three stories below.

"Quickly," she ordered, grabbing Caylin's arm and pulling her inside the room.

Caylin raised her eyebrows at her fellow Bondettes as they watched their host dart around the spacious office. The young woman was gorgeous, but her olive-skinned face was lined with worry as she stared out the window, scanning the club.

"Is the place bugged?" Theresa whispered nervously.

The so-called informant was looking under the telephone and between the leaves of a plant sitting on the large glass desk that dominated one side of the room. After another minute of seemingly aimless searching, she closed all the window blinds.

"Do you want to frisk us?" Jo asked dryly.

The young woman took a seat in a black leather armchair and folded her hands across her lap. "Please . . . sit down," she responded, ignoring Jo's inquiry.

Caylin plopped onto a long sofa. "Don't worry, we would know if someone were observing us."

The young woman looked doubtful. "One can never be too careful."

"Are you satisfied that the coast is clear?" Theresa asked.

The so-called informant smiled. "Yes, I'm sure now.

And I'm sorry to appear so paranoid . . . but I don't think I need to tell you what kind of stakes we're dealing with here."

"We're well aware that the stakes are high," Caylin answered quickly. There was no disputing *that* point.

"Good. Then we all understand each other."

Caylin was relieved that this girl—whoever she was— seemed as concerned with safety as the Spy Girls were. And she looked friendly. Caylin could usually spot a phony smile, but this one seemed genuine.

"I hope you are all enjoying your time in Rio," the young woman said calmly, as if the four of them had just sat down to participate in a tea party. "Our city offers many beautiful sights . . . not the least of which is our male population."

"So we've noticed," Jo answered.

Again the stranger's pretty face grew serious. "I'm thankful to all of you for being here—but I'm afraid I don't even know your names."

The Spy Girls exchanged a quick glance. Part of Caylin wanted to be totally honest with their paranoid hostess.

She seemed completely sincere and trustworthy—but as the girl herself had stated, one could never be too careful. Jo nodded in silent agreement.

"I'm Jacinta," Jo said, extending her hand. "And my friends are Corinne and . . . uh, Trixie." She paused. "For now, I think first names are enough."

The stranger grinned. "And even those are not your real names, I presume?"

"What's your name?" Theresa asked, dodging the question.

"I am Diva—first name only." She paused. "Now, I am guessing that the three of you would like to know a little about my situation."

"That's why we're here," Jo confirmed. "Tell us everything you can."

Diva leaned forward in her chair and looked each of the Spy Girls in the eyes. "Drugs—and the crimes associated with drugs—have ruined my family," she said softly. "My father is in grave danger."

"Go on," Jo urged. "We're listening." Her face softened; clearly Diva's words were affecting her deeply.

"This club looks wonderful on the outside," Diva continued. "People dance, laugh, enjoy the drinks and the music." She stood up and walked to the window, then peered through the blinds. "You all feel safe here, yes?"

"Yeah," Caylin agreed. "However. I'm guessing there's a pretty major 'but' coming."

Diva nodded. "This place is actually filthy with crime. The big boss of the most powerful drug ring in Brazil oversees El Centro."

"Uh, wow . . ." Theresa glanced around the office, then back at Diva. "What does that mean—exactly?"

"Information about the drug trade comes in and out of the club every single day. It's Underground Zero." Diva fell silent, allowing the girls time to absorb her statement.

Caylin felt yet another surge of adrenaline course through her veins. Could Diva be for real? If what she said was true, then all four of them were proverbial sitting ducks. And from the expressions on Theresa and Jo's faces, they were thinking the same thing.

"Should we really be sitting here discussing this, Diva?" The slight tremble in Jo's voice belied her calm exterior. "Frankly, it doesn't seem as if we should be here *period*."

"We have every right to be here," Diva countered. "This is my office."

"You work here?" Theresa asked.

Diva smiled. "I don't just work here. El Centro is mine. I own it."

Caylin sank into the cushions of the leather sofa. This new piece of information put an unexpected twist on the mission. Diva's information was certainly explosive—and more dangerous than Caylin had ever imagined.

"I say we pack our bags and head back to the States," Theresa suggested to her fellow Spy Girls. "Our training hasn't prepared us for anything this intense."

As soon as Diva had revealed that she owned El Centro, Jo had asked her to step out of the office so the girls could converse in private. This thing was seriously sticky.

"What do you think, Cay?" Jo asked, although she already had a feeling that Caylin was going to jump on the let's-run-like-the-wind bandwagon.

Caylin frowned. "If everything Diva says is true, we can assume that she's in business with this drug lord. I don't know how much we can trust her as an informant."

"Her motives are seriously doubtful," Theresa added. "I mean, if this dude goes down, who knows what happens to El Centro?"

"Not to mention the fact that the club was very likely built with drug money," Caylin pointed out. "Diva owes her livelihood to the Big Boss."

Jo sighed. She couldn't refute anything that Theresa and Caylin had said. But there was something in Diva's eyes that Jo responded to. She had recognized Diva's pain and desperation, her fervent wish to extricate her family from the clutches of the drug trade.

"I think we should stay," Jo said firmly. "I haven't been in Diva's exact situation, but I know where she's coming from."

"I don't know, Jo. . . ." Theresa bit her lip. "I mean, Jacinta."

"Drugs and crime killed my own father. I know the anguish these people cause and the power they wield."

Jo lowered her voice. "It's likely that Diva *can't* get out from under the hold of the Big Boss. Putting him in jail, where he can't hurt her family, is her only hope." She paused.

"In other words, *we're* her only hope," Caylin said.

"If we can help her bring down the drug lord, she can save her father and get her life back. If I were in her place, I would do whatever it took to accomplish that—no matter how dangerous it was." Jo was quiet as they all considered their dilemma.

"I guess we're going to have to give it a shot," Theresa said finally. "We'll do it in memory of Mr. Carreras."

"I'm in." Caylin walked to the door of the office. "Shall I invite Diva back inside?"

Jo nodded. Well, that was that. They would leave Brazil victorious—or in body bags.

Diva strode into the room and put her hands on her hips. "So? Will you help me?"

"We're all in this together now," Jo assured her. "We'll do whatever it takes."

"Thank you! Thank you so much." Diva beamed. "I

don't know exactly who you girls are, but I'm glad you showed up."

"So what's next?" Caylin asked. "We need a plan—a good one."

Diva nodded. "To pull off an effective sting operation, our story has to be airtight."

"Here's the deal," Jo explained to Diva. "As far as you know, the three of us are filthy rich American debutantes, out to expand our fortune by getting into the drug trade."

"We're rebelling against our parents and lusting after a taste of the glamorous life," Theresa added excitedly. "We love danger, adventure—"

"I get the picture," Diva said with a laugh. "And I think it's a perfect cover. I mean, who but spoiled American brats would have access to so much cash?"

"Not *all* Americans are shallow," Caylin reminded Diva. "Some of us care about more than money."

"Well, luckily for us, money is the *only* thing the boss cares about." Diva took out a pad and pen and began to take notes. "Now, we must decide what kind of offer you girls will make."

"Um, ten thousand dollars?" Theresa suggested. "That should buy the Big Boss enough cocaine to theoretically ruin the lives of every member of a small town."

Diva snorted. "Ten thousand is small change to these men, Trixie. I'm going to suggest that you offer him five hundred thousand dollars to start with."

Jo gasped. "Five hundred *thousand* dollars? Are we discussing American dollars?" She had never even conceived of that much money in one place at one time.

"Whoa . . . that's a lot of moolah," Caylin whispered. "Even for three rich debs."

"But Diva is right," Theresa said. "This man is probably used to trading millions of dollars' worth of cocaine at one time. If he's going to take us seriously as investors, we have to be in his league."

"Yes, now you understand." Diva smiled, her cheeks flushing. "If anyone questions the source of your income, you can say that you just came into the money from your trust funds, yes?"

Jo had to admire Diva. She was both smart and fearless—two of Jo's favorite qualities. For the first time, she began to feel confident about the mission. Thank goodness Diva thought the Big Boss would be interested in a straight cash investment. The trio wouldn't have to purchase drugs directly from anyone. Phew! Even if it was for a good cause, Jo didn't want to be on the receiving end of *any* amount of *anything* in the "this is your brain on" department.

"Half a mil it is," Jo said decisively. "What next?"

"I'll mention to the boss that you girls were around, looking to get into the business. I'll let him know that I have every reason to believe that working with you would be profitable."

"Do you think he'll bite?" Caylin asked.

Diva nodded. "The man is greedy. He won't let this opportunity pass him by."

"It's imperative that we meet with him personally," Jo said. "That's the only way we can ensure that the sting will work." She wasn't going to risk another lack-of-evidence case. Jo wanted to make a hundred percent sure that the creep got what was coming to him.

"I'm sure I'll be able to set up a meeting between you and the big boss . . . eventually," Diva allowed.

"What do you mean, 'eventually'?" Theresa asked.

"The man himself won't meet you face-to-face until you're approved by some of his underlings. If they give you the go-ahead, he'll invite you to his home."

"Underlings?" Jo pictured heavyset thugs with greasy hair and huge gold chains. Double gross.

Diva wiggled her eyebrows. "Believe me, that will be the most fun part of this adventure. The guys who work for the boss are . . . well, extremely attractive. And they'll take you to the most happening places in Rio."

"Hmmm . . . sounds interesting," Caylin said. "Do they like blond Americans?"

"I don't need to remind you two that the guys in question are dangerous *criminals*," Theresa piped up. "There will be no romantic encounters. None."

Leave it to Theresa. "Absolutely. No romance. Now . . . do we have plan A?" Jo looked from her fellow spy girlies to Diva.

"Yes, it's a plan," Diva answered. "Shall we shake on it?"

As Jo gripped Diva's hand in her own, she uttered a silent prayer. They needed all the help they could get.

· · ·

"What *time* is it at The Tower, anyway?" Theresa stifled a yawn as Caylin dialed Uncle Sam's private phone number.

"Who cares? Early, late . . . Uncle Sam never sleeps." Jo had kicked off her high heels and was stretched out on one of the luxurious oriental rugs that covered the floor of the living room.

"Kind of like us," Theresa commented. The short nap she had taken on the plane seemed a lifetime ago. But the girls wanted to share their information with Uncle Sam before they retired to their rooms. Staying in close and constant touch with The Tower was their best safety guard.

"Good evening, Spy Girls." Uncle Sam's voice came over the speakerphone. "Were you successful tonight?"

Caylin leaned toward the phone. "We met with the informant. She seems to be on the level."

"And you all agree on that score?" Uncle Sam asked. "One can never be too careful."

The girls giggled. "That's exactly what she said," Theresa told him.

There was a pause. "So the informant is a female. Interesting."

"You're not going sexist on us, are you?" Jo asked him.

He laughed—a rarity. "Never, Jo. Never."

"There's one thing," Caylin said hesitantly. "We're going to need five hundred g's—in cash."

"I expected as much. Consider it done."

Theresa could practically hear the wheels turning in Uncle Sam's mind. Get cash. Transport cash to Rio. Contact backup agents. Et cetera. Et cetera.

"Thanks, Uncle Sam—we knew we could count on you." Jo's voice caught in her throat. "We don't want anything to happen to screw up this mission."

"Nor do I," Uncle Sam responded. "Now get some sleep—and stay safe."

Caylin hung up the phone and leaned into the plush cushions of one of the living room's three sofas. "That's that. We've got the green light."

"So we proceed to the next stage," Theresa announced. "Operation Bring Down the Big Boss."

"Operation Revenge," Jo commented. "When I see this

guy heading to the clinker, I'm going to look up to heaven and smile."

"But this guy isn't the one who killed your father, Jo," Caylin reminded her. "You can't make this mish only about personal vendettas. It's too dangerous."

"Missions are *always* personal," Jo corrected her. "If they weren't, the three of us wouldn't be willing to risk our lives over and over again."

Theresa nodded. They all had their reasons for wanting to fight evil in the world. But this mission . . . this mission belonged to Jo.

FIVE

"At the *Co*-pa! Copa-ca-baaa-naaa!" Caylin had sung the song a hundred times, but the lyrics had never been so appropriate. It was Saturday night, and the trio was safely stashed in the Alfa Romeo, driving toward the location of their all-important first meeting with Mr. X's business operatives.

"I'm psyched Diva is going to come along on this rendezvous. I love you two, but it's nice to have someone different around." Theresa leaned forward from the backseat and looked from Jo to Caylin. "Know what I mean?"

"Yep." Jo turned off the radio, causing Caylin's insistent humming to be the only sound in the car. "I sort of wish we could make Diva an honorary Spy Girl. The chick defines cool."

"I couldn't believe those dances she was showing us,"

Caylin said. "I think I actually got the hang of that slow, slow, fast thing." She paused. "Or is it fast, fast, slow?"

"Maybe we'll get to samba tonight," Jo suggested. "I could use a little dancing to lighten my mood."

"You'll find out soon enough." Theresa pointed to the hand-drawn map Diva had given them that afternoon. "According to this, we take a left here. The place is down the street."

"I hope it's crowded," Caylin said, peering into the dark night. "I mean, these guys can't just *kill* us with hundreds of people around—can they?"

"They won't *want* to kill us," Theresa assured her. "There's no way they'll figure out who we really are."

"I just wish we knew the Big Boss's name," Jo said. "If Diva would give us a positive ID, we could have Uncle Sam do a background check."

"You heard her," Caylin responded. "She's dead set against telling us the guy's name until we meet him face-to-face. According to her, we'll be safer that way."

Jo swung the Alfa Romeo to the left, then slowed to a stop. "I can't believe the restaurant is actually called

La Americana," she commented. "Who knew we'd find such a home away from home?"

"Personally, I hope the *food* isn't American. I'm not in the mood for sunlamp burgers or cardboard pizza," Theresa commented as they got out of the sports car. "But I have to say, this place looks pretty darn empty of *americanas*—"

"As well as everyone of every *other* nationality, for that matter," Caylin finished. "Hey, look—there's a sign on the door."

"What's it say?" Theresa asked.

Jo led her *compadres* up to La Americana's front door and squinted through the darkness at the sign. "Uh-oh," Jo said. "The sign says the place is closed for a private party."

"Maybe we're at the wrong place," Caylin suggested.

"Or we have the wrong day," Theresa said. She took a few steps away from the door and glanced around the near empty parking lot.

"Great!" Jo kicked the door in frustration. "This isn't exactly the auspicious start I was hoping for."

The door opened. Standing on the other side of it was

one of the hottest guys Caylin had ever seen. Jet-black hair, coal-black eyes, deeply tanned skin. Yum, yum.

"Ah, you ladies are right on time," the guy said with just about the sexiest accent Caylin had ever heard.

"W-we are?" Theresa asked. "I mean, yes, of *course* we are."

"Diva arrived a few minutes ago," Señor Hottie continued. "She has assured us that we will all have a marvelous time this evening."

"I guess we're the private party," Theresa whispered as Jo introduced herself to their host in Portuguese.

Señor Hottie was bent over Jo's hand. An actual, real-live, old-school kiss on the hand took place right before Caylin's eyes.

"Jacinta, I am pleased to make your acquaintance."

It was incredibly hard to believe that this heartthrob was also a cold-blooded drug trader. If nothing else, his manners were exquisite.

"And who are you?" Jo asked flirtatiously.

"I am Juan." He turned to Theresa. "And you must be Trixie."

"Pleased to meet you," Theresa said, extending her hand.

He looked into Caylin's eyes. "And you, my dear, are Corinne." Yeow. If Juan's fellow operatives were half as cute as *he* was, the girls were going to have to work *mighty* hard to keep their minds on the mission.

"Shall we go inside?" Juan asked.

"Let the games begin," Jo said.

The Spy Girls exchanged glances, then followed Juan into La Americana . . . where their fate awaited them.

Theresa shut her eyes in order to *truly* savor the succulent beef dish that had been served as the third course. Boy, the SG's dinner companions sure gave new meaning to the expression "wine and dine." In addition to three different beef dishes, the table was laden with roast duck, stuffed lobster, and a melt-in-your-mouth cheese soufflé. Yummy! Theresa had never felt so pampered by a member of the male population—or by *any* member of the population, for that matter.

"You enjoy your meal, yes?" inquired Carlos, Theresa's de facto date for the evening.

She nodded and popped another piece of the thinly sliced beef into her mouth. "It's delicious."

"I'll never be able to look at a duck again . . . without wanting to eat it for dinner," Caylin commented.

"I know what I would like for *dessert*." That charming comment had come from Caylin's so-called date, Jorge.

Yeah, these guys were laying on the compliments so thick, Theresa could have cut them with a knife. And yes, they were largely relying on thousand-dollar suits and gourmet food to impress the girls. But Theresa had to admit that their tactics worked. She felt totally swept up in the glamour of the evening. Jeez, one of the best big bands in all of Rio—according to Diva, who *obviously* knew about such things—was playing just for the eight of them.

Life didn't get much sweeter than this—as long as Theresa didn't dwell too much on the fact that all of these guys were probably packing heat underneath their Prada suits. That notion had a really annoying way of bringing Theresa's giddiness meter down a few notches.

As two tuxedoed waiters circled the table, setting down

tiny cups of espresso in front of each of them, Armand cleared his throat.

"Let us talk for a moment, ladies," he said. "Then we can delight in the rest of the evening."

It had been clear from the start that Armand was the leader of this merry band. And Theresa's initial speculation had been confirmed earlier by Diva. While the two girls were reapplying lipstick in the bathroom, Diva had whispered to Theresa that Armand was *the* man to impress.

Theresa had passed along that tidbit of information to Jo, who had spent every minute since beguiling Armand. So far, Jo's performance had been a roaring success. No surprises there.

"Trixie, Corinne, and I are extremely anxious to explore the many opportunities that Rio has to offer," Jo purred as she sat back from the table and ran the tip of her index finger around the rim of her espresso cup. Flawless. Even *Theresa* was having a difficult time remembering that she and her compatriots weren't actually three debs looking for action.

"Yes, Brazil is a country filled with possibilities,"

Armand responded. "Of course, one has to have money—and spend money—in order to *make* money."

"So true," Caylin said. "Equally, it's important that we know *where* to spend that money."

"Which is why we're all here tonight," Diva broke in. "These young women are serious about exploring the options you have to offer."

"And what is the *extent* to which you three wish to explore?" Armand asked. He looked at each Spy Girl in turn, his eyebrows raised.

This was it. The Offer. Make-it-or-break-it time. Theresa held her breath as she waited for Jo to respond. She also offered silent thanks that Jo had become their designated spokeswoman. Theresa didn't think she would have been able to get the giant figure to roll off her tongue without gagging.

"On a scale of one to a million . . . we're at about five hundred thousand," Jo said calmly. "I'm referring to our level of interest, naturally."

Armand grinned, then bowed his head. "Naturally." He paused. "Now tell me, Jacinta, what sort of benefits are you all hoping to derive from . . . exploring your options?"

"At some point in the near future, we would like to see our money *grow*. We don't need to *see* the growth. . . . We just want to pick the fruit off the tree."

Theresa was tempted to applaud. Who knew that Jo was a master of veiled language? She sounded so *professional*. It was almost eerie.

Armand raised his espresso cup. "I think that our boss will be very interested in assisting you ladies in your quest for opportunity. Cheers."

There was an echo of cheers around the table. Glasses clinked, lips smiled, a couple of people giggled. As the hot, rich espresso warmed Theresa's stomach, she snuck a glance at Diva, who was seated next to Juan.

"You're in," Diva mouthed silently.

"We are done with business, yes?" Armand asked the girls.

"Yes," Caylin confirmed.

"Then let's party!" Armand stood up and turned toward the band. "Tonight—we samba!"

• • •

The evening had lulled Jo into a kind of satisfied stupor. As she listened to the big band's seductive tunes, Jo felt herself mentally slipping further and further away from the implications of this dangerous mission. For this moment, at least, she was nothing more than a young woman out for a good time. She closed her eyes, enjoying the sensation of Armand's arms around her waist as they danced.

"I have always felt American ladies were . . . how do you say . . . beneath me. But you are very beautiful," Armand said, his voice suggestive.

Talk about a backhanded compliment! Jo wanted to rebuke Armand for his rather outmoded attitude, but he was simply too gorgeous to resist. His dark eyes gave new meaning to the term *come hither.*

"You're not so bad yourself," Jo murmured. "I could dance all night."

"Ah, yes, but I have other activities in mind." Armand's voice was silky, his hands warm and insistent on her back.

"You do?" Jo knew she wasn't supposed to allow either romance or lust to cloud her objective. She'd made *that* mistake before—twice. But getting in good with the Big Boss's yes-men was a key aspect of their mission. She was practically *obligated* to flirt up a storm.

Armand pulled Jo even closer, then lowered his lips to hers. The kiss was sensual, soft, everything a kiss should be. At first. Then Armand pressed his body firmly against Jo's . . . and she felt cold, hard metal pressing against her ribs.

A gun. Reality came crashing down. This wasn't a romantic evening with a hot guy. This was the beginning of an elaborate sting operation designed to put these guys—and their boss—in jail. Armand had a gun, and Jo had no doubt that he would be willing to use it, no matter how polite his manners were over dinner and drinks.

Images flashed through Jo's mind. That steel gun pressed against her father's head. The vivid colors that had been spattered all over her white shirt—

Jo jerked out of Armand's arms. "No, no." Her breathing was ragged as Armand's face seemed to metamorphose into the face of her father's killer. A face she'd never forgotten.

"Jacinta, what is the matter?" Armand sounded irritated,

as if he couldn't imagine why someone of the female gender would so willingly, *forcefully* step out of his embrace.

"I just, um, have to go," Jo told him. Her stomach was churning, and she felt as if fainting were a distinct possibility.

Without a glance at Theresa or Caylin, Jo fled. Right now, she simply had to be alone.

Uh-oh. Jo had just freaked out—big time. Caylin tore her attention away from Jorge and watched Jo flee the dance floor.

"What is wrong with her?" Armand shouted. "She is like a crazy woman!"

Caylin gave Jorge an apologetic smile and slid out of his embrace. Out of the corner of her eye, she saw that Theresa was flashing Carlos a similar worried grin. It was official. They were facing a crisis.

"I demand to know what is going on!" Armand yelled.

For the first time that night, it was easy to believe that Armand was a powerful, dangerous, *vicious* man with a criminal mind. Caylin felt the hairs on the back of her neck rise as she stared at Armand's reddening face. Yikes. She wouldn't want to be on *his* bad side.

"Why does she react this way to my kiss?" Armand demanded.

She had to think fast. Very fast. "Um . . . she has a boyfriend?" Caylin offered.

Armand's face went from bright red to dark purple in three seconds flat. "Jacinta is a tease. How can she behave that way with me if she has a boyfriend? It is shameful!"

Caylin shot a significant glance at Diva, who slipped out of Juan's arms and headed off toward where Jo had made her impromptu exit. Thank goodness for their new friend. If anyone had the wherewithal to get Jo back on track right now, it would be her. In the meantime, it was up to "Corinne" and "Trixie" to try and soothe Armand's hackles, which were really, uh, *hackling*.

"Hey, Trixie, want to help me out here?" Caylin whispered out of the side of her mouth.

Theresa put a hand on Armand's shoulder and gave him a sympathetic squeeze. "The thing is, Jacinta is thinking about breaking up with her boyfriend. I mean, he's, like, totally mean to her. She doesn't like him at all."

Armand narrowed his eyes. "Where is he? I will kill him!"

Oops. Theresa's heart was in the right place, but provoking Armand's macho side probably wasn't the best idea under the circumstances.

Caylin stepped forward. "Listen, Armand, it's like this. . . ."

As Caylin babbled on, she prayed that Diva would be able to calm Jo down. If this mission was going to be a success, they had to play their hand carefully. And unless Jo came back for some major damage control, the Big Meeting with Armand's Big Boss could very well get called off—and the mission would be a Big Bust. Or worse.

SIX

"Jo?" Diva called from the other side of the bathroom door. "May I come inside?"

Jo quickly wiped the tears from her cheeks and took several deep, calming breaths. "Uh, sure," she answered weakly.

The door opened, and Diva slipped into the luxurious bathroom. She perched beside Jo on the red velvet settee and placed a comforting arm around her shoulders.

"Is there anything I can do?" Diva asked.

Jo sniffed. "Don't you even want to know why I ran off like a maniac?"

Diva shrugged. "I know what it is like to have dark shadows in one's life. Sometimes . . . well, sometimes the ghosts come out of the corners and one cannot fight them."

Jo couldn't have said it better herself—and Diva was speaking in her second language. "You and I have a lot in common," Jo said, brushing away one last tear. "My family was also torn apart by drugs."

Now it was Diva's turn to get weepy. "Sometimes I lie awake at night and imagine my life so differently. I picture myself and my family on a simple picnic, or going to church, or making dinner in the kitchen . . . all without the dark cloud of the *business* hanging over our heads."

"I don't understand why there's so much evil in the world." Jo rose from the settee and walked to a vanity table at the other side of the large bathroom. "When I was a little girl, my father protected me from that evil. But as I grew older, he taught me to fight it."

"Your father sounds like a wise man," Diva said.

Jo nodded. "He was."

"He passed away?" Diva asked. Her voice was hesitant, as if she were worried that her questions were getting too personal.

"Yes. He . . ." He was murdered. All because the justice system he loved had been corrupted by the drug trade.

"You don't have to tell me about it," Diva said softly. "I know how difficult it is to talk about these things."

In the reflection of the mirror over the vanity table, Jo saw Diva's face grow dark. "You obviously have your own tragedies to deal with," she said.

Diva sighed. "My hair used to be beautiful—it was a shiny, midnight black."

"It's still beautiful." Jo decided against pressing further. If Diva wanted to talk, she would.

"This—" She pointed to the stripe in her hair. "It hasn't always been there."

"No?" Now Jo's curiosity was uncontainable. "How did it get that way?"

"Part of my hair turned white the day my father—" Her voice broke, and she began to sob. They were the kind of deep, tearless sobs that tore apart one's insides.

Diva had appreciated Jo's privacy. Now Jo would return the favor. In time, she would probably discover the haunting secrets of Diva's past. Diva would tell her—when she was ready to.

"We're going to get this guy, Diva." In the mirror Jo's eyes locked with her new friend's.

Diva smiled weakly. "Yes. You three are my angels.

You are going to help me and my family get our lives back."

"And you're going to help. Like I said, we're all in this together." Jo looked at herself in the mirror again and found that she was smiling. As always, Jo found that once the Spy Girl inside her focused all her negative energy on the mission, she felt completely energized. Jo knew what she had to do—now for Diva as much as for herself. This mission was about justice for all.

Jo stood up and faced Diva. "Shall we go back to the party?"

Diva executed a small but graceful curtsy. "By all means."

The two touched hands for a brief moment, then left the bathroom, ready to grapple with their fears.

"You are like fire that is made of liquid," Carlos exclaimed as Caylin was twirled around for what felt like the thousandth time.

"No, she is like fire that spits!" Jorge claimed as he grabbed Caylin and dipped her close to the floor.

Caylin knew that people got carsick and seasick. But was it possible to become dance sick? Jo and Diva's abrupt departure had created a dearth of females in the crowd. So for almost half an hour now, Theresa and Caylin had been juggling two guys each—both on *and* off the dance floor.

"This is great, guys, but I think Trixie needs a turn on the floor now." Caylin was panting, and her hair felt as if it were plastered against her sweaty forehead.

"Trixie is *on* the floor," Theresa called from a few feet away. "Oh, and *please* forget that I *ever* said I wanted to learn the samba."

Juan pulled Theresa close, then picked her up and spun her around several times. "Trixie says she is not good at the Latin dance, but we prove her wrong!"

Caylin gaped at Theresa. Was this the same girl whose idea of an ideal evening was surfing the web for chat rooms? Theresa's dress was slipping off her shoulders, and her brown hair was swinging wildly around her face.

"Corinne, we must show Trixie and Juan how much

better *we* are on the floor, ah?" Armand had approached Caylin from behind. Without warning, he put his hands around her waist, then scooped her into his arms.

Well, at least Armand's nose had been wrestled back into its joint. Theresa and Caylin had fawned over him enough so that he seemed to have forgotten all about Jo's poorly timed freak-out. But enough was enough. If she and Theresa had to keep up this frenetic pace much longer, they weren't going to be able to get out of bed in the morning—much less work to bring down a drug lord.

"Whoaaa . . . !" Theresa cried. She had slipped out of Juan's grasp and was now careening toward Armand and Caylin on her stilettos. "Watch out!"

Smack! Theresa had plowed into Caylin, causing a three-body pileup on the dance floor.

"I think I'm going to die," Theresa moaned.

Caylin remained on the brick floor, thankful for a moment of rest, no matter how ill-gotten. And then . . . a light at the end of the tunnel. Diva and Jo were heading toward them, arm in arm.

"Why do I feel like I just walked into an episode of

The Gong Show?" Jo asked wryly, nearing the scene of the dance catastrophe.

Diva laughed. "Clearly we were missed out here."

"You have *no* idea." Caylin grabbed Jorge's outstretched hand and struggled to her feet.

"I think Trixie and Corinne need to hang up their pearls for the night," Jo said to Diva. "They're tough to be around if they don't get their beauty sleep."

"Gotcha." Diva placed her hand on Armand's shoulder and flashed him a flirtatious smile. "Armand, you gorgeous man, let's talk."

As if on cue, Jorge, Carlos, and Juan melted into the background. As the guys plunked into chairs around the dinner table, Theresa, Caylin, and Jo huddled.

"Do you think everything went according to plan?" Caylin asked. If the answer to that question was no, she had sacrificed both her feet and her equilibrium for no good reason.

"I think so," Jo answered. "Well, I *hope* so. Sorry for the glitch, guys. You know I didn't mean to let you down."

"You didn't," Theresa assured her. "Besides, your

absence meant that Corinne and I got to suck up all the male attention for once."

Jo didn't respond, and Caylin realized that she was listening in on the conversation—strictly Portuguese—that was taking place between Diva and Armand. Their voices were hushed, and Caylin couldn't determine the tone of what was being said.

"Do you think it's a go?" Caylin whispered to Theresa.

"I think we're about to find out," Theresa whispered back. "They're heading this way."

Jo flashed a thumbs-up. "The news is going to be good," she promised, turning back to Caylin and Theresa.

"It has been a most wonderful evening," Armand announced. "But, alas, the hour is late."

Instantly Jorge, Carlos, and Juan popped up from their seats and gravitated toward the girls. There seemed to be some kind of silent communication between the guys that dictated their actions. Did that mean a simple flick of Armand's wrist could result in one of Caylin's dance partners sticking a gun in her face?

"The pleasure has been ours, Armand," Jo said

smoothly. "Please forgive my fit of emotion earlier. It's just that . . . I find you very attractive. So strong . . . so . . ." Jo let her words linger suggestively, then fluttered her lashes. "It was a moment of weakness."

Caylin suppressed a wince. She knew Jo was merely working on Armand's delusional side, but . . . *ugh.*

Armand looked gratified. He shrugged. "It is no problem. I know women—these things happen." He paused, glancing around the group to make sure he had everyone's attention. "My new friends, I would like to tell you that I am going to do my best to set up a meeting between you and our boss. As we discussed, he has many *investment* opportunities to offer."

It was the longest speech of the night—and apparently the last. Without another word, Armand and his cronies filed out of La Americana's back patio and disappeared into the dark night.

"Congratulations, amigas," Diva said with a smile. "You're in business."

Theresa was beyond exhaustion, but she knew that she would lie awake for a long time before she fell asleep tonight. The events of the last few hours whirled in her brain as she listened to Caylin and Jo brief Uncle Sam on the all-important evening.

"I'm very pleased with the progress you've made," Uncle Sam was saying. "I didn't want to undermine your confidence, but to tell you the truth, I wasn't at all sure that these men would agree to give three young American women the opportunity to meet with their boss."

"Great. Now you tell us." Sometimes Theresa appreciated the way Uncle Sam let them find out whether or not a mission was a go on their own. Other times, she wished he would take a slightly more hands-on approach.

"If the rest of the mission goes as well as tonight, then this Big Boss—whoever he is—can look forward to spending the rest of his life in the ole hoosegow." The satisfaction in Caylin's voice was evident. Already each of the girls had poured her soul into their latest adventure.

"So what are our chances of making it out of this thing alive?" Theresa asked.

"The Tower is prepared to back you up every step of

the way," Uncle Sam assured them. "We can offer you a suitcase full of cash at a moment's notice."

"Cash is all well and good," Theresa responded. "But I think I'd like a bullet-proof vest, thank you very much. Or maybe a force field. Can you whip that up for me, Sammo?"

"Just sit tight, Theresa." Uncle Sam was using his patronizing I-know-everything-there-is-to-know-about-international-espionage voice. "A veritable army of Brazilian and United States agents are on twenty-four-hour call. When you need the team behind you, they'll be there."

Caylin sat up a little straighter. "Whoa. That sounds so official."

"It *is* official. Each of these men and women has received special training in order to maximize the effectiveness of their actions while minimizing any risk of bodily harm."

Theresa noted that the term *bodily harm* sounded significantly less clinical when applied to *her* body. Her pain threshold was high—but not *that* high.

"I'm just relieved everything turned out okay tonight," Jo said with a deep sigh. "I can't believe I flaked." She had told Uncle Sam about her "little moment," but he had assured her that sometimes it happened to even the best spies.

"There was no harm done, Jo, I assure you," Uncle Sam soothed. "But I *am* wondering what went down at the end of the night."

"Their convo was all in Portuguese," Caylin informed him. "I couldn't understand a word."

"Jo, were you able to hear what Diva said to this man Armand? Was it something to allay any of his remaining fears or questions about associating with you three?" Uncle Sam asked.

"Sort of," Jo replied. "Basically Diva said, 'Just get them set up. . . . It'll all be over soon, anyway.'"

Theresa frowned. "Doesn't that sound just a tiny bit suspicious?" she asked the group at large. "I mean, I'm not thrilled with the idea of us being so-called set up."

"Diva is on the level," Jo insisted. "I'm as positive about that as I am about my own dress size."

Uncle Sam cleared his throat, interrupting Jo's defense of Wonder Diva. "Let's not speculate too much. It's safer to act based on what we know. And what we know is that everything is going according to plan. At least for now."

"Amen to that," Caylin piped up.

"Get some rest, you three. You're going to need all of your strength." With that, Uncle Sam hung up with his usual lack of the niceties.

Jo reached over and squeezed Theresa's shoulder. "Don't worry, T. Diva's a stand-up chick. Like we said earlier, she could practically be a Spy Girl herself."

She was right. Diva had all of the qualities that made a good spy. She was smart, she was likable, and she had an innate ability to lie through her teeth. And *that* was what made Theresa so worried.

SEVEN

Caylin didn't want to open her eyes. She was in the middle of a particularly delicious dream starring herself, the lead hunk from the daytime soap *Pacific Sundown*, and a long, white, sandy beach. There was also a certain amount of suntan lotion being bandied about. Mmmm . . . Unfortunately, someone was pounding on her head. Wait, no. It wasn't her head. It was the door. Somebody was banging—loudly—on the front door of the mansion.

Caylin pried open her eyes and slid out of bed. She grabbed the fluffy terry cloth bathrobe hanging on the back of her bedroom door and stumbled into the hallway. From the other bedrooms, she heard the sounds of Theresa and Jo's soft snores. Lucky girls—probably still dreaming about superhotties of their own.

"I'm coming!" Caylin yelled as the pounding continued unabated. "And if you're selling magazines, we don't want any."

Caylin stumbled, still half asleep, to the bottom of the staircase. Now that she was at least semiconscious, she realized that this was one of those moments when a Spy Girl was wise to exercise caution. *Anybody* could be on the other side of that door. Then again, if someone really meant to burst in and slit her throat, he probably wouldn't announce his presence with such a flourish.

"Who is it?" Caylin called.

"I am Rocky," a guy called back. Okay, that was sort of a weird Brazilian name, but hey, what did she know?

"Uh, what do you want, Rocky?" Caylin asked. At least he spoke English—dealing with that pesky language barrier was a struggle she wasn't up for this early in the morning.

"I have an important message, miss. Please open the door." He sounded harmless enough. Brutal killers didn't usually say "please."

Caylin opened the door and tried to look as dignified as possible, considering the fact that she was wearing a bathrobe and fuzzy bunny slippers. "Yes?"

Rocky's eyes flickered down to her feet, then snapped back up to her face. He nodded formally. "My boss has requested the presence of Miss Corinne, Miss Trixie, and Miss Jacinta for lunch this afternoon." Ah. Rocky was obviously yet another emissary of the Big Boss. "He has business issues to explore with you."

"Will we be meeting your boss face-to-face, then?" Caylin asked. Her heart began to hammer within her chest as she realized that this might be It.

"A car will pick you up at one o'clock," Rocky said, ignoring her question. "Good day."

"Wait—" Caylin called. Where was the meeting taking place? How long would it last? Should they bring the money? She had a million questions, but Rocky was already jogging toward a large black Cadillac parked in the circle drive.

"I guess that wasn't an invitation," Caylin said softly, to no one but the grandfather clock in the front hall. "It was an order."

At 1:15 p.m. Jo sat in the back of the longest stretch limousine she had ever seen. The black leather interior was decked out with a TV, a high-tech stereo, and even a full wet bar. She felt like a cross between Princess Kate and a rock star's girlfriend. The girls were definitely traveling in style. And they were dressed to the proverbial nines. Each girl had picked out her best "power" suit and a strand of real pearls. Hello, Rodeo Drive!

"I hope our lunch is *satisfying*," Caylin commented, breaking the silence.

"Our host will probably be quite . . . uh, something," Theresa said, glancing at Jo.

Jo leaned back against one of the windows so that she could get a better look at the driver. Unlike most of the guys they had dealt with, the driver wasn't incredibly young and hot. He was more of a grandfather type— hopefully a grandfather who was losing his hearing.

Jo tapped on the glass. "Do you know where we're going?" she loudly asked the driver in Portuguese.

"Lunch," he answered in the same language, and Jo passed the news back to the peanut gallery.

"Do you think it's okay to *talk*?" Caylin wondered aloud.

Jo shrugged at Caylin and Theresa. "A lot of people in

Brazil speak English," she said pointedly. "So if we *talk,* maybe we should include them in our conversation. Would you like that?"

"This sucks," Theresa whispered. "I feel like we're lambs being led to the slaughter."

"Well, let's be quiet lambs," Caylin suggested.

Jo agreed. Even if the driver couldn't understand their conversation, it was very possible that the Big Boss had his limo bugged. And Jo wasn't about to blow the whole mission because the three of them couldn't keep their mouths shut for a short car ride.

For several minutes the back of the limo was quiet except for Caylin's whistled rendition of "Don't Cry for Me, Argentina." The tension was mounting by the second. At last the driver cleared his throat.

"Here we are, ladies," the driver announced in perfect English a few minutes later, parking the car on a deserted residential street.

Oops. Good thing they hadn't blathered on about the mission. Spy Girl Lesson Number 402: Assume everyone speaks English.

As the trio climbed out of the car, Jo stared at their luncheon spot in shock. If this was the Big Man's house, he wasn't doing as well as they all thought. Yeah, the house was on the large side. And certainly the porch wasn't sagging and the roof tiles weren't falling off. But the place was hardly a palace. The girls' HQ was way ritzier. Like, about a hundred times way ritzier.

"Somehow I don't think there's an indoor pool here," Theresa whispered to Jo as they walked up the path to the front door.

"What's going on?" Caylin hissed. "I'm getting a bad feeling about this friendly little lunch."

Jo forced herself to smile brightly in case someone was watching them from inside the modest home. "Well, it's too late to back out now."

The front door opened before they had a chance to knock. Standing on the other side was a pleasant-looking man in his late sixties. White hair, a small potbelly . . . this was Grandpa Number 1. He looked even older than the driver. Jo suddenly felt extremely conspicuous in her hot pink Chanel suit and matching pumps. Grandpa was wearing a cheap-looking seersucker suit and a pair of eye-glasses that looked as if they had been purchased circa 1965.

Jo was positive that Caylin and Theresa were thinking exactly what she was. Was it possible—at *all*—that the mild-mannered man standing before them was the Big Boss?

"Hello, girls!" he greeted them enthusiastically in English. "Corinne, Jacinta, Trixie, it is a pleasure to make your acquaintance."

Enough with the polite salutations already. Jo was ready for some *action*. "Hello, sir."

He smiled. "Please, call me Chico. All my friends do, yes, you understand?" He stepped away from the door and ushered the trio into the house.

Jo studied their surroundings as she followed Chico—whose walk bore a distinct resemblance to a duck's waddle—down a short hallway. The house wasn't ostentatious, to say the least, but it was clear that the people who lived there took great care to make the place homey and comfortable. There was children's artwork on the walls, crocheted throw rugs on the floor, and antique clocks tucked into many of the corners.

"Thank you for having us to lunch, uh, Chico," Theresa said as they walked into a small, cozy dining room. "This is quite an honor."

"The honor was ours," Chico responded, beaming from behind his thick eyeglasses. Okay, his English wasn't superb. But he had said "ours."

Ours. That could mean only one thing. Jo fully expected the Big Boss to emerge from another room with a sack full of white powder. Okay, maybe not the sack—the girls were strictly playing investor. But she at least expected to see The Man Himself at long last.

"You eat, yes?" Chico gestured toward a table laden with delicious-looking home-cooked food.

Jo could practically feel the pounds collecting on her hips. She exchanged glances with her fellow SGs as they took their seats around the table.

"Is anyone else joining us?" Caylin asked after an awkward moment of silence.

"Eat, eat," Chico said. He gestured toward the food, grinning and smacking his lips. "Is good, yes?"

Okay, it was beyond obvious that this guy wasn't the

Big Boss. There was just no way. It was also obvious that he wasn't going to impart any information that he didn't feel was absolutely necessary.

"You heard our host," Theresa said firmly. "Let's eat."

Chico sat down at the head of the table and piled his plate high with rice, beans, and beef. After a few minutes of enjoying his meal, he patted his chin with a white linen napkin.

"So, you tell me your plan, yes?" He looked from one girl to the next, awaiting their response.

Jo considered responding in Portuguese, then decided against it. Letting Chico believe that none of them spoke his native language could turn out to be an advantage. One never knew what kind of conversations one might overhear. . . .

"We have half a million dollars of disposable income," Jo said, getting right to the point. "We would like to . . . make an investment."

"Ah, yes, wonderful, wonderful." Chico beamed at them, but it wasn't clear whether or not he had understood a word of what Jo had said. The expression on his face was somewhere between "addled professor" and "beatific monk."

Covert mission or no covert mission, this situation was

beginning to border on the absurd. "Um, can you tell us what our next step is?"

Understanding flashed in Chico's electric blue eyes. "Yes, yes, soon," he responded. "Things take time, yes?"

Jo sighed. Talk about frustrating! The waiting was nothing short of excruciating. She would feel that way even if she really *were* a rich debutante looking to get into the drug business. Jo Carreras was *not* one to appreciate being lopped off on some dough-brained underling. She wanted to meet the Big Boss!

"No worry, Jacinta," Chico continued. "I think the boss like your plan, yes? You will meet him very soon. Very soon."

Jo took another bite of her black beans. That meeting better be worth the wait. She was beginning to feel as if the Spy Girls were playing an elaborate game of cat and three blind mice.

El Centro was a totally different place during the day. Theresa couldn't believe this was the same club the girls had visited their first night in Rio. The silence was almost eerie as the girls walked inside and called out for Diva.

She appeared at the bottom of the staircase that led to the DJ booth, dressed down in a pair of slacks and a scoop-neck T-shirt. "So? Tell me."

"We just came from a meeting with Chico," Theresa blurted out.

"Yes?" Diva said breathlessly. "And?"

Jo shrugged. "Well, according to Chico, we're a go."

"Great!" Diva smiled, but she made a quick watch-what-you-say gesture with her hands. Naturally. Now that the business transaction was switching into high gear, they had to assume that almost any place could be wiretapped.

"We'll be meeting our . . . benefactor . . . very soon," Jo said to Diva. "And we can conduct our . . . uh, stuff."

Diva's excitement was evident from the bright flush that had come to her cheeks. "This calls for a shopping trip!" she exclaimed. "I will take you all to the best shops in Rio."

Theresa wasn't usually prone to spending sprees, unless they involved gigabytes and megahertz. But hey, they were American debutantes. It would seem strange if they *didn't* go drop a load of cash on fancy shoes and Brazilian knickknacks.

"Sounds good to me," Jo said. "I think there's a dress for doing the samba with my name on it."

"I think the votes are unanimous," Caylin said. "Let's hit the shops!"

Once the girls were outside El Centro, Diva pulled them aside. "May I go with you all for the exchange?" she asked. "More than anything, I would love to see the Big Boss go down," she added fiercely.

Theresa's instinct told her to say no. But she saw from the look on Jo's face that protestation at this point would be fruitless.

"We'll see what we can do," Jo promised. "If it's at all possible, you'll be right by our sides."

Diva nodded. "Good. I would be so honored to make the stand with you. All three of you."

Theresa smiled in sisterhood, but deep inside she hoped Jo knew what she was doing.

"Greeting, O Doubtful One, we bring glad tidings." Jo was practically bursting with adrenaline as the girls greeted Uncle Sam via speakerphone.

"Do I detect progress?" Uncle Sam asked in his usual calm manner.

"Diva thinks tomorrow is the big day," Caylin told him.

As they had shopped, Diva had let all three of them in on some of the Big Boss's ways and means of doing business. Apparently having lunch with daffy old Chico was the final step a potential business associate needed to take before the deal with the Big Boss became final. It was some kind of tradition or something.

"Bravo!" Uncle Sam said. "Excellent work, Spy Girls."

"We just have one question," Jo said. "Can we bring Diva along on the sting?"

For several seconds Sam didn't respond. "I know this young woman is our informant, but we don't know whether or not she has ulterior motives. Allowing her in on the sting could prove hazardous."

"But Diva is in just as much danger as we are!" Jo insisted. "As soon as things get funky, the bad dudes are going to suspect that she had something to do with the setup."

"Good point, Jo." There was another pause. "On second thought . . . maybe bringing your friend Diva along is a good idea," Uncle Sam said slowly. "Her intimate knowledge of the Big Boss and his underlings could prove helpful if the situation gets sticky."

"And if it turns out that she's working for the other side, we can always use her as a human shield," Theresa added.

"Come on, T., don't question Diva," Jo said, sounding like a broken record. "She's totally on the up-and-up."

"Quiet down," Uncle Sam ordered. "Spy Girls, it's time to get serious. Now, here's the plan. . . ."

EIGHT

"Time to switch to decaf," Jo muttered to herself the next morning. She had been up since six o'clock, and her hands were shaking—either from anticipation or the three cups of coffee she had downed while reading a daily newspaper.

She had eaten breakfast. She had updated herself on current events. She had showered and dressed in one of her supreme debutante outfits, a fresh little number courtesy of Dolce & Gabbana and, oh yes, The Tower. Still there was no word from the Big Boss. Jo didn't think she could wait much longer. Her nerves were *seriously* on the verge.

Jo heard the whir of a car engine and the slam of a door before she heard the knock at the door. Ta-da! This was the moment she had been waiting for—the moment they had *all* been waiting for. As Jo walked toward the front door, she marveled at the fact that Caylin and Theresa were still asleep. For her, last night had been like Christmas Eve. Hopefully the emissary she was about to greet at the door was going to bring her the best present ever. A date with the Big Boss.

As Jo opened the door, her spirits rose even higher. The man had sent Armand, a sure sign that something major was about to go down. "Good morning, Armand."

Thank goodness she had taken the time to do up her face. If there was anyone who appreciated a pretty girl, it was Armand.

"Jacinta, it is lovely to see you again."

"Likewise." Man, when would the chitchat end? She was veritably *drowning* in polite small talk. But she had to be patient.

"I am happy to inform you that it is time to make the exchange," Armand stated formally. "There will be a car here to pick you up at five o'clock this evening." He paused. "As long as that is convenient for you ladies, of course."

Jo gave him one of her most dazzling smiles. "Well . . . we *are* expecting a shipment of new furniture this afternoon. But I'm sure we can arrange to be free by five o'clock."

"Wonderful. It's a date." Armand looked as if he would like to start the date—a *real* date—right that minute. He was looking at Jo as if she were a piece of pie on a dessert plate. "Your investment . . . is in American dollars, no?"

Jo nodded in understanding. Diva had already informed her that drug business was conducted with powerful American cash whenever possible. Speaking of which . . .

"Armand, may we bring Diva with us?" Jo asked sweetly. "She's been so instrumental in our business venture that we'd like to have her along for the celebration that will follow the . . . exchange."

Armand gave her a knowing smile. "Why, Jacinta, but of course. Diva is always welcome during business dealings." He paused. "She's practically one of the family."

Huh. Getting the okay to bring Diva in on the exchange had been easy. A more suspicious person—such as Theresa—might have even said that getting permission had been *too* easy. But Jo *wasn't* suspicious, not where Diva was concerned.

"Then we'll see you at five," Jo said.

She counted backward from ten to keep herself somewhere near a state of calm as she waited for Armand to get into his BMW convertible and peel out of the driveway. As soon as the BMW disappeared down the street, Jo raced to the speakerphone.

She pressed the button that automatically dialed Uncle Sam's number and waited breathlessly for him to come on the line.

"Speak to me," Uncle Sam greeted after only one ring.

"We're on!" Jo yelled. "Deploy the money, deploy the troops." She was torn between jumping for joy and shaking with fright. "Your Spy Girls are going into battle at precisely five o'clock this afternoon."

"Stand by," Uncle Sam ordered her. "The Tower is on its way."

Jo hung up the phone and collapsed on the sofa. Finally. The day she had been unconsciously anticipating for four years had arrived. At last Jo was going to claim justice for Judge Carreras. The man who actually pulled the trigger might remain free for the rest of his life, but thanks to Jo, a man just as bad was about to spend the rest of his life in lockdown.

Who ever said that revenge wasn't sweet?

• • •

By three o'clock in the afternoon Caylin had logged a good two hours in the window seat at the front of the mansion. The girls had paced nervously around the house all morning and afternoon, waiting, waiting, waiting for something to *happen*.

Out of nowhere, a huge furniture truck pulled into the driveway. "Hark!" Caylin screamed to the Spy Girls.

"Who goes there?" Theresa yelled back. She and Jo were now sprinting from the kitchen to the front of the house.

"Our furniture has arrived," Caylin announced excitedly. "And it looks like there's a lot of it."

"Yee haw!" Jo yelled. "It's about time." She paused. "I guess debutantes don't say 'yee haw,' huh?"

"Who cares?" Caylin shouted. "The *furniture* is here. Finally!"

The girls rushed to the door and threw it open. "Welcome!" Theresa called. "The ergonomically correct desk chair goes in my room—right next to my laptop."

A very tall, very familiar dark-haired woman stepped out of the cab of the truck. "Very funny, Theresa. I know that you actually ordered the king-sized water bed."

"Danielle!" The cry was delivered in chorus. Their guardian angel was dressed in navy blue coveralls and a baseball cap. She was definitely the prettiest furniture deliveryman that Caylin had ever seen.

Danielle Hall was a senior Tower agent who had been assigned to help the Spy Girls through the toughest parts of some of their missions. She was always just a phone call away, and Danielle's advice and support had been oh-so-valuable during the past few months. She also had the habit of showing up at precisely the moment when she was needed most—like now.

Danielle turned back toward the huge furniture truck. "Back her up to the door, Bernie!" she yelled.

The driver waved, then maneuvered the truck so that its back was as close to the front door of the mansion as possible. Caylin watched the proceedings, fascinated. This was The Tower at its most spy-licious.

Danielle handed Caylin the key to the back of the truck. "Will you do the honors, Miss Corinne?" she asked with a wink.

"But of course." Caylin jogged to the back of the truck, inserted the key in its lock, and heaved the heavy metal door upward.

Instantly dozens of agents poured from the back of the truck into the front hall of the mansion. Many were obviously Tower agents, but others were Brazilian, shouting instructions at one another in rapid-fire Portuguese.

"Wow!" Jo exclaimed. "The commandos have arrived!"

As suddenly as it had come, the truck pulled away and disappeared down the street. Instead of furniture the Spy Girls had received a shipment of highly trained agents, a battery of high-tech surveillance equipment, and a metal briefcase stuffed with unmarked hundred-dollar bills. Yeow . . . this really was the major leagues.

"Danielle, we had no idea you were coming to save the day," Theresa exclaimed. "We would have prepared a special fairy godmother snack."

Danielle laughed. "You girls are the ones who have to save the day. I'm just here for moral support."

"Do we really need this many agents?" Caylin asked. She felt as if she were in a war bunker.

Danielle nodded. "We need extra men—and women—because of the international status of your mission. It's imperative that we have all safety, not to mention legal, potholes covered."

"I think we could supply electricity to a small nation with the amount of stuff these guys are hauling around," Jo commented. "I mean, really, who needs a laptop computer the size of a credit card?"

"I do!" Theresa yelled enthusiastically. "That way I could do my hacking even if I were locked into a small dark box."

"If you're locked in a small dark box, there's going to be a lot more to worry about than checking your e-mail," Caylin said.

Jo walked over to a gadget-filled trunk and peered inside. "Is any of this supercool spy paraphernalia for us?"

A tall, good-looking American Tower agent stepped up to the trunk. "We've got more toys than Santa at Christmastime," he informed her.

Hmmm. Caylin had been digging the dudes in Rio, but there was nothing like an American guy who looked like he had stepped off the cover of *Surfing Magazine* to get the blood flowing.

Each of the Spy Girls reached into the trunk and pulled out a new spy gadget. Theresa got a stun gun that from all outward appearances was a lipstick. Jo acquired a variation of the mascara cam—this camera was fitted into a breath mint.

"Just make sure you don't swallow," the cute Tower dude advised.

"What's this?" Caylin asked, staring at what looked like an ordinary everyday ballpoint pen.

"That's a direct link to The Tower," Cute Agent explained. "If you click the pen, an alarm will sound at The Tower headquarters in the United States. Once Uncle Sam hears that alarm, he'll place a person-to-person call to none other than the president of the US of A."

Yikes. Caylin hoped she never had occasion to use the pen. She had no desire to create any kind of havoc in the White House.

"Listen up, Spy Chicks," Danielle called. "It's wire time."

The girls had been through this routine several times

before. Each Spy Girl lifted her arms and allowed a totally hot Tower agent to attach a tiny wire to her torso. They all knew the importance of the wires.

Inside the meeting with the Big Boss, the girls would be on their own. The agents would be waiting outside, ready to burst in and make their arrests once the girls had sufficient evidence on tape. They could also raid the place in the unfortunate event that the whole deal went sour and the Spy Girls were in imminent danger. If the agents lost their ability to hear what was going on inside the meeting—for whatever reason—the girls could kiss the mission good-bye.

"Do we know the meeting place?" Danielle asked, consulting her notes.

Caylin shook her head. "We don't even know the Big Boss's name, much less where the handover is going to occur."

Danielle nodded. "That's too bad . . . but we'll manage. The second you get into that car, we'll be on your tail— from a distance, of course."

"What happens if the driver figures out somebody is following us?" Theresa asked anxiously.

Danielle raised her eyebrows. "He won't." Caylin shivered with anticipation. The sting was elaborate, but the agents seemed to know what they were doing. As long as she and her *compadres* upheld their end of the operation, all would go smoothly. She hoped.

Danielle glanced at her watch. "It's four forty-five," she announced. "Showtime."

Ding-dong. The doorbell rang at exactly five o'clock. Theresa touched the wire taped to her body one last time, her heart beating wildly.

"We'll be fine," Caylin said.

"We'll be better than fine," Jo corrected her. "We're going to kick some major drug-lord butt."

Theresa nodded. They had been in tight situations before—and they had, indeed, kicked butt. "We look great, we feel great, and we have a metal briefcase filled with hundred-dollar bills."

Jo laughed. "I couldn't have said it better myself." She paused. "So why do I feel like I'm going to barf?"

Unfortunately for all of them, there was no time to run

to the nearest bathroom and throw up. As Danielle had put it so succinctly, this was showtime. Theresa opened the door and found herself face-to-face with the charming Armand.

"Good afternoon, lovely ladies. It is a glorious evening for business, no?" Armand walked into the foyer and bowed slightly from the waist.

"We can hardly wait," Caylin agreed. Only her fellow Spy Girls would have been able to detect the small tremor in her voice as she spoke.

"Shall we go?" Jo asked. Caylin noticed that her eyes had drifted toward the staircase.

"By all means," Armand replied. He stepped aside to allow the three of them to leave the house in front of him. There were those manners again.

Caylin and Jo stepped outside and headed toward the limo parked in the driveway. As Theresa followed, Armand lightly touched her arm.

"Where is your new furniture, Trixie?" Armand inquired, looking into the living room.

Theresa thought fast. Very fast. "Oh, it's all upstairs."

Well, it wasn't *exactly* a lie—all their human, technological, and otherwise resources had taken a powder to the second floor fifteen minutes previous. "We got new . . . um, bedroom sets."

"Maybe later you'll show me, yes?"

Theresa smiled and lowered her eyes demurely. Yeah, right, she thought. Maybe later he would be in *jail*.

As she walked out the front door, Theresa turned and glanced once more into the house. Danielle's head popped out from behind the door that led to the kitchen, and she flashed a big thumbs-up. Theresa smiled, taking a deep breath. This was it. They would either come back to the mansion victorious—or they wouldn't come back at all.

NINE

"Hello, friends. It's a glorious evening for doing business, no?" Diva greeted the Spy Girls as she slid into the back of the limousine.

Jo had a perverse urge to giggle. Armand had used almost exactly the same words less than twenty minutes ago. If he only knew how different they sounded coming from Diva's mouth . . .

"Hi, Diva," Theresa greeted her warmly. Thank goodness. At last Theresa seemed to have let go of her paranoid suspicion of their greatest ally.

The driver drove out of El Centro's parking lot and pulled into traffic. Wow—rush hour was the same all over the world, apparently. Jo knew that it was beyond important that her demeanor remain calm, cool, and collected, but the international agent in her worried about The Tower's ability to trail the limo in this much traffic. Why couldn't the summit meeting have been set for a time that coincided with afternoon siesta?

As Jo stared—surreptitiously, she hoped—out the back window, Diva reached over and squeezed her arm. "We're in this together, Jacinta," she whispered softly.

Jo felt herself relax. Diva was a kindred spirit. She would look out for the girls, no matter what went down.

Up in the front, Armand was humming a salsa tune. "How are you doing, lovely ladies?" He turned and stared at them.

"Peachy," Theresa squeaked. "This is the *best*."

Good thing Armand didn't know Theresa better than he did. The fact that she had uttered a word like *peachy* was a clear indication that she was way past nervous.

Armand snorted. "The American girls are a little unsure, yes?" He winked at Diva. "They are new at this game."

"Don't let our youth fool you," Caylin told him coolly. "We've been around more than a few blocks in our time."

"*Rrrow* . . . feisty." Armand growled flirtatiously in Caylin's direction. "Maybe yours is the bedroom set I would like to see later tonight, ah?"

Jo resisted the urge to roll her eyes. Armand, gorgeous or not, was one aspect of this mission she wouldn't miss. His blatant come-ons bordered on nauseating. Instead of the eye roll, she let her lids droop. Shutting out the rest of the world was essential at this particular moment. Otherwise all sorts of haunting images might mess with her focus.

"I'm here, Jacinta." Again Diva squeezed her arm.

Jo grinned. They had been right to bring Diva along. She was sure of that now. Their new friend was an integral part of this crime organization, and she knew better than any of them what was up. As long as Diva stayed cool, nothing could *possibly* go wrong. . . .

"And I thought *we* had nice digs," Caylin commented as the girls climbed out of the limo thirty minutes later. "This place isn't a home . . . it's a city."

They had arrived at one of the most ginormous estates Caylin had ever seen. The front lawn—if the term *lawn* applied to an expanse of grass that large— was perfectly manicured. Several fountains dotted the landscape, and there were no less than three incredibly expensive sports cars parked in the driveway-slash-road.

Armand brushed past the girls and opened the front door without knocking. "Honey, I'm home!" He smiled at Caylin. "That's a little bit of American humor for you, yes?"

Caylin didn't bother to respond. Instead she gaped at the massive, opulent foyer into which Armand had led them. Yowza! Floor-to-ceiling white marble and a chandelier big enough for all three Spy Girls *and* Uncle Sam to swing from. This was definitely the Big Boss's den. The place shouted *dinero*.

"Ah, ladies, how lovely is it to see you again." Chico doddered in from an unidentified room off the front hall.

He was looking significantly more suave than he had during their lunch meeting. Today he was wearing an Armani suit, and a shiny diamond ring glittered on his right pinky finger.

Chico's eyes lit up when he saw Diva. "Ah, my girl . . ." He clasped her arms and kissed her on each cheek. "We have been expecting you."

Diva returned the kisses. "So, where is the meeting to take place?" she asked Chico.

Good for her. Just like a real Spy Girl, Diva had gotten straight to the point. Caylin gave her a silent cheer. If they didn't get this meeting going pronto, Caylin wasn't going to be able to keep the butterflies in her stomach from flying free.

"This way." Chico turned and headed down a long, narrow hallway. The girls fell into line, following his footsteps in nervous silence.

There was a veritable gang of gangsters waiting for the debutante party in a large den. Caylin had rarely seen more men in expensive suits in one place at one time. All of the hotties from their night at La Americana were present, as well as several beefy bodyguard types who looked as if they had been recruited from World Wrestling Entertainment. Alas, there was still no sign of the Big Boss. Hopefully he was nearby.

Caylin sized up the situation. There were two doors. One was behind Chico, who had retreated to the back of the room immediately. The other was behind Jo, who still hovered in front of the door the girls had come through. Meanwhile the metal briefcase in Theresa's left hand was clearly the center of attention. Every man in the room was staring lustfully at that case full o' cash.

Chico cleared his throat—apparently to distract everyone's attention from the half a million dollars at the end of Theresa's arm. "Now . . . we do business."

Ready. Set. Run. The sting was on.

Jo had looked forward to a day like this one ever since the day her father's killer had been set free. But now that the moment had arrived, she felt almost paralyzed with fear.

Any one of these men could take out a gun at a moment's notice and blow her brains out. Literally. Then again, at a moment's notice the American and Brazilian agents could charge into the room and take each and every one of these men into custody. At least, they could charge in here as long as they had managed to tail the trio and the wires were operational. Otherwise backup was more or less powerless to come in and do its thing when the time was right. Otherwise the three of them were totally and completely on their own—and poor Diva would be added to the endangered species list.

"I believe you have five hundred thousand dollars for us?" Chico asked Theresa.

The gulp was almost audible. "And I believe that you're willing to offer us a guaranteed twenty-five percent profit on our investment?"

Diva had informed the girls that twenty-five percent was a standard return on an investment in the drug trade. Thank goodness Theresa had maintained the presence of mind to spell it out for the always important wiretap. At the moment Jo wasn't sure she could remember her own vital statistics.

"Yes, of course, Trixie. That *is* the industry standard." Hmmm. Apparently Chico's English was better than he had let on.

Theresa held out the briefcase. "It's all there, Chico."

Jorge stepped forward, took the briefcase, then handed it to Chico. "Heavy," Chico commented. He laid the case on a mahogany table and flipped open the lid. Every person in the room stared at the green-and-white bills.

Chico smiled. "Beautiful!" He reached into the briefcase and laid his hands on the money. "There is nothing like the smell of new American dollars to put spring in an old man's step." He shut the case and snapped the lock shut.

Jo's entire body tensed as Chico walked toward the door at the back of the room. He turned down the dimmer on the overhead light switch, then opened the door. "It's ready."

A moment later a man stepped through the door. His face remained in shadow, but it was clear to Jo that this was the long-awaited Big Boss.

"The young ladies have officially invested in our business," Chico informed the boss. "The money is all yours." Chico picked up the briefcase and held it out to his superior.

"Wonderful." The Big Boss accepted the money, then stepped out of the shadows.

Jo stared at the face of the man the Spy Girls were about to bring down. As she absorbed the details of his features, the world started to shift around her. No! It wasn't possible!

"I—" Jo looked into the man's coal black eyes . . . and recognized him. In a flash, she saw that he recognized her as well.

"What is it?" Theresa asked.

Jo blinked rapidly as her father's murder flashed through her mind in a series of rapid, surreal images. Yes, she knew this man. She had seen him in her nightmares for years.

"You—you killed my father!" Jo screamed.

Theresa felt as if time had stopped as she watched Jo scream at the Big Boss. "We need backup *now*!" she yelled into her wiretap.

"I remember! I saw you!" Jo was yelling at the Big Boss, but her words were broken with loud, hoarse sobs. Meanwhile Diva was shaking. Her face had gone deathly pale.

The Big Boss's eyes were wide and scared. He looked toward Chico. "What is this?" the man shouted.

Chico took a step backward, away from the Big Boss. "I don't know!"

Pandemonium erupted in the room as Jo continued to shout accusations at the man in front of her. Everything was happening so fast that Theresa could barely process the events. All she knew for sure was that the sting was in serious jeopardy—not to mention their lives.

"No!" The Big Boss turned from Jo and began to run toward the door at the back of the room.

"He killed my father!" Jo screamed again.

Every man in the room pulled a gun from the waistband of his suit. Armand shouted in Portuguese while Chico fixed Jo with a cold, brutal stare. Oh no. This was it. They were all going to die.

"Where are the agents?" Caylin hissed.

Suddenly the door behind Theresa burst open. Instantly dozens of agents poured into the room. "Freeze!" someone screamed.

In seconds the agents had each of the Big Boss's underlings on the floor and in handcuffs. But the Big Boss was escaping through the back door.

"Over there!" Theresa screamed, pointing in the direction of the Big Boss.

"What are you doing?" Diva screamed at Theresa. Her eyes were dark and wild. She looked like a desperate, trapped animal. "You've got the wrong man! That man is innocent!"

Diva clutched Theresa's arms, shaking her. "Do you hear me? He is *innocent!*"

"Get him!" Theresa ordered.

Two agents leaped over the desk and disappeared behind the door. Thirty seconds later they reappeared with the man who had killed Jo's father.

"You're going to the electric chair!" Jo shouted. "I'm going to see you *fry.*"

Jo's words seemed to be coming from some primal, previously unknown part of her soul. Theresa had never seen her friend break down like this—it was frightening.

"Jacinta, no!" Diva moaned. "He is innocent!" Diva collapsed into a chair and sobbed hysterically.

"What are you talking about?" Caylin yelled, shaking Diva's shoulders.

"*That* man is my *father!*" Diva cried. "Chico is the one you want!"

TEN

Caylin didn't know whether to cry or breathe a huge sigh of relief. The Big Boss had been taken into custody, but Jo was a basket case. Nothing seemed to make sense.

Chico was shaking his head as he studied Diva's tear-stained face. "Diva, how can you say such things? You know I commit no crime. I am a pawn in the game of your father—just like all these men."

"You liar!" Diva cried. "He's lying!"

Again Chico shook his head. "I trusted you, Diva . . . but I forget you are like your father—a cold-blooded killer."

"Explain yourself," barked the agent holding Chico by the arm.

"I have been faithful to Diva's father as his second in command for many years—on pain of death." He sighed deeply. "But that wasn't enough for this family. They wanted me put in jail so that Diva could take over at her father's right hand. It wouldn't be enough to kill me. No, they want to put me away for their crimes. They want me to die, an old man, alone in prison."

Diva stood up and took the place beside her father. "No, *we* are the pawns. Chico has been controlling our lives for as long as I can remember."

"They no longer want this old man around," Chico commented, shrugging at one of the agents. "No respect, they have. Too much trouble I cause for them. They find me weak—senile, yes? Thank goodness I call for your help. But they find out I give information to you, and all this"—he waved his arms around the den—"this plan with you ladies, with the money, this was to punish me for telling. But now you have made me safe. And now I can be free."

Danielle put a hand on Jo's shoulder and pointed toward Diva's father, who was staring at Jo in horror. "Are you absolutely sure that's the man who killed your father?" Danielle asked.

Jo nodded. "I'll never forget his face."

"Take him away, boys," Danielle instructed the agents. "We've got our man."

"No!" Diva tried to hold on to her father, but two agents grabbed her arms and held her tightly.

"I love you, Diva!" her father cried as the agents pushed him toward the door. "We'll get through this!"

Diva watched as her father disappeared with the agents. She seemed to be in as bad shape as Jo. Then she turned to Caylin and grabbed her arm. "You've got to listen!" Diva cried. "They're taking the wrong man!"

Armand smiled at Theresa, Jo, and Caylin, despite the fact that he was wearing a pair of handcuffs and had a gun pointed toward his shoulder. "Thank you, ladies. Your brave actions have saved the world from suffering at the hands of that man—the crudest man I have ever known. He thought with his business, he could control us all. Power hungry, I think you call it."

Caylin didn't know what to believe. She didn't even fully understand what was going on around her. There were a million unanswered questions. But the Spy Girls had a right to know the answers. Especially Jo. Caylin glanced at her weeping friend and felt her own eyes well up with tears. Sometimes it seemed as if there was simply too much tragedy in the world for one super-duper Spy Girl to bear.

Jo forced herself to stop crying. She had spent too many years shedding tears. Now was the time for anger. Righteous, indignant rage. Slowly everything was becoming all too clear.

Diva wasn't just trying to set up Chico. She had also been setting up Jo. Diva and her father had wanted to twist the knife into Jo and her family even further than they had when they killed Judge Carreras. They had wanted to sit back and *laugh* at stupid, gullible Jo. Oh yes. Diva had known all along that Jacinta was actually Josefina Mercedes Carreras.

Jo turned to Diva, who was still standing under an antique shield. She glared at her with all the hatred and venom she could muster. "How could you?" she asked. "You knew your father killed my father. And what do you do? You *used* that against me! All that stuff about 'my father is in danger'—what a load. All you wanted to do was play on my vulnerability and win my trust. You're disgusting."

"You're wrong!" Diva cried. "I don't even know what you're talking about!"

"Yes, you do," Jo said, her voice steely. "You used my father's memory to further your own evil schemes."

"I told you, I have no idea what you're talking about, Jacinta." Diva's cheeks were ashen, and her dark eyes were rimmed with red. "I only wanted us to help each other bring down the Big Boss!"

Jo let out a sound that was somewhere between a laugh and a sob. "Help me? How does killing my dad *help* me?" Jo walked toward Diva so that the traitor could see the disgust in Jo's eyes as she listened to her speak.

"Your father killed my father, Diva. Four years ago. In Miami. He killed him right in front of me."

"Oh . . . no!" Diva brought her hands to her face. "That day . . . oh, that horrible day. . . ." She paused. "You—you're Josefina Carreras?"

Josefina Carreras. Josefina Mercedes Carreras. Jo hadn't been called "Josefina" in years. Since the day her father had been killed, woe be to anyone who dared called her anything but "Jo."

"You know I am," Jo spat. "You've known that all along. And you cried those fake, crocodile tears over the treachery of the drug trade to win my trust."

Diva's face turned from pale to even paler. Her body began to sway back and forth, and for a moment it looked as if she were going to faint. "I needed you," she muttered. "I needed your help, and—"

"Take her," Danielle said suddenly. "She belongs in custody right beside her father."

Before Diva could fall to the floor, two agents grabbed her arms and propped her up.

As they dragged her toward the door, Jo waited to feel some small measure of satisfaction. But she didn't. All she felt was the deep, aching, vast loss of her father. It was as if she had just witnessed his murder all over again.

Jo felt Theresa place an arm around her shoulders. "Let's get out of here, Jo."

"I'm going to see that they get what they deserve," Jo told Theresa.

"We all will," Caylin promised.

Jo allowed her fellow Spy Girls to wrap her in a warm embrace. Diva had betrayed her, but Theresa and Caylin would be her friends forever. After several long moments Jo pulled away, feeling a bit more like herself.

"Five minutes alone with those two," she said. "That's all I want." She knew exactly what she would do and how she would do it. . . .

Three hours later Theresa fought the urge to pull an I-told-you-so on Jo. After the threesome had returned to the mansion for a depressurization break, Danielle had driven them to the ultrasecret holding area where Tower agents were now questioning Diva and her father. Safely ensconced behind a two-way mirror, Theresa, Caylin, Jo, and Danielle were watching the interrogation from just several feet away.

"I shouldn't have trusted her," Jo muttered for the fifth time. "How could I have been so stupid?"

"We all trusted her, Jo," Caylin said soothingly. "Diva seemed like a stand-up chick."

Theresa nodded. Yes, she had held on to her suspicions regarding Diva for a long time, but the truth was that she had eventually believed in their informant as much as Jo and Caylin had.

"Listen to them," Danielle said. "They're pros."

The girls redirected their attention to the interrogation. Diva and her father were all wide eyes and innocence as they talked to The Tower agents. Danielle was right. If Theresa didn't know better, she would have felt sympathy toward the pair.

"My daughter only wanted to help our family," the Big Boss was saying. "Even if you feel that I have done wrong, please let her go. She is an innocent child."

Yet another fake tear slid down Diva's cheek. "No, Father! I am not going to let them believe these evil lies about you. We must help them learn the truth!"

The Big Boss shook his head sadly. Man, he was good. "They will believe what they want to believe, Diva."

Diva clutched her father's arm as she stared into the face of her interrogator. "You have to listen to me! *I'm* the person who brought your agents to Rio! Not Chico! Why would I have done that if my father and I were guilty of all of these horrible crimes? We're victims . . . just like Josefina."

Jo snorted. "She makes me sick—and I make me sick. It was obvious all along that Diva was this close to the Big Boss."

"You're right, Jo," Caylin said. "I mean, we should have gotten a clue way back when we found out that Diva *owned* a nightclub that was basically a front for drug trafficking."

"Or when the Big Boss's emissaries were so cool about Diva coming with us for the money exchange," Theresa commented.

"The important thing is that you three came through in the end," Danielle said firmly. "Jo, you recognized Diva's father when the time was right. And now they're both going to spend a long time behind bars."

Danielle had a good point. Even though Diva turned out to be a bad guy, she *had* led them to her father. Without her involvement, the Spy Girls never would have gotten to him.

"I can't believe she took us for such fools," Jo said. "Did she really think I wouldn't recognize her dad?"

Theresa shrugged. "Criminals can be arrogant. Look at them—even now they're trying to maintain their innocent sob story."

"I'm just glad that the man who killed your father is finally going to be locked away forever," Caylin said.

"And Diva can rot in jail right along beside him," Jo added. "She's as bad as he is. . . . I don't think I've ever felt so betrayed by another human being."

"The agents are finishing up the interview," Danielle interrupted. "Any moment, father and daughter are going to be taken to the cells where they belong."

Once again Theresa turned her attention back to the room in front of them. Diva and the Big Boss were now on their feet, agents at their sides. Slowly they began to walk from the room.

"Wait!" Diva yelled suddenly. She broke free from the agents' grasp and lunged toward the mirror. Her eyes were wild as she pressed her face against the two-way glass.

"The gun!" Diva yelled. "Remember the gun!" Before she could say another word, the agents regained their control of her and led both suspects from the room.

"What did she mean by that?" Theresa wondered aloud. "Remember the gun. . . ."

Caylin shrugged. "Who knows? Maybe it's some kind of weird organized-crime slogan."

"I don't know, and I don't care," Jo said. "But at least this mission is over with."

Theresa nodded. The mission was over. Unfortunately, not one of them was in the mood to celebrate.

ELEVEN

Check out all the amazing clothes we acquired during this mission," Caylin said to Jo. "I can't wait to wear these duds back in the States."

"Maybe I'll change my image," Theresa added brightly. "I'll turn in my khakis for a dressy evening gown."

Jo shrugged. "You can have my stuff. I don't feel like dealing with the whole packing thing."

Caylin exchanged a glance with Theresa. This was *not* the Jo they knew and loved. But nothing they said or did seemed to be helping to bring her out of her funk. And they had said and done just about *everything.* The girls had come straight back to HQ after the interrogation, and they had spent the last hour trying to cheer up Jo while they got ready to head back to the United States. Unfortunately, nothing was working.

"Mind if I come in?" Danielle was standing at the door of Jo's room, looking more maternal than usual.

"Please do." Caylin hoped Danielle had the magic words because she and Theresa were crashing and burning over and over again.

Danielle sat down on the queen-sized bed and looked thoughtfully at Jo for a few moments. "I know this mission has been tough for you, Jo. But you should be extremely proud of yourself. Not many daughters of murder victims are able to be responsible for the ultimate conviction of their loved one's killer."

Jo sighed. "I know, Danielle. . . . I'm just so drained. After reliving all of those awful memories, I feel totally and completely tapped out—like I could get into bed and sleep for a hundred years."

"All of you girls deserve a—" Danielle's statement was cut off by the sound of someone knocking at the front door.

"Did anyone order a pizza?" Caylin asked, making yet one more attempt at a lame joke. When no one responded, she shrugged. "I'll get it."

"We'll all get it," Danielle said, heaving herself off the

bed. "You never know who might be paying us a not so friendly visit."

The group trooped downstairs, where Caylin opened the front door warily. Standing on the front step was none other than Chico—and he was holding one of the biggest vases of flowers Caylin had ever laid eyes on.

"I have come to express gratitude to you wonderful girls," Chico said. He bowed deeply. "Thanks to your courage, I can live like a normal person without fearing that horrible, horrible man."

"You have been totally exonerated, then?" Danielle asked.

Chico nodded. "The agents are now aware that it was I who make communication to The Tower. Diva, she discovered my betrayal and take control herself. But I was meant to be the one you meet in Rio."

"I'm glad your world is safe again," Jo said. For the first time since she recognized Diva's father, Jo sounded like her old self. Thank goodness.

Again Chico bowed. "You girls are my heroes."

Jo stepped forward and embraced Chico. "You know,

you remind me of my grandfather. He died when I was young, but he looked a lot like you."

"I am please to hear you said that," Chico responded.

Jo laughed. "I am please to have said it."

Chico grinned, his blue eyes twinkling. "How long will your visit to Brazil be?"

"We're leaving in the morning," Theresa answered. "We've got to get out of here to make way for the new occupants of this place . . . and I'm sure we've got some kind of duty calling for us back in America."

Chico frowned. "But this is nonsense! You must rest. And I would like to help you—in my own home."

"What do you mean?" Caylin asked. Her ears had perked up at the word *rest*. Jo wasn't the only one who was wiped out.

"My house is not large . . . but I would love to offer to you for vacation. In my appreciation, I can give you my home. And I have enough money save to offer you girls your every wish. If only for this short time."

"That does sound tempting," Jo admitted.

"Please, be my guest. My grandson will love me all

forever. He comes to visit tomorrow, and he would love these beautiful girls. . . . He is very handsome."

This scenario was sounding better and better. Great R and R, cute grandson, lazy afternoon by the pool . . . Caylin turned to Danielle.

"What do you say?" she asked.

Danielle smiled. "I *do* think you girls deserve a little time out—but only for a few days."

Jo grinned at Chico. Her first *real* smile all day. "You're on, Chico. For the next few days we're going to let our troubles melt in the sun." Caylin laughed aloud. This was exactly what they needed. Peace, quiet, and a chance for holiday romance. Before long, everything in the world o' the Spy Girls would be back to normal.

"Have I at all mentioned in the last five minutes just how totally awesome Danielle is?" Theresa asked the next afternoon. "I don't think I've been this relaxed since before Spy Girl training camp."

She picked up a bottle of SPF 30 to apply yet another layer of sunscreen to her face. The Brazilian sun wasn't something to mess around with, no matter how amazing it felt washing over Theresa's body.

Caylin flipped a page of a magazine that was Brazil's answer to *People* and glanced at Theresa over the top of her huge mirrored sunglasses. "If we had known what a way Danielle has with Uncle Sam, we could have begged her to scam us vacation time from day one."

"We didn't *need* the vacation on day one," Jo commented. "Now we do."

"Good point," Theresa said.

After Chico's visit the night before, Danielle had dialed up Uncle Sam and managed to wheedle a few Spy Girl vacation days from their demanding—if lovable—boss. Go, Danielle!

The trio had spent the rest of the evening packing and waxing nostalgic about the details of their previous missions. By the time they had arrived at Chico's this morning, Jo had been at least semirestored to her old self—which was evidenced by her promise to give yet one more go at trying to teach Theresa the samba.

Theresa had closed her eyes against the bright sun, but

now she felt a presence beside her chair. She opened her eyes and found herself staring at Chico—and the promised grandson. Yes, indeed, said grandson lived up to grandpa's handsome description. Even a self-confessed geek like Theresa could appreciate green eyes, jet-black hair, and well-sculpted chest muscles.

"Why, *hello*," Caylin greeted them, beating both of her fellow Spy Girls to the proverbial punch. "We have been *so* looking forward to making your acquaintance."

"Girls, this is my grandson, Pedro. He told me by the window that he never sees girls this beautiful."

"Pull up a lounge chair, Pedro," Jo said, stretching her legs in a way that practically made the grandson's oh-so-*very*-green eyes pop out of his head.

Chico laughed. "Good. You are all friends now, yes?"

"Yes," Theresa said quickly. She had to say *something* before one of the other SGs cornered their latest prey.

"I must go now," Chico said. "The other men and I . . . we have what you call to complete unfinished business at the boss's home."

Theresa shuddered. She wouldn't set foot in that vast

place again for a million dollars. She much preferred Chico's pad, which was just large enough, comfortable, and homey—not to mention loaded with yummy food and hottie grandsons.

"Good luck!" Caylin called to Chico, obviously eager to usher Chico past the pool and out to his car so that she could focus on reeling in Pedro.

Theresa giggled. At last things really were back to the way they should be. Ah . . . paradise.

Jo smiled and nodded and flirted as Theresa and Caylin anxiously studied her face for signs that she was over the trauma of the last few days. But she wasn't over it. Not even close.

In her mind, Jo replayed almost every word of every interaction she'd had with Diva over the past several days. How could Jo have been so naive as to trust someone with such a treacherous heart? It seemed impossible. And as for Diva—could even Meryl Streep have faked the kind of emotion that Jo had read on her face and in her eyes?

"Jo! Earth to Jo!" Caylin was snapping her fingers in front of Jo's dark sunglasses.

"Sorry . . . I guess I sort of spaced out."

"Would you like a limeade? Or fresh orange juice? Pedro is waiting for your answer."

Jo glanced at Pedro. Mmmm. He really was a cutie. At any other time, she would have been turning on the flirt. "Oh . . . limeade, I guess."

As she watched Pedro retreat into the house, Jo allowed her thoughts to wander back to Diva. Their so-called friend had been so adamant about her father's innocence and her desire to help the Spy Girls.

Was it possible . . . ? No. Definitely not. All of the evidence established Diva's guilt beyond a shadow of a doubt. But then again, Jo knew that sometimes evidence had a tendency to fall through the cracks.

Remember the gun. Diva's words echoed over and over in Jo's mind. The gun. What gun? Where? Clearly Diva had thought that the image of a gun would resonate with the Spy Girls. There had to be something there. . . .

Suddenly Jo sat up straight in her lounge chair. She

had a crazy, irrational, nutso idea. But it was an idea nonetheless.

"Hey, Trixie, do you have your laptop handy?" she asked Theresa.

"Sure. It's upstairs in my room. I never leave home without it. Why?"

Jo jumped off the lounger and grabbed her enormous beach towel. "I want to go upstairs to surf the Internet. There are some old *Miami Herald* articles I have to read."

"What articles?" Theresa asked.

"The ones about my father," Jo said gravely. "I think it's time we do a little more investigation—Spy Girl style."

TWELVE

"Are you sure you want to be doing this, Jo?" Theresa had turned on her laptop and logged onto the Internet, but she had made it clear that she wasn't convinced Jo had all her wits about her.

"Positive." Jo was hovering behind Theresa's shoulder, staring at the screen.

"You haven't had to dwell on the details of your dad's murder for a long time," Caylin pointed out. "Going through all of those articles is going to bring back a lot of awful memories."

"I appreciate your concern—I really do," Jo insisted. "But I live with the fact that my father was killed every day . . . and if there's even the slightest chance that I'm missing some piece of the puzzle, I want to find out."

"Okay . . ." Theresa clicked onto an Internet search

engine, then typed in instructions for the engine to browse archived issues of *The Miami Herald.*

Jo focused on the whir of the computer as she tried to mentally prepare herself for this journey into the past. Shortly after that joke of a trial for Diva's father, Jo had forced herself to shut out the specifics of the case. Pondering the evidence had been driving Jo crazy—so crazy that she'd had to forget the majority of the evidence just to put her life back together and find the strength to move on. Well, she had moved on. But as the saying went, the past had always been close behind. And now Jo was about to turn around and face it.

"Here you are, Jo," Theresa said, interrupting her thoughts. "I managed to narrow the search to *Miami Herald* articles specifically relating to the trial. Just click the mouse . . . and you can read as much—or as little—as you want to."

Theresa slid out of the desk chair, and Jo took her place. She clicked onto the first article: "Miami Judge Shot and Killed." And there it was, in black and white. The story of her father's murder, complete with a photograph of a blood-spattered Jo crying at the scene of the crime.

"Do you remember anything about the case?" Theresa asked quietly. "It might help to refresh your memory before you go any further with this."

Jo bit her lip. "There was something about a murder weapon—or a lack of a murder weapon. I remember that being mentioned over and over again on the local TV news."

"We'll find out soon enough," Caylin said. "If they talked about the murder weapon on the news, they'll definitely mention it in these articles."

Jo clicked quickly through several more articles, searching for one that discussed the details of the trial at length. Finally she found a feature that had been written shortly after Diva's father had been freed. Yes. This was exactly what she had been looking for. She perused the article while Caylin and Theresa read over her shoulders.

"Now I remember," Jo said slowly. "According to the police lab, my dad was killed with a bullet fired from a rare gun. There were only five of them made."

"Wow . . . that's a pretty strong piece of evidence," Theresa said. "I can't believe they couldn't convict the guy with that."

Jo shook her head. "That's the thing. Four of the guns were being kept in museums or stored away safely in known private collections at the time. There was no way any of them could have been used in the shooting."

"And the fifth gun was never located," Theresa read aloud. "Whoa . . . that's pretty creepy."

"The gun Diva's father had in possession at the time he was arrested was a different make," Caylin continued. "And lab reports proved that the second gun wasn't fired that day."

"Which is why that evidence was thrown out of court and the guy was ultimately acquitted," Jo concluded. "Have you ever heard such a suspicious story?"

"No kidding," Theresa said. "It sounds like *somebody* paid off a crooked judge or a dirty crime lab official."

"Exactly." Jo stared at the article, paragraph after paragraph explaining away the guilt of her father's murderer. "At the time, that's exactly what I thought. Which is why I had to make myself forget all of this."

"What do you think now?" Caylin asked hesitantly.

Jo sighed. "I don't know . . . but I think that fifth

gun might prove to be the key to learning the truth." She paused. "I *have* to know where that fifth gun is. Period. And something tells me it's somewhere in Rio."

Caylin glanced at Theresa. She knew that her friend was thinking exactly what Caylin herself was. Jo's interest in the fifth gun spelled trouble.

"Jo, your dad's killer is finally in jail. Don't you think it's time to let it go?"

"Maybe. But I can't." Jo left her post in front of the computer screen and flopped onto the large bed. "I want to know the truth."

"We understand where you're coming from," Theresa said, perching beside Jo. "But the mission is over. It's time for all of us to relax. We need to regain our strength so that we'll be properly geared up for the next mission— whatever it is."

"You guys can go ahead and relax all you want," Jo said firmly. "I want to find that gun."

"This is crazy, Jo. You know Uncle Sam wouldn't approve of us poking our noses into Tower business at this stage of the game." Caylin had raised her voice to emphasize her point.

Jo remained silent, staring into space with an eerie expression on her face. Caylin was about to try a different tack to get Jo's mind off the fifth gun—but she swallowed her words when there was a knock on Theresa's bedroom door.

"Yes?" Theresa asked, opening the door.

"Mr. Chico is home," Maria, Chico's housekeeper announced. Then she said something in Portuguese that Caylin couldn't follow whatsoever.

"She says dinner is in fifteen minutes," Jo translated. At last she seemed to have come out of her trance.

After Maria was gone, Theresa slung her arm around Jo's shoulders. "Will you promise us to let this go?" she asked.

Jo nodded. "I will. At least for now."

Caylin breathed a huge sigh of relief. Jo was a reasonable enough chick. Once she'd had a chance to sleep on her decision to find that gun, she would realize that she was making a big mistake . . . hopefully.

• • •

Jo had continued to ponder the missing fifth gun throughout the first and second courses of dinner. But she was careful to mask her thoughts behind a bright, interested exterior. Above all else, she didn't want Theresa and Caylin to know just how serious she was about her quest for the truth—whatever it was.

"Brazil really is a gorgeous country," Theresa was saying to Chico. "Someday I would love to come back and spend more time here."

"You will always be welcome as our guest, eh, Pedro?" Chico said, winking at his grandson.

"Of course," Pedro returned. "All of the girls are welcome."

Jo was handing her plate to a white-jacketed male servant as the telephone rang somewhere deep within the house. Instantly Jo tensed.

A moment later Maria appeared at the entrance of the dining room. "Excuse me, sir, the *telefone* is for Miss Jacinta." Although The Tower had been convinced that Chico was on the up-and-up, the girls had continued to use their aliases. By now, everyone was used to them.

"Who is it?" Caylin asked, her voice laden with suspicion.

"She say Danielle," Maria answered in her somewhat broken English.

Jo pushed her chair out from the table. "I'll just be a second," she told Chico. "Danielle probably just wants to talk about travel plans or something."

Jo followed Maria farther into the house and picked up the receiver of a phone in a small den off the living room. "Hello?"

"Josefina, it is me."

She had known, somewhere deep inside her, that Danielle wouldn't be on the other end of the line. And Jo had been right. She recognized the traitor's voice immediately.

It was Diva. Jo whispered, "Where are you? Why are you calling me?"

"I cannot talk now. But I need to speak with you as soon as possible. It's about the gun."

The gun. Diva had implored her to remember the gun. But Jo wasn't a fool. Diva wasn't going to win back her trust by mentioning a gun that turned up missing four years ago.

"Why should I talk to you?" Jo asked. "And last I heard, you were rotting in jail."

"Meet me behind the club at nine o'clock tonight." Diva's whispered voice was urgent, pleading. "Please. For the sake of my father . . . and the memory of yours."

The phone went dead, and Jo replaced the receiver in its cradle. She had known from the instant she heard Diva's voice on the other end of the line that she would listen to what the girl had to say. Something was driving Jo forward, and she owed it to herself—and her father—to find out what that something was.

Jo reentered the dining room and took her place at the table as if she didn't have a care in the world. But her appetite was gone, and her mind was already several miles away—several miles away and behind El Centro, to be exact.

"What did Danielle want?" Caylin asked.

Jo shrugged. "She left her favorite bikini at the other house. I told her I'd swing by and pick it up after dinner."

"We'll come along and keep you company," Theresa offered. "I haven't had a ride in the Alfa Romeo all day—a new record for us."

Uh. That wasn't going to work. Not at all. Theresa and Caylin would never approve of Jo going to talk to Diva without clearing the rendezvous with The Tower first. And Jo's gut instinct told her that Uncle Sam wasn't going to okay any clandestine meetings with the Big Boss's daughter.

"I'd like to hang here," Caylin said. "Pedro and I were going to take a dip in the pool."

Jo breathed an inner sigh of relief. Getting rid of her ever present comrades was going to be easier than she had expected. "If you guys don't mind, I think I'll go on my own. I think a little solo jaunt would help me clear out my head once and for all."

Theresa nodded understandingly. "I see what you mean." She leaned close to Jo. "And I'll keep an eye on Caylin—so she doesn't make too much headway in your absence," she added in a whisper.

Jo leaned back in her chair and surveyed the crowded table. Everyone continued to eat and drink as if some possibly momentous event wasn't about to take place. But Jo knew differently. She knew that tonight might change everything.

"Hello, Diva." Jo had fled Chico's home without a hitch and sped all the way to El Centro. Diva had been waiting in the shadows behind the club, just as she had promised.

"Josefina, you must listen to me. My father is innocent."

"How did you get out of jail?" Jo asked. "Did you escape?" Even in the darkness, Jo could see that Diva looked terrible. Her face was pale, and her eyes were swollen from crying. She even thought that more of Diva's hair had turned white.

"No, the agents let me go . . . at least for now. They believe that I only did what I did because my father forced me to."

"Is that true?" Jo asked.

Diva shook her head. "No. I did what I did because of Chico. He is the one who has held all of us hostage all of these years."

"You're not making any sense," Jo said. "Not that I should be surprised by that fact—I'm not prepared to believe a word you say."

"Josefina, my father was not responsible for your father's death. He was set up—you must believe that."

"What do you mean, he was set up?" Jo asked. "Who set him up?"

Diva shook her head. "I don't know all of the facts. What I do know is that Chico has made my father's life miserable ever since the murder of your father and the trial in Miami . . . but I don't know why."

"What does Chico have to do with all of this?" Jo was starting to feel slightly dizzy. This whole situation was completely insane.

"Chico rules everything in Rio," Diva explained. "And he rules everything up above it, too, into America. Yes, he has provided for my family, and he made sure that my father was not wrongly sent to prison for the murder of your father . . . but he has had his own reasons for doing these things."

"None of this makes sense. I don't understand." Jo was trying not to feel sympathy for Diva, but it was difficult. The girl was a wreck.

"All Chico wanted was to keep his own hands from getting dirty," Diva said, her voice heavy with hate. "And he has kept my father in forced servitude for all of these years."

The full scope of what Diva was saying finally sank in. "Are you trying to tell me that *Chico* is the Big Boss?" Jo asked. "That's . . . well, it's impossible."

Diva snorted. "Believe me, it's more than possible. It's true." She paused. "And I believe that Chico is the man who murdered your father."

No. This conversation was now beyond totally insane. Diva was either out of her mind or the best liar Jo had ever had the displeasure to meet.

"But Chico's house is so modest . . . I mean, for a drug lord. Your *father's* house is the one that's huge and opulent."

Diva shook her head. "Josefina, you are very naive. That house where you and your friends are staying isn't where Chico really lives. He uses it as a cover so that he won't seem like such a wealthy man."

Jo's eyes widened. "And the mansion . . . ?"

"It is also his," Diva confirmed. "Not to mention two more houses—in other parts of Brazil—that he has bought in other people's names. As well as several homes in the United States. One in Miami."

"I don't believe you," Jo insisted, her head spinning. "Chico is so sweet. . . . He's like someone's grandfather." Like her *own* grandfather, in fact.

Diva laughed, but it was a laugh heavy with bitterness

and frustration. "Aren't all evil men sweet on the surface, Josefina? Do you think they gain their power by showing their true selves to the world?"

Jo's head began to pound as she studied Diva's ravaged face. Once again, everything was spinning out of control. Jo had no idea who she could trust. Diva? Chico? The Tower agents? It was all a huge, ugly mess.

"Josefina, if you can find the gun that shot the bullet that killed your father, then we can bring Chico to justice. It is our only hope."

"I'll think about what you've said," Jo told Diva after several long moments of tense, awkward silence. "That's all I can promise."

"Please, Josefina. Call me soon." With that parting remark, Diva disappeared into the dark Brazilian night.

Jo stood alone, feeling more isolated and confused than she had in her whole life. Only one thing was clear. This mission wasn't over. And it wouldn't *be* over—not until Jo learned the absolute truth about her father's death.

THIRTEEN

"It's official," Theresa said to Caylin the next afternoon. "This is the best tan I've ever had." Her careful use of the sunscreen had paid off. She had managed to get a tan without getting fried to a crisp in the process.

"That makes two of us," Caylin responded. "But Jo's still got us beat, even though she hasn't even sat down in the sun long enough to get a tan line. That's just so not like her."

"No kidding. If I didn't know better, I'd think that Jo was still deep into the mish."

Theresa glanced at Jo, who was sitting in a corner of the patio, shielded by a large umbrella. On the table in front of her was Theresa's laptop. Every time one of the girls walked over to check on Jo, she was engaged in a serene game of computer Monopoly.

Caylin took a sip from her tall, frosted glass of lemonade. "Well, she hasn't said anything about that gun since last night. That's a good sign . . . right?"

"I guess so. . . ." Theresa sighed. "It's just too bad that there isn't something we can do to help Jo get out of this black mood."

"Jo is one of the strongest people I've ever known. She'll bounce back when she's ready."

Theresa hoped Caylin was right. Jo had been forced to deal with a lot of heavy issues during this mission. But she was taking Diva's betrayal so personally . . . almost as if she couldn't bear to believe that yet one more person was willing to do evil in the world. Who was to say Jo would ever really get over the effects of this mission?

"We're not going to do any good by hovering over Jo and asking her how she feels every five seconds," Caylin continued. "The best thing we can do is have a good time ourselves—you know, teach by example."

Theresa laughed. "In that case, pass me that gold nail polish. I think I need a pedicure."

· · ·

"Mind if I have a seat?" It was late afternoon by the time Jo had formulated a semifirm plan of action. And essential to that plan was a carefully orchestrated conversation with none other than Chico himself. She had found him in his den, smoking a pipe and relaxing with a café latte.

Chico glanced up from the Brazilian newspaper he had been reading. "Of course, Jacinta. Please, have a seat."

The man was the picture of a clean conscience. In loose cotton pants, a traditional Brazilian shirt, and a pair of wire-rimmed reading glasses, Chico looked like any semiretired middle-class businessman. Jo sat down on the love seat opposite Chico's couch.

"I just wanted to thank you again for all your help," Jo began. "I mean, if it weren't for you, the man who killed my father would still be walking the streets."

Chico shrugged. "Was nothing, Jacinta. I am just happy that evil man is away now. It was good that I call The Tower with my information, yes?"

"Yes." Jo nodded. Okay. They were talking. . . . What now? "Do you have plans for the future, Chico?" she asked cautiously. "I mean, now that you don't have to worry about Diva and her father forcing you to do their dirty work?"

"I am an old man now. I will just sit in the sun and be lazy." He paused for a few moments, seemingly lost in the notion of permanent rest and relaxation. "Of course, there is part of me who wish I could have job like yours."

"Like mine?" Jo asked. Hmmm. Now they were getting somewhere. "What do you mean?"

"Tell me what it is like, working for the government in United States." His gaze was mild, but intent. "You must have exciting life, yes?"

Jo took a moment to gather her thoughts before she responded. She wanted to go at this part of their conversation with more than a little bit of imagination. "My job *is* pretty incredible. We get to do all kinds of James Bond stuff—you know, assassinations, bombings, the usual."

Chico raised his eyebrows. "That must be very difficult. I don't think I could do those things."

Jo shrugged. "If the ends justify the means, who cares what the price is?"

"I don't think I understand. What do you say—ends

and means?" If Chico was faking the innocent routine, he was doing a darn good job of it.

"I'm just pointing out that sometimes it's necessary to kill someone. Not that I *want* to—we just have to." Lies, lies, lies. Diva wasn't the only person in Rio who could lie her tail off. Jo had gotten plenty of practice in the art of deception during her time as a Spy Girl.

"Oh, my, I could not do that. Never." Chico looked horrified by what Jo had said.

Jo put on a sad, almost tearful face. "Yes, it's awful." She paused. "But there are other parts of the job that are a lot of fun."

"Oh yes?" Chico asked. "Tell me. I am just an old man. I don't know what is fun anymore."

Okay, they had established that Chico thought of himself as an old man. What a crime! "Well, we get to use lots of cool spy gadgets," Jo said, which was true enough. "Like, tiny cameras and microphones shaped like earrings and mini-computer modems . . . all that stuff."

"My, you girls *are* like James Bond." Chico still looked clueless.

"And I've gotten to play with lots of neato equipment," Jo continued. "We have access to all of this old knights' armor. . . ." Not. But whatever. "And one time I got to fire a Jack Major Longhorn pistol—this totally rare kind of gun."

There. A flicker. She had definitely seen a flash of interest in Chico's eye. An eye twitch wasn't a lot to go on, but at the moment, it had to be enough. . . .

Caylin stared at herself in the mirror. She had followed a Brazilian fashion mag's directions for the smoky-eyelid look, and the effect was nothing short of dazzling. Theresa, on the other hand, resembled a raccoon.

"Jo, you've got to come with us," Caylin said for the third time since dinner. "If you agree to go out, I'll even do your eyes so you look like an Egyptian princess."

"Thanks, guys, but I'm still feeling pretty drained." Jo was lounging on Caylin's bed, reading a random Harlequin romance that she had pulled from one of Chico's many bookcases. "I'm just going to hang out here and lose myself in the story of Adrianna and Storm."

"But Pedro is bringing two friends," Theresa pointed out. "Without you, Cay and I are going to be outnumbered."

"Yeah, it'll be La Americana all over again," Caylin added. "We'll be left to juggle the guys without you. And you know, that ain't right."

Jo shut the book. "Look. I'd love to, but I really think I'd just fall asleep at the table. My flirt switch is off tonight."

Caylin set down her mascara wand and turned to Jo. "Are you sure? 'Cause we can cancel with the hotties and stay here with you."

"Don't go nuts on me," Jo insisted. "There's, like, less than no point for you guys to miss out on possible action just because I want to stay in and eat bonbons all night." She paused. "Besides, I think I'm going to feel a whole lot better by tomorrow."

"Your wish is our command," Theresa said. "But you'll be missing out—tonight I samba!"

Caylin laughed. She would have to remember to take some pictures of Theresa on the dance floor with her digital lash cam. If those photos wouldn't bring a smile to Jo's face, nothing would!

• • •

Storm had just ridden off on his white stallion, leaving Adrianna to take care of her family's farm all by herself. Ouch! Why were there always so many obstacles on the path to true love? Life just wasn't fair. Nor was it fair that Jo had to sit around and read this stupid book while she waited for Chico to hit the sack. She had been sitting in the den for almost two hours, waiting, waiting, waiting. . . .

"Jacinta, I leave now, yes?" Chico suddenly called from the doorway. Uh-oh. Was he going to the Big Boss mansion? That could spell major trouble. "Tonight I play cards at La Americana with my old friends."

It wasn't bed, but it would do. All she cared about was Chico staying as far away from her and Diva as possible. "Have a great time!" Jo said cheerily. "I'll see you tomorrow."

Chico frowned, his blue eyes concerned. "You will be good alone?"

Jo made a show of yawning and stretching her arms above her head. "Oh, don't worry about me. I'm just going to head up to bed and read for a while."

Chico nodded. "Have nice dreams, then, Jacinta."

Jo sat rigidly on the sofa as she waited for Chico's foot-steps to fade down the hall. A moment later the front door opened and closed. Phew. He was gone. Time to set into motion part B of this totally insane plan. Jo picked up the phone at her side and dialed the number of El Centro.

"Yes?" Diva answered the phone on the first ring.

"It's on," Jo said quietly. "Meet me behind the house." Then she hung up the phone. Three, two, one, zero. Showtime.

FOURTEEN

"Josefina? Is that you?" Diva's whispered voice was coming from somewhere behind a large patch of rosebushes.

"It's Jo, actually," she answered as Diva emerged from her hiding place. "Everyone calls me Jo—only my dad called me Josefina."

Diva smiled shakily. "Jo, then. Thanks for coming. I promise, I'm telling you the truth about Chico."

The girls walked toward the side of the house and crouched in the well of a door that led to the basement. "I don't know if you're telling the truth or not," Jo answered, not ready to risk being betrayed by her friend again. "But I'm here. So let's do this thing."

"We have to find the gun," Diva said. "The gun is the key."

Jo glanced around the backyard. "What's the security situation? Should we be expecting dogs, and alarms, and spotlights shining in our faces?" She hadn't noticed heavy-duty equipment during the last couple of days, but one never knew.

"Nope. Carlos is on duty tonight. He always drinks himself to sleep by eight o'clock or so."

Jo raised an eyebrow. "You don't say?"

Even in the dark, it was obvious that Diva was blushing. "What can I tell you? We went out for a while back when I was a rebellious young teenager."

Jo was tempted to laugh, but she didn't. "You're still pretty rebellious," she commented dryly. "Most good little girls would wind up arrested by government agents for participation in a major drug operation."

It was Diva's turn to glare. "Do you want to find the gun or not?"

"Any ideas on where it might be?" Jo asked. "This place is packed with stuff—a thorough search could take hours."

Diva nodded. "Chico showed me a secret door when I was a little girl. He was showing off for me . . . calling himself Uncle Chico and saying I was like his own daughter."

"What a scum." Slowly Jo was starting to buy Diva's

story. There was too much detail, too much pain in her voice whenever she mentioned Chico or her father for Jo to believe that Diva was lying.

"The door leads to a private den," Diva continued. "And at the back of the room there is another door—one that Chico warned me *never* to open."

"Do you think we'll find the gun in there?" Jo asked.

"Yes, that is what my heart tells me," Diva said. "If I'm wrong . . . well, then it could be anywhere."

"Do you remember how to open the secret door?" Jo asked.

"Yes—when I was young, we lived for a time in this house. I would sneak into that den often . . . but I never, ever had the *cojones* to go in that other room."

"No time like the present," Jo said. "You lead."

"This is it," Diva whispered ten minutes later. "This is the secret door."

The girls had slipped into the house through a first-floor window just in case Maria was still around and monitoring Jo's comings and goings. As Diva had predicted,

Carlos was snoring loudly in the TV room off the front hall. Without a moment's hesitation, Diva had guided Jo down several long hallways. Finally she had stopped in front of a large oak bookcase that Jo had noticed the day before. In fact, it had proved the home for *Storm Clouds through Town.*

"The door is disguised by a *bookcase?*" Jo whispered. "Man, this is like an episode of *Scooby Doo.* I just hope we have enough Scooby snacks to keep the dog quiet while we search for clues, Velma."

"What?" Diva stared blankly at Jo.

"Never mind. Just a bit of American pop culture humor." She pointed at the bookcase. "Open sesame." Jo was trying to keep the mood light, but her heart was racing a thousand beats a minute.

Diva removed a copy of Machiavelli's *The Prince*—how fitting—from the bookshelf. Then she reached to the back of the case and began to spin a combination lock. "I'll never forget this combination," she said. "Chico used to mouth the numbers as he opened the lock . . . and I've remembered them ever since."

"You really should be a spy," Jo commented. "Your instincts are amazing."

Jo heard a soft click from the back of the bookcase, and Diva smiled with satisfaction. "Stand back," she instructed.

As Jo stepped away from the bookcase, it began to move. After several seconds a door was revealed. "Wow!" Jo exclaimed softly. "This adventure is getting more Nancy Drewish by the second."

"Be serious, Jo," Diva warned. "You have no idea what Chico will do if he finds us. . . ."

Jo didn't need to be told twice that she was facing almost certain death if they were discovered by the wrong person. Whether or not that person was Chico . . . time would tell.

The girls slipped through the door and were immediately enveloped in one of the blackest blacks Jo had ever seen. She felt as if she were standing in a cave five miles below sea level. Yikes. Maybe she *should* have told Theresa and Caylin what she was up to. Until this moment she hadn't realized just how likely it was that she would never return from this leg of the mission. A girl could be locked up in this place a long time before anyone found her—especially if it turned out that Diva had lured her here on purpose out of sheer evil revenge. Now *that* would suck.

"Are you sure you're a good guy?" Jo whispered. "'Cause I'm putting a lot of trust in you right about now."

In the darkness Diva reached out and squeezed her hand. "Believe me, Jo, I'm in just as much danger as you are. It's only my love for my father that's allowing me to overcome my fears in order to prove his innocence."

"We'll do it for both of our dads, then," Jo said, echoing Diva's sentiments from the night before.

"Keep ahold of my hand and we'll go down the stairs together." Slowly the girls descended the steep stone staircase that led to the Big Boss's private sanctuary.

At the bottom of the stairs Diva stopped. "Aha!" She flipped a switch, and the room they had entered was immediately flooded with light.

"Nice clubhouse." The room was large, furnished with antiques and Tiffany lamps. A huge zebra skin rug covered much of the hardwood floor, and the heads of big-game animals lined the walls. Yep. This was pretty much what she'd expect the Big Boss's lair to look like. It was textbook.

Diva gazed around the room. "I used to come here and pretend that I was a princess locked away in a tower . . . waiting for my knight in shining armor. Back then, I didn't realize that I really was a prisoner."

"I guess that's the door with a capital *D*, huh?" Jo pointed to a normal-looking door at the back of the room.

Diva nodded. "Chico didn't even bother to put a lock on it. He knew that no one would ever dare go in there without permission."

"He didn't bet on us," Jo said. "Let's do it."

Her heart thumped painfully as the girls walked slowly toward the door. They had to find the gun. There were simply no ifs, ands, or buts about it. Jo didn't have a plan B. If she was ever going to discover the truth about her dad's murder, she was going to find it in that room.

"You do the honors, Jo," Diva said, gesturing toward the doorknob.

Jo grabbed the knob. It turned easily in her hand, and the girls tiptoed into no-man's-land. From the light in the den, Jo was able to spot a floor lamp next to the door. She turned on the light, then gasped.

"Holy mother . . . What is this place?" Diva whispered.

Jo was speechless. The room was nothing short of an arsenal. It was a weapons collector's heaven on earth. Swords, shields, and spears took up every inch of wall space. Several large gun cases dominated the small room. There was even an ancient suit of armor in the corner.

"I'm glad I never came in here," Diva whispered, her voice shaky. "I would have had nightmares for months—if I didn't accidentally shoot myself."

"The gun has to be here," Jo said. "I saw a picture of it in one of the articles I read online, so I'll know it when I see it."

"In that case, let's start the search," Diva said. "I'm starting to feel a little claustrophobic—not to mention terrified."

Jo walked to one of the gun cases and peered inside. The thing was secured shut, but Jo predicted she could pick the lock with one of her Spy Girl gadgets in under fifteen seconds. She began to reach into her pocket but froze when she felt an unfamiliar presence behind her.

Jo whirled around. And there was Chico, looking not at all like the mild-mannered retiree who had bid her sweet dreams an hour ago.

"Looking for this, Josefina?" Chico asked. In his hand was the Jack Major Longhorn pistol that Jo had been searching for.

"Uh . . ." Plan B! Why didn't she have a plan B? Jo gulped. Had Diva set her up after all?

Before Jo had time to react to Chico's presence, Diva leaped out from behind the suit of armor and rushed their intruder. Diva dove toward Chico's back, but she was too late. He raised his arm and banged her on the head with the pearl-plated butt of the pistol.

Diva crumpled silently to the floor, knocked completely unconscious. Chico shook his head sadly. "Tsk, tsk. I always treated little Diva like she was my own daughter. It's such a shame when the young ones turn out to be ungrateful brats." He stared at Diva's lifeless body. "Still, if she wakes up, I may let her live. After all, she does such a magnificent job running El Centro for me."

Suddenly Chico's broken English had turned fluid. His

whole persona had been a calculated, manipulative mask to protect himself from authorities. Dirtbag!

"You—you're evil," Jo said, staring into Chico's eyes. "How could anyone be so cruel?"

Diva had been telling the truth from the beginning. And Jo had doubted her. A wave of guilt washed over Jo as she remembered all the mean things she had said to her new friend during the last couple of days.

Chico was turning the gun over in his hand, studying the weapon from all angles. "You know, young Josefina, I found using this gun to take your father's life to be quite a pleasurable experience." He pulled a handful of bullets from his pants pocket and jingled them in the palm of his hand.

Jo felt a flush of blackness threaten to overtake her, but she fended it off. She wasn't going to give Chico the satisfaction of passing out. No, she was going to look into the eyes of her father's true murderer and tell him face-to-face how much she hated him.

"You are the lowest, most despicable form of human life," Jo said, her voice like stone. "You didn't deserve to walk the same planet as my father."

As she spoke, Chico had been carefully loading the bullets into the pistol. Now he raised the gun. "Hush, Josefina. You teenagers are so rude."

Jo shut her mouth. With that gun in his hand, her options were limited at best.

"In fact, I enjoyed killing Judge Carreras so much that I have been unable to find a subject as worthy of these priceless bullets since." He took a moment to flash her a cold, brutal smile. "But you'll do quite nicely. A fine bit of symmetry, don't you think?"

He pointed the antique weapon directly at Jo's head. She shut her eyes. "I love you, Dad," she whispered.

"Prepare to join your beloved father, Josefina." He laughed. "You're going to die."

FIFTEEN

"Tell me what you want, what you really, really want!" Theresa shouted along to the music blaring in Club 222. "I say, if you wanna be—"

"Trixie, I never knew your real name was Off-key Spice," Caylin yelled in her ear as she danced past Theresa with Pedro.

Okay, so Theresa was never going to be Barbra Streisand. Wasn't she allowed to have a little fun once in a while? Even geeks had to let loose after a superhard, superemotional mission. And she *was* having a good time with . . . well, she had forgotten his name. But as long as the guy kept telling her how great she was at the samba, Theresa didn't care if his name was Satan.

Theresa leaned close to Pedro's friend. "Hey, what's your—" She broke off as she felt her cell phone vibrating in the pocket of the ultratight black leather pants Caylin had persuaded her to wear. "Never mind."

She walked toward Caylin, struggling to get the phone out of her pocket. "We need to have a girl talk," she yelled in her fellow SG's ear. "Someone's calling."

Caylin danced away from Pedro, and the girls headed for a semiprivate, semi-well-lit corner of the club. "What's the message?" Caylin asked.

"I don't know. . . ." Theresa yanked on the phone one more time, and it came free from the pocket. "But I'm never wearing these pants again." She glanced down at the phone. Uh-oh. It was a text—from Danielle.

"Trouble," Theresa said to Caylin. They leaned over the phone and read the message:

> New evidence backup deployed
>
> arriving 2100 hours
>
> effect house arrest immediately

That was the sum total of the emergency message. It was both cryptic and terrifying—the worst combination.

"What the—" Caylin started. "Ohmigod." She stared at Theresa. "Do you think this means . . . ?"

"Jo's theory," Theresa confirmed. "She was convinced that there was more to the mission than we thought."

"Which almost d-definitely means that D-Diva was telling the truth—" Caylin stuttered.

"And Chico is the Big Boss!"

The girls froze.

"Jo is home alone with him!" Caylin yelled. She glanced at her watch. "And 2100 hours is in . . . fifteen minutes."

"We've got to find her!" Theresa grabbed Caylin's arm, and the girls sprinted toward the exit. Jo's life was in serious jeopardy . . . and she probably didn't even know it.

Click. Click. Click, click, click, click. The gun hadn't gone off. Jo opened her eyes, realizing that she was still alive. Yes!

In front of her Chico was fumbling with the Longhorn. Oops. Apparently the pistol wasn't in the same prime condition it had been the morning the old man had used it to kill Judge Carreras. What a pity.

"Out of commission for too long, huh?" Jo asked. "Get used to it, Chico, old boy."

She reached behind her and pulled a five-foot spear from the wall. In one fluid motion Josefina Mercedes Carreras whipped the spear through the air low to the floor and swept Chico's legs out from underneath him. A deep sense of satisfaction settled over her as she watched him crash toward the cement floor.

"Ohhh!" Chico grunted as his head hit the ground.

Bang! The heretofore defunct Longhorn discharged one of its rare bullets—which landed in Chico's left thigh. His grip on the gun loosened, and it flew from his hand and landed several feet away from his body.

"Ooohhh . . . ," Chico moaned in pain, writhing on the cement floor. "I'm hurt! I'm hurt!"

"A fine bit of symmetry," Jo commented, taking delight in throwing Chico's words back in his ugly face.

She took a step toward the pistol and bent over to pick it up. But her hand froze. No. She couldn't pick up the filthy weapon that had taken her father's life.

Chico was staring at Jo's motionless hand. "Go ahead,

Josefina. Pick up the gun. Point it right at my heart. Or blow my brains out if you prefer."

He was taunting her, daring Jo to sink to his own level. But she wasn't going to do it—she wouldn't give Chico the pleasure. "Forget it," Jo said. "I'm not scum like you. I'm not a killer."

Chico's face relaxed. She could read relief through the pain, and it infuriated her. "Aaahhh!" Jo screamed at the top of her lungs as she lifted the spear and held it over Chico's body.

"No!" Chico cringed in fear.

Jo let the spear drop to her side. "Psych." But Jo's heart wasn't really into her faked attack. This was no joke. She was looking for revenge—and justice.

"I can get the authorities here in a matter of minutes," Jo informed Chico. "This is it for you."

Chico was holding his leg, muttering to himself. "A girl. A man brought down by a useless girl. . . . Oh, the shame."

Jo glanced over at Diva, who had begun to moan. From this moment forward, she would think of her new friend as a sister. Truly, Jo owed her soul to the girl who had had the courage to pick up the phone and call The Tower. Maybe now there was something Jo could do to repay that favor.

"I will be the fool for all to see," Chico was blubbering. "Society will never again respect me. I will die in prison, a fool."

Jo leaned over Chico, still wielding the spear. "I'll make you a deal."

He stopped blathering long enough to look at her. "What is this deal?"

"If you vow that you and your associates will leave Diva and her family alone for the rest of their lives—that you'll never order revenge on them—I won't tell the authorities that I was the one who brought you down. I'll spare you the embarrassment."

Chico nodded. "Yes, on my honor, I vow. Just do not humiliate me before my people."

Jo stared at the pathetic old man in response. Let the Big Boss worry about his manhood for a few moments, she figured. Jo liked to see him squirm.

• • •

"Over here!" Caylin screamed. She and Theresa had just located the secret door.

Danielle raced to their side. "Here, people!" she cried.

Flashlights in hand, Caylin, Theresa, Danielle, and about twenty other American and Brazilian agents thundered down the stone stairway. At the bottom they rushed through Chico's private den and burst through yet another door.

"Jo!" Theresa yelled. "Jo!"

Caylin stopped short behind Theresa. Thank goodness. Jo was sitting on top of an antique desk, staring at a writhing Chico as if she were in shock—but by all appearance physically unharmed. On the floor Diva was lying down, her eyelids fluttering.

"Are you all right?" Caylin had run to Jo's side.

"I'm fine now. But I think Diva is going to have a headache in the morning."

Tower agents flooded the small room, surrounding Chico. There must have been a dozen semiautomatic guns pointed at the monster's head. "I was shot!" Chico yelled.

"Some men ran in here and shot me before those brats came in!"

Caylin glanced at Jo. "Is that what happened?"

Jo shrugged. "Close enough."

"Oh, Jo, we should have listened to you," Theresa said, approaching Jo and wrapping her in an embrace. "You were right about Diva all along!"

"Let's go, Chico," Danielle said. "We'll worry about the mystery men who shot you back at Tower headquarters." She turned to the Spy Girls. "By the way, I spoke to Uncle Sam on the way over here, and he assured me that you're all getting a raise."

Several agents hoisted Chico to his feet and more or less dragged him toward the door. "I don't know who they were. . . . They were wearing masks."

"You'll have plenty of time to think about the shooters' identities while you're rotting in jail," one of The Tower agents assured him.

Caylin knelt beside Diva as Chico's hysterical voice faded in the distance. "Diva? Are you okay?"

Danielle gently felt Diva's head, looking for signs of

injury. "I think she's going to be fine. But Jo is right—that'll be a nasty bump in the morning."

Caylin turned her attention back to Jo. "Are you really okay? Chico didn't hurt you?"

Jo smiled. It was a small, slightly sad smile, but a smile nonetheless. "I really think I am going to be okay now . . . better than okay."

Caylin grinned. At last, their friend had the answers she had been searching for. Now Jo could begin the healing process in earnest.

"*Papá!*" Diva suddenly screamed.

Caylin whirled around. The man they had mistakenly believed was the Big Boss was standing at the door of the arsenal, grinning at his daughter. Diva sprang off the floor and launched herself into her father's arms.

"I am free," he told Diva, holding her close. "At last, our whole family is free."

Caylin felt tears well in her eyes and turned to look at Jo. There was a smile on Jo's face and tears in her eyes as she stared at Diva's reunion with her father. Finally—they had found a happy ending.

· · ·

An hour later Theresa studied the faces of the people who had gathered in the conference room of The Tower's Rio headquarters. For the first time in days, she felt totally relaxed. Diva was sitting in between her father and Jo, alternately laughing and crying as the group pieced together the whole story of what had gone down—both during the mission and four years ago, the day Jo's father had been murdered.

"Chico wanted me to kill your father," Mr. Sanchez— yes, she had finally learned Diva's last name—was saying to Jo. "He told me that if I didn't do the job, he would make life very hard for me and my family."

"What happened?" Caylin asked.

"I saw Jo and her father, talking so happily with each other. I had a daughter—Diva—who was the same age as Josefina." He paused to give Diva a brief hug. "Well, as soon as I saw them, I knew there was no way I could go through with it. I could not kill a man."

"Go on," Theresa urged him.

"Chico was waiting in the getaway car. He sensed my hesitancy, and he followed me to the car where Jo and her father were sitting. Finally he came up behind me and shot Judge Carreras with that pistol."

"I knew I had seen your face," Jo said quietly. "But at the time I didn't realize that it was Chico who put the gun to my father's head. . . . Everything happened so fast that day." Tears were streaming down her face.

"Anyway, as soon as he pulled the trigger, Chico ran away and jumped into the getaway car. I was left there to be arrested at the scene of the crime."

Caylin continued to listen to Mr. Sanchez's story. It was a prime example of the truth being stranger than fiction. After Mr. Sanchez's arrest, Chico had hired a high-powered attorney. Between the lawyer, Chico's contacts in the Miami police department, and the truly insufficient evidence, Mr. Sanchez was eventually acquitted. After that, Chico had followed up on his promise to make Mr. Sanchez's life miserable. Since he had the real murder weapon, he swore that if Diva's father ever disobeyed him again, Chico would get in touch with American authorities and anonymously supply the missing pistol.

"But I have always been haunted by that day," Mr. Sanchez said. He turned to Jo. "I don't know if you can ever forgive me for being there that morning, Josefina, but I want you to know that I will live with the events of that morning for the rest of my life."

Jo turned to Diva's father. "I forgive you," she said. "And I think my father would have forgiven you too. Your family was as much a victim in all of this as mine."

"I'm just glad that Mr. Sanchez had enough hard evidence to identify Chico as the real Big Boss," Theresa commented. "If The Tower hadn't realized how much danger Jo was in from Mr. Sanchez's statements in jail, who knew what might have happened to our third Spy Girl?"

Jo smiled. "Don't forget those mystery men. They were there."

Danielle frowned. "I'm not even going to go there. . . ."

"Let's focus on the fact that Chico's reign of terror is finally over," Jo said. "I think we all have a reason to celebrate."

Diva leaned over and hugged Jo. "You are all our family now," she said, tears running down her face. "We are forever in your debt."

Caylin hadn't realized that her own cheeks were wet with tears. All of their missions had been amazing. But this one—it had been the best. Their week in Brazil was one the Spy Girls would remember forever.

"I feel truly peaceful for the first time in four years," Jo said quietly. "And I think my dad would be proud of me."

"I'm sure he *is* proud, Jo," Caylin assured her. "He's probably watching us right now and smiling."

After the post-post-sting debriefing, the girls had retired to a hotel close to the airport. They had changed into their pajamas, but all three of them were still wide awake. Especially Jo. She had come through this rite of passage intact, and she felt better for having faced the past. For the first time in four years, she felt that she could remember her father without dwelling on the tragedy of his death. And that was a gift for which she would always be grateful.

"I think we all learned a lot on this mission," Theresa commented. "For instance, in the future, if Jo tells me I can trust someone, I'll listen to her." She grinned sheepishly. "I can't believe I ever doubted Diva's sincerity."

"We all did," Caylin reminded her. "Let's face it. The evidence didn't exactly work in her favor."

Jo was about to chime in encouraging words to Theresa when there was a knock on the door of the hotel room. "Let me guess. It's the Avon lady."

She went to the door, half expecting to find one of Chico's emissaries waiting with a gun in his hand. Instead she opened the door and found an ultracute Tower agent.

"I have a little present for you girls," he told them. "Courtesy of Uncle Sam." He handed Jo a white envelope, then took off down the hall.

"What's in it?" Theresa asked, climbing off the bed. "Are we getting a bonus on top of our raise?"

Jo opened the envelope and pulled out three tickets. "They're VIP passes to the big Kinh-Sanh benefit concert that's going to be at Madison Square Garden next week," she announced.

Caylin bounced excitedly. "New York, New York! Hey, you think this is another vacation?"

"Maybe." Jo studied the tickets, a smile on her face. "Or maybe . . . we're about to start a new mission?"

"Fasten your seat belts, Spy Girls," Theresa said. "I think we're in for another thrill ride."

IF LOOKS COULD KILL

To The Dude:

The new adventure is about to begin.

ONE

"Somewhere there's a convertible missing its fuzzy dice," Caylin Pike remarked as she stroked the sleeve of an obnoxious purple mohair sweater.

"Some people pay a lot of money to look like fuzzy dice," Jo Carreras replied, glancing at the price tag on the garment. "But it's not *quite* me."

"Are you kidding?" Caylin said with a laugh. "It looks like someone skinned Barney."

Jo rolled her eyes. "I forgot who I was browsing with. If it can't be sweated in, it's not fit to be worn, right, Cay?"

She and Caylin continued their mondo browse fest, chatting and maneuvering between close-knit racks of endless fashion.

It's nice to have some downtime, Jo thought. Seems like we spend every waking moment trying to save the free world, but we hardly ever have a spare minute to enjoy our American-born right to shop till we drop.

But the time was *now.*

She and Cay were on the fifth floor of Bogart's, one of the biggest and most exclusive department stores in New York City. Although few and way too far between, shopping sprees were one of the many perks of being a Spy Girl. From the moment they had walked through the front door, they had been assaulted by infinite temptations and combinations: dresses, blouses, suits, sweaters. Cotton, polyester, wool, knit blends. Ah, but then they also had to accessorize: earrings, bags, shoes, fragrances, scarves. The sheer amount of merchandise was almost too much for a Spy Girl to comprehend.

Almost.

Jo was all over everything. Playing dress-up was her second-favorite contact sport, after saving the world. Which she had actually done a few times. As a Spy Girl she had defused bombs, been shot at from snowmobiles, and fallen out of airplanes. Not to mention the many times she had used her stunning good looks to turn the heads of several charming enemies of the state.

Could she help it that bad guys seemed drawn to her flowing dark hair? Her black eyes and Latina complexion? Her flawless fashion sense? The only problem was her tendency to fall for the wrong men at the wrong times.

Oh, well, she thought. No one said world peace was easy.

Caylin Pike wasn't so flighty, Jo knew. Her idea of a good time was slipping her long blond hair into a ponytail, slapping on the gloves, and having a long session of kick boxing. How savage. Her fashion desires ran more toward cross-trainers and running tights. But for this little excursion she had settled for jeans and a baseball jersey.

Sometimes Jo just didn't understand that girl. But baseball players *were* kind of cute. . . .

Caylin and Jo made up two-thirds of the team known as the Spy Girls. They had been recruited from their various real lives as teenagers and trained in the art of espionage.

If you asked Jo, they had become quite good, thank you very much.

During one late-night movie fest with the other girls, Jo had offered her theory why they had taken to spying so easily: Teenagers are already superspies. They are world-class information gatherers (gossip and secrets), superb infiltrators (sneaking into the movies and hot new nightclubs), and expert evaders (ditching school and ducking teachers). Just add in some language and weapons training and presto! Jane Bond is born.

Jo sighed and gazed helplessly at the endless racks all around her. "I'll need *at least* three days to do this store right."

"No dice," Caylin replied. "Uncle Sam gave us the afternoon, not the month."

"An afternoon in New York City is the equivalent of three seconds. You can't accomplish anything!"

"My heart pumps Prada for you, Jo," came a voice from behind them.

Jo and Caylin turned and saw a girl their own age. She had brown hair, girl-next-door good looks, and an armful of beautiful blouses. Like, *twenty* of them!

"Doing a little shopping, T.?" Caylin joked.

"Ha ha," Theresa Hearth replied. "These shirts have my mother's label inside."

"So?" Jo asked. "Your mother does some hot stuff. It deserves to be in Bogart's." Theresa's mother had designed a hot new line of clothing called Girl Talk. She'd been featured on everything from VH-1 to E! to *Access Hollywood*. *Very* cool.

But Jo knew that Theresa wasn't the type to get sucked into that fabulous world of haute couture and even more haute attitude. She'd rather have her nose pressed up against a computer monitor, hacking into the CIA or something—and she had several times, actually.

"That's the problem," Theresa said, dumping the pile on a display table full of gloves. "These are *supposed* to be my mother's. But they aren't."

"What do you mean? There's the Girl Talk label right under your nose," Jo pointed out.

Theresa shook her head. "They're fake. See the capital *G* and *I*?"

"So?" Caylin asked.

"My mom's label never has any capital letters," Theresa explained. "When I was little, I refused to ever use capital letters when I was learning the alphabet. So as a sort of inside joke, my mother made the labels that way. No one else knows about it."

"Stupid question," Jo said, folding her arms over her chic leather jacket. "Why wouldn't you use capital letters when you were little?"

"Because they beat up on the lowercase letters," Theresa replied, as if it were the most obvious reason in the world.

Jo rolled her eyes. "Whatever."

"What?" Theresa exclaimed. "It makes perfect sense to me!"

"Why don't you just use all capital letters?" Caylin suggested. "Then no lowercase letters will get hurt."

It was Theresa's turn to roll her eyes. "Yeah, right. Why don't you just call them 'lower-class' letters? No one would ever use them!"

"Girls—" Jo began.

"Well, if you had your way, no one would ever use capital letters. It's the same thing!" Caylin argued.

"It is not!"

"Girls—"

"It is, too!" Caylin exclaimed. "That's why they *have*

upper- and lowercase letters. So you use them both. Then no one gets hurt."

Theresa was all attitude. "That is so stupid. I never—"

"*Girls!*"

Caylin and Theresa glared at Jo. "*What?*"

"Were those letters capital enough for you?" Jo asked, hands on hips. "I think it's time to go."

"I thought we were shopping," Caylin said.

Jo sighed, planted a hand on each of their shoulders, and moved them along. "You've shopped enough."

Caylin Pike loved the city.

It's like a perpetual motion machine, she thought. No one ever stops. Not for a second. A subtle smile crossed her face. Just like me.

Outside Bogart's, Fifth Avenue was truly hopping. Tourists lined up everywhere for Rockefeller Center, St. Patrick's Cathedral, and an endless selection of the most deliciously shoppable boutiques this side of Beverly Hills.

Caylin threw her arm out to flag a cab.

"We'll never get a cab at this time of day," Jo said, struggling with two large shopping bags.

"Oh, ye of little or no faith," Caylin replied. "I've got a system."

"A system? For flagging cabs?" Jo commented. "I swear, between T.'s capital letters and your 'system,' you make Sheldon Cooper look like a well-adjusted human being."

Before she could say any more, a bright yellow minivan pulled up to the curb right in front of Caylin. She turned to Jo and grinned. "You were saying?"

Jo's mouth dropped open in surprise, but she recovered quickly. "I stand by my previous insult."

"I forgive you," Caylin replied, feeling triumphant.

The three Spy Girls piled in with their various bags, stuffing themselves into the backseat of the van like sardines. Finally Theresa managed to shut the door.

"Where to, baby cakeses?" growled the heavyset driver, who came complete with a tweed hat and chewed-up cigar.

Caylin blinked, unable to believe her ears. "Did I just hear . . . did you hear . . . did he just call us 'baby cakeses'?"

"Yes, he did," Theresa replied.

"Baby cakeses?" Caylin repeated.

"Relax, Cay, this is New York," Jo said. "He meant it as a compliment. Right, honey buns?"

The driver winked and puffed his cigar. "Whatever you say, cupcake."

"Yeah, right, scuzzlebutt," Caylin grumbled, folding her arms and sinking into her seat.

"Where are we going?" Theresa asked.

"We have some time," Jo replied. "Another store?"

Theresa suddenly grinned. "I have an idea. Tower department store! Get it?"

"Oh, har-dee-har-har," Caylin muttered.

The organization that had recruited them, trained them, and assigned them to various missions was known only as The Tower. Caylin and the Spy Girls didn't know much about the organization at all. Their contact was called Uncle Sam, and they *never* saw his face. He was usually just a distorted image on a TV screen. That was the extent of their knowledge. They were on a need-to-know basis, and apparently their need to know was considered needless.

"Sure, why not?" Caylin replied, looking out the window at the swiftly moving traffic.

"Abso-friggin'-lutely, apples of my eye," the driver said, setting the meter and roaring into traffic with a squeal of the tires. Horns blared angrily from behind them, and the girls scrambled for their seat belts.

Suddenly a voice filled the cab—what would normally be some New York celebrity reminding passengers to buckle up for safety. This voice was indeed familiar, but it didn't belong to a celebrity.

"Hello, Spy Girls, this is your Uncle Sam reminding you to buckle up and enjoy the ride. But I'm afraid shopping is no longer on the agenda."

"Uncle Sam!" Jo piped up, looking around for the speakers. "Are you cleverly tucked in the glove compartment again?"

"Not even close, Jo," Sam replied.

"Are you at least in the same time zone?" Caylin asked, smiling at her friends. They all knew they weren't getting any 411 out of Sammy-poo.

"I'm afraid I can't divulge that information," Sam said smoothly.

"Shocker," Caylin quipped.

"But I bet you're going to divulge the socks off our next mission, right?" Theresa surmised.

Sam chuckled. "Sometimes you girls are just too smart for me."

"What is it this time, Sam?" Jo asked, leaning forward in her seat. "London? Paris? Gstaad?"

"How about Kinh-Sanh?"

Caylin's heart dropped. The girls stared at each other. "Kinh-Sanh?" Theresa replied uneasily.

Kinh-Sanh was an island nation halfway around the world, not far from the Chinese coast. It wasn't exactly known for its glamour.

"Isn't that a long way to go for a trio of American girls with no knowledge of Asian languages?" Jo asked.

"Relax, Spy Girls," Sam said, laughter in his tone. "It's beautiful this time of year. And it's home to the perfect mission for you. Kinh-Sanh has become a prime tourist spot—especially for young European and American college students who backpack across Asia. It's quite the hotbed for rich young westerners looking for adventure."

"Yeah, we all read *The Beach,* Sammy," Jo replied.

"Of course. Apparently it seems that a good number of these rich young westerners are going to Kinh-Sanh but not coming home. They've joined with a man known as 'Luscious' Lucien West."

"'Luscious'?" Caylin asked, raising one perfectly shaped blond eyebrow. "You're joking."

Sam sighed. "You girls know I don't have a sense of humor."

"It's what we like best about you," Jo replied. "Continue, please."

"Right away, young lady," Sam said dryly. "It seems this West runs a religious sect from a compound a few miles outside the capital city. And it's plush. Very opulent, very private, and very hush-hush."

"My kind of joint," Jo remarked.

"Backpackers get word of this place from an underground network running throughout Southeast Asia, and they flock to Lucien West—along with the account numbers of their trust funds," Sam said.

"Sounds like a cult," Caylin said. She leaned back into

the seat as the taxicab left Manhattan for JFK Airport.

"Yes, it does," Sam agreed.

"So what does The Tower want with a self-professed holy man?" Theresa asked, squinting slightly.

The once surly driver slid a dossier through the opening in the Plexiglas partition. "Here you are, ladies," he said, harsh New York accent and chewed-up cigar now gone.

They flipped it open and read while Sam spoke. Several satellite photos—super-zoom lens close—were clipped to the dossier. "The problem is that Lucien West's physical profile matches that of an international con man known only by the name of Carruthers. He's a chameleon."

"So we see," Theresa said, passing several photos of men with blond hair, black hair, mustaches, beards, and a dozen kinds of glasses. "This is all the same guy?"

"Yes. For the past ten years Carruthers has been linked with various schemes in Europe and the United States. Mostly things like counterfeiting, con games, and gambling. But he's never been caught."

"Again I ask why The Tower cares about a con man fleecing some rich Euro-dweebs who don't know any better?"

Jo inquired, studying a photo of Carruthers wearing, of all things, a turban.

"Carruthers came to the attention of The Tower when he was linked to a group of terrorists trying to smuggle nuclear weapons out of Russia," Sam answered gravely.

"Whoa," Caylin replied. "Nukes?"

"Yes, Caylin. Nukes," Sam said. "The plot failed, but again he was not caught. It's been three years since Carruthers has surfaced, and there's a good chance that this 'Luscious' Lucien West is his latest guise. And as peace loving and charismatic as Lucien is purported to be, he could be hiding something sinister . . . and deadly."

"But what if this Lucien guy is the real deal?" Jo asked, glancing warily at her friends.

"That's precisely what you're going to find out," Sammy replied.

Nothing like walking in blind, Caylin thought. "Great," she said. "But what if he's not?"

"That, Spy Girls," Sam said ominously, "is precisely for you to take care of."

TWO

"This is *wild*," Theresa remarked as the Spy Girls slowly moved through the crowded streets of Kinh-Sanh's capital city. The culture shock was instantaneous—no matter how many countries they were sent to, Theresa never got over the first few minutes. "It's so alive!"

After the eternal flight across the Pacific, a taxi had sounded like torture. So to take them to their Kinh-Sanh digs, the Spy Girls hired a rickshaw—sort of a human-drawn cart. The driver just chugged along, seeming unfazed by the load he was carrying—three Spy Girls plus luggage. His only reaction when they flagged him was to glare at their pile of bags, roll his eyes, and say something unintelligible.

The capital was a beautiful city. Modern skyscrapers mingled with more traditional architecture, blending the

Old World with the New. According to the Spy Girls' briefing, the prime minister of Kinh-Sanh had set forth a bold plan to modernize his country so that it might grow into a major trading power with the United States. Kinh-Sanh was known for its clothing industry—as well as its burgeoning computer industry. The tiny nation wasn't far from becoming a young Singapore. The streets were clean and safe, the citizens were educated, and the country was definitely on the upswing.

No wonder all the Western kids traveling across Asia stopped off here, Theresa thought. *This place is so cool.*

The rickshaw driver rolled them through the market district, a zoo of merchants, tourists, and native shoppers haggling over fish, bread, and cheesy souvenirs. Theresa soaked it all up, knowing that they were about to undertake a mission in the most exotic locale yet.

Finally the streets thinned out, and the driver stopped in front of a squat apartment building.

"I guess this is it," Jo said. She peeled off some Kinh-Sanh currency—known as the *yingling*—and passed it to the driver. She also slipped him a U.S. ten-dollar bill with it. "Forgive the obnoxious American, buddy, but you deserve it after hauling *our* luggage."

The man smiled and jogged off.

"Looks like we lug our own bags," Theresa said, glumly staring at all her stuff, then at the building. "To the *third* floor."

Caylin slung her backpack over one shoulder.

"You girls really need to learn how to pack light."

"Show me some computer hardware that weighs less than a hundred pounds and I'll pack it," Theresa grumbled, hefting her twin duffels.

"No one said you had to bring HAL 9000," Jo muttered. "You *always* bring HAL 9000. And his family, too."

"You glam queens have no appreciation of the fine art of hacking," Theresa replied as they entered the building and began the long climb to the third floor. "This is precision equipment. Unlike your crate o' Esteé Lauder, Jo."

"A small price to pay for world peace," Jo replied with a sigh.

Several minutes of bickering later, the girls found their apartment. Theresa produced the key that had been included in their mission pouch and opened the door.

All three of them gasped.

Unbelievable, Theresa marveled silently, mouth gaping.

"Am I wrong, or is this pad the paddiest pad yet?" Jo asked breathlessly.

"Pretty paddy," Caylin agreed.

The whole place was decorated in traditional Kinh-Sanh, complete with what appeared to be antique vases, rugs, screens, and figurines. Huge windows illuminated the twelve-foot walls with streaks of late-afternoon sunlight, bathing the apartment in an exotic orange. There was no furniture per se. There were, however, dozens of huge throw pillows and mats. In fact, the sunken center of the living room was a sea of velvet and chenille.

"I feel like a stupid American," Theresa mumbled, shaking her head. "If I had taken the time to learn anything about Kinh-Sanh culture, I'm sure I'd appreciate this a whole lot more."

"I dunno," Jo replied incredulously. "I'm appreciating it pretty well over here. And I don't even know how to ask, 'Where's the bathroom?'"

Reluctantly they dispersed to find the bedrooms, the kitchen, and for Theresa what would serve as a computer and communications room. In this area there were ports for all her equipment, along with a normal desk and chair. There were also three ten-speed mountain bikes hanging from the ceiling. Once Theresa saw the computer ports, the spell was broken for her.

"Jackpot," she whispered.

She returned to the main room to fetch her bags so she could set up shop immediately.

"Well, I'm not unpacking," Caylin said with a sigh. "I've got to jam."

Jo raised her eyebrows. "Already?"

"We just got here," Theresa added.

Caylin nodded. "I know. But if I'm going to make Lucien's compound by nightfall, I have to head out now. The map says it's ten miles."

Caylin had been elected—actually, Uncle Sam did the electing—to infiltrate Lucien West's cult, posing as yet another American backpacking across Asia with a pile of cash burning a big hole in her pocket.

"What kind of toys did Sammy give you?" Theresa asked, referring to the special-ops equipment that they were each issued at the beginning of each mission.

Caylin smiled and held up an object the size of a lipstick.

"That's *it*?" Jo asked.

"That's it," Caylin replied, zipping up her hooded fleece sweatshirt. "One miniature cell phone for emergency use only."

"What's the number?" Theresa asked.

"No number," Caylin said as she pocketed the phone. "It's one-way only. I can call you, but you can't call me. It wouldn't be too cool if you called me and this thing went off in the middle of a prayer circle or something."

"Guess not," Jo said grimly. "You be careful."

"Tell that to Luscious," Caylin replied. Theresa watched as she went into the computer room and unhooked a mountain bike from the rack. Then she shouldered her backpack, pulled the straps tight, and grabbed the bike. At the door Caylin stopped and turned.

"Later, Spy Girls."

Jo and Theresa waved, and with a deep breath Caylin left to go infiltrate the compound of Luscious Lucien West. After she was gone, Theresa turned to Jo. "I hate it when we split up."

"I know," Jo replied, shoulders slumping. "It's like we're missing a wheel."

Theresa smirked. "That would make us a tricycle, Jo."

Jo nodded. "Yeah. So?"

"Nothing—forget it." Theresa shook her head. "Do you think Cay'll be all right?"

Jo flopped down onto a pile of luxurious pillows and sighed. "She's cut off from her network. She's alone in a foreign country with no knowledge of the language or customs. She's infiltrating the home of a criminal who may or may not be up to something incredibly tacky." Jo smiled. "Of course she'll be okay."

Theresa pounded away on the keyboard like Lady Gaga after a bad interview. Try as she might, she couldn't hack into Lucien West's files.

"I'm becoming *extremely* peeved," she warned the

room. "Nobody needs this much security on their files. Madonna doesn't have this much security."

Just then Jo sashayed into the computer room. She spun around to show off her freshly unpacked ensemble of ribbed cotton tank top, black leggings, and flowing black kimono with an intricate dragon design. "What do you think of my 'first-day-in-Kinh-Sanh' selection, T.?"

Theresa tore her eyes away from the screen long enough to look Jo over. "East meets West in a head-on collision. Call the paramedics."

Jo's hands went to her hips faster than you could say *unsolicited attack*. "Well, we're a walking pile of personal problems today, aren't we?"

"It's our buddy, Luscious," Theresa said, gesturing at her machine.

Jo came closer and squinted at the screen. "Problem, O Goddess of the Technogeeks?"

Theresa finished a particularly feverish bout of typing and turned to her partner. "It's like Fort Knox, Jo. It's like this Luscious is hiding the next big entry in the burger wars or something. I can't get in anywhere! Auuugh!" She growled and tapped more keys. Tapped. Growled. Tapped. Then pounded the keyboard in frustration. "And what kind of a name is *Luscious,* anyway? What is he, a professional wrestler?"

Suddenly Theresa's computer let out an angry beep.

Theresa gulped. "Uh-oh."

Jo stiffened. "What is it?"

It beeped again.

Theresa typed wildly, alternating between her keyboard and her mouse. "Whoa," she said. "Whoa . . . *whoa!*"

Theresa lunged across the desk and yanked the cord out of her modem. Then she kicked the power cord out of the wall. She reclined in her chair and sighed. "That was way uncalled for."

"What was?" Jo asked, clueless.

Theresa shook her head in disbelief. "I haven't seen anything like that since the CIA," she said.

"Come on, girl, speak!" Jo growled in frustration. "Anything like *what*?"

"Watch this." Theresa reattached all her wires and hit the power switch. Her laptop came on, but the screen was blank. No cursor, no intro screen, no nothing.

"What does that mean?" Jo asked with a shrug.

Theresa sighed and slumped into her chair. "It means I got nuked in a big way. The security program on Lucien's network destroyed my computer. Everything's gone. It's useless."

"Wow," Jo said, stroking her jaw. "He can do that?"

"He just did." Theresa shook her head. "This is some serious stuff. Whoever set up Lucien's net is a true ace. This is government-level watchdog programming. And it took a bite out of me. I need a new computer!"

"We'll have to request one from Sammy," Jo said.

Theresa chuckled. "He'll be happy to hear about that."

"Did you find anything at all?"

Theresa snapped up the lone printout she could extract from the computer. "It looks like Lucien's corporation has extensive holdings in the city. But the only thing concrete I could find was this." She handed over the page to Jo. "It's a warehouse down on the waterfront. Supposedly he's going to use it for some future recreation facility. But right now it's empty."

"Okay," Jo replied, nodding. "So that leaves us with two questions."

Theresa ran her hands through her dark hair and blew out an exasperated breath. "Two questions?"

Jo nodded. "One, what would a second-rate religious cult leader need with world-class security on his computer files?"

"Unless he had something world-class to hide," Theresa replied. "So what's the second question?"

"The second question is even simpler."

"Yeah?"

A smile crept onto Jo's face. "Why aren't we hauling buns down to the waterfront to check out that warehouse?"

Caylin huffed and puffed and pedaled. Normally a ten-mile bike ride wouldn't have been that big a deal for her. But add a big backpack to the equation and the steep hills of the Kinh-Sanh countryside, and Caylin was beat.

The road was paved, but narrow and winding. No cars passed her. In fact, once she left the city limits, she didn't see a single soul. It was creepy.

Finally a massive ten-foot wall came into view up ahead. But the wall was just the beginning. The setting sun bathed the whole valley in a deep orange light, reflecting off the wall and the buildings inside it. The compound was set off the road, down a long driveway. This had to be Lucien's place. What else could it be? It was stunning!

In the center of the compound was a temple. It was a large, pyramidlike building made of stone and glass, which gave it a sort of ancient-yet-modern feel. Many buildings sprouted up around it, but the temple was the main attraction. From the size of the place, it looked like it could support several hundred people, no problem.

"Here goes nothing," Caylin muttered.

She took a deep breath and pedaled down the driveway to the main gate—two huge wooden doors that must have been barred from the inside. She saw no signs of life.

"Anybody home?" she whispered. She dismounted her bike, stretched, and walked toward the gate.

No doorbell. Oh, well. There was a small door cut into the gate at eye level. Caylin knocked on it.

Seconds passed. She heard nothing.

She knocked again.

Uh-oh, she thought. What kind of a lame spy would

she be if she couldn't even get someone to answer the door!

Then as she raised her fist to knock again, the little square door popped open. A gruff-looking Asian man with a shaved head stared out at her. He said something she couldn't understand.

"Uh, hi!" she piped up in her best airhead English. "I'm from Omaha, Nebraska, and I'd like to see Luscious Lucien West, please!"

The man cocked an eyebrow and slammed the little door shut.

Great.

Caylin rapped on the door again. Harder this time. Time to go into Academy Award mode.

The same man's face appeared. Caylin waved dorkily.

"Uh, hi again. I don't think you understood me before," she said, tossing her long blond hair over her shoulder. "I'd like to come in. See, I came all the way from Omaha, Nebraska, to see Luscious Lucien West. It would mean so much if you could just close that little door and open the big door so I can come in. Would that be okay?"

"Go eat a Big Mac, you silly American bimbo," the man growled.

Caylin's jaw dropped. "Bim . . . um, I'm sorry, but I could've sworn you just called me a *silly American bimbo*."

The man grinned. "Smart girl."

Caylin's eyes narrowed as she smiled back. "I thought so. Okay, then." She threw up her arms and turned back to her bike. "I guess I'll have to take all this cash somewhere else. Maybe to a casino in Thailand or something."

"Cash?" came the voice from the little door.

Gotcha.

Caylin turned around. "*Cash.* A donation for Lucien's cause. I'd really hoped to deliver it in person. I hear that this is the place to be, at least in this time zone."

The man leered, sizing her up. "Let me see."

Caylin smiled and unzipped a side pocket of her backpack. She pulled back the flap, exposing a thick wad of U.S. currency. Cold, hard cash.

The man's eyes widened. "Those hundreds?"

"Yeah. Freshly printed and everything. It's always weird seeing new bills. They're so flat and crisp with no creases or wrinkles. They're almost like Monopoly bills, don't you think?"

But the man was gone from the window.

Caylin quickly rezipped her backpack, put it back on, and tensed up, preparing for the worst. These people could do whatever they wanted out here in the middle of nowhere. Mug her. Rip her off. She had to be ready for anything.

But the big wooden doors only gave a loud thump.

Then they opened wide.

THREE

"It really is a beautiful city," Theresa remarked as she and Jo made their way toward the waterfront.

She tilted back her head as a breeze lifted her hair from her neck and looked around. The town had everything a visitor could want, from restaurants to nightclubs to tour guides, all of them polished and open and friendly. But still, Kinh-Sanh was very much a country of East Asia, with traditional historic landmarks and a population that relied more on the bicycle than any other mode of transportation.

"It is beautiful," Jo agreed, hopping out of the way as a guy on a racing bike flew by. "But . . . I dunno."

"What?" Theresa asked.

"It just seems *too* nice," Jo replied, shrugging. "Like artificial nice. Even in the nicest parts of New York you still see the occasional homeless person. Not here. It almost seems too perfect. Like Disney World." She pointed to the street itself. "Check it out. No trash. Not even a cigarette butt. I mean, no place is *that* clean."

"That's a first," Theresa said with a laugh.

"What?"

"You're actually criticizing a place for being *too* nice."

"Very funny," Jo said, waving her off. "Which way's the warehouse?"

"We make a left at the next corner," Theresa replied, pointing. She gazed around her, noticing the locals passing by on their bikes. They would stare—but not so long as to be impolite. "Are we sticking out like the American sore thumbs that we are or what?"

"I know," Jo replied, leaning in close. "So much for being inconspicuous."

They made the left at the next corner. Within a few blocks the scenery started to change. Nightclubs became bars. Restaurants became tattoo parlors. And the average passerby became, well, more fragrant.

"Did you get a whiff of that guy with the beard?" Jo whispered, waving her hand in front of her nose. "Ugh!"

"Shhh," Theresa warned. "Remember—we're foreigners. You don't want to offend anyone."

"Then we shouldn't have showered," Jo replied, holding out her arms to show off her black Armani jacket and good taste. "We smell too good."

Theresa smirked. "You're a regular stand-up comedian."

As the sun set, the neighborhood gradually took on the odor of dead fish. Then the Spy Girls got their first glimpse of the harbor. Waves lapped against the docks, and buoy bells clanked out on the water. Massive cargo ships dominated the horizon, and seagulls battled over fish in midair.

"Is that the warehouse?" Jo asked, gesturing at a dark building that took up an entire block.

"It should be." Theresa nodded. "Let's check it out."

As they approached, Theresa noted that the area was strangely deserted. Maybe all the thirsty sailors had already found their dives of choice.

The warehouse loomed above. Most of the windows had wooden planks sloppily nailed over them. The bricks were grimy and weathered by the salt air, but the main doors of the place were recently repainted in a shiny green. Of course, the mondo padlock was shiny and new.

A gilded sign hung next to the main doors. In several languages it said: Future Site of the Lucien West Recreational Facility for Children.

"Awww, how sweet of him," Jo muttered.

"'Recreational facility,' huh?" Theresa scoffed. "We'll see about that."

The guard with the shaved head led Caylin across a huge courtyard. The compound was immaculate—from the new buildings surrounding the main temple, to the manicured lawns and gardens, to the gravel paths that crunched under their feet. All of it surrounded by a ten-foot stone wall topped with steel spikes.

Why would a religious sect need spikes on their wall? Caylin wondered. There didn't seem to be much riffraff to keep out. Was it to keep members in?

Before Caylin could decide, a girl approached her. She wore plain white pants and a matching long-sleeve shirt—almost like sweats, but perfectly clean. Little white slippers, too. Her light brown hair was pulled back from her face, and when she got close enough, Caylin saw that her eyes were jade green.

"Hi!" she said, shaking Caylin's hand. "I'm Jenny. Welcome to paradise."

"Paradise, huh?" Caylin replied, introducing herself and noting that Jenny was as American as apple pie. She was probably a cheerleader in a past life.

"You'll see," Jenny assured her. "You're American, too?"

Caylin nodded as Jenny took her by the arm and led her forward. The shaved-head guard disappeared. "I'm from Omaha. That's in Nebraska."

"I know. I'm from Bloomfield, Illinois," Jenny said with a sweet smile. "Which makes us practically neighbors."

Caylin grinned back. So, is Jenny the official hostess? she wondered. She seemed perfect for the job. There wasn't an inkling of stress in the girl's manner.

Caylin gazed in wonder at the layout. "This place is . . ."

"Amazing, yeah. You'll get to know your way around in no time. And you'll be so happy here. We all are."

Caylin blinked. "Really?"

"Don't sound so surprised," Jenny said with a laugh. She patted Caylin's arm gently. "You had to have been lost enough to want to find this place, right?"

"I guess so," Caylin said, casting down her gaze—as if to say that her whole life was meaningless up to this moment. "It took so long to get here."

"Well, you found us," Jenny replied softly. Her arm pat had become hand holding. "And I swear that you won't regret coming here, Caylin. Lucien has changed our lives."

Caylin gazed into Jenny's eyes, searching for sarcasm or insincerity. She found none. *She means it. She really means it,* Caylin thought.

Jenny sighed dreamily. "Before, it was all . . . I don't know, just one sleazy thing after another out there. I mean in the West. TV was depressing. Talk shows and *The Office* repeats. School was depressing. Like, I wasn't learning anything, you know?"

"Believe me," Caylin replied earnestly. "I know."

Jenny nodded vigorously. "Yeah, it was all the same, right? I mean, what was I going to do when I got out of college? Go to work for some faceless corporation that wouldn't even pay me as much as a man in the same job? I had enough. I said 'when.'"

Caylin smiled. "I totally know what you mean. Coming to East Asia can be a life-altering experience. You see things a little differently. But I have to be honest. I do miss *The Office* a little."

Jenny laughed. "That'll pass. Pretty soon you won't miss anything. The gardens and the mountains will be more than enough entertainment. And Lucien's gatherings are like the Super Bowl every week. You'll see."

"How many people are here?" Caylin asked, noting the perfect silence all around them.

"Seventy-two," Jenny declared proudly. "Everybody's from everywhere. The United States, Europe, Asia. The word is out on Lucien, and the quality of people is just great. I love them all. We're like a big family."

"Cool. I can't wait to meet them." And find out how brainwashed they are, Caylin thought.

"I've been here just over a year," Jenny continued. "I'm sort of a senior member. I'll be your mentor during your indoctrination period. But feel free to ask any of the other members anything. There are no secrets here."

I'll be the judge of that, Caylin thought. "Sounds good to me."

Jenny nodded, then grinned a little too enthusiastically. "So . . . I hear that you have a small donation for the cause?"

Caylin grinned back. "Yeah," she replied, unshouldering her pack and unzipping the money pocket. She flashed the bills. "But I don't know. . . . Do you think it's enough?"

Jenny's slack jaw said it all. But she recovered nicely, smiling away. "I'm sure Lucien will be very grateful. Unfortunately money is a necessary part of what he's creating here. Without it we'd be treated as just another hippie cult. If you just give it to me, I'll make sure—"

"Actually," Caylin cut her off, closing the pack, "I was hoping to give this to him personally."

Jenny's expression darkened slightly, an abrupt shift. "Well . . . that's not usually how it's done."

"Oh, please, Jenny?" Caylin whined. "I came all this way. And if it's as great as everyone says it is, I can help out even more. I turned eighteen a few months ago, and I control my trust fund now. There'd be a lot more where this came from. I don't mean to be a skeptic, but I'm afraid that Lucien is the one who will have to convince me."

"I don't know. . . . Lucien's a very busy man."

"*Pretty* please?" Caylin's tone was so sweet, she thought she might puke.

Jenny nodded reluctantly, then finally smiled.

"I understand, Caylin. I'll see what I can do. Wait here."

"That padlock weighs more than my makeup kit," Jo grumbled. "Any ideas how we're going to open it?"

"Just one," Theresa replied, looking over her shoulder to make sure the alley was still deserted. The sun was quickly setting, and the light was growing rusty and dim. She slipped a hand inside a hidden pocket, pulled out her reading glasses, and put them on.

"You going to read me a bedtime story?" Jo asked.

"Did anyone ever tell you that you're too cynical, Jo?" Theresa asked, examining the lock.

"Let's see, um, only *everyone*."

"Well, check this out, Miss Sarcasm." Suddenly twin red lasers shot out of Theresa's lenses. In seconds they burned through the steel clasp of the padlock. It burst open and clanked to the ground.

Theresa shut down the lasers and grinned at Jo.

"Holy Superman, Batman!" Jo marveled. "You have heat vision!"

"Just a little bit," Theresa replied, holding her thumb and index finger a smidgen apart.

"You sneak!" Jo exclaimed, whacking Theresa's arm. "How come Caylin and I didn't get glasses like those?"

Theresa shrugged. "Neither of you wear glasses. I need them to see my computer screen. Uncle Sam thought they might come in handy."

"Oh, that's fair. You're blind, so Cay and I get the shaft. Very nice."

"Shut your *boca,* girl. We have a warehouse to search. Or are you going to play the Spy Who Whined a Lot?" Theresa teased, raising an eyebrow.

"Fine," Jo growled, and opened the warehouse door. "But next time I'm requesting forty-four-magnum Gucci pumps."

The door creaked open, revealing a dark hallway. Jo and Theresa slipped inside and shut it behind them, plunging themselves in total darkness.

"I don't suppose you have little floodlights on your designer eyewear," Jo teased.

"You mean you didn't bring your flashlight?" Theresa muttered. She produced her own minilight. It was about the size of a cigarette lighter but very powerful. All the Spy Girls had one.

"I travel light," Jo replied indignantly.

"Too bad you don't travel flashlight," Theresa joked.

"You have absolutely no sense of style, Theresa, and it shows in your insults."

"Oh, rip my heart out, why don't you." Theresa shone the light at the far end of the dingy corridor. There was a rotted-looking door, peeling paint and all. "Come on."

They listened at the door but heard nothing. The hinges creaked angrily when they opened it, but no one seemed to be around to hear it. They found the main floor of the warehouse, a huge chamber half the size of a football field. It was big enough to hold an army of crates. And other than some splintered wood, foam peanuts, and rat drop-pings, it was empty.

"Yuck," Jo said, grimacing. "How about *that* smell?"

"Yep," Theresa replied, shining her light around. "That is definitely, without a doubt, a smell."

"And you call me a cynic," Jo muttered. "What now, Miss Dry Humor?"

"There are four or five more floors," Theresa suggested with a shrug.

Jo rolled her eyes. "Terrif."

The search continued, but all they found was more of the same—except for some live rats cluttering in the corners. Which didn't make either Spy Girl very happy. They also found an office on the second floor. But other than cobwebs, a desk, and a rickety old chair, it had been picked clean.

They returned to the first floor, near a series of rusty garage doors that served as the main loading dock.

Theresa sighed. "Well, that's it."

"What about the basement?" Jo asked, delicately risking a seat on a crate.

"I don't think there is one," Theresa said. "There's no way down. Maybe the building's too close to the water to have a basement."

Jo picked a piece of warehouse grit from her perfectly pressed Calvin Klein jeans. "Who knows. What's the next move?"

Theresa shrugged. "I guess we head back to the flat. Hopefully my new laptop has arrived. I can take another hack at Lucien."

"And I can have a bath," Jo replied, wiping her hands on her sweet Armani sleeves.

They moved toward the front door, but something she saw out of the corner of her eye stopped Theresa. Something on the floor a few yards away. She shone the light.

It was a bright piece of cloth, decorated with an intricate red-and-yellow pattern.

"Hold up, Jo." Theresa picked it up and showed her partner. Jo reached out and held it between her forefinger and thumb, rubbing the fabric.

"It's silk," she said. "*Nice* silk."

"Look, it's cut into a sleeve pattern," Theresa pointed

out. "But it hasn't been sewn yet. Maybe they were storing textiles here."

"Yeah, and maybe it was left from the previous owner," Jo replied. "I mean, silk in East Asia isn't all that rare, right?"

"Right," Theresa said, dropping the sleeve. "I think I'm just clue happy. I'm starving—let's get some dinner."

They hit the street, checking first to see if anyone was lurking. The coast seemed clear. Theresa tossed what was left of the padlock into the harbor, and they walked briskly toward the tourist district.

"I wonder how Caylin's doing," Jo said, looking out at the water.

"Probably up to her black belt in peace and love," Theresa replied. "Hope she doesn't go crazy. I bet—"

A loud roar cut Theresa off. The Spy Girls whirled at the sound. And froze.

Four motorcycles squealed around the corner. Each was driven by a mystery figure clad in black leather from head to toe. As Theresa and Jo watched, stunned, the motorcycles stopped in a row and sat there, revving their engines ominously.

"Friends of yours from home?" Theresa whispered.

"Not me," Jo replied with a gulp. "Maybe we look like old girlfriends."

"That must be it," Theresa said, taking a tentative step back. "Who says romance is dead?"

"Romance . . . or *us*?"

The riders' leather seemed darker than Darth Vader's in the dim light. Their helmets covered their entire heads, and the visors were mirrored. But that wasn't the worst part.

Each rider carried a weapon. One had a baseball bat. Another had a pair of nunchaku—two lengths of wood attached by a thick chain. A third had a telescoping steel baton. And the last rider?

He slowly reached over his shoulder and unsheathed a razor-sharp samurai sword. He held the sword high and spun his wheels in place, kicking up a cloud of gray smoke.

"Uh, T. . . ."

"Yeah, Jo?" Theresa said, staring at the blade.

"I think we're in trouble."

With a loud screech of rubber, all four riders roared toward the Spy Girls!

FOUR

Caylin traced circles in the gravel with her toe. Jenny had been gone for a while, disappearing into the main temple. Caylin hoped that Uncle Sam had spotted her enough money to catch Luscious Lucien's eye. If not, she'd be stuck in this compound a very long time until she could get close to him.

Ha, Caylin thought. The almighty buck. You could buy your way into just about anything these days.

Off to her right small groups of "members" made their way from one building to another across the compound. Chow time? Maybe. This looked like a parade of the whole crew. They were dressed in the same simple white clothes as Jenny. And from what Caylin could see in the dim light, Jenny was right. All were about her age—yet all the faces were different. A true mix of nationalities from across the planet. Their manner was calm and leisurely. Their laughter genuine. They didn't have a care in the world.

Interesting.

Then Caylin caught sight of three men with shaved heads walking in a different direction.

Hmmm. More interesting.

Caylin wandered off the gravel path to get a better look at the men.

They were dressed differently than the members. Black robes. Very loose fitting. They were also much older than the members, and they all seemed so intense. Priests? Caylin doubted that. Yes, priests could be very intense, but this was a different kind of intensity. These men focused on what was going on *around* them, not inside them.

She'd only seen that kind of look in one other place— on the faces of the Secret Service types that she sometimes sparred with in the Tower gym.

Security. Yeah, that made sense. There sure was an army surplus of them. And the guy at the front gate was definitely rude enough.

Caylin felt a twinge of adrenaline. With that many guards around, she'd have to watch herself. . . .

"Hey," came a voice.

Caylin turned to see Jenny. Smiling as always.

"You weren't thinking of wandering off, were you?" she asked not so innocently.

Caylin smiled. "Not at all. I just wanted to get a better look at the sunset."

Jenny nodded. "You'll get some positively amazing sunsets in these mountains. Enjoy them. We all do."

Of course you do, Caylin thought. No music, no gym, no TV. What else is there?

Jenny suddenly pulled Caylin close. "I have good news," she whispered. "Lucien has granted you an audience for a few brief moments."

"Awesome!" Caylin piped.

Jenny laughed and guided Caylin toward the main temple. "I know how you feel. I remember my first audience with Lucien. He's so . . . *in tune,* you know? It's like he can immediately read into your soul."

Hope not, Caylin thought, but forced herself to play up

the breathless excitement. "Oh, I can't believe I'm actually going to meet him. Do I look okay?"

That was such a Jo thing to say, Caylin thought. Ugh.

"You'll do fine," Jenny reassured her. "Just be open and natural. Everything will take care of itself."

"O-okay."

When they got close to the large, ornate doors of the main temple, they swung inward like doors on an ultratacky Las Vegas supermarket. Caylin nearly burst out laughing.

But that feeling evaporated when she got a peek inside.

The ceiling had to be a hundred feet high.

Thick pillows for kneeling were lined up in a circle, surrounding a raised sofalike structure that was no doubt for Lucien. The walls were decorated in silver and gold, with an extensive collection of vases and sculpture throughout. She also noticed a pair of shaved heads hovering in the shadows. Caylin thought it odd that she was technically in a house of worship, but she saw no traditional religious trappings. She wondered exactly what Lucien and his followers worshiped.

"This is one of the main meditation chambers," Jenny whispered. "You'll eventually think of this place as your natural center. This is where all wrongs inside you become right again."

What*ever*, Jennifer, Caylin thought. This girl was just too placid for her. Caylin's natural center would forever be a gymnasium. But she had to play along. "It's beautiful, Jenny. I can't imagine a more perfect place."

"I told you so. We meet here as a group once a day in the morning. That way you can face your day without any questions. You always know where you belong."

Caylin leaned in close. "Where's Lucien?"

Jenny patted her hand. "Be patient. He'll be here soon. And then you can begin your new life."

Caylin tried to convey a desperate smile—as if to say that this place was her last hope. But she didn't want to overdo it. Jenny seemed so insanely happy, but how much was too much with these people? And what would happen if they figured out Caylin was a fake?

Suddenly a gong sounded.

Jenny stiffened. "It's time." She patted Caylin's hand

once again and said, "Good luck." Then she retreated into the shadows.

Caylin whirled around. She didn't know which way to look. Then she spotted a set of double doors at the opposite end of the temple. With another deafening *gong,* the double doors slowly slid open.

She saw a silhouette, backlit by an intense floodlight. A tall, slim figure of a man. Flowing robes. Unearthly glow. An entrance fit for a king. The man stepped forward, and Caylin got her first good look at him. It was true. It was him.

Luscious Lucien West!

"Think it'll work if we play dead?" Theresa asked.

The motorcycles headed straight for them. The riders brandished their weapons, looking real ready to take the Spy Girls' heads off.

"That only works with grizzly bears!" Jo replied, shoving Theresa out of the way. "Look out!"

They split to each side of the alley, ducking between rusted garbage cans and mounds of junk. The cycles roared by, missing them by inches.

Jo and Theresa shared a look. This was serious.

The riders locked up their brakes fifty paces down the alley, stopping in a screech of burning rubber. They immediately turned the bikes around.

"What's the plan?" Theresa shouted to Jo.

"You're the smart one," Jo replied. "Talk to them."

"You're the flirt—*you* talk to them," Theresa yelled.

The bad guys gunned the engines once again and tore toward them. The weapons whirled above their heads— waiting to come down on the Spy Girls' own.

"I think hiding in the garbage is a bad idea!" Theresa hollered.

"I think you're *riiiiighhht! Whoa!*"

The baseball bat came within inches of Jo's skull as the bikers raced by again. They screeched to a halt like before, but this time they were much closer. The Spy Girls had seconds to act.

"That's *it*!" Jo screamed. "That came very close to the hair!"

"What are you going to do?" Theresa asked desperately, watching in obvious horror as Jo stood up, grabbed a hunk of discarded wood, and marched defiantly to the middle of the alley. "Jo! Are you *nuts*?"

"Hey!" Jo called. "You! Yeah, you, the ugly one with the bat!" Jo brandished her own rickety club. "If you're so tough, why don't you come fight like a man!"

"Jo! He'll kill you!" Theresa pleaded.

"I'm defending myself," Jo replied angrily. "Just like the manual says I should."

"The manual didn't mention swords and bats!" Theresa shouted.

But it was too late. The rider with the bat came forward alone, responding to Jo's taunt. The other three stayed back, probably enjoying the show.

Jo planted her feet and took her best A-Rod batting stance—but instead of a pitcher, she faced another hitter. One with a real bat.

"C'mon, meat, show me the cheese!" Jo called.

The biker gunned the engine. The cycle lurched forward, gaining more speed. Jo held the club high. The rider held the bat higher. There was no way Jo could survive it. This was it. This Spy Girl had gone too far.

Jo wanted to close her eyes. But she couldn't.

It happened: impact.

But at the last second Jo crouched. The bat whizzed over her head, hitting nothing. Jo's club, however, hit home. She slammed it upward as the guy passed, catching him under the jaw. He flew off the back of the bike, his helmet spinning twenty feet in the air. He landed hard. The bat clattered. The helmet clunked down a second later. And the guy, bald head and all, lay there unconscious in front of them.

"Whoa," whispered Theresa. "Home run."

"Come on," Jo urged, tugging Theresa's sleeve.

"Where?"

Jo pointed at the guy's bike, which had continued on for a few yards, then pitched over on its side. Theresa's eyes widened. "No way!"

"You want to stay with them?" Jo said, pointing to the now advancing bikers. "Be my guest."

Such a scummy individual doesn't deserve such a fine motorcycle, anyway, she thought excitedly. I'm riding this beautiful machine all the way home.

Jo grabbed the handlebars and mounted the bike, muttering machine specs as she went: "The MRZ 669, German made, top street speed 188, equipped with the Floydian Model 2 motor cross tires. . . . T, get the lead out!"

Theresa stared at the bike revving beneath Jo, shaking her head. "I can't do this, Jo. I *can't*."

Behind them the other bikes swooped in.

"Theresa."

She reluctantly met Jo's stare.

"Trust me."

Theresa glanced back at the approaching riders and hopped on behind Jo. "You're just lucky I don't have any other choice."

"I hope there's enough luck for both of us," Jo shouted above the revving engines. "Hang on!"

Jo peeled out, Theresa lurched, and the chase was on!

FIVE

Lucien West stepped forward from the doorway and strode toward Caylin. He walked with total confidence: slowly, deliberately. As if to let whoever was there know that no matter what room he entered, it immediately became *his* room.

He wore an intricate mass of white robes, with a tan top robe that would have seemed silly on anyone else. But Lucien pulled it off. He looked almost regal: black hair cut close, coming to a pronounced widow's peak over a strong brow . . . blue eyes, deep-set but piercing, focused at all times on Caylin . . . smooth, close shave. His smile widened as he approached.

"Caylin," he greeted her, enveloping her hand in both of his. His handshake was firm and warm. "Welcome to our sanctuary. I've heard so much about you that I feel we've already met."

"Hello, Mr. West," Caylin said breathlessly. "It's so nice to finally meet you. I've come such a long way."

"Yes, we all have. But you're home now, Caylin." Lucien's voice was deep, soothing. "I want you to feel as welcome here as you ever have anywhere."

"Thank you," she said. "You don't know how happy it makes me to hear that. I've been so . . . I dunno . . . lost, I guess."

Lucien's expression turned to concern. He put a hand on Caylin's shoulder and guided her. "Walk with me, Caylin," he said earnestly, slowly strolling around the perimeter of the temple. "I know how lost you must feel. I was, too. So lost. Every day faded into the next. I had no purpose. Everyone around me seemed determined to hold me back or bring me down to their level. It hardly seemed fair. Is that what you're feeling?"

Caylin nodded. "It's like a twenty-ton weight on my shoulders. It took all the courage I had just to find my way here."

"Jenny says you're from Nebraska," Lucien said, sounding sincerely interested.

"Yeah, Omaha." She chuckled. "There's not a lot going on in Omaha."

"I can imagine."

Caylin gazed up into Lucien's face. His eyes locked on to hers and held them. Beautiful blue eyes. Crystal clear. Honest. Understanding. It was as if he truly wanted to know what was going on in her heart and soul. Caylin thought she was putting on a pretty good act. But if Lucien was acting . . . well, he deserved to be right up there with De Niro.

What if Lucien was exactly what he said he was? What if this whole Carruthers thing was just a case of mistaken identity?

"You see, Caylin," Lucien said, holding her gaze, "it takes a long time to realize that where you stand on the planet really has nothing to do with where you are emotionally and spiritually."

"I'm not sure I understand," Caylin said.

"Well, someone who lives in Omaha who is perfectly happy with who they are probably thinks that it's the most wonderful place on the planet." He placed his hand against his chest. "Inside affects outside, you see?"

Caylin nodded. "I think so."

Lucien smiled and placed his hands on Caylin's shoulders. His ice blue eyes were clearer than ever. Enveloping her.

"That's mostly what we do here, Caylin. The people who come to me are lost like you. But that doesn't mean they're worthless, or useless, or cast aside. It just means they're lost. And when you find yourself, you'll come to think of this place as home. You belong here, Caylin. I can tell. You definitely belong here with us. . . ."

Caylin stared into Lucien's eyes. She saw nothing there that hinted at ill will or evil or whatever Uncle Sam was accusing him of. Lucien did this because he cared. Caylin, at that moment, was sure of it.

His eyes were so beautiful. . . .

She couldn't help staring into them. Couldn't help listening to the calmness of his voice as he made everything seem so much better. The grounds were peaceful, the surrounding countryside beautiful and calming.

This place really is a utopia, Caylin thought.

And Lucien was the perfect guide to its spiritual treasures.

But that's why he's so good at what he does, she thought, suddenly feeling very tired. The jet lag and the bike ride were catching up with her. . . .

So good . . . so very, very good . . .

The alleys zipped by at a speed too terrifying to consider. Jo was too busy driving to look. And Theresa was too busy cringing to care.

"Are they still there?" Jo called.

"What?" Theresa shouted.

"Are they still there? I don't have mirrors!"

"I'm not looking!" Theresa's eyes were squeezed shut.

"You have to look!" Jo demanded.

Theresa shook her head. "No way!"

"Way! Just look, for crying out loud!"

Theresa was frozen, but she forced herself to glance behind them. She was convinced that any movement on her part would send the bike into a violent spin and kill the both of them. But nothing happened.

Until the samurai sword sliced down into the taillight of their bike!

The red plastic shattered, spilling out behind them. The swordsman—mere inches off their back end—raised the blade for another strike.

"Are they still there?" Jo called.

"Yeah, they're still there! Gun it!" Theresa screamed.

Jo hammered the throttle, and the samurai sword swished open air.

Theresa's panic suddenly turned to red-hot anger. She pulled closer to Jo and yelled, "I've had it with these animals! Get us out of here!"

"Just lean into the turns more," Jo ordered. "This could get ugly."

Theresa nodded and tried to concentrate on the road. But it wasn't a road. It was a back alley in the seediest part of a foreign city. Filled with crates, Dumpster containers, and cargo trucks hauling fish.

In other words, lots to hit.

The bike swerved between debris. Theresa's stomach churned. Jo must have been hoping to catch one of the other riders in a mistake. But it didn't happen. They stayed a few feet off their tail, trying to maneuver into position for the killing strike.

"Time for something different," Jo said.

She swerved suddenly. Theresa thought her heart would come up her throat. She clamped her arms around Jo and tried to lean with her. The back tire of the bike kicked out with the swerve, slamming into a large stack of crates. The whole thing came down with a crash.

Theresa glanced behind them just in time to see the biker with the steel baton go flying over his handlebars and into a mass of rusty trash cans.

"Got one!" Theresa cheered.

The other two bikers seemed to take it personally. They revved and closed the distance between them in seconds. Jo wove in and out of more garbage and obstacles, trying desperately to stay in front of the men in black. But this was their town. They knew the alleys.

The biker with the nunchaku closed in. His front tire brushed Theresa's right foot, flinging it out in an involuntary kick. Panic gripped her and she screamed. In a terrifying instant she turned, saw the blur coming at her head, and lashed out in self-defense.

She screamed again. Blinding pain shot up her arm. Did the nunchaku hit her?

Then she saw it.

They hadn't hit her. *She'd caught them in mid-strike!*

Her hand gripped the business end of the weapon without her even knowing it. Now she and Jo were towing the other biker. He yanked back, but Theresa held on, playing a vicious tug-of-war.

"What's happening?" Jo called out.

The alley widened, allowing the biker to move up alongside Jo and Theresa. Now the nunchaku were pulled tight between the two bikes. Theresa refused to let go, yanking back harder every time the bad guy tried to pull her off the bike. They wobbled dangerously on each tug.

"Are you crazy, T.—let go!" Jo ordered.

But Theresa couldn't. Her hand was locked on, and there was nothing she could do about it.

Suddenly Jo saw something up ahead. She immediately swerved into the other biker. He instinctively swerved away, still holding the nunchaku tight between them like some unbreakable bridge.

Then he screamed, seeing what Jo had seen—a loading dock ramp.

Jo swerved away and the biker rolled up the ramp, letting go of the nunchaku just as he took to the air.

He flew off his bike, screaming, arms pin-wheeling, until the whole mess came down in a massive bin of dead fish.

The Spy Girls roared on, Jo laughing, Theresa holding the dangling nunchaku in her aching hand.

Before they could relax, the last biker—sword in hand—closed in.

"Lean!" Jo hollered, taking a wicked left turn. The bike skidded beneath them, nearly spilling them all over the pavement. But they held their balance and rolled on. Up ahead Theresa could see the harbor and water.

The sword slammed down into Theresa's seat—less than an inch from her back!

That was too close! A fresh surge of adrenaline went through her, and she lashed out with the nunchaku. They clattered against the steel of the sword, causing no damage. Theresa got a good look at the rider, the folds of his leather, the sheen of his mirrored visor. Faceless. Evil.

He raised the sword again, prepared to cut the head right off her shoulders.

Fear gripped her.

She actually caught sight of the razor edge, the line of surgical steel that would cut right through her body.

It was almost like a strange hypnosis. . . . Theresa could see the blow coming but could do nothing to stop it.

Suddenly the bike lurched again, making yet another left, away from the swordsman.

But he kept going straight.

Right into the harbor.

The bike slammed into a thick cement pylon, sending the biker and his sword spinning out over the water. The bike exploded in a spray of flames and steel chunks. The guy flipped over and over again and finally splashed down.

"He's gone!" Theresa blurted out. "We got them all!"

"Yeeeeeehaaaaa!" Jo cried at the top of her lungs. She gunned the engine in exultation.

Warehouses whizzed by on one side, the harbor on the other. The exhilaration of victory gripped Theresa as they cheered and laughed . . .

. . . until a large panel truck pulled out in front of them!

The Spy Girls screamed.

There was no way to stop!

Caylin shook her head suddenly. Blinked. What just happened?

Lucien still stared at her. "Are you okay, Caylin?"

"Yeah," she said, nodding, trying to clear her head. "It's just been a very long trip."

"Yes, of course. You must be exhausted," Lucien said in a kind voice.

Caylin smiled wanly. She couldn't believe what just happened to her. Lucien had tried to use some kind of hypnosis! Powerful stuff, too. Caylin Pike swooned for no man, no matter how (literally) hypnotic they were. She wasn't about to start now.

But still, she had to keep up a good front. She had to look like she was buying into his spiel—without truly falling under his spell. She had to keep focused, no matter what.

"Now, Caylin," Lucien said gently. "I understand you have something for me."

Caylin smiled and nodded. "Yes, I do." She went to her pack and pulled out five thick stacks of hundred-dollar bills. She handed them over to him—the first time that Lucien's eyes didn't lock on to hers.

Guess he sees something more interesting, she thought sarcastically.

"Sorry it's not wrapped or anything," she said lamely. "It seems . . . I dunno, kind of tacky just handing you a pile of cash."

"Nonsense," Lucien assured her. "Donations can come in all forms, Caylin. And this particular donation is quite generous. Thank you."

He somehow slid all five stacks of cash into his robe. Caylin wondered just how many inside pockets he had.

Caylin grinned, showing how happy she was to please him. "Um, I don't want to seem too pushy, Mr. West—"

"Call me Lucien, Caylin," he said with a smile.

"Okay. Lucien. But if this works out for me—and I'm not saying it won't or anything . . ."

"Of course not," Lucien reassured her.

". . . I can help out even more. With the money, I mean. I have a trust fund and—"

"Caylin, Caylin." Lucien stopped her. "Don't worry about that now. There will be plenty of time for that. Right now I want you to concentrate on your inner self. You must relax and find what you have lost. Do you understand?"

Caylin offered up a sheepish grin. "Yeah, I understand. Sorry for being too eager."

"That's fine. You're not in Omaha anymore. Here you have all the time in the world," Lucien said, gesturing grandly at the room around them. "Here you'll find what was lost. Call it what you want. Peace, harmony, enlightenment. Freedom from a bankrupt culture that values HDTV, DVD, and SUV. If you ask me, there's not enough LUV. I want you to think about that. Relax. Let nature take her course. You'll see. I promise you."

Caylin nodded. Boy, he talked the talk and walked the walk, didn't he? But Caylin wondered if this man was capable of true evil.

It was anyone's guess.

But she knew she was the only one who could find out for sure.

Jo jammed on the brakes and turned the bike sideways, spilling herself and Theresa onto the pavement. They flopped and rolled with the momentum, trying to shield their heads and faces.

The bike slid on, slamming into the rear tires of the truck.

The Spy Girls rolled to a stop, and Jo deliriously watched as the truck crunched over the remains of the bike. The driver stopped, got out of the truck, and surveyed the smoking wreckage. Then he started waving his arms and screaming obscenities in Kinh-Sanhian.

"Whoa," Jo moaned, rolling over.

"Beyond whoa," Theresa croaked, holding a bleeding elbow.

"You okay?" Jo asked, grimacing when she saw T.'s wound.

"I'll live . . . I think," Theresa muttered. "Where did you learn how to parallel park?"

"Now we're criticizing my driving?"

All Theresa could do was laugh. Jo scowled and then finally joined in.

"So, Caylin," Lucien said with a smile. "You've had a small introduction to our little section of the world here. But I'd like to discuss it further with you if that would be okay?"

"Okay?" Caylin gushed. "That would be great!"

"Splendid. I know you must be very tired from your journey, so take some time to clean up and get settled. Jenny will see to you. After that, I was hoping you would join me for a late supper in my quarters."

Uh-oh, she thought. Is this a date?

Caylin kept up her act, however, looking thrilled. "I'd *love* to, Lucien. It's more than I ever could have hoped for on my first day."

"It's the least I can do," Lucien replied. But he paused

when he spotted a shaved head approaching. "Excuse me, Caylin. Just for a moment."

He met the bald man and spoke to him in hushed tones. The man looked incredibly intense, his brow furrowed and his jaw set.

Then Caylin saw it—Lucien's visage turned to rage for a split second. Not displeasure or impatience. But rage. Something the man said truly ticked him off. And Caylin knew that the face that had been so calming and handsome could be just as frightening. Lucien's personality was incredibly powerful—in both extremes.

Finally Lucien dismissed the shaved head. He stood for a moment with his back to Caylin, composing himself. He straightened his robe, took a deep breath, and turned back to her.

He was all serene smile. "I apologize for the interruption, Caylin."

"Is something wrong?" she asked innocently.

"Not at all," Lucien replied with a wave of dismissal. "I believe we were discussing dinner?"

"Yeah, it sounds too good to be true!" Caylin gushed,

even going so far as clapping excitedly. Lucien stared at her hands.

For a split second panic gripped her—she'd gone too far. The clapping was *way* over the top.

But Lucien simply grinned at her enthusiasm.

"Wonderful!" he exclaimed. "It's settled. When it's time, you'll be called. Until then, I hope you're comfortable."

"I'm sure I will be. Thanks so much, Lucien. It means the world."

He smiled in total confidence. "Your world, Caylin, is about to change dramatically. Both our worlds are. The worlds in here"—he touched his head and chest—"and the real world that surrounds us all." His eyes grew sparkly and playful and—Caylin was sure of it—a little sinister. "The world is ripe for a colossal change . . ."

Lucien's grin intensified.

". . . and I, beautiful Caylin, am going to make that happen."

SIX

Jo and Theresa returned to the flat in peace. And pieces.

Actually, besides some scrapes and cuts—a particularly nasty one on Theresa's elbow—they were basically okay. But when she looked in the mirror inside the front door, all Theresa could see were two girls buried under a layer of dirt, grease, and fish oil.

"So how many lives do you have left?" Jo asked as they limped into the living room. "I think this cat's down to about three."

"And we were worried that we were too clean," Theresa grumbled in reply.

Jo ripped her once beautiful Armani jacket off and threw it across the room in disgust. "I can't believe those slimeballs totaled my jacket! Do you know how long it took me to find a tailor who could press it just right?"

"About as long as it's going to take me to strangle you," Theresa replied wearily. "I can hardly lift my arms . . . but in your case, I'll make an exception."

Jo glared at her. "Hey, I got us out of there. And we're the ones still walking."

"You call that walking?" Theresa said of Jo's exhausted limp. "You look like Yoda trying to be a runway model."

"Oh, shut up."

She and Jo shuffled in and slumped down on the throw pillows. After a few minutes of exhausted silence, they had enough energy to get up for some beverages and food. But the throw pillows were like magnets. Soon they were lounging again, listening to the hustle and bustle on the street outside. Staring at the exotic nighttime skyline through the long windows that lined the far wall.

"Is it me," Theresa said, "or was that attack a little too smooth to be a random run-in with a bike gang?"

"That was a professional hit," Jo replied. "No doubt about it. Those MRZ bikes are too pricey for your average hood. They're racing bikes. They start in the mid-five-figure range." She smirked. "And oh, what a treat to ride."

Theresa fished an ice cube out of her soda and held it against a bruise on her forehead. She winced. "Then we are definitely onto something. Do you think the warehouse is a front?"

Jo shrugged. "For what? It's empty."

"Empty. Yet guarded by killer bikers," Theresa pointed out.

Jo sighed and rubbed her sore back. "Nothing adds up."

"Well, let's try some of that math," Theresa offered. "Between the warehouse and my poor nuked computer, you have a second-rate cult leader who wears high security like a bullet-proof vest."

"But for what?" Jo pressed. "Bilking rich college kids out of their inheritances?"

"It has to be something bigger." Theresa shook her head slowly. "You're talking about attempted murder and government-level encryptions. Not to mention four brand-new MRZ motorcycles. That's some slick financing. That tells me Lucien's not so second-rate."

"Great," Jo grumbled. "And as usual, we don't know squat."

Theresa rolled over and gazed grimly at her partner. "Whatever it is, Jo, we better find out soon. Because our best friend is right in the middle of it."

After receiving Lucien's gracious invitation to dinner, Caylin was turned over to Jenny, who showed Caylin to her quarters. Outwardly Jenny was still just as friendly, but Caylin immediately noticed a chillier air from her.

"Lucien has never done that before," Jenny pointed out as they crossed the compound to the members' quarters.

"Done what?" Caylin asked.

"Asked a new arrival to have dinner with him—in *his* quarters." Jenny smiled slyly. "You must have made quite an impression."

Caylin shrugged. "I'm just going with the flow."

They crossed the courtyard and entered a stone building. Jenny led her to the second floor and down a long hallway that resembled a college dorm. She opened a door about halfway down the hall and flipped on the light. Inside was a bed, already made, a desk and chair, and a small closet. A set of white garments was laid out on the bed for her.

"I guessed at the size," Jenny said as Caylin lifted her white top from the mattress. "I hope they fit."

"I'm sure it will be fine," Caylin replied. They're so baggy they might as well be one size fits all, she thought.

"Everyone gets their own room," Jenny said. "Everything you'll need is provided for you. Someone will come along and take your backpack."

Caylin paused. "They will?"

"Don't worry. All our personal belongings are put into storage, but you have access to them anytime you want to. But believe me, after a while you'll forget you ever brought anything with you." Jenny chuckled. "I haven't gone through my stuff in about four months."

Wow, Caylin thought. She's truly let it all go. I wonder what Jenny was like before she got here.

Caylin smiled at her. "This place really is your home."

Jenny smiled back. "It's hard to remember what life was like before I came to Lucien's world. Yes, it really is home."

Caylin dumped her pack on the bed and sat down, glancing around the nearly bare room. She couldn't believe that people actually lived without stimulus from the out-side world. She'd go nuts without her workouts, her sparring, and the occasional cheesy Jean Claude Van Dammage flick. Thankfully, this arrangement was temporary. But she still had to keep up a solid front.

"If you want to take a shower, the shower room is down the hall," Jenny said before leaving. "It's expected that you wear the whites for your first audience with Lucien. First official audience, that is."

"Thanks," Caylin said. "A shower sounds good."

Ha, she thought, that's the first honest thing I've said since I got here.

"Good luck, Caylin," Jenny said, her hand on the door-knob. "You can meet the others tomorrow. Until then, enjoy what Lucien has to say."

"He's very charming, isn't he?" Caylin said, looking Jenny in the eye.

Jenny couldn't suppress her grin. "Lucien is . . . *every-thing,* Caylin. It's the only way to describe him. You'll see. Good night."

"Good night," Caylin said with a wave.

Jenny closed the door without a sound.

Whoa. That girl is either seriously programmed or has a serious crush . . . or both, Caylin thought.

She prepped for her shower. But before leaving the room, she slipped the tiny Tower cell phone out of her backpack and carried it with her. She wasn't going to call the Spy Girls just yet, but she didn't want the phone out of her sight until she could find a safe hiding place for it.

It was a good thing, too. For when she returned from her shower, her backpack—including all of her personal effects—was gone. Creepy. She donned the white vestments, which proved to be quite comfortable.

A few minutes later a shaved head came to her door.

It was time for dinner.

The guard—Caylin couldn't help but think of the shaved heads as guards—led her back across the compound to the main temple. But this time she was led to the far side, behind a curtain and down a long hall. At the end was an open elevator. The guard gestured for her to get in.

When she did, the door shut and she shot upward. The

ride was brief. As far as Caylin could tell, she was on the top floor of the temple building.

The doors opened, and she stepped out into paradise, part two.

Lucien's private quarters were breathtaking. A twenty-foot-long window stretched from floor to ceiling all around them, offering a view of the compound and surrounding mountains that was worth a stack of cash.

The center of the room was sunk into the floor, with three steps leading down into it. This was the dining area, apparently. The table was round but with short little legs. They would have to squat on pillows to eat. The smell of oriental cooking wafted to her, and immediately Caylin's stomach growled. She'd forgotten that she hadn't eaten all day.

"Caylin," came Lucien's voice.

She turned, and there he was. He must have come out from behind one of the many curtains that lined the wall behind her. He still wore his white robes but had dumped the tan one. Leisure wear, Caylin mused.

"So . . . do you approve of the view?" he asked.

"It's amazing," Caylin replied. "Leadership sure has its privileges."

Watch it, she warned herself. That comment sounded a little too much like the real Caylin. She had to be more lame and humble.

But Lucien laughed at the quip. "It certainly does. I find this place so peaceful. It grounds me. And reminds me that even though I act as mentor to many people, I'm still just a simple man. The mountains out there are a lot bigger than I am."

That's funny, Caylin thought. An hour earlier he was talking about being the one who would change the world.

Lucien approached her and felt the fabric of her sleeve. He smiled. "These suit you, I think. Are they comfortable?"

Caylin tried not to squirm. As handsome and charming as he was, she didn't like him being so close.

"Yeah. It's nice not to have to think about what to wear to dinner," Caylin said.

Lucien chuckled. "One of the many advantages of simple clothing is lack of distraction." He gestured at the table. "Shall we eat?"

"Yeah, I'm starving."

They sat down at the table. Caylin imitated Lucien, tucking her legs underneath her. It wasn't very comfortable. What she wouldn't have given for a regular old kitchen chair and a real table.

They dined on an exotic variety of local dishes. Noodles, fish, root vegetables, and a very bitter tea. "Decaffeinated, of course," Lucien said with a smile.

"Of course," Caylin replied, hoping he wasn't drugging her. After that hypnotic episode, she wasn't trusting this guy any farther than she could throw his bankbook. She tried to get him to talk—which wasn't a problem. Lucien seemed to like the sound of his own voice. "So how did you start this?"

Lucien took a sip of tea. "I was like you, Caylin. Lost," he said, replacing his cup on the table. "Wandering the world from place to place, looking for something that meant something. You know, as different as each country in the world can be, they are all basically the same. The East, the West, virtually anywhere you go—you work for money and material gain. You try to find a job that is somehow fulfilling. But most people just find something they can tolerate. So you can have the beautiful apartment, the 'phat flat,' so to speak."

This made him chuckle, and Caylin did, too. Politely.

"Then what?" Lucien continued. "Start a family? Work even harder. To what end? Most jobs break your back and your heart. When I got here, I found this compound. It was an old temple that was just falling apart. The local government had no interest in it, so I took what money I had left and I bought it." He smiled, and his eyes grew distant. "You have no idea how that one act changed my life. It was as if I suddenly took control of everything. As if I finally grabbed the helm of my own life and started steering. Soon others started to come. We'd talk, and they'd find that they were just like me. All they had to do was take control and steer their own course. I helped them do that. Now there are over seventy people here. We've built something that's not only beautiful but meaningful."

Caylin honored his long speech with a moment of reverent silence—it seemed appropriate.

"That's amazing," Caylin said finally. "You make it sound so easy."

"It is!" Lucien said, his beautiful eyes sparkling. "All you have to do is take the last step. You know in your heart what's always been the problem. Now you're here. Take the step."

She smiled shyly. "This is a little weird for me. I mean, no one ever told me I was ever good enough to accomplish anything." As she said the words, she thought about how sad they sounded and was suddenly glad she hadn't led the type of life that would actually force her to come here for help.

Lucien stared deep into her eyes, his expression both passionate and sympathetic. "It's time to leave all that behind, Caylin. Here you can accomplish anything you desire. You just have to let yourself."

They stared at each other for a few intense moments. Caylin felt the hypnotic trance creeping in again, and she fought it off. She blinked and looked away.

Lucien smiled and sipped his tea. "I hope you decide to

stay for a while, Caylin. Things are only going to get more exciting. I have many plans."

Caylin's ears perked up at this. "Really?"

He nodded. "*Big* plans. I hope to help beautify this whole country. I've been dealing closely with the prime minister himself. He's seen what I've done with this site. In fact, he sat exactly where you're sitting and told me how impressed he is."

"That's amazing, Lucien."

"Yes, it is pretty impressive. It wasn't something I expected. But we've struck up a spiritual partnership, so to speak."

"A partnership?" Caylin prodded.

"Absolutely," Lucien replied earnestly. "I want to expand and help beautify the country the way I have this place. I want to help the children of Kinh-Sanh as well. I have plans for a large recreational center in the capital city."

"Really?" Caylin asked, faking breathlessness.

Lucien nodded, smiling. "Yes, it's really going to be wonderful. Eventually I want to build a spiritual retreat in the capital city that is even larger than this one. Sort of a playground for the enlightened. After that, I'm even thinking about franchises."

Caylin's eyes widened. "Wow. Franchises?" Kentucky Fried Enlightenment? she thought.

"Why not? Why should this kind of paradise be restricted to Kinh-Sanh? There are so many places that would benefit from what we have here. It's definitely—"

He paused, looking over Caylin's shoulder. She turned.

A grim-looking shaved head was motioning for Lucien.

"Excuse me, Caylin," Lucien said calmly. "I won't be but a moment."

He stood and trotted over to the bald man. They conferred briefly, and then Lucien followed the man to one of the curtains in the corner.

Then they disappeared behind it.

Adrenaline surged through Caylin. She needed to find out what was back there. From how Lucien was talking, he was a spiritual emperor waiting to happen. That wasn't necessarily evil, but the ambition in this man was not to be taken lightly. *Franchises?*

She looked around. No other guards, as far as she could see. She quickly and gracefully covered the distance to the curtain. She smiled, so happy that she was able to *move* again. She paused, listening.

No sound.

Wait—

She heard low talking.

Between the curtains Caylin could see a sliver of light. Did she dare peek through? What if she was caught?

Well, she could just say she was looking for the bathroom. That always seemed to work. She was new here, after all. An innocent. At least, she was trying to put up that front. She assumed Lucien believed her. The little naive girl from the Midwest.

She could plead innocence. Sorry, Lucien. I just didn't know any better.

That was the ticket.

Excitement boiled within her. She reached up to the curtain. Pinched it gently. Pulled it slightly. The sliver of light grew larger.

Caylin took a deep breath . . . and peeked through.

• • •

"Maybe that silk sleeve meant something," Theresa wondered aloud. She sipped her soda and winced as her hurt elbow gave her a jolt of pain. "It was the only thing tangible in the whole building."

"You mean other than splinters and rat poops," Jo replied. She rolled onto her back and stared at the ceiling. "Sorry, T., I don't buy it. What would a possible nuke smuggler want with high-end silk? I think we're so desperate for a clue that we'll consider anything at this point."

"I hate it when you're right," Theresa muttered.

"Then you must hate just about everything I say, huh?" Jo quipped.

Theresa burst out laughing. "Yeah, you just keep on believing that, Jo. Then it must be true."

"Oh, it's true," Jo said, smiling slyly.

"Whatever. I think we owe it to ourselves to let Uncle Sam in on all this."

Jo nodded. "Good idea. He might have a helpful hint."

Theresa wrinkled her nose. "Helpful? Sammy? All he

ever does is bark at us. It's like he's a demented parent and high-level civil servant all rolled into one."

"You're being too hard on the old guy," Jo said. Her eyes narrowed playfully. "I bet he's hot."

Theresa looked horrified. "Uncle Sam? Are you nuts?"

"Come on," Jo protested. "That voice, that authoritarian manner. I bet he's a handsome man."

Theresa shook her head. "No way. I think he hides behind that digital distortion because he looks like the Phantom of the Opera."

"Look at *Charlie's Angels*," Jo argued. "Charlie turned out to be Blake Carrington, this totally sexy billionaire."

Theresa rolled her eyes. "Charlie turned out to be the *voice* of John Forsythe, a handsome character actor who *played* a billionaire on TV. I think you're taking your spy fantasy just a little too far. And another thing, the flat is probably bugged. Uncle Sam now knows that you have a crush on him."

Jo's jaw dropped. "I do not!"

"What did you just say?" Theresa asked, grinning. "Two key words: hot and sexy."

Jo shook her head violently and turned her voice up several decibels. "If you're listening, Sammy, *I do not have a crush on you*. T.'s making the whole thing up. She's bored since she broke her computer."

"Very nice, Jo. Now you're talking to walls."

Jo sank back into her pillows. "As long as they don't answer me."

"Anyway, we still should call Uncle Sam. I need to remind him that the encryptions on my new computer need to be top-shelf." Theresa's jaw ground at the thought of being hoodwinked by another programmer. "With this new gear I'll be able to hack into Bill Gates's pocket protector. No huckster hacker is going to keep me out of Luscious's files."

She smiled a deliciously evil smile.

"His little empire is coming down."

Caylin gasped as she peeked between the curtains.

It was a computer room!

The entire right wall was a complex system of spinning, humming, clicking hard drives. An air conditioner blew frigid air from the ceiling. Several bald techies pecked away on various keyboards or pulled apart circuit boards.

A few feet away Lucien and the man who must have been the head techie were having a heated discussion.

"You have to understand, Mr. West," he said firmly—placatingly. "No files were compromised. All information is intact."

"How were they able to break in as far as they did in the first place?" Lucien demanded, his blue eyes flashing.

The techie shrugged. "They were very good." He smiled in satisfaction. "We were better."

Lucien smiled back sarcastically. "You were better. Yet you weren't good enough to track this thief down. I need to know where they are if I'm to prevent this from happening again."

"I can tell you that whoever hacked in was an expert," Baldie explained, glaring at the computers. "They left no trail. No footprints. But our security programs are quite vicious. The culprits won't be back anytime soon unless they have access to another machine with the same power." He grinned. "They got nuked in a big way. Their machines wouldn't even be able to tell them the date and time."

Caylin smiled. They *had* to be talking about Theresa. She must be furious that they nuked her precious laptop!

Suddenly Lucien got in the man's face, pointing a threatening finger. "You listen to me, Max. If this happens again, I don't just want their computers nuked. I want their location. Do you understand me? These security breaches stop immediately."

Max nodded his bald head. "I understand. But I need to upgrade the programming. The CIA has some new encryptions that will help. But it'll take some cash. And some contacts."

"You do whatever you have to do to make those files safe," Lucien warned. "No one, but no one, must know of my plans. If they find out, we're all out of business."

Lucien turned toward the curtain.

Caylin sprinted back to the table. She hurdled a cushion and the three steps down to land right where she had been sitting before.

Lucien walked out and took a moment to straighten his robes. Then he calmly strode back to his seat.

Caylin smiled at him and sipped her tea. Her cheeks were red-hot, but in this light she didn't think Lucien would notice.

"Now, beautiful Caylin," he said brightly. "Where were we?"

Caylin grinned, primed for more info. "Franchises!"

SEVEN

The morning light blasted through the tall windows of the flat. Jo emerged from her room fully dressed and ready to take on the world if need be.

"Yo, T.!" she called.

"In here," Theresa replied.

Jo found her in the computer room, pecking away on a new laptop. The machine was also hooked into a strange square black box. Theresa's glasses had slid down her nose, and her hair was a snakelike mass. Her flannel pj's and T-shirt were rumpled.

"What's with you?" Jo asked.

Theresa didn't look up from her work. "The computer got here about four in the morning. I couldn't wait to hook it up."

Jo looked at her watch. "You've been sitting there for *six hours?*"

Theresa scratched her head. "I dunno. You tell me."

"Okay. You've been sitting there for six hours. Don't you want to get out for a while?" Jo suggested.

"Not a chance." She furiously typed away. "I've got this sucker on the run. I can feel it." She patted the black box next to her. "This little puppy can wreak more havoc than a Death Star run by Dennis the Menace."

Jo rolled her eyes. "Well, I'm not going to sit around all day watching you type. I'm heading out for a walk. Do you think maybe we can save the world or something tonight? If the rest of this adventure is all cyberstalking, I'm going home."

Theresa typed and typed. Her answer was distant, as if she didn't even hear herself speaking. "Sure, okay."

Why do I bother? Jo wondered. She threw up her arms and left.

Once on the street, Jo headed toward the market district they'd passed through on the rickshaw ride in. The city was bustling. People on bicycles darted in and out of slow-moving traffic. Tourists aimed their cameras and said *"fromage."* And the whole place generally went about its business.

The market district was about a twenty-minute walk. Once Jo got there, it was unmistakable. The smell of spiced noodles was overpowering. The temperature seemed to rise as the quarters suddenly got very close. Everyone was pushed together, shuffling between rickety tables and drab tents. The tourists didn't look nearly so comfortable here. They browsed, but they were obviously wary of being scammed. They haggled in many different languages but never in the native tongue. The vendors just did their business and tried to get as many bills off the people's piles as possible.

Jo poked around the little bits of Kinh-Sanhian junk—and junk from a dozen other countries. She found Chinese fans and handcuffs. Little Eiffel Towers. A vendor selling nothing but pirated American music on CDs. And clothes. Lots and lots of clothes.

Some of it wasn't too tacky, either.

Hmmm, maybe this country isn't such a nightmare after all, Jo thought. She browsed through a few racks, inspecting cuffs, hemlines, and collar styles with a trained eye.

Suddenly someone tapped her on the shoulder.

"Help you, pretty miss?" a wizened old Kinh-Sanh man asked. "Twenty dollar."

Jo grinned wide, immediately slipping into superflirt mode. She spoke with a slight Spanish accent. "Ah, hello. You speak English?"

The man nodded. "Little enough."

"Fantastic. I've been all over this city, and no one wants to help me," she pouted.

"I help," the vendor replied with a proud smile. "I get you supercool T-shirt. Twenty dollar."

Jo grinned. "I'll buy five T-shirts if you can help me."

The vendor's eyes lit up. "You make me very happy. I help!"

"Oh, thank you," Jo said, touching the man's arm. "I've come all the way from Madrid, and I'm totally lost. Do you know anything about a man named West? Lucien West?"

The vendor's expression turned to disgust. "Ugh! You mean stinkball Luscious."

Jo's heart jumped. "Yes, that's him. Luscious Lucien West. I've come to find him. I hear he's the superguru of Kinh-Sanh." Jo leaned in close and elbowed the angry vendor.

"I hear Lucien West can sell inner peace to the Dalai Lama himself."

"Beh!" the vendor growled, spitting. "All he do is set up shop in our beautiful country. Steal money. Steal lives. He evil man. I not help." The man waved her away. "You go now."

Jo slowly sulked away, pretending to be disappointed.

Hmmm. *That* was interesting. Not everyone thought Lucien was the cat's nip.

She moved on through the crowd. She tried to space them out, putting on her little Spanish girl lost act for a few more vendors. The reactions were all the same. "He set up shop. He evil man." One supergenerous woman tried to convince Jo to come home with her rather than go to Lucien. Jo politely refused but bought a couple of the plastic key chains she was selling.

After a while Jo glanced at her watch. Wow! She'd spent three hours in the market. Well, she figured, that's nothing new. This was Kinh-Sanh's version of the mall, and three hours in a mall was just a warm-up for Jo. She was about to head back to the flat when she spotted something familiar.

A flash of color.

Silk blouses on a rack. The exact same pattern as the sleeve scrap they found in the warehouse!

Jo hurried over and snagged one off the rack. It was nice enough, but the print wasn't her at all. She checked the label—and her jaw dropped. The label said Girl Talk!

And it was in capital letters. It was a knockoff of Theresa's mother's design!

Well, the fact that it was a cheap copy explained the obnoxious print. But how would a rackful of bogus Girl Talks find their way into a seedy market when they should be hanging out at Bogart's fifth floor?

Jo immediately bought one of every color for about ten U.S. dollars each.

As she hightailed it back to the flat, she couldn't help but grin. She had just combined the thrill of shopping, the excitement of finding an extreme bargain, and the rush of saving the world all at once!

Did she have the life or *what?*

The noonday sun beamed happily down on the garden near the main temple. Caylin sat with Jenny and a half

dozen other members she had just met. Her indoctrination had begun in earnest, and the members sat in the
warm sun reminiscing about their first days in the compound. The one common thread Caylin found between
all of them?

Too much money.

But Lucien was doing his best to help cure them of it.

"I feel so free," a girl named Concetta said, holding
her arms out to soak in the sunbeams. "Everything I used
to worry about means nothing. It is true freedom, Caylin.
You'll know what we mean very soon."

Concetta came from Milan. From what she had said
before, her father owned a vineyard that produced some of
the finest wine in northern Italy. Big bucks. But for some
reason, wine barrels full of cash weren't enough to fulfill
Concetta's sense of self-worth.

"Listen to her, Caylin," Barry from London advised.
"She was one of the most lost causes you ever saw when
she came in here. But look at her now. A veritable font of
tranquility."

The others laughed. Barry came from a distinguished

British publishing family. He fled Cambridge for a chain-smoking trip across Asia. Then he found Lucien, smoked his last butt, and never left. He didn't even miss the nicotine.

"Inner peace can be catching," added Stanislaus from Prague.

There were others: Molly from Seattle (her father was a computer game designer); Ito from Nagasaki (his father was into Japanese steel and golf course development); Gunther from Zurich (banking); Heddy from Iceland (designer soft drinks); Louis from Jamaica (resort development and agriculture).

What was amazing to Caylin was that there were over sixty others who she hadn't met yet. What did *their* parents do? Best-selling authors? Tax lawyers? Senators? It boggled the mind.

She'd learned more about Jenny, too. Her mother was a real estate developer in the Chicago suburbs. Jenny had begun college but quickly fell into the wrong crowd. Drinking. Partying. Learning very little except how to skip class. Eventually Jenny scammed a hunk of money from one of her tuition accounts and headed out. By the time she got to Lucien, the rest of her tuition money was safely in her bag, in cash, waiting for the proper moment to be spent.

That moment came on Jenny's second day at the compound. Since then she was able to get Lucien some other account numbers belonging to her mother. Jenny justified this by swearing that her mother had more than she could ever need. She said it with such shocking disgust that Caylin had to wonder what her mother ever did to deserve it.

"So what does your father do?" Ito asked her.

Caylin shrugged. "He's an oil rancher. So was my grandfather and my great-grandfather."

"There's oil in Nebraska?" Molly from Seattle asked skeptically.

"No," Caylin replied. "In Texas. We just live in Nebraska."

"I hope you realize how important it is for us to help Lucien any way we can," Jenny told her. "We were all unlucky to be born into unbelievable materialistic situations. Luckily we don't have to live with it."

"It's also lucky that most of us are able to siphon some of

that wealth to Lucien," Barry said. "I don't know what I would do if this place ever shut down. I'd have no place to go."

Caylin smiled and nodded in agreement. But inside, she just couldn't believe it. Were their lives so bad? So empty? Actually, they sounded too *full*. The way she saw it, they were just a bunch of spoiled rich kids who suddenly realized that they were at an age when people expected them to take responsibility for their lives. Get the expensive degrees. Take over the family businesses. Make something of themselves.

Grow up.

None of them wanted to do that. They had taken their deep-seated aversion to real life and used it as a springboard to brainwashing. Lucien was a dream of an authority figure—he put no pressure on them as long as the cash rolled in. It was as if they were paying him to protect them from the real world.

Ha. Not a bad setup.

But Caylin also realized that she was being harsh. She doubted that any of their decisions had been conscious. They looked ahead at their responsibilities and couldn't handle what they saw. Instinctively they rebelled. Fled to a place where the pastures were greener than any they had ever seen. Greener than cold, hard cash at any rate.

Yet down to the last one she had met, they seemed happy. Their "inner peace" was genuine. Inside these walls, stress was extinct.

Caylin couldn't really fault them for wanting true inner peace.

A bell rang from the temple. The group slowly got to their feet.

"What's that?" Caylin asked.

"The midday gathering," Jenny said, offering a hand to help her up. "Come on."

The group made their way toward the front of the temple. Small crowds of other members came out of buildings and copses of trees and other gardens. It was like a slow, serene stampede of white cloth.

Lucien calls, Caylin mused, and they come running.

She purposely lagged back from the group to watch them all more closely. But something distracted her.

A pair of sparkly white Range Rovers entered the

compound and drove toward them. Their arrival was rather shocking since Caylin hadn't seen any hint of outside technology within the compound (other than Lucien's computer room). The SUVs' windows were tinted black. As they passed, Caylin tried to see inside. But no dice.

The Rovers proceeded to the back of the main temple, disappearing around the corner.

Hmmm.

Caylin glanced around. The rest of the group was intent on getting to the gathering. No one paid any attention to her.

Perfect.

She edged through some shrubbery to the side of the building and peered around the corner to check it out. The Range Rovers were backing up to a pair of steel double doors. When the SVUs stopped, the drivers—both burly shaved heads—dismounted and went straight for the doors. One knocked while the other opened the hatchbacks of the Rovers. Something wasn't right with these guys. What was it—?

Caylin stiffened.

They wore the regular "spiritual" garb like all the others.

But in her spy training Caylin had seen enough concealed weapons to know that these two peace lovers were packing heat. The bulges were unmistakable.

What would cult members need with guns?

The double doors swung wide, and several more shaved heads carried out a bunch of large duffel bags. Judging by the effort, Caylin guessed the bags were full of something heavy. The guards tossed them into the back of the Range Rovers without a word.

In seconds the transaction was complete. The hatchbacks were slammed shut, the double doors closed, and the armed drivers got back in and put the SUVs in gear.

This was huge. She wasn't exactly sure what she'd seen, but weapons and bags and secret exchanges sure *felt* huge. Caylin had to get to her phone. She'd stashed it in her room, frustrated like crazy because she didn't have anywhere to carry it. But this definitely deserved a phone call to the other Spy Girls.

"Hey!" a voice called from behind her.

Caylin froze, fear streaking down her spine.

Somehow a phone call didn't seem to be in her future.

EIGHT

Caylin whirled.

Jenny!

"What are you doing?" she demanded.

Caylin grinned. "Just looking around. I'm still kind of lost around here."

Jenny shook her head. "All you had to do was follow us. Come on, we'll miss the gathering!"

Caylin nodded and went with her, reminding herself to let out a really heavy sigh of relief later. That was close!

She had to be more careful. The new person would arouse the most suspicion if she were continuously caught poking her nose around corners.

The only problem was that there always seemed to be something suspicious going on around those pesky corners.

But, Caylin thought desperately, what did it all mean?

• • •

"Eureka!" Theresa shouted.

Jo bolted into the flat's computer room, wondering who won the lottery. There was Theresa, hair shooting up in all directions, bags under her bloodshot eyes, arms raised in victory. Her ridiculous grin made her look insane.

"What?" Jo asked.

"I did it!" She held up a sheaf of laser printouts. "I hacked that sucker wide open! Just call me Madam Machete!"

"If you don't get a grip, I'm going to start calling you Darla Demento," Jo said.

"Jo, do you realize what I've just gone through?" Theresa said, her eyes wild. "The security? The dead ends? The mazes? I've just done an iron woman triathalon of a hack! And I got a ton!"

"A ton of what?" Jo asked, wrinkling her nose.

Theresa wiggled her eyebrows. "Numbers, my dear. Lots and lots of numbers. Take a look."

Theresa scrolled down a screen filled with numerical entries. Figures flew by in a blizzard.

"Slow down!" Jo ordered. "What is all this?"

"It's one of Lucien's financial ledgers," Theresa explained, brandishing a crumpled printout. "This is what we've been looking for."

"That's great, but what's in it?" Jo repeated.

"Millions." Theresa clicked the mouse as the numbers continued to fly. "He's got millions of dollars passing back and forth to various accounts. They all seem to start out as this vague description called 'donations.' But that doesn't make any sense at all."

"Why not?" Jo asked. "He's running a spiritual retreat, after all."

Theresa shook her head. "We're talking nine figures here, Jo. Even if all the rich kids in the Western Hemisphere got together and pooled their trust funds, they'd never be able to slap together this kind of money. And they're all 'cash' transactions that are basically untraceable."

"So he is into something crooked," Jo declared.

"Well, his books are crooked, that's for sure," Theresa said, leaning back in her chair. "Just from an accounting standpoint, he's a first-rate con artist. But the real question is, where does the money come from?"

"Drugs?" Jo speculated, squinting at the screen.

Theresa shook her head doubtfully. "I think Uncle Sam would've known about that. No, this is something different. But what?"

"Have you saved all this stuff?" Jo asked.

"Are you kidding? I downloaded it as soon as I found it. I wasn't going to let this guy get the best of—"

Theresa's eyes bugged at her screen.

"Oh no, not again!"

She typed frantically, then dove across the desk and yanked the cords out of the back of her little black box. The system shut down with an electronic thunk.

"They nuke you again?" Jo asked.

Theresa stood, frozen. "No. That was something different. Someone was tracking my hack. Not just back to my computer, but to our actual address."

"Did you get out in time?" Jo asked nervously.

"I think so," Theresa said, looking at the black box as if the bad guys were going to pop out of it.

"You *think* so?" Jo screeched. "If a bunch of bald bikers pull up outside, I'm handing you over."

Theresa laughed. "Don't worry, Jo. I got out."

Jo slumped against the wall. "So what do we do now?"

"We can show all this data to Sammy. He might have a suggestion. Or . . ."

"Or what?" Jo prompted.

"Well . . . there was something else in that ledger," Theresa said, rubbing her weary eyes. "But I have no idea what it means. Something called 'the Purchase.'"

Jo shrugged. "What is it?"

"Earth to Jo," Theresa said, waving a hand in front of Jo's eyes. "I just said I don't know. But think about it. What do you buy with that much money?"

"The Yankees," Jo replied.

"I doubt it," Theresa said. "But I bet all that cash would go a lot further in a third world country like Kinh-Sanh than it would in the United States. A *lot* further."

"That makes sense," Jo agreed. "But other than that, what do we really have?"

Theresa smiled lamely. "Nothing."

"Right. Which either means you're going to have to do some more creative hacking, or we're going to have to find an alternate means of fact-finding," Jo said.

Theresa deflated and plopped back into her chair. "I'm done with the laptop for a while. Even if I could keep my eyes open, Lucien's computer squad is looking for me now. I wouldn't get anywhere."

"I thought so," Jo said with a nod. "That's why I took it upon myself to hit the streets while your nose was pressed up against your screen."

She tossed a rumpled garment into Theresa's lap.

"What's this?" Theresa asked.

Jo grinned. "I don't know if it has anything to do with anything, but check out the print."

Theresa's eyes widened in recognition. "It's the same silk pattern we found in the warehouse!"

"Correct-amundo," Jo said, leaning against the desk. "Now check out the label."

Theresa's eyes grew even wider. "My mom's label! It's a total rip-off!"

"Two for two," Jo said, holding up her hands in two peace signs. "Aren't you glad you told that stupid story about the capital letters to us?"

"It's not stupid." Theresa scowled. "It's a very fond memory of my childhood."

"Then you had a lame childhood," Jo teased. "The point is, I wouldn't have recognized it otherwise. But don't you think it's a little strange that the same pattern that is on the floor in Lucien's warehouse is available for ten bucks in the market district?"

Theresa blinked. "You paid ten bucks for this? Even the knockoffs are fifty in the States."

"Can I sniff the bargains or what?" Jo said triumphantly.

Theresa smirked. "You're going to wear this?"

"Are you nuts?" Jo blurted out. "I wouldn't wear that to your funeral. I wouldn't wear that to Mike Schaeffer's funeral!"

"Who's Mike Schaeffer?" Theresa asked, her brow furrowing.

Jo scowled. "Nobody."

"Jooooooo . . . ," Theresa sang.

"He's nobody. Just an old—no, make that an *ancient* flame. He's the reason the word *jerk* is so deeply tattooed on my brain."

Theresa's grin widened. "So . . . a little chunk of the past life breaks loose. Was he cute?"

Jo growled impatiently. "We're not talking about this now. End of story. *Finito.* Sign off, Little Miss Modem."

"Well, pardon me all over town," Theresa said, grinning up at Jo. "All I asked was if you'd wear my mother's designs."

Jo held up one of the obnoxious knockoffs. "Your mother didn't design this! She'd keel over if she saw it. This is what frat boys wear to their spring flings."

She tossed it over her shoulder in disgust.

"But Jo," Theresa said playfully. "You bought *six* of them. Why did you buy so many if you weren't going to wear them? One would've been plenty if you were just going to show me the bogus label."

"I was *not* going to wear them," Jo said in a threatening voice. "I stand by my previous statements regarding funerals. Which is what you'll be attending if you don't lay off."

"Oh yeah, the Mike Schaeffer affair," Theresa replied. "Who was he again?"

"Auuuuuggggggghhhhh!" Jo bellowed. She scooped up

the other obnoxious shirts and hurled them at Theresa. T. giggled and slipped out of her chair to the floor. Shirts hung off her as if she were a brightly dressed scarecrow.

After a few seconds of staring, all the two of them could do was sit there and laugh.

Finally Jo slumped to the floor with Theresa. "Before you took me on that charming trip down bad-memory lane, I did have a point."

"I see," Theresa replied. "And what might that point be?"

"I think a return trip to the warehouse is in order," she suggested. "But we'll be a little more professional this time. We go under cover of night. With the proper gear. And the proper attire."

"You mean the shirts?" Theresa asked.

"I mean proper evening wear," Jo said, a sly grin appearing on her face. *"All black."*

It was nearly midnight when they were ready.

Jo emerged from her room clad in a black turtleneck and tight black jeans. She clicked on a leather fanny pack that held a few basics: pepper spray perfume, compact communicator, mascara dart gun with sleep-tipped darts. You know, the essentials.

She caught a look at herself in the mirror. "Ooh, baby, you are just too hot to handle." She smooched at her reflection.

"You're gonna make me puke," Theresa muttered. She had opted for a black sweater and loose-fitting black jeans rather than the skintight outerwear.

"I'd love a black leather cat suit," Jo remarked, inspecting her profile. She ran a hand over her stomach. "Sort of an Emma Peel thing."

"The sailors down on the wharf would love it," Theresa said. She tucked a minicamera and her glasses into a zipper pouch in the sweater. "But that *is* your crowd."

Jo applied some lipstick and puckered her lips to even it out. "I am unappreciated in my own time. Are we ready to go yet?"

"I've been ready for ten minutes," Theresa complained. "The bad guys could've taken over the Alamo by now, and you're primping."

"I refuse to go into battle with a shiny nose," Jo declared, applying powder.

"You're gonna go with a bloody nose if you don't—"

A loud beeping cut Theresa off. What was that? The phone. But who would be calling at this hour?

Jo and Theresa realized it simultaneously: "Caylin!"

They dove for the phone and snapped it up, holding it between their ears.

"Hello!" they said in unison.

"Hey, guys," came Caylin's hushed voice. "It's me."

"Where are you?" Jo asked.

"I'm in a shower stall. Everyone's asleep. I figured I should check in. It's been . . . interesting."

"What happened?" Theresa asked, whispering, too.

Caylin quickly ran down her string of events, from meeting Lucien to seeing the computers to the men with guns and duffels.

"Yeah, well, those computer geeks are probably in it up to here," Theresa said proudly. "I broke in tonight. And we got an eyeful."

She and Jo shared their side of the story, down to the last brush burn from the cycle chase.

"So what do you think 'the Purchase' is?" Jo asked.

"Your guess is as good as mine," Caylin replied. "The only thing Lucien talked about was a recreation facility downtown and a new retreat. Oh yeah, and franchises."

"Franchises?" Jo asked. "Sheesh."

Theresa frowned and shook her head. "That's small fries compared to the amounts of money we're talking about. This is going to be big, whatever it is."

"I don't know," Caylin said. "*Something* is going on. We just have to dig deeper."

"Actually, we were just about to do that," Jo replied. "We're hitting the warehouse again tonight."

"That's probably a good idea," Caylin said. "Be careful. There might be something worse than killer bikers this time."

"Will do," Theresa said. Then she smiled. "It's good to hear your voice. How are they treating you?"

Caylin laughed. "The place really is paradise, if you're

into that kind of thing. I prefer something a little more down-to-earth mys—"

Suddenly Caylin's voice was cut off. "Cay?" Jo called.

No answer. Something came across from the background. A gruff voice.

"Caylin, are you there?" Theresa asked.

There was a thunk. Some static.

Then the line went dead.

NINE

Caylin huddled in the cramped shower stall, smelling the mildew, gripping her tiny cell phone, and staring up at Jenny.

"What are you doing?" Jenny demanded, scowling. "That's an unauthorized phone. That should be in storage with the rest of your personal belongings. And you know the rules: No outside contact until your indoctrination period is over!"

Caylin slumped down farther. "I know, but . . ."

"But what?" Jenny scolded, obviously trying not to raise her voice. "If any of the others wake up and find us in here, we could both be excommunicated! I worked too hard, and I'm not going to get thrown out because of you."

Easy, girl, Caylin thought angrily. This isn't NASA. The only hard work it took for you to get through the gate was carrying a bag of cash and memorizing a Swiss account number.

Caylin stopped herself. She was undercover. But Jenny was really here, in every sense of the word. This was her world, no matter how Caylin felt about that.

"I'm sorry," Caylin whispered, her shoulders sagging.

"Who are you talking to?" Jenny demanded.

Caylin fidgeted. "My, um . . . my boyfriend."

Jenny rolled her eyes. "I should've known. If it's not parents, then it's boyfriends. Well, we haven't lost anyone yet to a boyfriend, and I'm not about to start now. Come out of there."

"I'm sorry, Jenny," Caylin said lamely. "He's in Berlin, and I just miss him so much. My parents were a nightmare, but he was the only person I could really talk to."

Jenny nodded and offered her hand. "They always are. Come on."

Caylin took her hand and stood, not quite sure how to take Jenny's reaction. So far, this seemed like a pretty normal thing. Even kids who hate their homes can get homesick.

"What's his name?" Jenny asked, hands on hips.

Caylin thought quickly. "Sam."

"What's he doing in Berlin?"

Caylin smiled awkwardly and shrugged. "The same thing I'm doing in East Asia. Wandering around. He likes Europe too much to wander anywhere else."

"How much did you tell him about this place?" Jenny asked, her tone very serious.

"Nothing," Caylin replied, shivering. The cold and dampness of the shower room was taking its toll on her. "If he knew I'd joined up with something like this, he'd go nuts. He'd probably even tell my parents. As far as he knows, I'm just wandering from place to place."

Jenny thought about her answer for a moment and apparently decided to accept it because she didn't ask anything else. Then she put out her hand.

"Give me the phone," Jenny ordered.

She sounds like Miss Buszko in kindergarten, Caylin thought. Sheesh.

"Aw, Jenny," Caylin whined. "Just let me keep it, huh? I promise I won't use it."

"Then what's the point of keeping it?" Jenny challenged.

Caylin deflated. "Come on. . . ."

"Caylin, if you're going to stay here, you have to abide by the rules. Even the ones you don't agree with. That's part of the sacrifice we all make."

"I'm trying, Jenny," Caylin replied. "Really."

"I know," Jenny said, nodding. "But to find true inner peace, you must forget about the outside world. Even Sam in Berlin. He can't help you from thousands of miles away. When you have a problem or feel weak, come talk to me. I've been through it all, trust me." Just when Caylin thought Jenny was softening, the glorious mentor held out her hand again. "But you have to start by giving up the phone. Right now."

Caylin wasn't worried about losing the phone. She was worried about giving it up to Jenny. It was a Tower communications device, with all the bells and whistles. If Jenny decided to play with it, she might hit the wrong button and ring Uncle Sam's vacation home in Monte Carlo. Or worse.

She simply couldn't give Jenny that phone.

"I'll tell you what. I'll go you one better," Caylin offered.

She set the tiny phone down on the tile floor. Then she stomped on it with all her might. The plastic gave a loud crunch. The soft white shoes didn't give much padding, and a bolt of pain shot up Caylin's leg. But she'd felt worse and didn't flinch.

The phone was toast.

Caylin smiled. "That way no one is tempted. Right?"

Jenny returned the smile. "Maybe you'll fit in here after all. Come on. You need your rest. Tomorrow's a big day."

Caylin nodded and followed. But the blissful smile on her face was false as a cosmetic eyelash. The lump in her throat was real. For now she had absolutely no way of contacting the Spy Girls!

"What do we do?" Jo asked, fear gripping her heart. "Caylin could be busted!"

"There's nothing we can do, Jo." Theresa shook her head. "And you know it. Cay's on her own. If she blows her cover, then she has to handle it. Our mission parameters are clear. Read your manual."

"You know what you can do with your manual, O Goddess

of the Geeks," Jo said, eyes flashing. "We're talking about Caylin here!"

Theresa frowned. "I know. Don't think for a second that I don't. But you know there is nothing we can do. We don't know if she was busted or not."

Jo slumped down into the mountain of pillows. She sighed in futility. "I know. But it makes me crazy sometimes."

"Me too. But all we can do is head to the warehouse as scheduled. If she can, she'll make contact with us soon enough."

Jo looked up at Theresa with worried eyes. "And if she can't?"

Theresa smiled lamely. "I didn't hear that, Jo. Let's roll."

The night air was chilly, but Theresa and Jo were dressed for it: scalp-to-toe black. Even T. had to admit that they looked pretty hot—true superspies if there ever were any. As they passed from the thin late-night crowds of the tourist district to the deserted alleys of the waterfront, no one paid them any mind. Just two more wandering souls trying to find the best place to hole up for the night, right?

They passed by the site where the truck ran over their motorcycle. The whole mess had been cleaned up. Not a speck of broken glass remained.

"Wow," Theresa marveled. "In my hometown they can't even fix potholes."

"It's pretty amazing when a city keeps the streets clean even in the neighborhoods that smell like dead fish," Jo agreed.

They arrived at the warehouse just before 1 a.m.

Theresa paused. "Someone's been here."

"How do you know?" Jo asked.

"Check it out." A shiny new padlock hung from the main door.

"Should we burn it off again?" Jo asked.

Theresa shook her head. "They might be watching. Or waiting inside. Let's go around the other side and see if there's another way in."

They crept around to the side facing the docks. A massive cargo ship was moored a few hundred feet down the pier. And a large panel truck was backed up against the warehouse's loading platform. One of the garage doors was open.

Uh-oh, Theresa thought. Someone's home.

Suddenly a lighter flickered in the darkness.

Jo and Theresa flattened themselves against the wall of the warehouse.

Theresa made out the silhouette of a large, bald man. He lit a cigarette and puffed away. He didn't see them.

Theresa fished out a tiny pair of binoculars and flipped them open. They were equipped with green night vision, which allowed her to see just about everything in the dark.

"I still think you get the coolest gear," Jo whispered.

"If you'd show up at your surveillance training classes, they might actually trust you with some of this stuff," Theresa replied.

"Yeah, yeah, yeah, Lucy Lecture," Jo muttered. "What do you see?"

Theresa squinted through the lens, her heart pounding. "Three guys. They're unloading something from the truck into the warehouse."

"Are they duffel bags?" Jo asked, remembering what Caylin had seen.

"No," Theresa said, trying to focus better. It didn't help that her hands were shaking. She forced herself to concentrate. "These look like heavy-duty suitcases. Metal. There's some writing on the side. I can't really make it out. It's not English, though."

"Asian lettering?"

Theresa shook her head. "Maybe Russian."

One of the men on the loading dock tripped. His suitcase clanked to the ground, and he went flying. The big man tossed his cigarette aside angrily and let out a string of curses in some foreign language. At least, it sounded foreign. And they sounded like curses.

The clumsy man stood up, grabbed the big suitcase, and continued on his way.

"They're all going inside," Theresa said, following them with her night vision.

"Let's go," Jo replied, tugging T.'s sleeve.

Theresa yanked loose. "Okay, okay. But *quietly*."

"No duh," Jo grumbled.

"They have guns, Jo," Theresa warned. "Aren't you the least bit nervous?"

Jo grinned in the moonlight. "*Nervous* is not in my vocabulary."

"I'll take that as a big yes," Theresa muttered. "Come on."

They slipped onto the loading dock and cautiously peeked inside the truck. It was empty.

Whatever they're delivering is inside already, Theresa thought. Which means we have to go inside, too. Great.

Theresa made fists to keep her hands from trembling. She jerked her head toward the door, motioning for Jo to go. Slowly the girls tiptoed into the warehouse. Both of them wore special soft-soled, Tower-issued shoes that masked most sound. But even they couldn't prevent the occasional creaking of the ancient warehouse floor—which sent rivers of ice up Theresa's spine every time.

"Shhh," Jo warned.

"We should've brought wings and flown in," Theresa remarked.

They waited until the last man disappeared around a corner, then advanced. The men paid no attention to anything around them, shooting comments back and forth and laughing occasionally. When the big cigarette guy cursed at them again, they shut up.

The men eventually stopped in front of a wall on the main floor of the empty warehouse. Theresa noticed that it wasn't far from where they had picked up the silk sleeve. Two more men waited for them. Five in all. With three suitcases.

What are they doing? Theresa wondered, her pulse pounding in her ears. And what's in the Samsonite?

The big man stepped forward and clicked something on the wall—and a whole section swung inward!

"Secret door," Jo whispered, grabbing Theresa's arm like a vise. "*That's* why we couldn't find a basement. It's hidden."

Theresa nodded excitedly. They crept closer, pausing behind a pile of splintered wood next to a cement pillar. Theresa felt the grit grinding beneath her feet, but the special shoes kept it silent. Thank God.

The men bobbed and sank into the floor as they went through the door—as if they were going down a flight of steps. Finally the last man slipped through the door, and it swung shut with a clunk.

The girls hurried over to it.

"Give them a second to move on," Theresa warned, holding Jo's arm. "We don't want to run up their backs."

"We still don't know where the switch is," Jo reminded her, running her fingers along the smooth wall. Bits of soot fell through her fingers to the floor. She found nothing.

"It has to be here somewhere," Theresa said, picking at every little imperfection in the paint. She probed the specific section of wall that she saw the man touch. "The big guy touched right here. Or close to here."

"Better hurry, or we'll lose them," Jo said.

"Yeah, they might take those steps all the way down to China," Theresa replied. "Or Toledo. Or whatever's currently on the opposite side of the planet."

"You're not nice," Jo quipped.

"Aw, you just don't know me," Theresa answered.

Adrenaline shot through her veins when her fingers brushed over a small imperfection in the wall. She frantically dug in her fingernails and pulled down a small lever made of the same plaster as the wall.

"Got it!" she said triumphantly, instantly regretting how loud she was.

But it was too late for that—the wall swung inward.

Beyond was a pitch-black staircase. All Theresa could see were a few steps leading down. Then nothing. The men ahead must have moved on—there wasn't a sound to be heard.

Theresa peeked through her night vision binocs.

"It's blurry because we're so close," she whispered. "But the stairs go down."

Jo rolled her eyes. "I'm blind, and I can see that. How far?"

"About twenty feet. I can't tell for sure, but it looks like a dead end."

They started down. The steps and walls were made of interlocking stone. It smelled damp and ancient. They ran their hands along the side for support.

"I don't hear them," Theresa said, bumping Jo's shoulder.

"All I hear is you," Jo replied, shoving her back.

"Watch it, Spy Girl," T. warned. "It's a long way down."

Jo chuckled nervously. "How do you know that?"

"Gut feeling," Theresa said with a shrug no one could see.

Finally they reached the bottom. There was a square yard's worth of landing, but no way out. They were surrounded by stone walls.

"There has to be another secret door," Theresa said.

"You think?" Jo joked.

They searched, but in the dark all they could do was feel. Crumbs of old mortar fell away from the joints. They did everything—they pulled, they pushed, they felt for something other than stone. Jo even checked for a good old doorknob. But nothing.

"You know what would be a cool gadget?" Jo asked.

"What?" Theresa replied, feeling along the top of the wall.

"A secret door detector."

Theresa chuckled. "Good point. Make a note of it."

"T., we checked every inch of these walls," Jo said, crossing her arms across her chest. "It's just not here."

"It has to be," Theresa grumbled. "Five steroid thugs

with Russian Samsonites can't just evaporate. We have to check again. We must have missed—"

Theresa paused.

"What?" Jo asked.

"We didn't check the floor."

"Grrr," Jo growled. She sank to her knees. "Now I'm reduced to feeling around on my hands and knees?"

"No, no, stand up," Theresa told her. "It's probably just a little pressure plate. Something quick and simple that you could find in the dark."

She began tapping every little stone she could feel.

"Hey—I have a loose one over here!" Jo said excitedly. She hopped up and down on it, but nothing happened. "No fair."

"Keep hopping. It just might be—"

Theresa's toe tapped a stone, and she heard a click.

The wall to their left popped outward several inches. A crack of light seeped through.

"That's it!" Theresa said. "Open sesame seed buns."

"What do you mean 'that's it'? My rock opened the door."

"No way," Theresa argued. "I felt a distinct click when I stepped on this rock right here."

She tapped her toe for emphasis.

"I don't hear any click," Jo said.

Theresa rolled her eyes. "The door's not going to click when it's *open,* brain cell. Can we move on, please?"

"Glory hog." Jo shoved past her and slowly pushed on the open door.

"Return to stealth mode," Theresa whispered.

The stone door swung easily on greased hinges. The light ahead was dim, but sunlike compared to the dungeon they just came from.

The secret door clicked shut behind them.

When their eyes adjusted, they found themselves on a rusty steel balcony at the top of a long metal staircase, like a fire escape. But they weren't on the side of a building— they were deep inside the subbasement of the warehouse. The floor was two stories below. So far down that it might as well have been two miles.

Jo and Theresa stared at the scene below, mouths gaping.

"Oh my gosh . . . ," Theresa whispered.

TEN

Twenty feet below Jo and Theresa lay a massive chamber full of Kinh-Sanhians. Two hundred. Maybe three. And each was chained to a grimy sewing machine. Men, women, children even—they all hunched over their machines, churning out piece after piece of flashy clothing. Grime coated the workers. The scraps they wore looked like they were made from unusable bits of the cloth they worked on.

Armed guards—all of them with shaved heads—walked among the rows of machines. They barked occasional orders but mostly just hung back, made jokes, and smoked cigarettes.

The place sounded like a demented barnyard. One machine ran for a few seconds, then another one across the room answered it. The air smelled like stale cigarette smoke, machine oil, and sweat. Bad sweat. The kind of sweat that was tinged with fear.

"Look at them all," Jo whispered. "They're like zombies."

Her eyes fell on one worker in particular, a skin-and-bones child who mindlessly fed cloth into her machine. A combination of anger and pity rose in Jo. Her mouth filled with the taste of copper. The taste of pure adrenaline.

"Underfed zombies," Theresa replied angrily. "This is a sweatshop, Jo. A real, live sweatshop."

"So that's Lucien's secret," Jo reasoned. "But those people . . . they look like they're right off the street."

"They probably are," Theresa replied. "Think about it. The city streets seemed so nice and clean. Especially in the tourist district. I bet Lucien and his thugs kidnap homeless people and throw them down here to make his designer knockoffs."

"And he pockets the cash," Jo finished.

"Exactly." Theresa scowled. "Courtesy of my mother's good name and label. This guy makes me want to barf. He deserves to die for what he's doing to these people."

"T., how PG-13 of you," Jo replied. "I think we'll just

have to settle with destroying his operation, unmasking him as a sham, and sending him to prison for the rest of his life."

"That's like winning the lame half of *The Price Is Right* showcase. But it'll have to do." Theresa rubbed her chin. "Still, something doesn't add up."

"What's that?"

"Let's get out of here and I'll tell you. We're sitting ducks up here." Theresa turned to the secret door, but it was just a blank wall. "Oh no."

Panic gripped Jo as the two of them ran their hands over the rough surface, trying to slip into the cracks where the door met the wall.

It was no use.

There was no latch on this side.

They were trapped!

Finishing her Tower training was easy. The triathlon in Greece, that was easy, too. And Caylin's final test for her black belt? The moves were so natural to her that that had been the easiest challenge of all.

So was slipping out of the dorm. All she'd needed was a little speed, a little stealth maneuvering, and the ability to hide around corners as baldies patrolled the hallways.

Now came the hard part.

Caylin couldn't get an exact time (they took her watch), but it had to be around one or two in the morning. Everyone was asleep. From what she could see, there were no guards roaming the compound.

But there were plenty of cameras.

She had spent most of the afternoon in the compound with Jenny and her cronies. Plenty of time to note the location of each camera. And how long it took to make its mechanical sweep.

Now all she had to do was run it like an obstacle course. She would wait for the camera to turn away, then dart to the next bit of cover.

Simple, right?

Caylin hoped so.

She fixed on the first camera, and after a moment sprinted across the grass to a pair of trees. There she waited.

She wished she had something other than her bright whites to wear. But maybe that was the point. They were easy for the baldies to spot. There was never any question who wore them. Oh, well, it wasn't like she had a choice.

Caylin had grown quite sick of sitting around in her room. No books. No music. No gym. It was prison for her—and she'd only been there for twenty-four hours! She tried to imagine what it would be like to actually *live* there. Breakdown time!

Now that she had lost her phone, she figured it was time to get a little more aggressive. She had to do some serious snooping. She'd never find anything out during the light of day. There were too many peace-and-love activities, and she'd had more than enough of that.

The next camera turned away.

Caylin bolted, covering the distance to the next group of trees in seconds.

The next camera was high above her, attached to the main temple. That would be the tricky one—it didn't move. It was aimed along the side of the building, toward the rear. Which was exactly where Caylin was going. She would have to take the chance that no one was looking at that monitor at that moment. Because she really didn't have an excuse if she got caught this time.

No boyfriend. No searching for the bathroom. No taking a midnight stroll. She'd be as busted as busted can be.

Oh, well, better busted than bored, she figured.

She took a deep breath. Willed whoever was watching to look away.

And she ran.

The moon cast a long shadow on that side of the temple, helping her hide. Would it be enough? It had to be.

Her legs pumped hard. The grass passed beneath her, and her hair whipped back from her face. She felt like she was going a hundred miles an hour. But she was still so slow, so slow.

They had to see her.

A guard dozing on a bench. The security guy checking the cameras. Lucien gazing out his beautiful windows. Someone.

Finally Caylin reached the spot where she'd seen the Range Rovers that day. She slipped around the corner of the temple and plastered herself against the wall. Her breathing was controlled, steady. The adrenaline was exhilarating.

Now *this* is what I call inner peace! she thought.

She held her breath for a few seconds, listening.

Nothing.

Looks like I pulled it off. For now . . .

She padded across the gravel to the steel double doors at the back of the temple and pulled on the large handle. Locked, naturally.

Caylin reached up and produced the last piece of hardware she had. The only thing she could hide from Jenny and the vulture who took all her stuff—a bobby pin.

She hoped she could do it. Jo had done it once, in a wine cellar in Prague, of all places. Over time, it became a kind of competition between the Spy Girls. Jo was the master. Even Theresa could do it if her life depended on it.

But Caylin had never been able to pull it off.

Now it counted. Now it was for real.

"Here goes nothing," she whispered.

Caylin bent the pin like she was supposed to. She slid

it into the lock. Jiggled it. Pushed it. Jiggled it. Tried to turn it but couldn't. She jiggled it some more.

Something clicked.

A wave of hope swept through her. She tried to turn the pin like a key.

It didn't budge.

Caylin sighed. Wiped her hands on her pants. Told herself to take her time, even though she knew that was the one thing she *couldn't* do. How long until a guard strolled by?

She jiggled it again. Wiggled, jiggled, squiggled—nothing worked.

Finally she took a deep breath. Held it. Closed her eyes. And slid the pin into the lock again. Gave it a gentle tug. Then twisted.

The pin turned!

The lock clicked aside, and the door opened!

Caylin beamed in triumph. Wait until the others heard about that! Picked a lock on a field mission! She was a true spy now!

She slipped through the door and quietly closed it

behind her, then slid the lucky bobby pin back into her hair, vowing never to go anywhere without it.

Caylin took a quick look around. She was in a brick hallway. A short flight of concrete stairs ran down in front of her. Fluorescent lights were mounted in the walls every ten feet. Very plain, compared to the Taj upstairs.

Caylin snuck down the stairs and made her way along a corridor. Turned right. Turned left. She passed a series of doorways. The chambers were mostly empty and dim, save for some tables and folding chairs. The air smelled like a bad frat house cigar.

She paused before one doorway. A light shone out into the hall. Someone hummed inside.

Uh-oh, Caylin thought nervously. We've made contact. Intelligent life exists in the basement.

Slowly, carefully, she dared a peek around the corner.

A shaved head sat with his back to her, puffing a cigar. But he wasn't wearing his robes. He wore a tank top and boxer shorts with big red hearts on them. A bunch of empty beer cans were stacked in a pyramid in front of him. Well-worn playing cards covered the table—a half-finished game of solitaire. A rack of poker chips sat to his left. The song he hummed was "What Makes You Beautiful," of all things.

He was cleaning a nine-millimeter pistol with a soiled rag. Two full magazines were within reach.

Some holy man, Caylin thought. Just as she suspected. They packed heat. She hadn't exactly expected the valentine undies, though.

Caylin tiptoed across the doorway and moved on.

She took a left and headed down another corridor. Actually, Caylin had no idea where she was going. All she knew was that she was somewhere underneath the main temple. Getting lost didn't really worry her—this maze had to open up *somewhere*. Getting caught, however, did worry her.

That's the real trick, isn't it? she thought as her slippered feet slid along the tile floor.

This particular hallway dead-ended at a steel door. When Caylin put her ear to it and listened, she heard nothing. The metal of the knob was cold and smooth on her palm—and turned easily.

She opened the door and peeked in.

Pitch-black.

She felt the wall inside and found a light switch. But she slipped in and shut the door before flipping it on.

Caylin turned, and when she did, her mouth dropped open.

Holy college tuition, Batman, she thought.

The room was full of cash. Large bills, small bills, stacked, piled, bagged, and more. The far wall was literally a wall of money. The bundles were held together by bank bands and rubber bands. The stacks in turn were held together by plastic wrap. These cash "cubes" were about a foot square. Caylin figured there had to be at least fifty of them against the far wall alone. That didn't include the unwrapped millions all around her. A table held a counting machine and an adding machine big enough for Donald Trump's accountant. And in the corner to her left?

A big box filled with brand-new duffel bags—not even out of the wrapper yet.

"Whoa," she whispered.

There was enough cash here to finance a three-week Spy Girl shopping spree across London, Paris, and Milan!

So that's what was in the duffel bags. These cash cubes. It looked like they could fit about three cubes per bag. Which meant that they threw twelve cubes of cash in the back of those Range Rovers that afternoon.

Where was it going? And where did it come from?

Caylin knew that there was no way that much pure American currency could come from the cult members, as rich as they were. The short stack she handed over to Lucien was a cool ten grand of Tower money, and that was just a drop in the bucket compared to what was here.

This was huge. She had to find a way to contact the Spy Girls. Somehow. There must be some kind of communication device in Lucien's penthouse. If she could con her way up there again . . . Lucien seemed to take a shine to her. . . . Maybe she could sneak a call—

Something pressed against the back of her neck. The tiny hairs stood up around it.

Caylin gulped, knowing immediately what the object was from her training.

A gun barrel.

"Hiya, toots," came a gruff, shaved-headed voice.

ELEVEN

"Don't tell me." Jo moaned, trying to block out the wails of the sewing machines below them.

"Okay, I won't," Theresa promised, running her hand along the door. "But we're trapped."

"I told you not to tell me!" Jo hissed.

"Since when do I listen to you?" Theresa said. "We have to get off this platform before one of the guards sees us."

"Or someone else comes through the secret door," Jo added, scanning the sweatshop below for a miracle. "What are the options?"

"Only one, Jo, and you know it," Theresa said, all business. "You see that dark archway at the far end of the shop?"

Jo squinted through the smoky air. There it was—a dark doorway in the very far wall. Jo gulped. They would have to sneak the length of the entire place to get there. It might as well have been a hundred miles across whoopie cushions.

Great, Jo thought. Just great.

"Yeah, I see it," she replied glumly. "But I don't believe it. Not for a second."

"We can do it," Theresa assured her.

"No, we can't."

"Jo, take a listen," Theresa ordered, nudging her. "We don't have to be quiet. They'll never hear us with all this racket. All we have to do is sneak around those carts with the clothes piled high. Invincible, invulnerable, invisible, remember?"

"You forgot inconceivable," Jo said, her eyes wide.

"Well, I'm going for it," Theresa said, reclipping her hair at the back of her head in preparation. "If we stay up here, we're definitely busted. By my count, there's six guards. They're lazy and scummy, and the last thing they'll expect to see is a couple of hot little spies running through their sweatshop. Let's go. On three."

"I hate this," Jo said angrily, checking the laces on her shoes. "And by osmosis I have come to hate you."

"Hate me later, Jo," Theresa said with a reassuring smile. "When we're sipping Earl Gray back at the flat."

Jo rolled her eyes. "On three," she replied, resigned.

Theresa nodded. "Three."

Then she started down the stairs.

"Hey!" Jo exclaimed. "Where's one and two?"

She moved quickly after Theresa, heart pounding, trying desperately to keep below the level of the railing. She figured their black forms would blend with the rusty black steel of the stairwell. Well, she *hoped* they did.

Suddenly Jo stumbled. Her stomach lurched into her throat as the long flight of steps rushed up to her.

She clawed for the railing, but it was too late.

Her arms pinwheeled helplessly and she pitched forward!

Caylin took a long, deep breath as Luscious Lucien West entered the cash room with two more shaved heads. He was dressed in full robes and looked relaxed and refreshed. His hair was perfect.

Does the man sleep? Caylin wondered.

He took one look at the guard who had found Caylin—the soiled-tank-top-and-valentine-boxers guy. "Good work, Lou. Go get some clothes on, will you?"

"Sure ting, boss," Lou replied. "Too much beauty'll burn yer eyes, right?"

"You're a charming man, Lou," Lucien said, his eyes boring into Caylin.

"Tanks, boss." He left.

"Well, well, well." Lucien shook his head. "Beautiful Caylin. You have no idea how disappointed I am to find you here."

"You have no idea how happy I am to disappoint you," Caylin replied, relieved to finally drop the simpering student act.

"A sharp wit to go with your charm," he replied with a smile. "What a waste. I thought we were becoming good friends." He raised her chin with his finger and looked into her eyes. "*Very* good friends."

Caylin yanked her chin out of his grip. "Once again, happy to disappoint you, Lucien. Or should I call you Carruthers?"

Caylin caught a glimpse of alarm on Lucien's face. But that's all it was—a glimpse. He ignored her accusation. "I suppose it's useless to ask what exactly you are doing down here?"

Caylin shrugged. "I wanted my money back."

Lucien chuckled. "Did you really think you could sneak around here without getting caught? I mean, you seem like such a clever girl."

"Not clever enough, I guess," Caylin replied. "But at least I don't have a cellar full of stolen cash keeping me up at night. And a dorm full of brainwashed kids hanging on my every word. I wouldn't be able to live with myself."

"So, then, I disappoint you, too?" Lucien asked, appearing amused.

"*Disgust* is more the word I'd use."

Lucien nodded, as if to accept it. He held up an inquiring finger. "Let me ask you this, Caylin, or whatever your name may be. Do you see anything in that temple to suggest that my students are unhappy? Brainwashed? Being held against their will?"

Caylin didn't answer.

"I'll take your silence as a no," Lucien said. "You see, they're devoted. But not devoted the way you might be devoted to whatever agency sent you here. They are . . . saturated. There isn't any part of them that isn't completely dedicated to what we're teaching here. Most of them have forgotten that another world exists outside these walls. They have found true peace. A true utopia. A true home."

"A place to stash their parents' cash," Caylin corrected, fists balled tightly.

Lucien rolled his eyes. "If you found your version of paradise, wouldn't you offer every penny you had to keep it?"

"Every penny converted into unmarked hundred-dollar bills," Caylin countered, her expression defiant. "Shipped out in small deposits to banks in the city. Marked down as donations. Then run through a complex computerized accounting system that makes every transaction untraceable. A system guarded by government-level watchdog security. Probably pirated from the CIA off the black market." She folded her arms and smirked. "Stop me if I'm wrong."

"I couldn't stop you if you were," Lucien replied dryly. A smile curled his lips. "You were definitely one of my gabbier students."

"Shame you didn't teach me anything," she said, gesturing to the roomful of cash. "I had to do an independent study to get what I was looking for."

"Okay, Caylin," Lucien said darkly, stepping forward menacingly. "The insult game is over. Who are you working for?"

At last, Caylin thought. The ruthless criminal comes out.

She took an instinctive step back but held up a brave front, saying nothing.

Lucien's expression intensified. His sparkling blue eyes nearly simmered in their sockets. "I ask again, who are you working for?"

Caylin glared at him, but kept silent.

"Well, it seems that this conversation is now over." He smirked, stroking his chin. "Such a pity. You brought me such nice, crisp hundred-dollar bills."

"Can we kill her?" one of the shaved heads asked.

A chill ran up Caylin's spine.

Lucien thought about it. A smile curled his lips. "No," he said. "Bring the car around. Let's take her to work."

TWELVE

Jo slammed into the back of Theresa, and the two of them belly flopped down the rusty stairs. Theresa's hand shot out and snagged the steel railing, bringing both of them to a tense, panicky halt.

Whoa, she thought. That was close. Another inch and she would've rolled right to the bottom of the steps.

"You okay?" Jo whispered from behind her.

"You mean other than my arm being torn from its socket?" Theresa asked angrily. "I see those ballet lessons are finally paying off."

"Sorry, T.," Jo said. "I slipped."

"I noticed."

Theresa continued forward shakily, trying to flex the pain from her limbs. She was going to have bruises on bruises after this mission. She reached the bottom of the steps without tripping over her own feet, then ducked to the side behind a large canvas cart full of cloth. Jo was next to her in seconds.

"See?" Theresa said breathlessly, her heart hammering. "Piece of cake."

"Yeah, but you're about as graceful as a cow. Keep going—I want to get out of here." Jo pointed to the next cart. "That way."

They shuffled to the next cart almost on their hands and knees. They paused when a huge guard sauntered by, puffing on a nasty-looking cigar. His teeth were brown, and he wore no shirt. Streams of oily sweat ran down his torso, and he had hair up his back to his shoulders.

He paused momentarily not five feet in front of them. But he was intent on several workers down the aisle who weren't hustling as fast as he liked.

Then the smell hit Theresa. Pure body odor. So intense that it felt like a dirty hand clamped over her nose.

Jo gripped Theresa's arm. "I think I'm gonna puke," she whispered.

"Steady," Theresa said, holding her nose.

The guard moved on down the aisle, barking in some unknown language. The smell lingered like a deep footprint.

Theresa glanced at Jo. Her hand was clamped over her mouth and nose, and her eyes were watering.

"It's *on* me, T.," Jo moaned. "The smell is on me—I can feel it!"

"Come on," Theresa urged. "Let's go find a nice sewer somewhere."

They peeked around the cart. The nearest guard was a dozen paces away. No better chance. They crawled to the next cart and paused. The guard had moved farther away.

Theresa was about to bolt for the doorway when she caught the eye of one of the workers. She froze, and Jo slammed into her. But Theresa couldn't move.

The slave was a middle-aged woman, but she looked much older. A young boy—probably her son—sat next to her. They worked the fabric through the machines together because they were obviously too exhausted to do it separately. The woman seemed to look right through Theresa, her face blank. Then she turned back to her work without a word.

Theresa gulped.

This was insane. She scanned some of the other workers. Men who looked like they were starving. Women who looked ancient. Children who looked ready to pass out at their machines.

"Look," Jo whispered, pointing.

There was a young woman not far away, maybe nineteen or twenty. But she looked more like forty.

"Is she American?" Jo asked.

Theresa shrugged. It was possible. But who could tell for sure with all the dirt and sweat?

Theresa forced herself to move on, her jaw set grimly.

Soon it was in sight. The only thing that stood between them and the archway was another cart, a pile of discarded cloth, and ten feet of open floor.

"Ready?" Theresa asked.

"Of course not," Jo replied.

Theresa smirked and got in position. The only guard

near them had moved off. Several carts now blocked his line of sight.

"Now's our chance—go!" Jo urged.

Theresa bolted to the last cart. She slid along its far side and started climbing the pile of discarded cloth.

Someone groaned. A puff of smoke rose from the other side of the pile.

She froze.

What was that? Theresa inched farther up the pile, trying to see—

A guard sat up on the other side of the pile! Bits of cloth clung to his back like leeches. He groaned again, brushed some away, and stretched.

Theresa's eyes bugged, and panic shot through her like a thunderbolt.

He'd been dozing on the cloth pile! His stinky cigar was less than two feet from Theresa's face!

Theresa slid back down the pile and went into a fetal position. She frantically started burying herself in the pile of scrap. In seconds she was partially concealed—as long as she stayed still. She glared back at Jo. She had taken refuge behind the last cart. She was totally pale.

The guy looked around, still sleepy. He held his cigar, yawned, and smacked his lips.

He didn't see me, Theresa thought. He would've flipped by now.

But how were they going to get by him?

A voice barked from across the room. The guard scowled and looked that way. The voice came again. The guy grunted something back and waved. Then he stood and stretched. He shook his head like a dog and belched.

From the foul look on Jo's face, she was thinking the same thing as Theresa: What a pig!

The guard turned around then and marched right up and over the pile of scrap. On his way down the other side one big boot came down next to Theresa's nose. The other came down on her left hand.

It took all of her willpower not to scream.

The guy moved on, but Theresa pulled her hand back and held it. It throbbed hotly but seemed to be okay. Rage blossomed within her, and she wanted to pop that guy right in the kisser. After a flea bath, of course.

Then Theresa froze again.

The guard had paused next to the cart Jo was hiding behind. She could've reached out and tugged on his greasy pants.

Jo glared at Theresa as if to ask, What now?

Theresa mouthed "don't move" and flexed her hurt hand. All either of them could do was stay still.

The guard fished in his pocket and pulled out a lighter. He flicked it, but nothing happened. Flicked it again. And again.

Theresa rolled her eyes. Come *on*.

Finally the lighter blazed to life. He put the flame to his dying cigar to freshen it. Puffs of smoke came up. Then he snapped the lighter shut, pocketed it, and admired his smoke. A dreamy look came over his face, and he puffed on it some more.

Then fresh panic rose in Theresa. From her angle she could see another guard—the big hairy head guard—approaching. He looked ticked. The other guard was too busy enjoying his cigar to see him.

He marched right up and smacked the stogie out of the

guy's mouth! Red ashes and smoke shot up from the guy's face in a blizzard . . . and the cigar flipped over the cart and came down right on Jo's head!

Jo spazzed and knocked the chewed-up stump away, not stopping until all the burning ashes were out of her hair. Theresa had never seen such a look of pure rage on Jo's face. Her hair—in a tight ponytail before—was now everywhere. Her nostrils were flared nearly as wide as her eyes, and her breaths came in deep, heaving gulps.

The head guard bellowed a litany of insults. The smaller guard could only sit there and take it. But Theresa could see his eyes. . . . He was searching the floor for his cigar. And it was smoldering a few inches from Jo's right hand.

If he found the cigar, she was snagged for sure!

Theresa frantically tried to signal Jo, but she wasn't looking. She was too busy brushing the residual ashes from her hair.

"Come on, Jo, look!"

Finally Jo glanced her way. Theresa caught her eye and made sure she was paying attention. She held up her own right hand and pointed to it. Then she pointed at Jo's hand.

Jo looked down. And her eyes went wide.

The head guard finished screaming and walked away from the smaller guard. Immediately the smaller guard started searching for his lost cigar.

At that instant Jo flicked it with her finger. It spun out from behind the cart and came to a stop right by the guy's foot.

He smiled, picked it up, and put it back in his mouth. The guard walked away, happily flicking his dead lighter.

Theresa let out a huge sigh and crawled out from under the cloth. Jo shuffled forward and met her behind the last cart. She immediately parted her hair for Theresa and bared her skull.

"Do I have a burn?" she demanded. "I swear it feels like I have a burn."

"I don't see anything, Jo," Theresa replied wearily. "Let's go."

"Ooh, I wanted to hit that guy! What a walking trash bag!"

"Come on," Theresa pleaded, tugging Jo's arm.

She took one last look around. The coast was as clean as could be, all guards' hygiene considered.

They bolted across the last ten feet and through the archway. Once outside the shop they stopped for a breath.

"I don't think anyone saw us," Theresa said.

"Except that woman and her son," Jo replied, her face full of disgust. "I mean . . . T., we have to *do* something—"

"I know, Jo. I know. But we can't do anything until we get out of here and contact Uncle Sam. Okay?"

Jo nodded. "Yeah. Let's go."

The corridors were damp and fetid. Being so close to the harbor brought in the moisture. The rats had to be huge. Luckily they didn't see any—it was too dark. Unfortunately that meant that they couldn't see any guards up ahead. They would literally run right into them. And that would be the end of them.

But Theresa and Jo knew they didn't have a choice. If they didn't make it out of this maze, then no one would ever know what was going on underneath that warehouse. It would open up as that recreation center, and pampered children of all ages would be playing games up there while people of all ages rotted away down here.

They *had* to make it out. It was that simple.

Soon Theresa felt a breeze from up ahead.

"Is that a way out?" Jo asked, peering through the gloom.

"I don't see any lights," Theresa whispered. "And that air isn't exactly fresh. I wouldn't get your hopes up."

With that, they stepped into a wide chamber. A few propane torches hung along the walls, but not much to see by. Yet Theresa saw all she needed to see.

They were in a cell block. Prison bars ran along both walls, and behind them hundreds of workers slept. But the conditions were hardly humane. They slept in tight groups on cloth mats woven from scraps. Bowls and jars lined the floors of the cells, but Theresa couldn't tell if the workers ate out of them, drank out of them, or . . .

"Oh no," Jo moaned. "Oh, Theresa . . ."

Theresa squeezed Jo's hand. "Shhh, I know. Let's keep moving."

They moved down the corridor between the cells, careful not to make a sound. It would've been bad enough to wake up the workers, who would no doubt beg to be set free. But it would've been worse to wake up the two snoring guards at the far end of the chamber. They were stretched out in their chairs, feet and arms crossed, heads back and mouths open. Sawing away.

"When we get out of here, T., I'm going to make it my mission in life to see that Lucien West never sees another ray of sunlight for the rest of his life. I'm going to bury him," Jo seethed.

"We all are, Jo. I promise you. But we have to get out of here first."

They edged closer to the snoring guards. Jo tiptoed up to them and delicately stepped over them. Then she turned back to Theresa and motioned for her to do the same.

Theresa did. But in midstep one of the guards stopped snoring.

She froze, one foot dangling in the air.

The guard grunted, shifted, smacked his lips, and continued snoring.

Carefully Theresa licked her lips and stepped over him.

They moved on into the darkness. The tunnels seemed endless. The warehouse took up an entire block, but this maze went on and on. They had to be beyond the borders of the warehouse. Who knew where they would come out?

Finally Theresa saw a light up ahead.

"I hope that's a door," Jo said. "And there's a spa on the other side of it. A spa with Swedish masseurs and hot mud and a mineral water Jacuzzi."

"I'll settle for the door," Theresa replied.

But it wasn't a door. It was another chamber. It was better lit than the others, with half a dozen electric bulbs hanging from the ceiling. There were three tables in the room, with two bulbs above each one.

But that's not what stopped the Spy Girls dead.

It was the three army-green suitcases, one on each table. The ones with the Russian writing on the side. Poised nice and neat. As if in respect. Or on display.

No guards were there to greet them. Just the girls and the suitcases.

"Those are the cases from the truck," Jo whispered.

"I knew there had to be gold at the end of this nightmare rainbow," Theresa replied.

They opened one and flipped back the lid. Then another. And another.

And froze.

Theresa's heart felt like it was in her throat, and Jo stood there with her mouth hanging open.

No one said a word. No one had to.

Theresa knew from her training what she was looking at. It seemed impossible. But it wasn't. The proof was right there in front of her.

The cases held the components of a nuclear warhead, ready for assembly!

THIRTEEN

"Oh no," Theresa muttered, gripping a table for support.

"Is that what I think it is?" Jo asked wearily, pointing at a section of the device and hoping, hoping that it wasn't . . .

But she knew it was.

"It sure isn't lost luggage from Siberia," Theresa replied.

Jo thought about that. "Actually, it is."

"The real question is, what do we do about it?" Theresa asked, delicately fingering a piece of hardware.

"Do you remember when Uncle Sam briefed us on Carruthers?" Jo asked, allowing herself to touch the device as well, knowing in the pit of her stomach what it was capable of. "He said the guy was affiliated with a terrorist group trying to smuggle nuclear weapons out of Russia."

"Looks like he succeeded," Theresa commented, gesturing to the cases.

"Indeed, he did," came a voice from behind them.

They whirled.

An extremely handsome man stood before them. He had black hair that came to a pronounced widow's peak. His eyes were deep-set, but incredibly bright and piercing. He was dressed in a pair of slacks and a pullover shirt. Very neat, yet not what they expected from a renowned religious leader.

He was surrounded by half a dozen armed guards, all with shaved heads.

And next to him stood a familiar form, dressed in white sweats and slippers.

Caylin!

"Mr. Carruthers, I presume," Jo said with a smile.

Lucien chuckled. "I'm sorry, dear. You must have me mixed up with someone else. My name is West. Lucien West."

"You don't look so 'luscious' to me," Theresa muttered.

"He's not," Caylin agreed.

At that comment Lucien shoved Caylin forward. She stumbled over to her comrades. "Why don't you stand with your friends, Caylin. I've had quite enough of you."

"Yeah, you're a real one-man party yourself, Carruthers," Caylin replied. She smiled at Jo and Theresa. "How are you guys doing?"

"We were fine until *you* got here," Theresa replied.

"When did you get busted, Cay?" Jo asked.

"About an hour ago," Caylin replied.

"Sloppy," Jo chided. "That's a whole hour before us. We win." She grinned triumphantly.

"Maybe so," Caylin responded. "But I picked a lock with a bobby pin in less than a minute. And that's in the field!"

"You're lying," Theresa muttered, shaking her head. "No way. Not in under a minute."

"I sure did!" Caylin protested.

"Not a chance," Jo agreed.

"Just ask Lucien, girls. His security cameras have it on tape." Caylin glared at Lucien. "Tell them, Lucien. And while you're at it, tell them about the rec room in your basement that's filled to the ceiling with hundred-dollar bills."

"Cool," Theresa said.

"That's my kind of rec room," Jo added.

"If you girls are quite finished, we have some business

to attend to," Lucien said with a smile. "So if you'll just tell me who you're working for, we can get on to the unpleasant part of the evening."

"Working for?" Theresa asked, raising her eyebrows.

"We don't think of this as work," Jo said, buffing her nails. "It's more of a spiritual thing."

"Yeah," Caylin agreed, clapping a hand on Theresa's shoulder. "We go around the world exposing trash bag con men for the vermin that they are. Then—*bam*—instant inner peace. You understand, don't you?"

Lucien shut his eyes and rubbed his head like it hurt. "No, I don't think I do," he muttered.

Theresa stepped forward. "Why don't I give it a try?" she asked. "It goes something like this. The cult is a front for the sweatshop. You launder all the cash that comes in from knockoff clothing by running it through the cult's books. You make all the money look like cash donations. Nice and legal."

"But the one question that's been nagging us," Jo went on, arms held out expansively, "is, why all the cash? I mean, you have way more cash than you could ever generate from knockoffs. So where did it all come from?" Her eyes narrowed, and she pointed at the nuke. "Our answer's right there on those tables, isn't it?"

Caylin nodded. "You've been using your terrorist contacts to get the nukes. Then you're selling them to the highest bidder."

"That's what you're calling 'the Purchase' in all your ledgers," Theresa said. She folded her arms across her chest and smiled. "By the way. Your computer security systems stink. I broke right in and downloaded the whole thing. You really should have your security beefed up. Any old moron can hack in there. Very sloppy."

"So," Jo asked, shrugging. "Does that just about cover it?"

Lucien broke out into gales of laughter. The girls didn't even crack a smile. "No," he said, snickering. "You're wrong. You're completely wrong."

Theresa's brow furrowed. "I doubt it," she replied. "We're pretty good at this stuff. And you're not that smart."

Lucien beamed. "Oh yes, I am."

"Prove it," Jo challenged.

"As I told Caylin, the temple is quite legitimate," Lucien

replied. He paced the floor as he spoke, slipping into preacher mode. "All the students are there because they want to be. I don't brainwash. I just happen to have something that they crave."

"It can't be charm," Jo said with a disgusted scowl.

"No, Jo," Caylin said as she leaned closer to her friend. "The word's *smarm*."

Lucien shook his head. "Try empathy, ladies. Empathy. I feel their pain. I accept them for who they are. I let them become who they've always wanted to be. It's really very simple." Lucien ran a hand along the lid of one of the green cases and gently shut it. Then he smiled. "As for the money-laundering part, yes, that's true. But that's just on the surface. It's how I got started in Kinh-Sanh five years ago."

"Is he always this wordy?" Theresa asked Caylin.

"Oh yeah," Caylin answered immediately.

"Great. Should we sit down?" Jo asked sarcastically.

"No," Lucien ordered, pointing a menacing finger at them. "Stand. For it's really quite fascinating."

"It is?" Jo griped.

"Shhh, Jo," Theresa whispered. "The guy's giving it all up."

Lucien moved to the remaining cases as he spoke, shutting and latching them in turn. "The shop and the temple ran smoothly for a few years. But then the Kinh-Sanh government tried to shut down the shop as a goodwill gesture to the United States. You know, a little brownnosing by the third world country to impress the Yanks. I was desperate. I would've been out of business. And this was the best operation I had ever set up. It was perfect."

"So you *are* Carruthers," Caylin pointed out.

"If you say so, Caylin," he replied, shrugging. "It hardly matters. Anyway, I had to find a way to keep the dream alive. So I went to the prime minister of Kinh-Sanh and made him an offer he couldn't refuse."

"And that was?" Theresa asked.

Lucien's grin was sinister. "I would help him make Kinh-Sanh a major world power overnight. A country that would be more powerful than all of its neighbors. A country that could stand proudly and point to its beautiful capital city, its clean streets, and its friendly natives, and say, 'Kinh-Sanh's voice will now be heard around the world.'"

The realization hit Jo like a thunderbolt. It must have hit the other girls as well because Theresa blurted out: "You're selling the prime minister the nukes!"

"Selling?" Lucien asked impatiently.

Jo chuckled. "Oh, sorry, I guess you're just *giving* them to him," she mused.

"That's exactly what I'm doing," Lucien replied, patting one of the cases. "Make no mistake, he's paying for them. But I'm acting as a broker, so to speak."

Great, Jo thought. Just what the world needs. A trash bag of nuclear proportions.

"The almighty middleman," Caylin muttered.

"Precisely," Lucien said. "I get a hefty 'finder's fee' and the eternal gratitude of the prime minister. He immediately saw the light when it came to my other operations. The shop keeps his streets free of unsightly homeless people, which brings in the tourists, which brings in the cash. In exchange, I get a cut of the pie."

"So that's it?" Theresa asked.

"Not quite," Lucien replied smugly. "I also get to operate my businesses unchallenged. You see, believe it or not, I *am* a spiritual man. But I am also a big believer in free enterprise. And this nuclear-sized deal will not just tip the scales of world order, it'll make me a billionaire in the process."

"At the cost of hundreds of lives in your shop," Theresa said in disgust.

"Or millions if those nukes ever get used," Caylin added grimly.

Lucien only smiled and spread his arms. "Name a billionaire who hasn't squashed a few hundred lives in his day?"

Jo started laughing. Laughing hard. She felt the other girls staring at her, probably wondering if she'd snapped.

"Something amusing?" Lucien asked, glaring at her.

Jo giggled, nodding. "Yeah, big time. You've formulated the perfect plan here, Carruthers. But it's not quite perfect."

Lucien smiled pleasantly. "No?"

"No. You left out one tiny but crucial detail."

Lucien's smile became a smirk. "Well? Are you going to enlighten me?"

"Showers, Lucien. Showers for your guards! They stink!

They stink worse than my high school football team, and they practiced in a cow pasture!"

Lucien couldn't suppress his own chuckle. He turned to his guards. "Well, gentlemen, what do you think about that?"

The biggest, hairiest guard stepped forward.

He smiled at Jo. Jo smiled back nervously. Then her nervousness turned to horror as she watched the man lift his arm and literally blow his body odor toward them!

"How disgusting!" Jo moaned, fanning with her hand. "Why don't you just cut me in half with a laser or something quick?"

The guards chuckled and slapped their smelly comrade on the back for his ingenuity.

"What a shame that all this is for nothing," Theresa said to Lucien. "Our people will be along any minute now. And then it's bye-bye, Carruthers."

Lucien laughed even harder. "So what? Let them come. What do you think they'll find? An empty warehouse. Meanwhile you three will be earning back all the money you've cost me by standing here talking."

"What do you mean?" Caylin asked uneasily.

Lucien nodded to his guards. "Put these young ladies to work. Give them their own machines. And let them sew until they either die of exhaustion or dehydration." The smile widened on his face. "Whichever comes first."

FOURTEEN

Caylin squinted at her dark, murky surroundings as the Spy Girls were led back to the sweatshop. All the tired, tortured eyes of the workers focused on her and her friends as they were searched.

The guards took all their gear. Everything. Then they sat the girls down in a row in front of three decrepit sewing machines and shackled their ankles to a steel bar underneath.

Caylin tested the bonds. Solid. Very solid. And heavy. Caylin knew she was in shape—but she wondered how the slaves could even move their feet on the sewing machine pedals. They looked so skinny and weak.

We'll look like that, too, if we don't do something, she thought.

Huge piles of unsewn sleeves were slapped down

before them. The big hairy guard ran down the instructions, plain and simple. The Spy Girls were to sew the long hem the length of the sleeve, making a tube. Someone else would be sewing them to the body.

The guard lit a new cigar and spit on the floor. "Here are rules," he barked in a thick accent. "Work or else. That's it. Simple, no?"

"No," Jo replied. "We don't know how to sew."

The guard, obviously knowing how much he turned Jo on, leaned in real close and puffed his cigar. Jo looked as if she wanted to puke then and there. "Is even more simple. Learn or else."

The guard blew a massive cloud of smoke in Jo's face. He walked away, laughing.

"I'll never wash this stink off me," Jo moaned. "It'll be on me forever, I know it."

"If we don't get out of here," Theresa warned, "forever will be sooner than you think."

The guard snapped his fingers at them.

"Guess we better start sewing," Caylin suggested, picking up a sleeve. "How do we do this?"

"T., your mom's a designer," Jo said. "Did she ever teach you anything about sewing?"

Theresa shrugged, awkwardly holding a piece of fabric. "As far as I know, all you do is take the sleeve, fold it over like this, and run it straight through the machine like this."

She pressed the pedal and ran it through the machine. The needle chomped into the fabric and ate it up in seconds. Theresa held up her work so they could see.

"Nice work, T.," Jo replied. "Olive Oyl couldn't even get her hand through that cuff."

She was right, Caylin saw. Theresa had sewn a crooked line to the end, leaving a one-inch hole where someone's hand was supposed to come through.

"Oh, well," Theresa said, shrugging. "That's the theory."

They all started sewing their sleeves. Badly. Very, very badly. But Caylin didn't care. Jo reasoned that the more sleeves they ruined, the less business Lucien would have. So they kept sewing and didn't make any attempt to improve. But after a few minutes something was strange.

"Do you suddenly feel like a celebrity?" Jo asked.

"I know what you mean," Caylin replied, creeped out.

All around them the workers stared. It must have been a big event—three American girls being brought in at gunpoint and chained. But after a while, and a little prodding from the guards, everyone settled back into their routine of ordinary, everyday slave labor. And the guards resumed their lounging and joking among themselves.

That's when the Spy Girls came to life.

"It's time for a plan," Caylin said out of the side of her mouth.

"Any suggestions?" Jo asked, glancing at the guards.

"They took everything," Theresa replied.

The girls spoke in low voices, not looking at each other. Caylin and the others tried to make it seem as if they were working, working, working, just like everyone else.

"Not everything," Jo said with a sly grin.

"Really?" Theresa asked. "What do you have left?"

"My heel."

Realization dawned on Caylin. Of course! Theresa and Jo still wore their Tower-issue shoes. Each pair was equipped with one homing beacon in the left heel. All you had to do was slide it out—which they both did nonchalantly—touch it with your thumbprint, and slide it back into place. Supposedly a distress signal was now being sent to the nearest Tower receiver. But who knew where that was? Or if the signal could get out of the subbasement at all?

"Let's hope the cavalry is on its way," Caylin said, sloppily running a sleeve through her machine.

"We can't count on it," Theresa said gravely. "I have another idea."

Caylin watched as Theresa motioned to the nearest guard. He scowled and reluctantly came over.

"Hello, sir," Theresa said sweetly. "I hate to bother you, but you guys confiscated my glasses. I can't see a thing without them. Look at this terrible job I'm doing." She held up some of the useless sleeves she'd sewn. "Silly me. I'm blind as a bat!"

The guard shrugged. He didn't speak English. And he obviously didn't care.

Jo grinned as soon as she heard the word *glasses*.

Caylin scowled. What's going on? she wondered. What's with the glasses?

Theresa raised her voice. "Do you understand me? I need my glasses! I can't see anything without them! Blind. Do you understand the word *blind*? It means I can't see what I'm doing. I could be setting world underground sewing records if I could just see what I was doing! Where's your boss? Bring him over." Theresa stood and waved to the big hairy guard with the cigar. "Yoo-hoo! Hairy guard! You speak English. Can you get my glasses for me? Please?"

The cigar-chomping guard shambled over, a look of supreme rage on his face. "What you want?"

"My glasses." Theresa traced circles around her eyes and pointed at the pile of Spy Girl gear over by the stairs. "I need them to see. See?" She squinted for emphasis.

"You get glasses. You shut up and work."

Theresa nodded vigorously. "Oh yes, absolutely. I promise."

The guard chewed on his cigar for a moment, thinking. Then he marched over to the pile of gear. He held up Jo's fanny pack.

"No, that's not it," Theresa said. "It's the one underneath. Yeah, that's the one. My glasses are in there. Thanks so much."

The guard brought Theresa her glasses. She gratefully

put them on and picked up a sleeve. "Oh, what a beautiful pattern. I hadn't noticed it before."

"You work now," the guard growled, threatening to backhand her. "Or else."

Theresa humbly bowed and smiled. "Oh yes, I promise. You're a very nice man. I take away all the things she said about you." Theresa pointed to Jo. "She didn't mean it, really."

When the guard was out of earshot, T. added, "Except the part about you *stinking*."

"What's the big deal about your glasses?" Caylin demanded.

Theresa turned to Caylin and smiled. "Watch your feet, Spy Girl. The heat's on."

With that, she began to laser through Caylin's shackles.

"Yow!" Caylin barked as the red beams cut into the steel around her ankles. "What's *that*?"

"That's hot," Theresa warned, her eyes focused intensely. "So don't move."

Caylin grimaced, waiting for the laser to cut into her flesh. But it never did. The whole process took only a few seconds. Suddenly the shackles clanked open at her feet.

Theresa quickly did the same for Jo's and her own.

They were free . . . sort of.

"What do we do about the guards?" Jo whispered. "We can't just sneak out."

Caylin smiled. "Hey, T."

Theresa looked at her. Caylin subtly pointed at the ceiling. Theresa saw what she meant and grinned.

"Hold on to your butts," Theresa warned.

She fixed her laser gaze skyward and activated it. A red beam shot up to the ceiling. Caylin's smile widened as Theresa hit her target.

"What's she doing?" Jo whispered.

"Watch," Caylin answered.

It became quite clear when the sprinkler head Theresa hit got hot enough to go off.

Within seconds the whole sprinkler system went off, drenching the whole shop.

A fire alarm sounded, and the guards scrambled around in confusion.

Caylin grinned in the downpour.

"Let's get out of here!" she cried.

FIFTEEN

Caylin looked around at the sheer madness breaking out around her. The guards were too busy trying to figure out where the fire was—and how to shut off the sprinklers—to care that the Spy Girls sprinted across the shop to the archway. The girls ran through, leaving the screaming workers pulling at their shackles as the place was soaked.

But the storm didn't stop at the exit. The sprinkler system ran throughout the tunnels, and the Spy Girls raced through them, covering their eyes and trying not to slip on the slimy stone floor.

"Do you guys know where you're going?" Caylin yelled, hoping against hope.

"Trust us," Jo called back. "We've done this before."

Two soaked guards met them head-on, but they didn't stop them. The confused men ran right past them.

"Did they even see us?" Theresa asked.

"Who cares?" Jo cried. "Go!"

Soon they reached the prison block. The water and screaming alarm had awakened the workers. They waved their arms and cried out to be freed. Some slammed cups and debris against the bars, trying to get their attention.

"Oh no," Jo wailed. "The workers! We have to help them!"

"How do we let them out?" Theresa asked, looking around helplessly.

"Over there," Caylin said, pointing to a series of levers on the far wall.

"Are you sure?" Theresa called.

"Of course not!" Caylin sprinted over and began yanking every lever on down the line. Sure enough, one by one the cell doors clanked open!

"You did it!" Jo screamed as scores of slaves poured out of their cells.

They all jumped around and celebrated in the sprinkler-induced rainfall, letting it douse them in newfound freedom. They howled their thanks to the Spy Girls in words they couldn't understand. But the message was obvious.

Just then a pair of guards entered.

The slaves took one look at their captors and charged them. The guards' eyes bulged, and they scrambled to escape. But there was nowhere to go. Twenty slaves landed on top of them.

The men screamed, but they were overmatched. Soon they were just the bottom of a huge human pile. A twisted mass of limbs and fists.

Finally a skinny Kinh-Sanh man stood up, holding his fist high. In it he held a ring of shackle keys.

He screamed something and pointed back toward the sweatshop. His brethren roared their approval. The sea of slaves headed in that direction, no doubt intending to free all their friends and relatives on the sewing machines.

As the riot moved away Caylin noticed the two guards. They staggered to their feet and moved in a panicked daze toward the shop, ignoring the Spy Girls.

"That should keep those guards busy for a while," Jo said, beaming.

"Keep them busy?" Caylin scoffed. "Those cowards will hightail it to the nearest horizon the first chance they get."

"Let's go get that nuke," Theresa said, pointing down the hall.

"And a certain trash bag, too," Caylin added, jaw set.

They sprinted down the tunnel. When they burst into the well-lit chamber, it was empty.

And so were the tables!

Caylin's heart sank. Her fists involuntarily balled at her sides, and she wanted to throw something. Hard.

"He's got the nuke," Jo said helplessly.

"You don't say," Caylin responded, rage in her voice.

Theresa pointed at a doorway in the far wall. "That's the only way out. He had to go that way."

"Let's roll!" Caylin cried, racing forward.

The tunnel grew very dark very quickly. The sprinkler system didn't reach that far, but the moisture was intense. The stone floor was as slick as ice in some places. And the smell of dead fish grew unbearable. Where were they going?

Soon Caylin heard lapping waves along with their labored breathing.

"The harbor must be close," Jo said, puffing.

Finally the trio emerged in a stone, cavelike chamber. The ceiling was low and wet. Before them was a dock. Two massive powerboats were moored there. The water came in from the mouth of the cave, which seemed to open into the harbor. The first light of dawn made the mouth seem like a glowing portal to another world.

In a way, it was.

"Hold it right there, ladies!" came an angry voice.

Lucien stood up in one of the powerboats. He leveled a submachine gun at them.

The Spy Girls came to a dead stop, nearly sliding right into the water on the slick stone.

A black tarp covered much of the seating area of Lucien's powerboat. No doubt where he had stashed the nuclear suitcases.

"Give it up, Carruthers," Theresa warned, stepping forward. "It's all finished."

"Are you *kidding*?" Lucien asked incredulously. "I'm the

one holding the gun. I'm the one holding the nuclear weapon and a ton of cash. I'm not finished. I'm just getting started."

"That's a Furious Shepherd," Jo whispered to Caylin.

"What?" Caylin asked.

"The boat," Jo replied. "Both of them. The Furious Shepherd 76. One of the fastest boats on the water." She smiled at Lucien. "I'm impressed, sleazeball."

"How sweet," Lucien replied, rolling his eyes. "Then you probably won't understand it when I do this."

He turned the machine gun on the other boat and opened fire. Bullets sprayed the control panel and driver's seat of the beautiful boat, shredding it. He also raked the gun across the boat's stern, riddling the fuel tank until the gun was empty. The boat was now useless.

"You are truly a criminal," Jo said, staring forlornly at the ruined machine.

Lucien yanked the empty clip from the gun. "I can't very well have you coming after me, can I? You know, in the big climactic boat chase? No, I'm afraid not. I'm afraid I'll just have to set sail into a beautiful sunrise. The perfect beginning to a brand-new day."

"How can you live with what you have done?" Caylin asked.

Lucien shrugged. "It's just a boat."

Caylin scowled. "Not that. Your students. Your disciples. Your devoted followers who have invested everything they have—financially and spiritually—just to be a part of your world?"

Caylin stood defiantly, and Lucien paused. He seemed to think about it. Really think about it.

"It wasn't fake," he said softly, eyes distant. "They're good kids. They've learned a lot. I've helped them."

Caylin's lip curled into a snarl. "And now you're dumping them. Do you have any idea what's going to happen to them when they find out what you really are?"

Lucien's eyes regained their focus, once again zeroing in on Caylin. "They're young. They'll get over it."

"You disgusting piece of—" Caylin began.

"Oh, spare me, Caylin," Lucien snapped, grabbing a fresh clip for his gun. "People expect way too much from leaders. They need to think for themselves." He chuckled humorlessly. "No one was ever around to help *me*."

"It shows," Caylin replied stiffly.

Lucien smiled and hefted the clip. "Good-bye, beautiful Caylin."

Just as Lucien was about to shove the fresh clip into the gun, the doorway behind the Spy Girls exploded with slaves.

They poured through the opening, aiming all their pent-up rage at the man in the boat. The man responsible for their slavery. For the torture and the inhuman living conditions. For *everything*.

Lucien couldn't get the gun loaded fast enough. And even if he did, he never would have had enough bullets. They stormed the boat and beat him down, tearing the gun away and tossing it into the water. They ripped at his clothes and hair. Blood poured from his nose, and finally Luscious Lucien West screamed in true fear. He went into a fetal position and waited for the bitter end.

"We can't let them do it," Jo whispered. "As much as he deserves it. As much as *they* deserve it. We can't let it happen."

Caylin glanced at Theresa, who nodded. Unfortunately Jo was right.

The Spy Girls ran forward and began pulling the slaves from Lucien. They held them back and explained that he must go to jail. It was only right. They explained that if they killed Lucien, then they would be no better than Lucien. The Kinh-Sanh government couldn't and wouldn't protect him. The government was in as much trouble for conspiring with him.

"But what do we have if we let him live?" asked one freed slave in broken English.

"Your freedom," Theresa explained.

"That's lame," Caylin said. She reached under the tarp and pulled out one of Lucien's infamous cash cubes. All U.S. hundred-dollar bills. "How about your freedom . . . and a big hunk of money!"

The people cheered, and Caylin started handing out thick wads of bills. The people grabbed the money, pouncing and fondling it like a belated Christmas gift. Ben Franklins fluttered everywhere, and the joyous workers scrambled for the dropped cash as if they were on a game show.

"Well, I feel a lot better," Jo said. She nudged Lucien with her elbow. "How about you?"

"Leave me alone," Lucien mumbled, trying to hold back the blood from his nose.

"Hey, Jo," Caylin said. "You say this is one of the fastest boats on the water?"

"You know it," Jo said.

Caylin smiled. "Well, then fire the puppy up!"

"No!" Theresa piped up. "No way! She is not driving this thing. I almost got squashed by a truck because of her driving. *I'll* drive."

"You?" Jo asked. "You couldn't find the ignition switch in this rig. And it was your fat rear end that kept me from being able to swing around that truck!"

"Yo, Spy Girls, chill your engines," Caylin said. "Let's just get out of this cave. I'm getting claustrophobic."

Jo fired up the twin engines and slowly guided the Furious Shepherd into the harbor. The sun was just rising over the eastern horizon, bathing them in a warm orange light.

That's when Jo floored it.

"That's far enough," Caylin said.

Jo cut the engines. The bow of the monster boat slowly

returned to the surface of the water. They had run out to the middle of the harbor, about a mile from shore.

Jo shut down the engines completely. All they heard was the lapping of the waves and the cries of seabirds.

After a few minutes Lucien looked up at them. "Are you going to kill me?"

Jo laughed.

"Nope," Caylin said. "Not to say that you don't deserve it."

"Then what are we waiting for?" he asked, mopping blood from his upper lip.

Suddenly a huge disturbance in the water made the boat rock.

"*That's* what we're waiting for," Theresa said.

She grabbed the nearest railing. "Better hold on tight, Luscious."

The sea churned all around them, bubbling and roaring as if Godzilla himself was coming up.

But it wasn't Godzilla. In seconds they saw a huge black shape rise up not far off their starboard side. Then something slammed the boat from underneath. Something *huge*.

It lifted the boat clear out of the water. The craft pitched to one side and came to rest on the deck of a long, black sea monster. A steel sea monster known as the U.S.S. *Manhattan,* a nuclear submarine.

Soon the waves settled as the sub surfaced completely. All was calm around them. Then they heard a familiar voice come over the sub's loudspeaker.

"Welcome aboard, Spy Girls," Uncle Sam declared. "Mission accomplished!"

EPILOGUE

I can't believe you're actually wearing that," Theresa scolded Jo as she paraded shamelessly around the Kinh-Sanh flat. It was their last day in the country, after a long and boring debriefing.

"Why not?" Jo asked, modeling one of the obnoxious designer knockoffs she'd bought at the street market. "It's fabu."

"I knew it!" Theresa exclaimed. "You are such a liar. You said it was a clue, and that was it. You said you wouldn't be caught wearing it at your own funeral, remember?"

"Shut up, T.," Jo warned, holding up a finger.

"In fact," Theresa continued, marching forward, "you said you wouldn't be caught dead wearing it—"

"Theresa, shut up!" Jo said.

"At Mike Schaeffer's funeral!" Theresa finished, getting in Jo's face.

"Who's Mike Schaeffer?" Caylin asked, guzzling a soda.

"An old flame, apparently," Theresa teased. "I couldn't get it out of her."

"Jo, how interesting," Caylin said, playing with her straw. "Tell me more."

"Since when do you care about my love life?" Jo grumbled.

Caylin shrugged and smiled. "Since it makes you so uncomfortable."

The Spy Girls were understandably punchy. The week following Lucien's capture had been one long meeting after another. The scam they had uncovered reached all the way to the prime minister of Kinh-Sanh himself. Upon the country's learning of the scandal, he was immediately arrested. The capital city exploded in celebration at the news. It was like one long Mardi Gras that the Spy Girls couldn't enjoy because they were telling so many bureaucrats exactly what had happened. Ugh, how utterly boring.

"Do you know that I've shampooed twice a day for a week, and I still smell cigar smoke in my hair?" Jo grumbled, holding a few strands in front of her face for inspection. "It's amazing. I told you it would happen. I'm going to have to carry this around with me like luggage. No guy will ever want to come near me."

"Enough about the cigar smoke!" Caylin bellowed, holding up her hands. "I've had it up to here with the cigar smoke!"

Jo grabbed up her own soda and sipped it. "If you have something better to talk about, Cay, let's hear it."

"How about Mike Schaeffer?" Theresa asked, arching an eyebrow.

"*Except* Mike Schaeffer," Jo warned.

"How about our next mission?" Caylin suggested, kicking aside one of the throw pillows. "All the stupid meetings are over. World peace reigns once again. What's our next move?"

"Sammy hasn't said anything," Theresa replied. "Maybe we're just heading back home for now."

"Good. I could use the sleep," Jo muttered, massaging her temples.

"Not so fast, Spy Girls," came Sammy's familiar voice.

Caylin jumped up from the sea of pillows. "I *hate* when you do that, Uncle Sam," she bristled, shaking her fist at the ceiling. "How long have you been listening to us?"

"Long enough to know I don't want to know a thing about Mike Schaeffer."

"You're the only one," Jo commented.

"So what's the deal, Sammy?" Theresa asked, glancing around the room. "Where are we off to this time?"

Sammy chuckled. "Well, Spy Girls, you handled your-selves so well on this mission, we've come up with some-thing even more interesting."

"Is world peace in danger?" Theresa asked hopefully.

"Definitely," Sam answered.

"Is it in an exotic foreign land?" Caylin asked.

"Absolutely."

Jo mugged at her partners mischievously. "Will there be cute guys to stare at?"

Theresa and Caylin moaned and threw pillows at her.

"Can't you keep your mind out of the gutter for ten seconds?" Caylin asked.

"Oh, like you weren't thinking it," Jo replied, shoving pillows away. "I mean, really. Sometimes I think I'm the only one who tells it like it is around here."

"Excuse me, girls," Sam interrupted. "Should I come back later?"

"Of course not," Theresa replied. "If Jo would shut up long enough for you to talk."

Jo tossed a pillow back at Theresa but didn't reply.

"Very well," Sam continued. "You would like to know the location of your next mission?"

"Yes," they said simultaneously.

Uncle Sam chuckled. "Okay, Spy Girls. Your wish is my command. Hang on to your socks because you're off to . . ."

ABOUT THE AUTHOR

Elizabeth Cage is a saucy pseudonym for a noted young adult writer. Her true identity and current whereabouts are classified.

GAIA MOORE IS BRILLIANT AND BEAUTIFUL.

SHE'S TRAINED IN THREE KINDS OF MARTIAL ARTS,

HAS A REFLEX SPEED THAT'S OFF THE CHARTS, AND CAN

BREAK CODES IN FOUR DIFFERENT LANGUAGES.

SHE'S ALSO MISSING THE FEAR GENE.

TURN THE PAGE FOR A SNEAK PEEK AT *FEARLESS* BY FRANCINE PASCAL.

GAIA

Losers with no imagination say that if you start a new school, there has to be a first day. How come they haven't figured out how to beat that? Just think existentially. All you do is take what's supposed to be the first day and bury it someplace in the next month. By the time you get around to it a month later, who cares?

When I first heard the word *existential*, I didn't know what it meant, so I never used it. But then I found out that no one knows what it means, so now I use it all the time.

Since I just moved to New York last week, tomorrow would have been my first day at the new school, but I existentialized it, and now I've got a good thirty days before I have to deal with it. So, like, it'll be just a regular day, and I'll just grab my usual school stuff, jeans and a T-shirt, and throw them on. Then just like I always do, I'll take them off and throw on about eighteen different T-shirts and four different pairs of jeans before I find the right ones that hide my diesel arms and thunder thighs. Not good things on a girl, but no one else seems to see them like I do.

I won't bother to clean up when I'm done. I don't want to trick my new cohabitants, George and Ella, into thinking that I'm neat or considerate or anything. Why set them up for disappointment? I made that mistake with my old cohabitants and . . . well, I'm not living with them anymore, am I?

George Niven was my dad's mentor in the CIA. He's old. Like fifty or something. His wife, Ella is much younger. Maybe thirty. I don't know. And you certainly can't tell from the way she dresses. Middle of winter she finds a way to show her belly button. And she's got four hundred of these little elastic bands that can only pass for a skirt if you never move your legs. Top that with this unbelievable iridescent red hair and you've got one hot seventeen-year-old. At least that's what she thinks. We all live cozy together in Greenwich Village in a brownstone—that's what they call row houses in New York City. Don't ask me why, because it isn't brown, but we'll let that go for now.

I'm not sure how this transfer of me and my pathetic possessions was arranged. Not by my dad, He is Out of the Picture. No letters. No birthday cards. He didn't even contact me in the hospital last year when I almost fractured my skull. (And no, I didn't almost fracture my skull to test my dad, as a certain asshole suggested.) I haven't seen him since I was twelve, since . . . since—I guess it's time to back up a little. My name is Gaia. Guy. Uh. Yes, it's a weird name. No, I don't feel like explaining it right now.

I am seventeen. The good thing about seventeen is that you're not sixteen. Sixteen goes with the word sweet, and I am so far from sweet. I've got a black belt in kung fu and I've trained in karate, judo, jujitsu, and *muay thai*—which is basically kick boxing. I've got a reflex speed that's off the charts. I'm a near perfect shot. I can climb mountains, box, wrestle, break codes in four languages. I can throw a 175-pound man over my shoulders, which accounts for my disgusting shoulders. I can kick just about anybody's ass. I'm not bragging. I wish I were. I wish my dad hadn't made me into the . . . thing I am.

I have blond hair. Not yellow, fairy-tale blond. But blond enough to stick me in the category. You know, so guys expect you to expect them to hit on you. So teachers set your default grade at B-minus. C-plus if you happen to have big breasts, which I don't particularly. My friend from before, Ivy, had this equation between grades and cup size, but I'll spare you that.

Back in ninth grade I dyed my way right out of the blond category, but after a while it got annoying. The dye stung and turned my hands orange. To be honest, though (and I am not a liar), there's another reason I let my hair grow back. Being blond makes people think they can pick on you, and I like when people think they can pick on me.

You see, I have this handicap. Uh, that's the wrong word. I am hormonally challenged. I am never afraid. I just don't have the gene or whatever it is that makes you scared.

It's not like I'll jump off a cliff or anything. I'm not an idiot. My rationality is not defective. In fact, it's extra good. They say nothing clouds your reason like fear. But then, I wouldn't know. I don't know what it feels like to be scared. It's like if you don't have hope, how can you imagine it? Or being born blind, how do you know what colors are?

I guess you'd say I'm fearless. Whatever fear is.

If I see some big guy beating up on a little guy, I just dive in and finish him off. And I can. Because that's the way I've been trained. I'm so strong, you wouldn't believe. But I hate it.

Since I'm never afraid of anything, my dad figured he'd better make sure I can hold my own when I rush into things. What he did really worked, too. Better than he expected. See, my dad didn't consider nature.

Nature compensates for its mistakes. If it forgot to give me a fear gene, it gave me some other fantastic abilities that definitely work in my favor. When I need it. I have this awesome speed, enormous energy, and amazing strength all quadrupled because there's no fear to hold me back.

It's even hard for me to figure out. People talk about danger and being careful. In my head I totally understand, but in my gut I just don't feel it. So if I see somebody in trouble, I just jump in and use everything I've got. And that's big stuff, and it's intense.

I mean, you ever hear that story about the mother who lifted the car off her little boy? That's like the kind of strength regular people can get from adrenaline. Except I don't need extra adrenaline because without fear, there's nothing to stop you from using every bit of power you have.

And a human body, especially a highly trained one like mine, has a lot of concentrated power.

But there's a price. I remember once reading about the Spartans. They were these fantastic Greek warriors about four hundred something BC. They'd beat everybody. Nobody could touch them. But after a battle they'd get so drained they'd shake all over and practically slide to the ground. That's what happens to me. It's like I use up everything and my body gets really weak and I almost black out. But it only lasts a couple of minutes. Eventually I'm okay again.

And there is one other thing that works in my favor. I can do whatever I want 'cause I've got nothing to lose.

See, my mother is . . . not here anymore. I don't really care that my dad is gone because I hate his guts. I don't have any brothers or sisters. I don't even have any grandparents. Well, actually, I think I do have one, but she lives in some end-of-the-world place in Russia and I get the feeling she's a few beans short of a burrito. But this is a tangent.

Tangent is a heinous word for two reasons:

1. It appears in my trigonometry book.

2. Ella, the woman-with-whom-I-now-live-never-to-be-confused-with-a-mother, accuses me of "going off on them."

Where was I? Right. I was telling you my secrets. It probably all boils down to three magic words: I don't care. I have no family, pets, or friends. I don't even have a lamp or a pair of pants I give a shit about.

I Don't Care.

And nobody can make me.

Ella says I'm looking for trouble. For a dummy she hit it right this time.

I *am* looking for trouble.

THE POINT

Don't go into the park after sunset. The warning rolled around Gaia Moore's head as she crossed the street that bordered Washington Square Park to the east. She savored the words as she would a forkful of chocolate cheesecake.

There was a stand of trees directly in front of her and a park entrance a couple hundred feet to the left. She hooked through the trees, feeling the familiar fizz in her limbs. It wasn't fear, of course. It was energy, maybe even excitement—the things that came when fear should have. She passed slowly through a grassy stretch, staying off the lighted paths that snaked inefficiently through the park.

As the crow flies. That's how she liked to walk. So what if she had nowhere to go? So what if no one on earth knew or probably cared where she was or when she'd get home? That wasn't the point. It didn't mean she had to take the long way. She was starting a new school in the morning, and she meant to put as much distance between herself and tomorrow as she could. Walking fast didn't stop the earth's slow roll, but sometimes it felt like it could.

She'd passed the midway point, marked by the miniature Arc de Triomph, before she caught the flutter of a shadow out of the corner of her eye. She didn't turn her head. She hunched her shoulders so her tall frame looked smaller. The shadow froze. She could feel eyes on her back. Bingo.

The mayor liked to brag how far the New York City crime rate had fallen, but Washington Square at night didn't disappoint. In her short time here she'd learned it was full of junkies who couldn't resist a blond girl with a full wallet, especially under the cover of night.

Gaia didn't alter the rhythm of her steps. An attacker proceeded differently when he sensed your awareness. Any deception was her advantage.

The energy was building in her veins. Come on, she urged silently. Her mind was beautifully blank. Her concentration was perfect. Her ears were pricked to decipher the subtlest motion.

Yet she could have sensed the clumsy attacker thundering from the brush if she'd been deaf and blind. A heavy arm was thrown over her shoulders and tightened around her neck.

"Oh, please," she muttered, burying an elbow in his solar plexus.

As he staggered backward and sucked for air, she turned on him indignantly. Yes, it was a big, clumsy stupid him—a little taller than average and young, probably not even twenty years old. She felt a tiny spark of hope as she let her eyes wander through the bushes. Maybe there were more . . . ? The really incompetent dopes usually traveled in packs. But she heard nothing more than his noisy X-rated complaints.

She let him come at her again. Might as well get a shred of a workout. She even let him earn a little speed as he barreled toward her. She loved turning a man's own strength against him. That was the essence of it. She reversed his momentum with a fast knee strike and finished him off with a front kick.

He lay sprawled in a half-conscious pile, and she was tempted to demand his wallet or his watch or something. A smile flickered over her face. It would be amusing, but that wasn't the point, was it?

Just as she was turning away, she detected a faint glitter on the ground near his left arm. She came closer and leaned down. It was a razor blade, shiny but not perfectly clean. In the dark she couldn't tell if the crud on the blade was rust or blood. She glanced quickly at her hands. No, he'd done her no harm. But it lodged in her mind as a strange choice of weapon.

She walked away without bothering to look further. She knew he'd be fine. Her specialty was subduing without causing any real damage. He'd lie there for a few minutes. He'd be sore, maybe bruised tomorrow. He'd brush the cobwebs off his imagination to invent a story for his buddies about how three seven-foot, three-hundred-pound male karate black belts attacked him in the park.

But she would bet her life on the fact that he would never sneak up on another fragile-looking woman without remembering this night. And that was the point. That was what Gaia lived for.

"Who can come to the board and write out the quadratic formula?" Silence.

"A volunteer, please? I need a volunteer."

No. Gaia sent the teacher telepathic missiles. *Do not call on me.*

"Come on, kids. This is basic stuff. You are supposed to be the advanced class. Am I in the wrong room?"

The teacher's voice—what was the woman's name again?—was reedy and awful sounding. Gaia really should have remembered the name, considering this was not the first day.

No. No. No. The teacher's eyes swept over the second-to-back row twice before they rested on Gaia. *Shit.*

"You, in the . . . brown, is it? What's your name?"

"Gaia."

"Gay what?"

Every member of the class snickered.

The beautiful thing about Gaia was that she didn't hate them for laughing. In fact, she loved them for being so predictable. It made them so manageable. There was nothing those buttheads could give that Gaia couldn't take.

"Guy. (Pause) Uh."

The teacher cocked her head as if the name were some kind of insult. "Right, then. Come on up to the board. Guy (pause) uh."

The class snickered again.

God, she hated school. Gaia dragged herself out of her chair.

Why was she here, anyway? She didn't want to be a doctor or a lawyer. She didn't want to be a CIA agent or Green Beret or superoperative *X-Files* type, like her dad had obviously hoped.

What did she want to be when she grew up? (She loved that question.) A waitress. She wanted to serve food at some piece-of-crap greasy spoon and wait for a customer to bitch her out, or stiff her on the tip, or pinch her butt. She'd travel across the country from one bad restaurant to the next and scare people who thought it was okay to be mean to waitresses. And there were a lot of people like that. Nobody got more shit than a waitress did. (Well, maybe telemarketers, but they sort of deserved it.)

"Gaia? Any day now."

Snicker. Snicker. This was an easy crowd. Ms. What's-her-face must have been thrilled with her success.

Gaia hesitated at the board for a moment.

"You don't know it, do you?" The teacher's tone was possibly the most patronizing thing she had ever heard.

Gaia didn't answer. She just wrote the formula out very slowly, appreciating the horrible grinding screech of the chalk as she drew the equals sign. It sounded a lot like the teacher's voice, actually.

$$x = \frac{-b \pm \sqrt{b^2 - 4ac}}{2a}$$

At the last second she changed the final plus to a minus sign. Of course she knew the formula. What was she, stupid?

Her dad had raced her through basic algebra by third grade. She'd (begrudgingly) mastered multivariable calculus and linear algebra before she started high school. She might hate math, but she was good at it.

"I'm sorry, Gaia. That's incorrect. You may sit down."

Gaia tried to look disappointed as she shuffled to her chair.

"Talk to me after class about placement, please." The teacher said that in a slightly lower voice, as if the rest of the students wouldn't hear she found Gaia unfit for the class. "Yes, ma'am," Gaia said brightly. It was the first ray of light all day. She'd demote herself to memorizing times tables if meant getting a different teacher.

Times tables actually came in pretty handy for a waitress. What with figuring out tips and all.

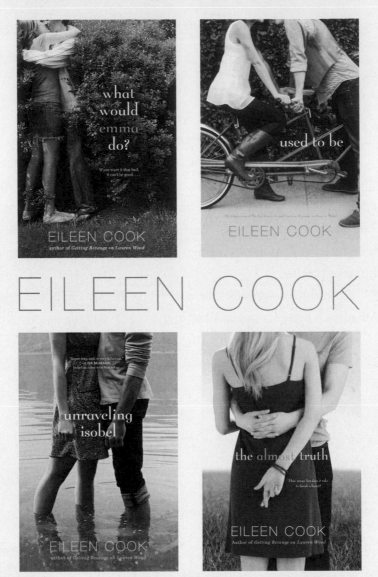

IN A WORLD WHERE SUICIDE HAS BECOME AN EPIDEMIC, THE ONLY CURE IS . . .

THE PROGRAM.

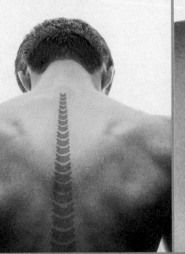

SIMON TEEN

Simon & Schuster's **Simon Teen**
e-newsletter delivers current updates on
the hottest titles, exciting sweepstakes, and
exclusive content from your favorite authors.

Visit **TEEN.SimonandSchuster.com** to
sign up, post your thoughts, and find out what
every avid reader is talking about!

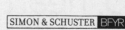